Isabel Ostrander

William J. Burns

The Crevice

CLASSIC PAGES

Isabel Ostrander

William J. Burns

The Crevice

Reihe: classic pages

1. Auflage 2010 | ISBN: 978-3-86741-387-9

© Europäischer Hochschulverlag GmbH & Co KG

www.classic-pages.de

CONTENTS

CHAPTER I PENNINGTON LAWTON AND THE GRIM REAPER	2
CHAPTER II REVELATIONS	14
CHAPTER III HENRY BLAINE TAKES A HAND	25
CHAPTER IV THE SEARCH	33
CHAPTER V THE WILL	46
CHAPTER VI THE FIRST COUNTER-MOVE	57
CHAPTER VII THE LETTER	67
CHAPTER VIII GUY MORROW FACES A PROBLEM	84
CHAPTER IX GONE!	89
CHAPTER X MARGARET HEFFERMAN'S FAILURE	99
CHAPTER XI THE CONFIDENCE OF EMILY	114
CHAPTER XII THE CIPHER	130
CHAPTER XIII THE EMPTY HOUSE	144
CHAPTER XIV IN THE OPEN	162
CHAPTER XV CHECKMATE!	175
CHAPTER XVI THE LIBRARY CHAIR	190
CHAPTER XVII THE RESCUE	203
CHAPTER XVIII THE TRAP	216
CHAPTER XIX THE UNSEEN LISTENER	231
CHAPTER XX THE CREVICE	247
CHAPTER XXI CLEARED SKIES	262

LIST OF ILLUSTRATIONS

"I supposed that father was working late over some papers and I knew that I must not disturb him." 1

With the cunning of a Jimmy Valentine he manipulated the tumblers. Ramon Hamilton, his discomfiture forgotten, watched with breathless interest. 81

Her head was thrown back, her eyes blazing: and as she faced him, she slowly raised her arm and pointed a steady finger at the recoiling figure. 222

"I supposed that father was working late over some papers and I knew that I must not disturb him."

CHAPTER I
PENNINGTON LAWTON AND THE GRIM REAPER

Had New Illington been part of an empire instead of one of the most important cities in the greatest republic in the world, the cry "The King is dead! Long live the King!" might well have resounded through its streets on that bleak November morning when Pennington Lawton was found dead, seated quietly in his arm-chair by the hearth in the library, where so many vast deals of national import had been first conceived, and the details arranged which had carried them on and on to brilliant consummation.

Lawton, the magnate, the supreme power in the financial world of the whole country, had been suddenly cut down in his prime.

The news of his passing traveled more quickly than the extras which rolled damp from the presses could convey it through the avenues and alleys of the city, whose wealthiest citizen he had been, and through the highways and byways of the country, which his marvelous mentality and finesse had so manifestly strengthened in its position as a world power.

At the banks and trust companies there were hurriedly-called directors' meetings, where men sat about long mahogany tables, and talked constrainedly about the immediate future and the vast changes which the death of this great man would necessarily bring. In the political clubs, his passing was discussed with bated breath.

At the hospitals and charitable institutions which he had so generously helped to maintain, in the art clubs and museums, in the Cosmopolitan Opera House — in the founding of which he had been leading spirit and unfailingly thereafter, its most generous contributor — he was mourned with a sincerity no less deep because of its admixture of self-interest.

In aristocratic drawing-rooms, there were whispers over the tea-cups; the luck of Ramon Hamilton, the rising young lawyer, whose engagement to Anita Lawton, daughter and sole heiress of the dead financier, had just been announced, was remarked upon with the frankness of envy, left momentarily unguarded by the sudden shock.

For three days Pennington Lawton lay in simple, but veritable state. Telegrams poured in from the highest representatives of State, clergy and finance. Then, while the banks and charitable institutions momentarily closed their doors, and flags throughout the city were lowered in respect to the man who had gone, the funeral procession wound its solemn way from the aristocratic church of St. James, to the graveyard. The last extras were issued, detailing the service; the last obituaries printed, the final pæans of praise were sung, and the world went on its way.

During the two days thereafter, multitudinous affairs of more imperative public import were brought to light; a celebrated murder was committed; a notorious band of criminals was rounded up; a political boss toppled and fell from his self-made pedestal; a diplomatic scandal of far-reaching effect was unearthed, and in the press of passing events, the fact that Lawton had been eliminated from the scheme of things faded into comparative insignificance, from the point of view of the general public.

In the great house on Belleair Avenue, which the man who was gone had called home, a tall, slender young girl sat listlessly conversing with a pompous little man, whose clerical garb proclaimed the reason for his coming. The girl's sable garments pathetically betrayed her youth, and in her soft eyes was the pained and wounded look of a child face to face with its first comprehended sorrow.

The Rev. Dr. Franklin laid an obsequious hand upon her arm.

"The Lord gave and the Lord hath taken away; blessed be the name of the Lord."

Anita Lawton shivered slightly, and raised a trembling, protesting hand.

"Please," she said, softly, "I know — I heard you say that at

St. James' two days ago. I try to believe, to think, that in some inscrutable way, God meant it for the best when he took my father so ruthlessly from me, with no premonition, no sign of warning. It is hard, Dr. Franklin. I cannot coordinate my thoughts just yet. You must give me a little time."

The minister bent his short body still lower before her.

"My dear child, do you remember, also, a later prayer in the same service?" — unconsciously he assumed the full rich, rounded, pulpit tones, which were habitual with him. "'Lord, Thou hast been our refuge from one generation to another; before the mountains were brought forth or ever the earth and world were made — '"

A low knocking upon the door interrupted him, and the butler appeared.

"Mr. Rockamore and Mr. Mallowe," Anita Lawton read aloud from the cards he presented. "Oh, I can't see them now. Tell them, Wilkes, that my minister is with me, and they must forgive me for denying myself to them."

The butler retired, and the Rev. Dr. Franklin, at the mention of two of the most prominent and influential men in the city since the death of Lawton, turned bulging, inquiring eyes upon the girl.

"My dear child, is it wise for you to refuse to see two of your father's best friends? You will need their help, their kindness — a woman alone in the world, no matter how exalted her position, needs friends. Mr. Mallowe is not one of my parishioners, but I understand that as president of the Street Railways, he was closely associated with your dear father in many affairs of finance. Mr. Rockamore I know to be a man of almost unlimited power in the world in which Mr. Lawton moved. Should you not see them? Remember that you are under my protection in every way, of course, but since our Heavenly Father has seen fit to take unto Himself your dear one, I feel that it would be advisable for you to place yourself under the temporal guidance of those whom he trusted, at any rate for the time being."

"Oh, I feel that they were my father's friends, but not mine.

Since mother and my little sister and brother were lost at sea, so many years ago, I have learned to depend wholly upon my father, who was more comrade than parent. Then, as you know, I met Ramon — Mr. Hamilton, and of course I trust him as implicitly as I must trust you. But although, on many occasions, I assisted my father to receive his financial confrères on a social basis, I cannot feel at a time like this that I care to talk with any except those who are nearest and dearest to me."

"But suppose they have come, not wholly to offer you consolation, but to confer with you upon some business matters upon which it would be advantageous for you to inform yourself? Your grief and desire for seclusion are most natural, under the circumstances, but one must sometimes consider earthly things also." The minister's evidently eager desire to be present at an interview with the great men and to place himself on a more familiar footing with them was so obvious that Anita's gesture of dissent held also something of repugnance.

"I could not, Dr. Franklin. Perhaps later, when the first shock has passed, but not yet. You understand that I like them both most cordially. Those whom father trusted must be men of sterling worth, but just now I feel as must an animal which has been beaten. I want to creep off into a dark and silent place until my misery dulls a little."

"You have borne up wonderfully well, dear child, under the severe shock of this tragedy. Mrs. Franklin and I have remarked upon it. You have exhibited the same self-mastery and strength of character which made your father the man he was." Dr. Franklin arose from his chair with a sigh which was not altogether perfunctory. "Think well over what I have said. Try to realize that your only consolation and strength in this hour of your deepest sorrow come from on High, and believe that if you take your poor, crushed heart to the Throne of Grace it shall be healed. That has been promised us. Think, also, of what I have just said to you concerning your father's associates, and when next they call, as they will, of course, do very shortly, try to receive them with your usual gracious charms, and should they offer you any advice upon worldly matters, which we must not permit ourselves to neglect, send for me. I will leave you now. Mrs. Franklin will call upon you to-morrow. Try to be brave and calm, and pray for the guidance which will be vouchsafed you, should you ask it, frankly and freely."

Anita Lawton gave him her hand and accompanied him in silence to the door. There, with a few gentle words, she dismissed him, and when the sound of his measured footsteps had diminished, she closed the door with a little gasp of half relief, and turned to the window. It had been an effort to her to see and talk with her spiritual adviser, whose hypocrisy she had vaguely felt.

If only Ramon had come — Ramon, whose wife she would be in so short a time, and who must now be father as well as husband to her. She glanced at the little French clock on the mantel. He was late — he had promised to be there at four. As she parted the heavy curtains, the telephone upon her father's desk, in the corner, shrilled sharply. When she took the receiver off the hook, the voice of her lover came to the girl as clearly, tenderly, as if he, himself, stood beside her.

"Anita, dear, may I come to you now?"

"Oh, please do, Ramon; I have been waiting for you. Dr. Franklin called this afternoon, and while he was here with me Mr. Rockamore and Mr. Mallowe came, but I could not see them. There is something I feel I must talk over with you."

She hung up the receiver with a little sigh, and for the first time in days a faint suspicion of a smile lightened her face. As she turned away, however, her eyes fell upon the great leather chair by the hearth, and her expression changed as she gave an uncontrollable shudder. It was in that chair her father had been found on that fateful morning, about a week ago, clad still in the dinner-clothes of the previous evening, a faint, introspective smile upon his keen, inscrutable face; his eyes wide, with a politely inquiring stare, as if he had looked upon things which until then had been withheld from his vision. She walked over to the chair, and laid her hand where his head had rested. Then, all at once, the tension within her seemed to snap and she flung herself within its capacious, wide-reaching arms, in a torrent of tears — the first she had shed.

It was thus that Ramon Hamilton found her, on his arrival twenty minutes later, and without ado, he gathered her up, carried her to the window-seat, and made her cry out her heart upon his shoulder.

When she was somewhat quieted he said to her gently, "Dearest, why will you insist upon coming to this room, of all others, at least just for a little time? The memories here will only add to your suffering."

"I don't know; I can't explain it. That chair there in which poor father was found has a peculiar, dreadful fascination for me. I have heard that murderers invariably return sooner or later to the scene of their crime. May we not also have the same desire to stay close to the place whence some one we love has departed?"

"You are morbid, dear. Bring your maid and come to my mother's house for a little, as she has repeatedly asked you to do. It will make it so much easier for you."

"Perhaps it would. Your mother has been so very kind, and yet I feel that I must remain here, that there is something for me to do."

"I don't understand. What do you mean, dearest?"

She turned swiftly and placed her hands upon his broad shoulders. Her childish eyes were steely with an intensity of purpose hitherto foreign to them.

"Ramon, there is something I have not told you or any one; but I feel that the time has come for me to speak. It is not nervousness, or imagination; it is a fact which occurred on the night of my father's death."

"Why speak of it, Anita?" He took her hands from his shoulders, and pressed them gently, but with quiet strength. "It is all over now, you know. We must not dwell too much upon what is past; I shall have to help you to put it all from your mind — not to forget, but to make your memories tender and beautiful."

"But I must speak of it. It will be on my mind day and night until I have told you. Ramon, you dined with us that night — the night before. Did my father seem ill to you?"

"Of course not. I had never known him to be in better health and spirits." Ramon glanced at her in involuntary surprise.

"Are you sure?"

"Why do you ask me that? You know that heart-disease may attack one at any time without warning."

Anita sank upon the window-seat again, and leaned forward pensively, her hands clasped over her knees.

"You will remember that after you and father had your coffee and cigars together in the dining-room, you both joined me?"

"Of course. You were playing the piano, ramblingly, as if your thoughts were far away, and you seemed nervous, ill at ease. I wondered about it at the time."

"It was because of father. To you he appeared in the best of spirits, as you say, but I, who knew him better than any one else on earth, realized that he was forcing himself to be genial, to take an interest in what we were saying. For days he had been overwrought and depressed. As you know, he has confided in me, absolutely, since I have been old enough to be a real companion to him. I thought that I knew all his business affairs — those of the last two or three years at least — but latterly his manner has puzzled and distressed me. Then, while you were in the dining-room, the telephone rang twice."

"Yes; the calls were for your father. When he was summoned to the wire he immediately had the connection given to him on his private line, here in the library. After he returned to the dining-room he did seem slightly absent-minded, now that I think of it; but it did not occur to me that there could have been any serious trouble. You know, dearest, ever since the evening when he promised to give you to me, he has consulted me, also, to a great extent about his financial interests, and I think if any difficulty had arisen he would have mentioned it."

"Still, I am convinced that something was on his mind. I tried to approach him concerning it, but he was evasive, and put me off, laughingly. You know that father was not the sort of man whose confidence could be forced even by those dearest to him. I had been so worried about him, though, that I had a nervous headache, and after you left, Ramon, I retired at once. An hour or two later, father had a visitor — that fact as you know, the coroner elicited from the servants, but it had, of course, no bearing on his death, since the caller was Mr. Rockamore. I heard his voice when I opened the door of my room, after ringing for my maid to get some lavender salts. I could not sleep, my headache grew worse; and while I was struggling against it, I heard Mr. Rockamore depart, and my father's voice in the hall, after the slamming of the front door, telling Wilkes to retire, that he would need him no more that night. I heard the butler's footsteps pass down the hall, and then I rose and opened my door again. I don't know why, but I felt that I wanted to speak to father when he came up on his way to bed."

Anita paused, and Ramon, in spite of himself, felt a thrill of puzzled wonder at her expression, upon which a dawning look, almost of horror, spread and grew.

"But he did not come, and after a while I stole to the head of the stairs and looked down. There was a low light in the hall and a brighter one from the library, the door of which was ajar. I supposed that father was working late over some papers, and I knew that I must not disturb him. I crept back to bed at last, with a sigh, but left my own door slightly open, so that if I should happen to be awake when he passed, I might call to him.

"Presently, however, I dozed off. I don't know how long I slept, but I awakened to hear voices — angry voices, my father's and another, which I did not recognize. I got up and by the nightlight I saw that the hands of the little clock on my dresser pointed to nearly three o'clock. I could not imagine who would call on father so very late at night, and I feared at first it might be a burglar, but my common sense assured me that father would not stop to parley with a burglar. While I stood wondering, father raised his voice slightly, and I caught one word which he uttered.

Ramon, that word sounded to me like 'blackmail!' Why, what is it? Why do you look at me so strangely?" she added hastily, at his uncontrollable start.

"I? I am not looking at you strangely, dear; it is not possible that you could have heard aright. It must have been simply a fancy of yours, born of the state of your nerves. You could not really have understood." But Ramon Hamilton looked away from her as he spoke, with a peculiarly significant gleam in his candid eyes. After a slight pause he went on: "No one in the world could have attempted to blackmail your father. He was the soul of honor and integrity, as no one knows better than you. Why, his opinion was sought on every public question. You remember hearing of some of the political honors which he repeatedly refused, but he could, had he wished, have held the highest office at the disposal of the people. You must have been mistaken, Anita. There has never been a reason for the word 'blackmail' to cross your father's lips."

"I know that I was not mistaken, for I heard more — enough to convince me that I had been right in my surmise! Father was keeping something from me!"

"Dear little girl, suppose he had been? Nothing, of course, that could possibly reflect upon his integrity, — don't misunderstand me — but you are only twenty, you know. It is not to be expected that you could quite comprehend the details of all the varied business interests of a man who had virtually led the finances of his country for more than twenty years. Perhaps it was a purely business matter."

"I tell you, Ramon, that that man, whoever he was, actually dared to threaten father. When I heard that word 'blackmail' in the angriest tones which I had ever heard my father use, I did something mean, despicable, which only my culminating anxiety could have induced me to do. I slipped on my robe and slippers, stole half-way downstairs and listened deliberately."

"Anita, you should not have done that! It was not like you to do so. If your father had wished you to know of this interview, don't you think he would have told you?"

"Perhaps he would have, but what opportunity was he given? A few hours later, he was found dead in that chair over there; the chair in which he sat while he was talking with his unknown visitor."

The young man sprang to his feet. "You can't realize what you are saying; what you are hinting! It is unthinkable! If you let these morbid fancies prey upon your mind, you will be really ill." His tones were full of horror. "Your father died of heart-disease. The doctors and the coroner established that beyond the shadow of a doubt, you know. Any other supposition is beyond the bounds of possibility."

"Of heart-disease, yes. But might not the sudden attack have been brought on by his altercation with this man? His sudden rage, controlled as it was, at the insults hurled at him?"

"What insults, Anita? Tell me what you heard when you crept down the stairs. You know you can trust me, dear — you must trust me."

"The man was saying: 'Come, Lawton, be sensible; half a loaf is better than no bread. There is no blackmail about this, even if you choose to call it so. It is an ordinary business proposition, as you have been told a hundred times!'"

"'It's a damnable crooked scheme, as I have told you a hundred times, and I shall have nothing to do with it! This is final!' Father's tones rang out clearly and distinctly, quivering with suppressed fury. 'My hands are clean, my financial operations have been open and above-board; there is no stain upon my life or character, and I can look every man in the face and tell him to go where you may go now!'

"'Oh, is that so!' sneered the other man loudly. Then his voice became insinuatingly low. 'How about poor Herbert — ' His tones were so indistinct that I could not catch the name. Then he went on more defiantly, 'His wife — ' He didn't finish the sentence, Ramon, for father groaned suddenly, terribly, as if he were in swift pain; the man gave a little sneering laugh, and I could hear him moving about in the library, whistling half under his breath in sheer bravado. I could not bear to hear any more. I put my hands over my ears and fled back to my room. What could it mean, Ramon? What is this about father and some other man and his wife which the stranger dared to insinuate! reflected upon father's integrity? Why should he have groaned as if the very mention of these people hurt him inexpressibly?"

"I don't know, dear." Ramon Hamilton sat with his honest eyes still turned from her. "You must have been mistaken; perhaps you even dreamed it all." Anita Lawton gave an impatient gesture.

"I am not quite the child you think me, Ramon. Could that man have meant to insinuate that father in his own advancement had trod upon and ruined some one else, as financiers have always done? Could he have meant that father had driven this man and his wife to despair? I cannot bear to think of it. I try to thrust it from my thoughts a dozen times a day, but that groan from father's lips sounded so much like one of remorse that hideous ideas come beating in on my brain. Was my father like other rich men, Ramon? He did not live for money, although the successful manipulation of it was almost a passion with him. He lived for me, always for me, and the good that he would be able to do in this world."

"Of course he did, darling. No one who knew him could imagine otherwise for a moment." He hesitated, and then added, "No one else discovered this man's presence in the house that night? You have told no one? Not the doctor, or the coroner, or Dr. Franklin?"

"Oh, no; if I had it would have been necessary for me to have told what I overheard. Besides, it could have had no direct bearing on daddy's death; that was caused by heart-disease, as you say. But I believe, and I always will believe, that that man killed father, as surely, as inevitably, as if he had stabbed or shot or poisoned him! Why did he come like a thief in the night? Father's integrity, his honor, were known to all the world. Why did that reference to this Herbert and his wife cause him such pain?"

"I don't know, dear; I have no more idea than you. If you

really, really overheard that conversation, as you seem convinced you did, you did well in keeping it to yourself. Let that hour remain buried in your thoughts, as in your father's grave. Only rest assured that whatever it is, it casts no stain upon your father's good name or his memory." He rose and gathered her into his arms. "I must go now, Anita; I'll come again to-morrow. You are quite sure that you will not accept my mother's invitation? I really think it would be better for you."

She looked deeply into his eyes, then drew herself gently from his clasp. "Not yet. Thank her for me, Ramon, with all my heart, but I will not leave my father's house just yet, even for a few days. I am sure that I shall be happier here." He kissed her, and left the room. She stood where he had left her until she heard the heavy thud of the front door. Then, turning to the window, she thrust her slim little hand between the sedately drawn curtains, and waved him a tender good-by; then with a little sigh, she dropped among the pillows of the couch, lost in thought.

"Whatever was meant by that conversation which I overheard," she murmured to herself, "Ramon knows. I read it in his eyes."

The young man, as he made his way down the crowded avenue, was turning over in his mind the extraordinary story which the girl he loved had told him.

"What could it mean? Who could the man have been? Surely not Herbert himself, and yet — oh! why will they not let sleeping dogs lie; why must that old scandal, that one stain on Pennington Lawton's past have been brought again to light, and at such a time? I pray God that Anita never mentions it to anyone else, never learns the truth. By Jove, if any complications arise from this, there will be only one thing for me to do. I must call upon the Master Mind."

CHAPTER II
REVELATIONS

For two days Anita wandered wraithlike about the great darkened house. The thought that Ramon was keeping something from her — that he and her dead father together had kept a secret which, for some reason, must not be revealed to her, weighed upon her spirits. Conjectures as to the unknown intruder on the night of her father's death, and his possible purpose, flooded her mind to the exclusion of all else.

In the dusk of the winter afternoon she was lying on the couch in her dressing-room, lost in thought, when Ellen, tapping lightly at the door, interrupted her reverie.

"The minister, Miss Anita — the Rev. Dr. Franklin — he is in the drawing-room."

"Oh!" Anita gave a little movement of dismay. "Tell him that I am suffering from a very severe headache, and gave orders that I was not to be disturbed by anyone. He means well, Ellen, of course, but he always depresses me horribly, lately. I don't feel like talking to him this afternoon."

The maid retired, but returned again almost immediately with a surprised, half-frightened expression on her usually stolid face.

"Please, Miss Anita, Dr. Franklin says he must see you and at once. He seems to be excited and he won't take no for an answer."

"Ramon!" Anita cried, springing from the couch with swift apprehension. "Something has happened to Ramon, and Dr. Franklin has come to tell me. He may be injured, dead! Ah, God would not do that; He would not take him from me, too!"

"Don't take on so, Miss Anita, dear," the faithful Ellen murmured, as she deftly smoothed the girl's hair and rearranged her gown; "the little man acts more as if he had a fine piece of gossip to pass on — fidgeting about like an old woman, he is. Begging your pardon, Miss, I know he is the minister, of course, and I ought to show him more respect, but he forever reminds me of a fat black pigeon."

The remarks of the privileged old servant fell upon deaf, unheeding ears. Anita, sobbing softly beneath her breath, flew down to the drawing-room, where the pompous black-cloaked figure rose at her entrance. But — was it purely Anita's fancy or had some indefinable change actually taken place in the manner of her spiritual adviser? The rather close-set eyes seemed to the girl to gleam somewhat coldly upon her, and although he took both her hands in his in quick, fatherly greeting, his hand-clasp appeared all at once to be lacking in warmth.

"My poor child, my poor Anita!" he began unctuously, but she interrupted him.

"What is it, Dr. Franklin? Has something happened to Ramon?" she asked swiftly. "Please tell me! Now, without delay! Don't keep me in suspense. I can tell by your face, your manner, that a new misfortune has come to me! Does it concern Ramon?"

"Oh, no; it is not Mr. Hamilton. You need have no fears for him, Anita. I have come upon a business matter — a matter connected with your dear father's estate."

Anita motioned him to a chair. Seating herself opposite, she gazed at him inquiringly.

"The settlement of the estate? Oh, the lawyers are attending to that, I believe." Anita spoke a little coldly. Had Dr. Franklin come already to inquire about a possible legacy for St. James'?

She was ashamed of the thought the next moment, when he said gently, "Yes, but there is something which I must tell you. It has been requested that I do so. It is a delicate matter to discuss with you, but surely no one is more fitted to speak to you than I."

"Certainly, Doctor, I understand." She leaned forward eagerly.

"My dear, you know the whole country, the whole world at large, has always considered your father to have been a man of great wealth."

"Yes. My father's charities alone, as you are aware, unostentatiously as they were conducted, would have tended to give that impression. Then his tremendous business interests — "

"Anita, at the moment of your father's death he was far from being the King of Finance, which the world judged him to be. It is hard for me to tell you this, but you must know, and you must try to believe that your Heavenly Father is sending you this added trial for some sure purpose of His own. Your father died a poor man, Anita. In fact, a bankrupt." The girl looked up with an incredulous smile.

"Dr. Franklin, who could ever have asked you to come to me with such an incredible assertion? Surely, you must know how preposterous the very idea is! I do not boast or brag, but it is common knowledge that my father was the richest man in the city, in this entire part of the country, in fact. The thought of such a thing is absurd. Who could have attempted to perpetrate such a senseless hoax, a ridiculous insult to your intelligence and mine?"

The minister shook his head slowly.

"'Common knowledge' is, alas, not always trustworthy. It is only too true that your father stood on the verge of bankruptcy. His entire fortune has been swept away."

"Impossible!"

Anita started from her chair, impressed in spite of herself. "How could that be? Who has told you this terrible thing?"

"The unfortunate news was disclosed to me confidentially by your late father's truest friends and closest associates. Having your best interests at heart, they feel that you should know the state of affairs at once, and came to me as the one best fitted to inform you."

"I cannot believe it!" Anita Lawton sank back with white, strained face. "I cannot believe that it is true. How could such a thing have happened? They must be mistaken — those who gave you such information. Father was worth millions, at least. That I know, for he told me much of his business affairs and up to the last day of his life he was engaged in tremendous deals of almost national importance."

"Might he not have become so deeply involved in one of them that he could not extricate himself, and ruin came?" Dr. Franklin insinuated. "I know little of finance, of course; and those who wished you to know gave me none of the details beyond the one paramount fact."

"I know, of course, who were your informants," Anita said. "No one except my father's three closest associates had any possible conception of how much he possessed, even approximately, for he was always secretive and conservative in his dealings. Only to Mr. Mallowe, Mr. Rockamore and Mr. Carlis did he ever divulge his plans to the slightest extent. A bankrupt! My father a bankrupt? The very words seem meaningless to me. Dr. Franklin, there must be some hideous mistake."

"Unfortunately, it is no mistake, my poor child. These gentlemen you mention, I may admit to you in confidence, were my informants."

"You say they gave you no details beyond the paramount fact of my father's ruin? But surely they must have told you something more. I have a right to know, Dr. Franklin, and I shall not rest until I do. How did such a catastrophe come to him? There have been no gigantic failures lately, no panics which could have swept him down. What terrible mistake could he have made, he whose judgment was almost infallible?"

The minister hesitated visibly, and when he spoke at last, it was as if with a conscious effort he chose his words.

"I do not think it was any sudden collapse of some project in which he was engaged, Anita, but a — a general series of misfortunes which culminated by forcing him, just before his death, to the brink of bankruptcy. You are a mere child, my dear, and could not be supposed to understand matters of finance. If you will be guided by me you will accept the assurance of your friends who truly have your best interests at heart. Their statements will be confirmed, I know, by the lawyers who are engaged in settling up the estate of your father. Do not, I beg of you, inquire too closely into the details of your father's insolvency."

Anita rose slowly, her eyes fixed upon the face of the minister, and with her hands resting upon the chair-back, as if to steady herself, she asked quietly:

"Why should I not? What is there which I, his daughter, should not know? Dr. Franklin, there is something behind all this which you are trying to conceal from me. I knew my father to be a multi-millionaire. You come and tell me he was a pauper instead, a bankrupt; and I am not to ask how this state of affairs came about? You have known me since I was a little girl — surely you understand me well enough to realize that I shall not rest under such a condition until the whole truth is revealed to me!"

"I am your friend." The resonance in the minister's voice deepened. "You will believe me when I tell you that it would be best for your future, for the honor of your father's memory, to place yourself without question in the hands of your true friends, and to ask no details which are not voluntarily given you."

"'Best for my future!'" she repeated, aghast. "'For the honor of my father's memory.' What do you mean, Dr. Franklin? You have gone too far not to speak plainly. Do you dare — are you insinuating, that there was something disgraceful, dishonorable about my father's insolvency? You have been my spiritual adviser nearly all my life, and when you tell me that my father was a bankrupt, that the knowledge comes to you from his best friends and will be corroborated by his attorneys, I am forced to believe you. But if you attempt to convince me that my father's honor — his good name — is involved, then I tell you that it is not true! Either a terrible mistake has been made or a deliberate conspiracy is on foot — the blackest sort of conspiracy, to defame the dead!"

"My dear!" The minister raised his hands in shocked amazement. "You are beside yourself, you don't know what you are saying! I have repeated to you only that which was told to me, and in practically the same words. As to the possibility of a conspiracy, you will realize the absurdity of such an idea when I deliver to you the message with which I was charged. Your father's partner in many enterprises, the Honorable Bertie Rockamore, together with President Mallowe, of the Street Railways, and Mr. Carlis, the great politician, promised some little time ago that they would stand in *loco parentis* toward you should your natural protector be removed. They desire me to tell you that you need have no anxiety for the immediate future. You will be cared for and provided with all that you have been accustomed to, just as if your father were alive."

"Indeed? They are most kind — " Anita spoke quietly enough, but with a curiously dry, controlled note in her voice which reminded the minister of her father's tones, and for some inexplicable reason he felt vaguely uncomfortable. "Please say to them that I do sincerely appreciate their magnanimity, their charity, toward one who has no right, legal or moral, to claim protection or care from them. But now, Dr. Franklin, may I beg that you will forgive me if I retire? The news you have brought me of course has been a terrible shock. I must have time to collect my thoughts, to realize the sudden, terrible change this revelation has made in my whole life. I am deeply grateful to you, to my father's three associates, but I can say no more now."

"Of course, dear child." Dr. Franklin patted her hand perfunctorily and arose with ill-concealed relief that the interview was at an end. He could not understand her attitude of the last few moments and it troubled him vaguely. She had received the news of her father's bankruptcy with a girlish horror and incredulousness — which had been only natural under the circumstances; but when it was borne in upon her, in as delicate a way as he could convey it, that dishonor was involved in the matter, she had, after the first outburst, maintained a stony, ashen self-poise and control that were far from what he had expected. It was the most disagreeable task he had performed in many a day and he was heartily glad that it was over. Only his very great desire to ingratiate himself with these kings of finance, who had commissioned him to do their bidding, as well as the inclination to be of real service to his young and orphaned parishioner, had induced him to undertake the mission.

"You must rest and have an opportunity to adjust yourself to this new, unfortunate state of affairs," he continued. "I will call again to-morrow. If I can be of the slightest service to you, do not hesitate to let me know. It is a sad trial, but our Heavenly Father has tempered the wind to the shorn lamb; He has provided you with a protector in young Mr. Hamilton, and with kind, true friends who will see that no harm or deprivation comes to you. Try to feel that this added grief and trouble will, in the end, be for the best."

The alacrity with which he took his departure was painfully obvious, but Anita scarcely noticed it. Her mind was busy with the new, hideous thought, which had assailed her at that first hint of dishonesty on the part of her father — the thought that she was being made the victim of a gigantic conspiracy.

As soon as she found herself alone, she flew to the telephone. "Main, 2785," she demanded.... "Mr. Hamilton, please.... Is that you, Ramon?... Can you come to me at once? I need your advice and help. Something has happened — something terrible! No, I cannot tell you over the 'phone. You will come at once? Yes, good-by, Ramon dear."

She hung up the receiver and paced the floor restlessly. Almost inconceivable as it had appeared to her consciousness under the first shock of the announcement, she might in time have come to accept the astounding fact of her father's insolvency, but that disgrace, dishonor, could have attached itself to his name — that he, the model of uprightness, of integrity could have been guilty of crooked dealing, of something which must for the honor of his memory be kept secret from the ears of his fellow-men, she could never bring herself to believe. Every instinct of her nature revolted, and underlying all her girlish unsophistication, a native shrewdness, inherited perhaps from her father, bade her distrust alike the worldly, self-interested pastor of the Church of St. James and the three so-called friends, who, although her father's associates, had been his rivals, and who had offered with such astounding magnanimity to stand by her.

Why had they offered to help her? Was it really through tenderness and affection for her father's daughter, or was it to stay her hand and close her mouth to all queries?

Why did not Ramon come? Surely he should have been there before this. What could be detaining him? She tried to be patient, to calm her seething brain while she waited, but it was no use. Hours passed while she paced the floor, restlessly, and the dusk settled into the darkness of early winter. Wilkes came to turn on the lights, but she refused them — she could think better in the dark. The dinner-hour came and went and twice Ellen knocked anxiously upon the door, but Anita, torn with anxiety, would pay no heed. She had telephoned to Ramon's office, only to find that he had left there immediately upon receiving her message; to his home — he had not returned.

Nine o'clock sounded in silvery chimes from the clock upon the mantel; then ten and eleven and at length, just when she felt that she could endure no more, the front door-bell rang. A well-known step sounded upon the stairs, and Ramon entered.

With a little gasp of joy and relief she flung herself upon him in the darkness, but at an involuntary groan from him she recoiled.

"What is it, Ramon? What has happened to you?"

Without waiting for a reply she switched on the light.

Ramon stood before her, his face pale, his eyes dark with pain. One arm was in a sling and the thick hair upon his forehead barely concealed a long strip of plaster.

"Nothing really serious, dear. I had a slight accident — run down by a motor-car, just after leaving the office. My head was cut and I was rather knocked out, so they took me to a hospital. I would have come before, but they would not allow me to leave. I knew that you would be anxious because of my delay in coming, but I feared to add to your apprehension by telephoning to you from the hospital."

"But your arm — is it sprained?"

"Broken. I had a nasty crash — can't imagine how it was that I didn't see the car coming in time to avoid it. It was a big limousine with several men inside, all singing and shouting riotously, and the chauffeur, I think, must have been drunk, for he swerved the car directly across the road in my path. They never stopped after they had bowled me over, and no one seemed to know where they went."

"Then the police did not get their number?"

"No, but they will, of course. Not that I care, particularly; I'm lucky to have got off as lightly as I did. I might have been killed."

"It was a miracle that you were not, Ramon. Do you know what I believe? I don't think it was any accident, but a deliberate attempt to assassinate you; to keep you from coming to me."

"What nonsense, dear! They were a wild, hilarious party, careless and irresponsible. Such accidents happen every day."

"I am convinced that it was no accident. Ramon, I feel that I am to be the victim of a conspiracy; that you are the only human being who stands in the way of my being absolutely in the power of those who would defraud me and defame father's name."

"Anita, what do you mean?"

"Dr. Franklin called upon me this afternoon; he left just before I telephoned to you. He told me an astonishing piece of news. Ramon, would you have considered my father a rich man?"

"What an absurd question, dear! Of course. One of the richest men in the whole country, as you know."

"You say that he consulted you about his business affairs, and that you knew of no trouble or difficulty which could have caused him anxiety? His securities in stocks and bonds, his assets were all sound?"

"Certainly. What do you mean?"

"I mean that my father died a pauper! That on the word of Mr. Rockamore, Mr. Mallowe, Mr. Carlis and Dr. Franklin, he was on the verge of dishonorable bankruptcy, into which I may not inquire."

"Good Heavens, they must be mad! I am sure that your father was at the zenith of his successful career, and as for dishonor, surely, Anita, no one who knew him could credit that!"

"Mr. Rockamore and the other two who were so closely associated with him made a solemn promise to my father shortly before his death, it seems, that they would care for and provide for me. They sent Dr. Franklin to me this afternoon to explain the circumstances to me, and to assure me of their protection. Save for you, they consider me absolutely in their hands; and when I sent for you, you were almost killed in the attempt to come to me. Ramon, don't you see, don't you understand, there is some mystery on foot, some terrible conspiracy? That unknown visitor, my father's death so soon after, and now this sudden revelation of his bankruptcy, together with this accident to you? Ramon, we must have advice and help. I do not believe that my father was a pauper. I know that he has done nothing dishonorable; I am convinced that the accident to you was a premeditated attempt at murder."

"My God! I can't believe it, Anita; I don't know what to think. If it turns out that there really is something crooked about it all, and Rockamore and the others are concerned in it, it will be the biggest conspiracy that was ever hatched in the world of high finance. You were right, dear, bless your woman's intuition; we must have help. This matter must be thoroughly investigated. There is only one man in America to-day, who is capable of carrying it through, successfully. I shall send at once for the Master Mind."

"The Master Mind?"

"Yes, dear — Henry Blaine, the most eminent detective the English-speaking world has produced."

"I have heard of him, of course. I think father knew him, did he not?"

"Yes, on one occasion he was of inestimable service to your father. I will summon him at once."

Ramon went to the telephone and by good luck found the

detective free for the moment and at his service.

He returned to the girl. She noticed that he reeled slightly in his walk; that his lips were white and set with pain.

"Ramon, you are ill, suffering. That cut on your head and your poor arm — "

"It is nothing. I don't mind, Anita darling; it will soon pass. Thank Heavens, I found Mr. Blaine free. He will get to the truth of this matter for us even if no one else on earth could. He has brought more notorious malefactors to justice than any detective of modern times; fearlessly, he has unearthed political scandals which lay dangerously close to the highest executives of the land. He cannot be cajoled, bribed or intimidated; you will be safe in his hands from the machinations of every scoundrel who ever lived."

"I have read of some of his marvelous exploits, but; what service was it that he rendered to my father?"

"I — I cannot tell you, dearest. It was very long ago, and a matter which affected your father solely. Perhaps some time you may learn the truth of it."

"I may not know! I may not know! Why must I be so hedged in? Why must everything be kept from me? I feel as if I were living in a maze of mystery. I must know the truth."

She wrung her hands hysterically, but he soothed her and they talked in low tones until Wilkes suddenly appeared in the doorway and announced:

"Mr. Henry Blaine!"

CHAPTER III
HENRY BLAINE TAKES A HAND

A man stood upon the threshold: a man of medium height, with sandy hair and mustache slightly tinged with gray. His face was alert and keenly intelligent. His eyes shrewd, but kindly, the brows sloping downward toward the nose, with the peculiar look of concentration of one given to quick decisions and instant, fearless action.

His eyes traveled quickly from the young girl's face to Ramon Hamilton, as the latter advanced with outstretched hand.

"Mr. Blaine, it was fortunate that we found you at liberty and able to assist us in a matter which is of vital importance to us both. This is Miss Anita Lawton, daughter of the late Pennington Lawton, who desires your aid on a most urgent matter."

"Miss Lawton." Mr. Elaine bowed over her hand.

When they were seated she said, shyly: "I understand from Ramon — Mr. Hamilton — that you were at one time of great service to my father. I trust that you will be able to help me now, for I feel that I am in the meshes of a conspiracy. You know that my father died suddenly, almost a week ago."

"Yes, of course. His death was a great loss to the whole country, Miss Lawton."

"Something occurred a few hours before his death, of which even the coroner is unaware, Mr. Blaine. I told Mr. Hamilton what I knew, but he advised me to say nothing of it, unless further developments ensued."

"And they have ensued?" the detective asked quietly.

"Yes."

Anita then detailed to Mr. Blaine the incident of her father's nocturnal visitor. As she told him the conversation she had overheard, it seemed to her that the eyes of the detective narrowed slightly, but no other change of expression betrayed the fact that the incident might have held a significance in his mind.

"The voice was entirely strange to you?" he asked.

"Yes; I have never heard it before, but it made such an impression upon me that I think I would recognize it instantly whenever or wherever I might happen to hear it."

"You caught no glimpse of the man through the half-opened door?"

"No, I was not far enough downstairs to see into the room."

"And when you fled, after hearing your father groan, you returned immediately to your room?"

"Yes. I closed my door and buried my face deeply in the pillows on my bed. I did not want to hear or know any more. I was frightened; I did not know what to think. After a time I must have drifted off into an uneasy sort of sleep, for I knew nothing more until my maid came to tell me that Wilkes, the butler, wished to speak to me. My father had been found dead in his chair. No one in the household seemed to know of my father's late visitor, for they made no mention of his coming. I would have told no one, except Ramon, but for the fact that this afternoon my minister informed me that my father, instead of being the multi-millionaire we had all supposed him, had in reality died a bankrupt."

The detective received this information with inscrutable calm. Only by a thoughtful pursing of his lips did he give indication that the news had any visible effect upon him.

Anita continued, giving him all the details of the minister's visit, and the magnanimous promise of her father's three associates to stand in *loco parentis* toward her.

It was only when she told of summoning her lover, and the accident which befell him on his way to her, that that peculiar gleam returned again to the eyes of Mr. Blaine, and they glanced narrowly at the young man opposite him.

"As I told Ramon, I cannot help but feel that it is not true. My father could not have become a pauper, much less could he, the soul of honor, have been guilty of anything derogatory to his good name. Until a few days prior to his death, he had been in his usual excellent spirits, and surely had there been any financial difficulties in his path he would have retrenched, in some measure. He made no effort to do so, however, and in the last few weeks has given even more generously than usual to the various philanthropic projects in which he was so interested. Does that look as if he was on the verge of bankruptcy? He bought me a string of pearls on my birthday, two months ago, which for their size are considered by experts to be the most perfectly matched in America. A fortnight ago, he presented me with a new car. Only three days before his death he spoke of an ancient château in France which he had desired to purchase. Oh, the whole affair is utterly inexplicable to me!"

"We will take the matter up at once, Miss Lawton. The main thing that I must impress upon you for the present is to acquiesce with the utmost docility and unsuspicion in every proposition made to you by the three men, Carlis, Mallowe and Rockamore; in other words, place yourself absolutely in their hands, but keep me informed of every move they make. You understand that the most important factor in this case is to keep them absolutely unsuspecting of your distrust, or that you have called me to your assistance. I must not be seen coming here or to Mr. Hamilton's office, nor must you come to mine. I will have a private wire installed for you to-morrow morning, by means of which you can communicate with me, or one of my operatives, at any hour of the day or night, in the presence of anyone. This telephone will connect only with my office, but the number will be, supposedly, that of your dressmaker, and if you require aid, advice, or the presence of one of my operatives, you have merely to call up the number and say: 'Is my gown ready? If it is, please send it around immediately.' Let me know through this medium whatever occurs, and take absolutely no one into your confidence."

"I understand, Mr. Blaine; and I will try to follow your instructions to the letter. Oh, by the way, there is something I wish to tell you, which no one, not even Mr. Hamilton, knows, much less my father's friends, or my minister. Four years ago, my father financed a philanthropic venture of mine, the Anita Lawton Club for Working Girls. It is not a purely charitable institution, but a home club, where worthy young women could live by paying a nominal sum — merely to preserve their self-respect — and be aided in obtaining positions. Stenographers, telephone and telegraph operators, clerks, all find homes there. No one knew, however, that under my management, the club grew in less than a year not only to have paid for itself, but to have yielded a small income, over and above expenses. I did not tell my father — I don't know why, perhaps it was because I inherited a little of his business acumen, but I manipulated the net income in various minor undertakings, even in time buying small plots of unimproved real-estate, meaning after a year or two more to surprise my father with the result of my venture, but his death intervened before I could tell him about it."

"Your father's associates, then, believe you to be without funds or private income of your own?" the detective asked.

"Yes, Mr. Blaine. And whatever money is necessary for the investigation, will, of course, be forthcoming from this source."

"Let me strongly advise you to make no mention of it to anyone else; let these men believe you to be utterly within their power financially. And now, Miss Lawton, I will leave you, for I have work to do." The detective rose. "The private wire will be installed to-morrow morning. Remember to be absolutely unsuspicious, to appear deeply grateful for the kindness offered you; receive these men and your spiritual adviser whenever they call, and above all, keep me informed of everything that occurs, no matter how insignificant or irrelevant it may seem to you to be. Keep me advised on even the smallest details — anything, everything concerning you and them."

Thus it was, that when two days later, President Mallowe of the Street Railways, called upon his new ward, she received him with downcast eyes, and a charmingly deferential manner. His long-nosed, heavy-jowled face, with the bristling gray side-whiskers, flushed darkly when she placed her trembling little hand in his and shyly voiced her gratitude for his great kindness to her.

"My dear young lady, this has been a most sad and unfortunate affair, but I have come to assure you again of the sentiments of myself and my associates toward you. We come, your self-appointed guardians; we will see that no financial worriments shall come to you. Remember, my dear, that I have three married daughters of my own, and I could not permit the child of my old friend to want for anything. You may remain on here in this house, which has been your home, indefinitely, and it will be maintained for you in the manner to which you have always been accustomed."

"Remain here in my home?" Anita stammered. "Why it — it is my home, isn't it?"

"You must consider it as such. I do not like to tell you this, but it is necessary that you should know. I hold a mortgage of eighty thousand dollars on the house, but I have never recorded it, because of my friendship and close affiliation with your father. I shall not have it recorded now, of course, but there is a slight condition, purely a matter of business, which in view of the fact that through your coming marriage you will have a home of your own, Mr. Rockamore, Mr. Carlis and myself, feel that we should agree upon. Your father has a shadowy interest in some old bonds which have for years been unremunerative. Should they prove of ultimate value, we feel that they should be transferred to us as our reimbursement for the present large sum which we shall lay out for you."

"Of course, Mr. Mallowe. That would only be just. I am glad that I may perhaps have an opportunity to repay some of the kindness which in your great-hearted charity, you are now bestowing upon me. I will see that my father's attorneys attend to the matter, as soon as possible. It may be some little time before the estate is settled, as of course it must be horribly complicated and involved, but I will bring this to their immediate attention."

"You are a very brave young woman, Miss Lawton, and I am glad that you are taking such a clear-sighted view of this double catastrophe which has come upon you. Ah, I had almost forgotten; here is a duplicate of the mortgage which I hold upon this house, which your father made out to me some months ago."

Anita scarcely glanced at it, but laid it quietly by upon the table, as though it were of small interest to her.

"Mr. Mallowe, although I understand that Mr. Rockamore, being a promoter, was more closely associated with my father in various projects than you, I believe that he always considered you his best friend. Can you tell me what it was which brought my father's affairs to such a pass as this?"

"Dear young lady, do not ask me. It is a painful subject to discuss, and as you are a mere child, you cannot be supposed to understand the financial manœuvres of a man of your father's passion for gigantic operations. Years of success had possibly made him overconfident; and then you know, we are none of us infallible; we are liable to make mistakes, at one time or another. Your father interested himself daringly in many schemes which we more conservative ones would have hesitated to enter; indeed, we not only hesitated, but repeatedly declined when your father placed the propositions before us. As you know, unfortunately, he was a man who would have resented any attempt at advice, and although for a long time we have seen his approaching financial downfall, and have helped him in every way we could to avert it, he would not relinquish his plans while there was yet time. Do not ask me to go into any further details. It is really most distressing. Your father's attorneys will understand the matter fully when the estate is finally settled."

"I cannot understand it," Anita murmured. "I thought my father's judgment almost infallible. However, Mr. Mallowe, I cannot express my gratitude to you and my father's other associates for your great kindness toward me. Believe me, I am deeply affected by it. I shall never forget what you have done."

"Do not speak of it, dear Miss Lawton. I only wish for your sake that your poor father had heeded poorer heads than his, but it is too late to speak of that now. We will do all in our power to aid you, rest assured of that. Should you require anything, you have only to call upon Mr. Rockamore, Mr. Carlis or myself."

When he had bowed himself out, Anita flew to the table, seized the duplicate of the mortgage which he had given her, and slipped it between the pages of a book lying there. Then she went directly to her dressing-room where on a little stand near her bed reposed a telephone instrument which had not been there three days previously.

"Grosvenor 0760," she demanded, and when a voice replied to her at the other end of the wire, she asked querulously, "Is not my new gown ready yet? If it is, will you kindly send it over at once? I have also found your last quarterly bill, and I think there is something wrong with it. I will send it back by the messenger, who brings my gown. Thank you; good-by."

She took an envelope from the desk and returning to the drawing-room slipped the duplicate mortgage within it and sealed it carefully.

When, a few minutes later, a tall, dark, stolid-faced young man appeared, with a large dressmaker's box, she placed the envelope in his hand.

"For Mr. Blaine," she whispered. "See that it reaches him immediately."

A half hour afterward, Ramon Hamilton went to the telephone in his office, and heard the detective's voice over the wire.

"Mr. Hamilton, have you among the letters and documents at your office the signature of the person we were discussing the other day?"

"Why, yes, I think so. I will look and see. If I have do you wish me to send it around to you?"

"No, thank you. A messenger boy will call for it in a few minutes."

Wondering, Ramon Hamilton shuffled hastily through the paper in the pigeon-holes of his desk until he came to a letter from Pennington Lawton. He carefully tore off the signature, and when the messenger boy appeared, gave it to him. He would not have been so puzzled, had he seen the great Henry Blaine, when a few minutes had elapsed, seated before the desk in his office, comparing the signature of the torn slip which he had sent with that affixed to the duplicate mortgage.

A long, close, breathless scrutiny, with the most powerful magnifying glasses, and the detective jumped to his feet.

"That's no signature of Pennington Lawton," he exulted to himself. "I thought I knew that fine hand, perfectly as the forgery has been done. That's the work of James Brunell, by the Lord!"

CHAPTER IV
THE SEARCH

Henry Blaine, the man of decision, wasted no time in vain thought. Instantly, upon his discovery that the signature of Pennington Lawton had been forged, and that it had been done by an old and well-known offender, he touched the bell on his desk, which brought his confidential secretary.

"Has Guy Morrow returned yet from that blackmail case in Denver?"

"Yes, sir. He's in his private office now, making out his report to you."

A moment later, there entered a tall, dark young man, strong and muscular in build, but not apparently heavy, with a smooth face and firm-set jaw.

"I haven't finished my report yet, sir — "

"The report can wait. You remember James Brunell, the forger?"

"James Brunell?" Morrow repeated. "He was before my time, of course, but I've heard of him and his exploits. Pretty slick article, wasn't he! I understand he has been dead for years — at least nothing has been heard of his activities since I have been in the sleuth game."

"Did you ever hear of any of his associates?"

"I can't say that I have, sir, except Crimmins and Dolan; Crimmins died in San Quentin before his time was up; Dolan after his release went to Japan."

"I want to find Brunell. His closest associate was Walter Pennold. I think Pennold is living somewhere in Brooklyn, and through him you may be able to locate Brunell — "

Morrow shrugged his shoulders.

"A retired crook in the suburbs. That's going to take time."

"Not the way we'll work it. Listen."

The next morning, a tall, dark young man, strong and muscular in build, with a smooth face and firm-set jaw, appeared at the Bank of Brooklyn & Queens, and was immediately installed as a clerk, after a private interview with the vice-president.

His fellow clerks looked at him askance at first, for they knew there had been no vacancy, and there was a long waiting list ahead of him, but the young man bore himself with such a quiet, modest air of *camaraderie* about him that by the noon hour they had quite accepted him as one of themselves.

During the morning a package came to the bank and a letter which read in part:

... I am returning these securities to you in the hope that you may be able to place them in the possession of Jimmy Brunell. They belong to him, and my conscience is responsible for their return. I don't know where to find him. I do know that at one time he did some banking at the Brooklyn & Queens Institution. If he does not do so now, kindly hold these securities for Jimmy Brunell until called for, and in the meantime see Walter Pennold of Brooklyn.

With the package and letter came a request from Henry Blaine which those in power at the Brooklyn & Queens Bank were only too glad to accede to, in order to ingratiate themselves with the great investigator.

In accordance with this request, therefore, the affair was made known by the bank-officials to the clerks as a matter of long standing which had only just been rediscovered in an old vault, and the subordinates discussed it among themselves with the gusto of those whose lives were bounded by gilt cages, and circumscribed by rules of silence. It was not unusual, therefore, that the new clerk, Alfred Hicks, should have heard of it, but it was unusual that he should find it expedient to make a detour on his way to work the next morning which would take him to the gate of Walter Pennold's modest home. Perhaps the fact that Alfred Hicks' real name was Guy Morrow and that a letter received early that morning from Henry Blaine's office, giving Pennold's address and a single line of instruction may have had much to do with his matutinal visit.

Be that as it may, Morrow, the dapper young bank-clerk, found in the Pennold household a grizzled, middle-aged man, with shifty, suspicious eyes and a moist hand-clasp; behind him appeared a shrewish, thin-haired wife who eyed the intruder from the first with ill-concealed animosity.

He smiled — that frank, winning smile which had helped to land more men behind the bars than the astuteness of many of his seniors — and said: "I'm a clerk in the Brooklyn & Queens Bank, Mr. Pennold, and we have a box of securities there evidently belonging to one Jimmy Brunell. No one knows anything about it and no note came with it except a line which read: 'Hold for Jim Brunell. See Walter Pennold of Brooklyn.' Now you're the only Walter Pennold who banks with the B. & Q. and I thought you might like to know about it. There are over two hundred thousand dollars in securities and they have evidently been left there by somebody as conscience-money. You can go to the bank and see the people about it, of course. In fact, I understand they are going to write you a letter concerning it, but I thought you might like to know of it in advance. In case this Mr. Brunell is alive, they will pay him the money on demand, or if dead, to his heirs after him."

The middle-aged man with the shifty eyes spat cautiously, and then, rubbing his stubby chin with a hairy, freckled hand, observed:

"Well, young man, I'm Pennold, all right. I do some business with the Brooklyn & Queens people — small business, of course, for we poor honest folk haven't the money to put in finance that the big stock-holders have. I don't know where you can find this man Brunell, haven't heard of him in years, but I understand he went wrong. Ain't that so, Mame?"

The hatchet-faced woman nodded her head in slow and non-committal thought.

Pennold edged a little nearer his unknown guest and asked in a tone of would-be heartiness. "And what might your name be? You're a bright-looking feller to be a bank-clerk — not the stolid, plodding kind."

Morrow chuckled again.

"My name is Hicks. I live at 46 Jefferson Place. It's only a little way from here, you know." He swung his lunch-box nonchalantly. "Of course, bank-clerking don't get you anywhere, but it's steady, such as it is, and I go out with the boys a lot." He added confidentially: "The ponies are still running, you know, even if the betting-ring is closed — and there are other ways — " He paused significantly.

"I see, a sport, eh?" Pennold darted a quick glance at his wife. "Well, don't let it get the best of you, young feller. Remember what I told you about Jimmy Brunell — at least, what the report of him was. If I hear anything of where he is, I'll let the bank know."

"I'll be getting on; I'm late now — " Morrow paused on the bottom step of the little porch and turned. "See you again, Mr. Pennold, and your wife, if you'll let me. I pass by here often — I've been boarding with Mrs. Lindsay, on Jefferson Place, for some time now. By the way, have you seen the sporting page of the *Gazette* this morning? Al Goetz edits it, you know, and he gives you the straight dope. There'll be nothing to that fight they're pulling off Saturday night at the Zucker Athletic Club — Hennessey'll put it all over Schnabel in the first round. Good-by! If you hear anything of this Brunell, be sure you let me or the bank know!"

For a long moment after his buoyant stride had carried him out of sight around the corner, Walter Pennold and his wife sat in thoughtful silence. Then the woman spoke.

"What d'ye think of it all, Wally?"

"Dunno." The gentleman addressed drew from his pocket a blackened, odoriferous pipe and sucked upon it. "Must be some lay, of course. I'll go up to the bank and find out what I can, but I don't think that young feller, Hicks, is in on it. I've been in the game for forty years, and if I'm a judge, he's no 'tec. Fool kid spendin' more'n he earns and out for what coin he can grab. I'll look up that landlady of his, too, Mame; and if he's on the level there, and at the bank — "

"And if those securities are at the bank, he ought to be willin' to come in with us on a share," the wife supplemented shrewdly. "But it seems like some kind of a gag to me. You knew all Jimmy Brunell's jobs till he got religion or somethin', and turned honest — I can't think of any old crook who'd turn over that money to him, two hundred thousand cold, because his conscience hurt him, can you? You know, too, how decent and respectable Jimmy's been livin' all these years, putting up a front for the sake of that daughter of his; suppose this was a put-up game to catch him — what do the bulls want him for?"

"I ain't no mind-reader. I'll look up this business of securities, and then if the young feller's talked straight, we'll try to work it through him, if we can get to him, and I guess we can, so long as I ain't lost the gift of the gab in twenty years. We'll be as good, sorrowing heirs as ever Jimmy Brunell could find anywheres."

Before Walter Pennold could reach the bank, however, an unimpeachably official letter arrived from that institution, confirming the news imparted by the bank-clerk concerning the securities left for James Brunell. Pennold, going to the bank ostensibly to assure those in authority there of his cordial willingness to assist in the search for the heir, incidentally assured himself of Alfred Hicks' seemingly legitimate occupation. A later visit to Mrs. Lindsay of 46 Jefferson Place convinced him that the young man had lived there for some months and was as generous, openhanded, easy-going a boarder as that excellent woman had ever taken into her house. Just what price was paid by Henry Blaine to Mrs. Lindsay for that statement is immaterial to this narrative, but it suffices that Walter Pennold returned to the sharp-tongued wife of his bosom with only one obstacle in his thoughts between himself and a goodly share of the coveted two hundred thousand dollars.

That obstacle was an extremely healthy fear of Jimmy Brunell. It was true that there had been no connection between them in years, but he remembered Jimmy's attitude toward the "snitcher," as well as toward the man who "held out" on his pals; and behind his cupidity was a lurking caution which was made manifest when he walked into the kitchen and found Mrs. Pennold with her shriveled arms immersed in the washtub.

"Say, Mame, the young feller, Hicks, is all right, and so is the bank; but how about Jimmy himself? If I can fix the young feller, and we can pull it off with the bank, that's all well and good. But s'pose Jimmy should hear of it? Know what would happen to us, don't you?"

"If he ain't heard of them securities all this time they've been lyin' forgotten in the bank, it's safe he won't hear of 'em now unless you tell him," retorted his shrewder half, dryly. "Of course, if he's lived straight, as he has for near twenty years as far as we know, and he finds it out, he'll grab everything for himself. Why shouldn't he? But s'pose the bulls are after him for somethin', and the bank's hood-winked as well as us, where are we if we mix up in this? Tell me that!"

"There's another side of it, too, Mame."

Pennold walked to the window, and regarded the sordid lines of washed clothes contemplatively. "What if Jimmy has been up to somethin' on the quiet, that the bulls ain't on to, and this bunch of securities is on the level? If I went to him on the square, and offered him a percentage to play dead, wouldn't he be ready and willin' to divide?"

"Of course he would; he's no fool," returned Mrs. Pennold shortly. "But let me tell you, Wally, I don't like the look of that 'See Walter Pennold of Brooklyn,' on the note in the bank. S'pose they was trying to trace him through us?"

"You're talkin' like a blame' fool, Mame. Them securities has been there for years, forgotten. Everybody knows that me and Brunell was pals in the old days, but no one's got nothin' on us now, and he give up the game years ago."

"How d'you know he did?" persisted his wife doggedly. "That's what you better find out, but you've gotter be careful about it, in case this whole thing should be a plant."

"You don't have to tell me!" Pennold grumbled. "I'll write him first and then wait a few days, and if anyone's tailing me in the meantime, they'll have a run for their money."

"Write him!"

"Of course. You may have forgotten the old cipher, but I haven't. You know yourself we invented it, Jimmy and me, and the police tried their level best to get on to it, but failed."

"You can't address it in cipher, and if you're tailed you won't get a chance to mail it, Wally. Better wait and try to see him without writing."

For answer Pennold opened a drawer in the table, drew forth a grimy sheet of paper and an envelope, and bent laboriously to his task. It was long past dusk when he had finished, and tossed the paper across the table for his wife's perusal. This is what she saw:

```
ⱳLJF ⴖEⴝ JⴖΛ
     JOↄ ꓶⴖꓶLΛ Uⴖꓶoꓶↄ >ⴖ ΛⴖV
ⱡFⴖꓶ ⴖEⴝ >UⴖFL ELⱡ> VꓶꞀJOⴝ
    <ↃJ> O> ꓶΛ >ↃJFL ⱡⴖF UⴖEELU>‐
Oꓶↄ ⱡⴖF ΛⴖV Ɂⴖ FO>E <OEE ⴝJEE ⴖꓶ
VⴖV >ↃVF>ⴝJΛ J> ⱡⴖVF ⴖLꓶ
```

When she had gazed long at the characters, she shook her head at him, and a slow smile came over her face.

"You've forgotten a little yourself, Wally. You made a mistake in the *k*."

He glanced half-incredulously at it, and then laid his huge, rough hand on her thin hair in the first caress he had given her in years.

"By God, old girl, you're a smart one! You're right. Now listen. You've got to do the rest for me, the hardest part. Mail it."

"How? If we're tailed — "

"There'll be only one on the job, if we are, and I'll keep him busy to-morrow morning. You go to the market as usual, then go into that big department store, Ahearn & McManus'. There's a mail chute there, next the notion counter on the ground floor. Buy a spool of thread or somethin', and while you're waitin' for change, drop the letter in the box. You used to be pretty slick in department stores, Mame — "

"Smoothest shoplifter in New York until I got palsy!" she interrupted proudly, an unaccustomed glow on her sallow face. "I'll do it, Wally; I know I can!"

The next morning Alfred Hicks was a little late in getting to his work at the bank — so late, in fact, that he had only time to wave a cordial greeting to his new friends in their cages as he passed. He paused, however, that evening, with a pot of flowering bloom for Mrs. Pennold's dingy, not over-clean window-sill, and a packet of tobacco which he shared generously with his host. He talked much, with the garrulous self-confidence of youth, but did not mention the matter of the securities, and left the crafty couple completely disarmed.

Neither on entering nor leaving did Hicks appear to notice a short, swarthy figure loitering in the shadow of a dejected-looking ailanthus tree near the corner. It would have appeared curious, therefore, that the lurking figure followed the bank-clerk almost to his lodgings, had it not been for the fact that just before Jefferson Place was reached the figure sidled up to Hicks' side and whispered:

"No news yet, Morrow. Pennold went this morning to old Loui the Grabber and tried to borrow money from him, but didn't get it. I heard the whole talk. Then he went to Tanbark Pete's and got a ten-spot. After that, he divided his time between two saloons, where he played dominoes and pinochle, and his own house. I've got to report to H. B. when I'm sure the subject is safe for the night. Have you found anything yet?"

"Only that I've got him on the run. If he knows where our

man is, Suraci, he'll go after him in a day or two. Meantime, tell H. B., in case I don't get a chance to let him know, that the securities stunt went, all right, and my end of it is O. K."

The next day, and the following, Pennold did indeed set for the young Italian detective a swift pace. He departed upon long rambles, which started briskly and ended aimlessly; he called upon harmless and tedious acquaintances, from Jamaica to Fordham; he went — apparently and ostentatiously to look for a position as janitor — to many office-buildings in lower Manhattan, which he invariably entered and left by different doors. In the evenings he sat blandly upon his own stoop, smoking and chatting amiably if monosyllabically with his wife and their new-found friend, Alfred Hicks, while his indefatigable shadow glowered apparently unnoticed from the gloom of the ailanthus tree.

On Thursday morning, however, Pennold betook himself leisurely to the nearest subway station, and there the real trial of strength between him and his unseen antagonist began. From the Brooklyn Bridge station he rode to the Grand Central; then with a speed which belied his physical appearance, he raced across the bridge to the downtown platform, and caught a train for Fourteenth Street. There he swiftly turned north to Seventy-second Street — then to the Grand Central, again to Ninety-sixth, and so on, doubling from station to station until finally he felt that he must be entirely secure from pursuit.

He alighted at length at a station far up in the Bronx, and after looking carefully about he started off toward the west, where the mushroom growth of the new city sprang up in rows of rococo brick and stone houses with oases of green fields and open lots between. He turned up a little lane of tiny frame houses, each set in its trim garden, and stopped at the fourth cottage.

With a last furtive backward glance, Pennold mounted the steps and rang the bell nervously. The door was opened from within so suddenly that it seemed as if the man who faced his visitor on the threshold must have been awaiting the summons. He stepped quickly out, shutting the door behind him, and for a short space the two stood talking in low tones — Pennold eagerly, insistently, the other man evasively, slowly, as if choosing his words with care. He was as erect as Pennold was shambling and stoop-shouldered, and although gray and lined of features, his eyes were clear and more steady, his chin more firm, his whole bearing more elastic and forceful.

He did not invite his visitor to enter, and the colloquy between them was brief. It was significant that they did not shake hands, but parted with a brief though not unfriendly nod. The tall man turned and re-entered his house, closing the door again behind him, while Pennold scuttled away, without a farewell glance. It might have been well had he looked once more over his shoulder, for there, crouching against the veranda rail where he had managed to overhear the last of the conversation, was that short, swarthy figure which had followed so indefatigably on his trail for three days — which had clung to him, closely but unseen, through all his devious journey of that morning. Suraci had not failed.

He tailed Pennold to his home, then went in person with his report to the great Blaine himself, who heard him through in silence, and then brought his mighty fist down upon his desk with a blow which made the massive bronze ink-well quiver.

"That's our man! You've got him, Suraci. Good work! Now wait a little; I want you to take some instructions yourself over to Morrow."

The next day the Pennolds missed the cheery greeting of their new friend, the bank-clerk. Since the acquaintanceship had been so recently formed, it was odd that they should have been as deeply concerned over his defection as they were. They said little that evening, but when his absence continued the second day, Pennold himself ambled down to the Brooklyn & Queens Bank and reluctantly deposited twenty dollars, merely for the pleasure of a chat with young Hicks. The latter's cheery face failed to greet him, however, within its portals, and a craftily worded inquiry merely elicited the information that he was no longer connected with that institution.

"What do you make of it, Mame?" he asked anxiously of his

wife when he reached home. His step was more shambling than ever, and his hands, clutching his hat-brim, trembled more than her gnarled, palsied ones.

"I'll tell you what I think when I've been around to Mrs. Lindsay's this afternoon — to 46 Jefferson Place."

"What're you goin' to do there? You can't ask for him, very well," objected her spouse.

"Do?" she retorted tartly. "What would I do in a boarding-house? Look for rooms for us, of course, and inquire about the other lodgers to be sure it's respectable for a decent, middle-aged, married couple. Do you think I'm goin' lookin' for a long-lost son? The life must be gettin' you at last, Wally! Your head ain't what it used to be."

But Mrs. Pennold's vaunted astuteness gained her little knowledge which could be of value to her in their late acquaintance. Mrs. Lindsay was a beetle-browed, enormously stout old lady, with a stern eye and commanding presence, who looked as if in her younger days she might well have been a police-matron — as indeed she had been. She had two double rooms and a single hall bedroom to show for inspection, and she waxed surprisingly voluble concerning the vacancy of the latter, at the first tentative mention of her other lodgers, by her visitor.

"As nice a young man as ever you'd wish to see, ma'am. I don't have none but the most refined people in my house. Lived with me a year and a half, Mr. Hicks did, except for his vacation — regular as clockwork in his bills, and free and open-handed with his tips to Delia. Of course, he wasn't just what you might call steady in his goings-out and comings-in, but there never was nothin' objectionable in his habits. You know what young men is! He had a fine position in a bank here in Brooklyn, but I don't think the company he kep' was all that it might have been. Kind of flashy and sporty, his friends was, and I guess that's what got him into trouble. For trouble he was in, ma'am, when he paid me yesterday in full even to the shavin' mug which I'd bought for his dresser, and meant him to keep for a present — and picked up bag and baggage and left. I always did think Friday was an unlucky day! He stood in the vestibule and shook both my hands, and there wasn't a dry eye in his head or mine!

"'Mis' Lindsay!' he says to me, just like I'm tellin' it to you. 'Mis' Lindsay, I can't stay here no longer. I wisht to heavings I could, for you've given me a real home,' he says, 'but I'm not at the bank no more, and I'm going away. I'm in trouble!' he says. 'I needn't tell you where I'm goin' for I ain't got a friend who'll ask after me or care, but I just want to thank you for all your kindness to me, an' to ask you to accept this present, and give this dollar-bill to Delia, when she comes in from the fish-store.'

"This is what he give me as a present, ma'am!" Mrs. Lindsay pointed dramatically to a German silver brooch set with a doubtful garnet, at her throat. "And I was so broke up over it all, that I forgot and give Delia the whole dollar, instead of just a quarter, like I should've done. I s'pose I'd ought to write to his folks, but I don't know where they are. He comes from up-State somewheres, and I never was one to pry in a boarder's letters or bureau-drawers. I'm just worried sick about it all!"

Mrs. Lindsay would have made a superb actress.

When the interview was at an end and Mrs. Pennold had rejoined her husband, they discussed the disappearance of Alfred Hicks from every standpoint and came finally to the conclusion that the young bank-clerk's sporting proclivities had brought him to ruin.

Meanwhile, in a modest cottage in Meadow Lane, in the Bronx, a small card reading "Room to Let" had been removed from the bay window, and just behind its curtains a young man sat, his eyes fastened upon the house across the way — the fourth from the end of the line. He was a tall, dark young man with a smooth face and firm-set jaw, and his new land-lady knew him as Guy Morrow.

All at once, as he sat watching, the door of the cottage opened, and a girl came out. There was nothing remarkable about her; she was quite a common type of girl: slender, not too tall, with a wealth of red-brown hair and soft hazel eyes; yet there was something about her which made Guy Morrow catch his breath; and throwing caution to the winds, he parted the curtains and leaned forward, looking down upon her. As she reached the gate, his gaze drew hers, and she lifted her gentle eyes and looked into his.

Then her lids drooped swiftly; a faint flush tinged her delicate face, and with lowered head she walked quickly on.

Guy Morrow sank back in his chair, and after the warm glow which had surged up so suddenly within him, a chill crept about his heart. What could that slender, brown-haired, clear-eyed girl be to the man he had been sent to spy upon — to Jimmy Brunell, the forger?

CHAPTER V
THE WILL

Henry Blaine sat in his office, leisurely turning over the pages of a morning newspaper; his attitude was one of apparent idleness, but the occasional swift glances he darted at the clock and a slight lifting of his eyebrows at the least sound from without betokened the fact that he was waiting for some one or something.

His eyes scanned the columns of each page with seeming carelessness, yet their keen glances missed not one significant phrase. And suddenly his gaze was transfixed by a paragraph tucked away in a corner of the second page.

It was merely an account of trouble between capital and labor in a distant manufacturing city, and a hint of an organized strike which threatened for the immediate future. The great detective was not at all a politician, and the social and economic conditions of the day held no greater import for him than for any other conscientious, far-seeing citizen of the country, yet he sat for a long moment with wrinkled brow and pursed lips, musing, while the newspaper dropped unheeded upon the desk.

His reverie was suddenly interrupted by the sharp, insistent tinkling of the telephone; a clear, girlish voice came to him over the wire:

"Is this Grosvenor 0760? This is Miss Lawton speaking. An alteration must be made at once in that last gown you sent me, and it is imperative that I see you in person concerning it. It will be inconvenient for me to have you come here this morning. Where shall I see you? At your establishment or — "

She paused suggestively, and he replied with a hurried question.

"It is absolutely necessary, Miss Lawton, that you see me in person? You are quite sure?"

"Absolutely." Her voice held a ring of earnestness and something more which caused him to jump to a lightning-like decision.

"Very well. I will meet you in twenty minutes at your Working Girls' Club. I am an architect, remember, and you wish to build a new and more improved institution of the same order on another site. Therefore, you have met me there to show me over the old building and suggest changes in its plans for the new one. You understand, Miss Lawton? My name is Banks, remember, and — be a few minutes late."

"I understand perfectly. Thank you. Good-by."

The receiver at the other end of the line clicked abruptly, and the detective sprang to his feet.

A quarter of an hour later Blaine presented himself at the Anita Lawton Club, where a trim maid ushered him into a tiny office. There, behind the desk, sat a girl, and at sight of her, the detective, master of himself as he was, gave an imperceptible start.

There was nothing remarkable about her; she was quite a common type of girl: slender, not too tall, with a wealth of red-brown hair, and soft hazel eyes; yet she reminded Blaine vaguely but insistently of some one else — some one whom he had encountered in the past.

He recovered himself at once, and presented the card which announced him as the senior member of the firm of Banks and Frost, architects.

"Whom did you wish to see, sir?" The girl turned slowly about in her swivel chair and regarded him respectfully but coolly. Her voice was low and gentle and distinctly feminine, yet it brought to him again that haunting sense of resemblance which the first vision of her had caused.

"Miss Lawton," he replied, quietly.

"But Miss Lawton is not here." The girl's surprise was unfeigned.

"I have an appointment to meet her here at this time. She may perhaps have been detained. She has arranged to go over the club building with me. As you see by my card, I am an architect and she is planning more extensive work, I believe, along the lines instituted here — at least that is the impression she has given my firm. I will wait a short time, if I may. You are connected with the official work of the club?"

"I am the secretary." The girl paused and then added, "I understand perfectly, sir. Will you be seated, please? Miss Lawton had not told me of her appointment here with you. She will without doubt arrive shortly."

Henry Blaine seated himself, and as she started to turn back to her desk, he asked quickly:

"You must find the work here very interesting, do you not? We — our firm — have erected several philanthropic institutions of learning and recreation, but none precisely on this order. Miss Lawton has shown us the plans of this present club and we consider the arrangement of the dormitories particularly ingenious, with regard to economy of space and the requisite sunlight and air."

"Oh, yes!" The girl turned toward him swiftly, her face suffused with interest. "Miss Lawton drew all the plans herself, and they were not changed in the least. I don't see how they could possibly be improved upon. Miss Lawton has done splendid work here, sir; the club has been a wonderful success since it was first opened."

"It must have been." The detective paused, then added easily, "I know that her late father was very proud of her executive ability. You — er — you educate young women here, do you not, and train them for positions?"

"We not only train the members of the club, but obtain positions for them, with reputable business firms," the girl answered.

"Indeed?" Blaine asked, with apparent surprise. "What sort of positions do the members of your club fill?"

"Whatever they are capable of acquiring a working knowledge of. Filing clerks, stenographers, secretaries, switchboard operators, telegraphers, even governesses. We have never had a failure, and I think it is because Miss Lawton gives not only her personal attention, but real love and faith to each girl. She is — wonderful."

The face of the young woman was rapt as she spoke, and Blaine could guess without further explanation that she herself was a protégée of Miss Lawton's, and a grateful one — unless she were playing a part. If so, she was an actress of transcendent ability.

"You say that you have never had a failure. That must, indeed, be encouraging," Blaine remarked, tentatively. "Perhaps we might arrange later with you or Miss Lawton to place one or two of your clerks or stenographers. We are enlarging our offices — "

"Good morning!" a fresh young voice interrupted him, and Anita Lawton stood upon the threshold. "Did Mr. Banks come yet? — ah, yes, I see. How do you do?"

Blaine arose, and Anita gave him her hand cordially. His quick eyes observed that in passing she patted the shoulder of her secretary affectionately, and the girl looked up at her quickly, with eyes aglow. The truth was no longer concealed from his discernment. The girl was staunch in every fiber of her being.

"Miss Lawton, I am sorry, but I have really not any too much time this morning. If we could proceed to business at once."

"Certainly. If you will come this way, Mr. Banks — " At the door she paused, and turned to the secretary: "I will see you later, dear."

Anita led the detective swiftly through the wide, clean halls and up the stairs, explaining in clear, distinct tones the floor-plan. On the second floor she opened the door leading into a little anteroom at the front of the house just over the office, and when they were seated, she said quickly, with rising excitement, although her voice was carefully hushed.

"Mr. Bl — Banks, I have something to show you — my father's will! It was discovered, or rather, produced, yesterday. The lawyers who have charge of the estate — Anderson & Wallace, you know — seem to me to be perfectly disinterested, and honest, but I am so hedged in on every hand by a stifling feeling of deceit and treachery that I feel I can trust no one save you and Mr. Hamilton — not even poor old Ellen, my maid, who has been with me since I was born!"

"I quite understand, Miss Lawton, and I realize how difficult the situation is for you, but I want you to trust no one — at least, to the extent of giving them your confidence. Now about the will; it was produced by your late father's attorneys?"

"No, by President Mallowe, of the Street Railways. It appears that Father left it in his charge. Mr. Anderson drew it; his partner, Mr. Wallace, witnessed it; and they both assure me that it is absolutely authentic. Here it is."

She opened her bag and handed a long envelope to him, but at first his attention was held by what she had said, and he frowned as he repeated quickly:

"'Authentic?' I trust you did not show any suspicion that you doubted for a moment that it was genuine?"

"Oh, by no means! It was Mr. Anderson himself who took especial pains to assure me of its authenticity."

Blaine regarded the envelope reflectively for a moment before he raised the flap. Why had the attorney considered it necessary to assure his late client's daughter that the will which he had himself drawn was genuine?

The will was short and to the point. In it Pennington Lawton left everything of which he died possessed to his daughter, unconditionally and without reservation.

"Of course, Miss Lawton, since you are only twenty, and your father has named no guardian or trustee, the courts will at once appoint one, and I have no hesitation in saying that I believe the guardian so appointed will be one of your father's three associates, presumably Mr. Mallowe. However, that will make little difference in our investigation, and, since it is claimed that all your father's huge fortune is lost, the matter of a guardian cannot tie our hands in any way. Now, just a moment, please."

He drew from his pocket a small but powerful magnifying glass and the slip of paper which Ramon Hamilton had sent him, on which was the signature of the late Pennington Lawton. Through the microscope he carefully compared it with that affixed to the will and then looked up reassuringly.

"It is quite all right, Miss Lawton. In my estimation the will is authentic and your father's signature genuine." He folded the paper, slipped it in its envelope and returned it to her. "There is one thing now which I must most earnestly caution you against. Do not sign any paper, no matter who wishes it or orders it — no matter if it is the most trivial household receipt. Do not write any letters yourself, or notes to any one, even to Mr. Hamilton; you understand they might be intercepted. If anyone wishes you to sign a paper relating to the matter of your father's estate, say you cannot do so until you have shown it in private to Mr. Hamilton — that you have promised you will not do so. Any other papers you can easily evade signing. As for your private correspondence, obtain a social secretary, and permit her to sign everything — one whom you can trust — say, one of your girls from here, that girl downstairs, for instance. What is her name?"

Anita Lawton rose, and a peculiar pained expression passed over her features.

"I am sorry, Mr. Blaine — really, really I am sorry. I cannot tell you her name. That was one of the conditions under which she came to us here — that is why I have given her an official position here in the Club. She is staunch and faithful and true; I know it, I feel it; and she is too high-principled to pass under any name not her own. I know and am heartily in sympathy with the reason for her secretiveness. You know that I trust you implicitly, but I know you would not have me go back on my word when once it has been given."

"Certainly not, Miss Lawton. I realize that many of your protégées here may come of unfortunate antecedents. If you feel that you can trust her, use her. Do you feel equally sure of the other members of your Club?"

"Absolutely. I feel that they all really love me; that they would do anything for me they could in the world, and yet I have done so little for them — only given them the little help which I was able to bestow, which we should all do for those less fortunate than ourselves.... Why did you ask me, Mr. Blaine, if I felt that I could trust the girls who have placed themselves under my care?"

"Because we may have need of them in the future. They may be of the most vital assistance to us in this investigation, should events turn out as I anticipate and they prove worthy of the charge it may be necessary for me to impose on them. But enough of that for now. If at any time you wish to see me, personally, telephone me as you did this morning and I will meet you here."

The detective left her in the office of the secretary, and as he made his adieus to them both he cast a last quick, penetrating glance at the girl behind the desk. Again that vague sense of resemblance possessed him. With whom was she connected? Why was her name so significantly withheld?

In the meantime Guy Morrow, from his post of observation in the window of the little cottage on Meadow Lane, had watched the object of his espionage for several fruitless days — fruitless, because the actions of the man Brunell had been so obviously those of one who felt himself utterly beyond suspicion.

The erect, gray-haired, clear-eyed man had come and gone about his business, without the slightest attempt at concealment. A few of the simplest inquiries of his land-lady had elicited the fact that the gentleman opposite, old Mr. Brunell, was a mapmaker, and worked at his trade in a little shop in the nearest row of brick buildings just around the corner — that he had lived in the little cottage since it had first been erected, six years before, alone with his daughter Emily, and before that, they had for many years occupied a small apartment near by — in fact, the girl had grown up in that neighborhood. He was a quiet man, not very talkative, but well liked by his neighbors, and his daughter was devoted to him. According to Mrs. Quinlan, Guy Morrow's aforesaid land-lady, Emily Brunell was a dear, sweet girl, very popular among the young people in the neighborhood, but she kept strictly at home in her leisure hours and preferred her father's companionship to that of anyone else. She was employed in some business capacity downtown, from nine until six; just what it was Mrs. Quinlan did not know.

Morrow kept well in the background, in case Mr. Pennold should put in an appearance again, but he did not. Evidently that conversation overheard by Suraci had been a final one, concerning the securities at least, and no one else called at the little cottage door over the way, except a vapid-faced young man to whom Morrow took an instant and inexplicable dislike.

Morrow made it a point to visit and investigate the little shop at an hour when he knew Brunell would not be there, and found in the cursory examination possible at that time that its purpose seemed to be strictly legitimate. A shock-headed boy of fifteen or thereabout was in charge, and the operative easily succeeded in engaging his stolid attention elsewhere while, with a bit of soft wax carefully palmed in his left hand, he succeeded in gaining an impression of the lock on the flimsy door. From this he had a key made in anticipation of orders from his chief, requiring a thorough search of the little shop — orders which for the first time in his career, he shrank from.

He made no effort to scrape an acquaintance with Brunell himself, but frequently encountered, as if by accident, the daughter Emily, on her way to and from the subway station. If she recognized in him the young lodger across the street, she made no sign, and as the days passed, Morrow, the man, despaired of gaining her friendship, save through her father, whom Morrow — the operative — had received orders not to approach personally.

Before he had seen her, had he known that the old forger possessed a daughter, he would have laid his plans to worm himself into the confidence of the little family through the girl, but having once laid eyes upon her face in all its gentle, trusting purity, every manly instinct in him revolted at the thought of making her a tool of her father's probable downfall.

There was a third member of the Brunell household whom Morrow had observed frequently seated upon the doorstep, or on one of the lower window sills — a small, scraggly black kitten, with stiff outstanding fur, and an absurdly belligerent attitude whenever a dog chanced to pass through the lane. It waited in the doorway each night for the return of its mistress, and in the soft glow of the lamplight which streamed from within, he had seen her catch the little creature up affectionately and cuddle it up against her neck before the door closed upon them.

One afternoon in the early November twilight, as Morrow was returning to his own door after shadowing Brunell on an aimless and chilly walk, he saw the kitten lying curled up just outside its own gate, and an inspiration sprang to his ingenious mind. He seated himself upon the steps of Mrs. Quinlan's front porch and waited until the darkness had deepened sufficiently to cloak his nefarious scheme. Then, with soft beguiling tone — and a few *sotto voce* remarks, for he hated cats — Morrow began a deliberate attempt to entice the kitten across to him.

"Come here, kitty, kitty," he called softly. "Come, pussy dear! Come here, you mangy, rat-tailed little beast! Come catty-kins."

At his first words the kitten raised its head and regarded him with yellow eyes gleaming through the dusk, in unconcealed antagonism. But, at the soft, purring flattery of his voice, the gleam softened to a glow of pleased interest, and the little creature rose lazily, stretched itself, and tripped lightly over to him, its tail erect in optimistic confidence.

Morrow picked it up gingerly by the neck and tucked it beneath his coat, stroking its head with a reluctant thumb, while it purred loudly in sleepy content, at the warmth of its welcome. The hour was approaching when Emily Brunell usually made her appearance, and he trusted to luck to keep the little animal quiet until she had entered her home and discovered its loss, but the fickle goddess failed him.

The kitten grew suddenly uneasy, as if some intuition warned it of treachery, and tried valiantly to escape from his grasp, and never did Spartan boy with wolf concealed beneath his tunic suffer more tortures than Morrow with the wretched little creature clawing at his hands.

Would Emily Brunell never come? What could be keeping her to-night, of all nights? Morrow gripped the soft, elusive bundle of fur with desperate firmness and looked across the street. Evidently he was not the only one impatient for her arrival. The doorway opposite had opened, and Jimmy Brunell stood peering anxiously forth into the darkness.

At that moment the kitten emitted a fearsome yowl, which Morrow smothered hastily with his coat. He fancied that the old man turned his head quickly and glanced in his direction, and never had the operative felt guiltier.

Brunell, however, retired within, closing the door after him, and the kitten's struggles gradually grew weaker and finally ceased.

Morrow felt a horrible fear surging up within him that he had strangled the little beast, and his grasp gradually relaxed. Then he opened his overcoat cautiously and peered within. The kitten was sleeping peacefully, and he heaved a sigh of relief, glancing up just in time to see Emily Brunell pass quickly through her own gate and up to the door.

He sat motionless on the steps of Mrs. Quinlan's, and his patience was rewarded when after a few moments the Brunell's door re-opened and he heard the girl's voice calling anxiously: "Kitty! Kitty!"

Morrow rose with unfeigned alacrity and crossing the road, opened the little gate without ceremony and mounted the steps of the porch.

"I beg your pardon," he said blandly. "Is this your kitten? It — er — wandered across the street to me and fell asleep under my coat. I board just over the way, you know, with Mrs. Quinlan. My name is Morrow."

The girl gave a little cry of relieved anxiety, and caught the kitten in her arms.

"Oh, I am so glad! I was afraid it was lost, and it is so tiny and defenseless to be out all alone in the cold and darkness. Thank you so much, Mr. Morrow. I suppose it was waiting for me, as it usually does, and grew restless at my delay, poor little thing! It was kind of you to comfort it!"

Feeling like an utter brute, Morrow stammered a humble disclaimer of her undeserved gratitude, and moved toward the steps.

"Oh, but it was really kind of you; most men hate cats, although my father loves them. I should have been home much earlier but I was detained by some extra work at the club where I am employed."

"The club?" he repeated stupidly.

"Yes," replied the girl, quietly, cuddling the kitten beneath her chin. "The Anita Lawton Club for Working Girls."

She caught herself up sharply, even as she spoke, and a look almost of apprehension crossed her ingenuous face for a moment, and was gone.

"Thank you again for protecting my kitten for me," she said softly. "Good-night."

Guy Morrow walked down the steps and across to his own lodgings with his brain awhirl. The investigation, through the medium of a small black kitten, had indeed taken an amazing turn. Jimmy Brunell's daughter was a protégée of the daughter of Pennington Lawton!

CHAPTER VI
THE FIRST COUNTER-MOVE

The little paragraph in the newspaper, which, irrelevant as it would seem, had caught the keenly discerning eye of Henry Blaine, grew in length and importance from day to day until it reached a position on the first page, and then spread in huge headlines over the entire sheet. Instead of relating merely the incidents of a labor strike in a manufacturing city — and that city a far-distant one — it became speedily a sociological question of almost national import. The yellow journals were quick to seize upon it at the psychological moment of civic unrest, and throw out hints, vague but vast in their significance, of the mighty interests behind the mere fact of the strike, the great financial question involved, the crisis between capital and labor, the trusts and the common people, the workers and the wasters, in the land of the free.

Henry Blaine, seated in his office, read the scare-heads and smiled his slow, inscrutable, illuminating smile — the smile which, without menace or rancor, had struck terror to the hearts of the greatest malefactors of his generation — which, without flattery or ingratiation, had won for him the friendship of the greatest men in the country. He knew every move in the gigantic game which was being played solely for his attention, long before a pawn was lifted from its place, a single counter changed; he had known it, from the moment that the seemingly unimportant paragraph had met his eyes; and he also knew the men who sat in the game, whose hands passed over the great chessboard of current events, whose brains directed the moves. And the stakes? Not the welfare of the workingmen in that distant city, not the lifting of the grinding heel of temporal power from the supine bodies of the humble — but the peace of mind, the honorable, untarnished name, the earthly riches of the slender girl who sat in that great darkened house on Belleair Avenue.

Hence Blaine sat back quietly, and waited for the decisive move which he knew to be forthcoming — waited, and not in vain. The spectacular play to the gallery of one was dramatically accomplished; it was heralded by extras bawled through the midnight streets, and full-page display headlines in the papers the next morning.

Promptly on the stroke of nine, Henry Blaine arrived at his office, and as he expected, found awaiting him an urgent telegram from the chief of police of the city where the strike had assumed such colossal importance, earnestly asking him for his immediate presence and assistance. He sent a tentative refusal — and waited. Still more insistent messages followed in rapid succession, from the mayor of that city, the governor of that state, even its representative in the Senate at Washington, to all of which he replied in the same emphatic, negative strain. Then, late in the afternoon, there eventuated that which he had anticipated. Mohammed came to the mountain.

Blaine read the card which his confidential secretary presented, and laid it down upon the desk before him.

"Show him in," he directed, shortly. He did not rise from his chair, nor indeed change his position an iota, but merely glanced up from beneath slightly raised eyebrows, when the door opened again and a bulky, pompous figure stood almost obsequiously before him.

"Come in, Mr. Carlis," he invited coolly. "Take this chair. What can I do for you?"

It was significant that neither man made any move toward shaking hands, although it was obvious that they were acquainted, at least. The great detective's tone when he greeted his visitor was as distinctly ironical as the latter's was uneasy, although he replied with a mirthless chuckle, which was intended to be airily nonchalant.

"Nothing for me, Mr. Blaine — that is, not to-day. One can never tell in this period of sudden changes and revolt, when our city may be stricken as another was just a few hours ago. There is no better, cleaner, more honestly prosperous metropolis in these United States to-day, than Illington, but — " Mr. Carlis, the political boss who had ruled for more than a decade in almost undisputed sway, paused and gulped, as if his oratorical eloquence stuck suddenly in his throat.

The detective watched him passively, a disconcerting look of inquiring interest on his mobile face. "It is because of our stricken sister city that I am here," went on the visitor. "I know I will not be in great favor with you as an advocate, Mr. Blaine. We have had our little tilts in the past, when you — er — disapproved of my methods of conducting my civic office and I distrusted your motives, but that is forgotten now, and I come to you merely as one public-spirited citizen to another. The mayor of Grafton has wired me, as has the chief of police, to urge you to proceed there at once and take charge of the investigation into last night's bomb outrages in connection with the great strike. They inform me that you have repeatedly refused to-day to come to their assistance."

Blaine nodded.

"That is quite true, Mr. Carlis. I did decline the offers extended to me."

"But surely you cannot refuse! Good heavens, man, do you realize what it means if you do? It isn't only that there is a fortune in it for you, your reputation stands or falls on your decision! This is a public charge! The people rely upon you! If you won't, for some reason of your own, come to the rescue now, when you are publicly called upon, you'll be a ruined man!" The voice of the Boss ascended in a shrill falsetto of remonstrance.

"There may be two opinions as to that, Mr. Carlis," Blaine returned quietly. "As far as the financial argument goes, I think you discovered long ago that its appeal to me is based upon a different point of view than your own. You forget that I am not a servant of the public, but a private citizen, free to accept or decline such offers as are made to me in my line of business, as I choose. This affair is not a public charge, but a business proposition, which I decline. As to my reputation depending upon it, I differ with you. My reputation will stand, I think, upon my record in the past, even if every yellow newspaper in the city is paid to revile me."

Carlis rested his plump hands upon his widespread knees, and leaned as far forward, in his eager anxiety, as his obese figure would permit.

"But why?" he fairly wailed, his carefully rounded, oratorical tones forgotten. "Why on earth do you decline this offer, Blaine? You've nothing big on hand now — nothing your operatives can't attend to. There isn't a case big enough for your attention on the calendar! You know as well as I do that Illington is clean and that the lid is on for keeps! The police are taking care of the petty crimes, and there's absolutely nothing doing in your line here at the moment. This is the chance of your career! Why on earth do you refuse it?"

"Well, Mr. Carlis, let us say, for instance, that my health is not quite as good as it was, and I find the air of Illington agrees with it better just now than that of Grafton." Blaine leaned back easily in his chair, and after a slight pause he added speculatively, with deliberate intent, "I didn't know you had interests there!"

The Boss purpled.

"Look here, Blaine!" he bellowed. "What d'you mean by that?"

"Merely following a train of thought, Mr. Carlis," returned the detective imperturbably. "I was trying to figure out why you were so desperately anxious to have me go to Grafton — "

"I tell you I am here at the urgent request of the mayor and the chief of police!" the fat man protested, but faintly, as if the unexpected attack had temporarily winded him. "Why in h — ll should I want you to go to Grafton?"

"Presumably because Grafton is some fourteen hundred miles from Illington," remarked Blaine, his quietly unemotional tones hardening suddenly like tempered steel. "Going to try to pull off something here in town which you think could be more easily done if I were away? Cards on the table, Mr. Carlis! You tried to bribe me in a case once, and you failed. Then you tried bullying me and you found that didn't work, either. Now you've come again with your hook baited with patriotism, public spirit, the cry of the people and all the rest of the guff the newspapers you control have been handing out to their readers since you took them over. What's the idea?"

The Boss rose, with what was intended for an air of injured dignity, but his fat face all at once seemed sagged and wrinkled, like a pricked balloon.

"I did not come here to be insulted!" he announced in his most impressive manner. "I came, as I told you, as a public-spirited citizen, because the officials of another city called upon me to urge you to aid them. I have failed in my mission, and I will go. I am surprised, Blaine, at your attitude; I thought you were too big a man to permit your personal antagonism to me to interfere with your duty — "

For the first time during their interview Blaine smiled slightly.

"Have you ever known me, Mr. Carlis, to permit my personal antagonism to you or any other man to interfere with what I conceive to be my duty?"

Before he replied, the politician produced a voluminous silk handkerchief, and mopped his brow. For some reason he did not feel called upon to make a direct answer.

"Well, what reason am I to give to the Mayor of Grafton and its political leaders, for your refusal? That talk about me trying to get you out of Illington, Blaine, is all bosh, and you know it. *I'm* running Illington just as I've run it for the last ten years, in spite of your interference or any other man's, and I'm going to stay right on the job! If you won't give any other reason for declining the call to Grafton, than your preference for the air of Illington, then the bets go as they lay!"

He jammed his hat upon his head, and strode from the room with all the ferocity his rotund figure could express. The first decisive move in the game had failed.

The door was scarcely closed behind him, when Blaine turned to the telephone and called up Anita Lawton on the private wire.

"Can you arrange to meet me at once, at your Working Girls' Club?" he asked. "I wish to suggest a plan to be put into immediate operation."

"Very well. I can be there in fifteen minutes."

When the detective arrived at the club, he was ushered immediately to the small ante-room on the second floor, where he found Anita anxiously awaiting him.

"Miss Lawton," he began, without further greeting than a quick handclasp, "you told me, the other day, that your girls here were all staunch and faithful to you. Your secretary downstairs had previously informed me that they were trained to hold positions of trust, and that you obtained such positions for them. I want you to obtain four positions for four of the girls in whom you place the most implicit confidence."

"Why, certainly, Mr. Blaine, if I can. Do you mean that they are to have something to do with your investigation into my father's affairs?"

"I want them to play detective for me, Miss Lawton. Have you four girls unemployed at the moment? — Say, for instance, a filing clerk, a stenographer, a governess and a switchboard operator, who are sufficiently intelligent and proficient in their various occupations, to assume such a trust?"

"Why, yes, I — I think we have. I can find out, of course. Where do you wish to place them?"

"That is the most difficult part of all, Miss Lawton. You must obtain the positions for them. These three men who stand in *loco parentis* toward you, as you say, and your spiritual adviser, Dr. Franklin, who so obviously wishes to ingratiate himself with them, would none of them refuse a request of this sort from you at this stage of the game, particularly if they are really engaged in a conspiracy against you. Go to these four men — Mr. Mallowe first — and tell them that because of the sudden, complete loss of your fortune, your club must be disorganized, and beg them each to give one of your girls, special protégées of yours, a position. Send your filing clerk to Mr. Mallowe, your most expert stenographer to Mr. Rockamore, your switchboard operator to Mr. Carlis, and your governess into the household of your minister. I have learned that he has three small children, and his wife applied only yesterday at an agency for a nursery governess. The last proposition may be the most difficult for you to handle, but I think if you manage to convey to the Reverend Dr. Franklin the fact that your three self-appointed guardians have each taken one of your girls into their employ, in order to help them, and that his following their benevolent example would bring him into closer *rapport* with them, no objection will be made — provided, of course, the young woman is suitable."

"I will try, Mr. Blaine, but of course I can do nothing about that until to-morrow, as it is so late in the afternoon. However, I can have a talk with the girls, if they are in now — or would you prefer to interview them?"

"No, you talk with them first, Miss Lawton, and to-morrow morning while you are arranging for their positions I will interview them and instruct them in their primary duties. I will leave you now. Remember that the girls must be absolutely trustworthy, and the stenographer who will be placed in the office of Mr. Rockamore must be particularly expert."

After the detective had taken his departure, Anita Lawton descended quickly to the office of the secretary.

"Emily," she asked, "is Loretta Murfree in, or Fifine Déchaussée?"

"I think they both are, Miss Lawton. Shall I ring for them?"

"Yes, please, Emily; send them to me one at a time, in the ante-room, and let me know when Agnes Olson and Margaret Hefferman come in. I wish to talk with all four of them, but separately."

Loretta Murfree was the first to put in an appearance. She was a short, dumpy, black-haired girl of twenty, and she bounced into the room with a flashing, wide-mouthed smile.

"How are you, dear Miss Lawton? We have missed you around here so much lately, but of course we knew that you must be very much occupied — "

She stopped and a little embarrassed flush spread over her face.

"I have been, Loretta. Thank you so much for your kind note, and for your share in the beautiful wreath you girls sent in memory of my dear father."

"Sure, we're all of us your friends, Miss Lawton; why wouldn't we be, after all you've done for us?"

"It is because I feel that, that I wanted to have a talk with you this afternoon. Loretta, if a position were offered to you as filing clerk in the office of a great financier of this city, at a suitable salary, would you accept it, if you could be doing me a great personal service at the same time?"

"Would I, Miss Lawton? Just try me! I'd take it for the experience alone, without the salary, and jump at the chance, even if you weren't concerned in it at all, but if it would be doing you a service at the same time, I'm more than glad."

"Thank you, Loretta. The position will be with an associate of my father's, I think, President Mallowe of the Street Railways. You must attend faithfully to your duties, if I am able to obtain this place for you, but I think the main part of your service to me will consist of keeping your eyes open. To-morrow morning a man will come here and interview you — a man in whom you must place implicit confidence and trust, and whose directions you must follow to the letter. He will tell you just what to do for me. This man is my friend; he is working in my interests, and if you care for me you must not fail him."

"Indeed I won't, Miss Lawton! I'll do whatever he tells me.... You said that I was to keep my eyes open. Does that mean that there is something you wish me to find out for you?" she asked shrewdly.

"I cannot tell you exactly what you are to do for me, Loretta.

The gentleman whom you are to meet to-morrow morning will give you all the details." Anita Lawton approached the girl and laid her hand on her shoulder. "I can surely trust you? You will not fail me?"

The quick tears sprang to the Irish girl's eyes, and for a moment softened their rather hard brilliance.

"You know that you can trust me, Miss Lawton! I'd do anything in the world for you!"

Anita Lawton held a similar conversation with each of the three girls, with a like result. To Fifine Déchaussée, a tall, refined girl, with the colorless, devout face of a religieuse, the probability of entering a minister's home, as governess for his children, was most welcome. The young French girl, homesick and alone in a strange land, had found in Anita Lawton her one friend, and her gratitude for this first opportunity given her, seemed overwhelming. Margaret Hefferman rejoiced at the possible opportunity of becoming a stenographer to the great promoter, Mr. Rockamore; and demure, fair-haired little Agnes Olson was equally pleased with the prospect of operating a switchboard in the office of Timothy Carlis, the politician.

Meantime, back in his office, Henry Blaine was receiving the personal report of Guy Morrow.

"The old man seems to be strictly on the level," he was saying. "He attends to his own affairs and seems to be running a legitimate business in his little shop, where he prints and sells maps. I went there, of course, to look it over, but I couldn't see anything crooked about it. However, when I left, I took a wax impression of the lock, in case you wanted me to have a key made and institute a more thorough investigation, at a time when I would not be disturbed."

"That's good, Morrow. We may need to do that later. At present I want you merely to keep an eye on them, and note who their visitors are. You've been talking with the girl you say — the daughter?"

"Yes, sir — " The young man paused in sudden confusion.

"She's a very quiet, respectable, proud sort of young woman, Mr. Blaine — not at all the kind you would expect to find the daughter of an old crook like Jimmy Brunell. And by the way, here's a funny coincidence! She's a protégée of Miss Lawton's, employed in some philanthropic home or club, as she calls it, which Pennington Lawton's daughter runs."

"By Jove!" Blaine exclaimed, "I might have known it! I thought there was something familiar about her appearance when I first saw her! No wonder Miss Lawton had promised not to divulge her name. It's a small world, Morrow. I'll have to look into this. Go back now and keep your eye on Jimmy."

"Very well, sir." Guy Morrow paused at the door and turned toward his chief. "Have you seen the late editions of the evening papers, Mr. Blaine? They're all slamming you, for refusing to accept the call to Grafton, to investigate those bomb outrages last night."

Henry Blaine smiled.

"There won't be any more of them," he remarked quietly. "That strike will die down as quickly as it arose, Morrow; the whole thing was a plant, and the labor leaders and factory owners themselves were merely tools in the hands of the politicians. That strike was arranged by our friend Timothy Carlis, to get me away from Illington on a false mission."

"You don't think, sir, that they suspect — "

"No, but they are taking no chances on my getting into the game. They don't suspect yet, but they will soon — because the time has come for us to get busy."

CHAPTER VII
THE LETTER

The next morning, when Ramon Hamilton presented himself at Henry Blaine's office in answer to the latter's summons, he found the great detective in a mood more nearly bordering upon excitability than he could remember having witnessed before. Instead of being seated calmly at his desk, his thoughts masked with his usual inscrutable imperturbability, Blaine was pacing restlessly back and forth with the disquietude, not of agitation, but of concentrated, ebullient energy.

"I sent for you, Mr. Hamilton," he began, after greeting his visitor cordially and waving him to a chair, "because we must proceed actively with the investigation into the alleged bankruptcy of Pennington Lawton. We have been passive long enough for me to have gathered some significant facts, but we now must make a salient move. The time hasn't yet come for me to step out into the open. When I do, it will be a tooth-and-nail fight, and I must be equipped with facts, not theories. I want some particulars about Mr. Lawton's insolvency, and there is no one who could more naturally inquire into this without arousing suspicion than you."

"I don't need to tell you, Mr. Blaine, how anxious I am to do anything I can to help you, for Miss Lawton's sake," Ramon Hamilton replied eagerly. "I should like to have looked into the matter long ago — indeed, I felt that suspicion must have been aroused in the minds of Mallowe and his associates by the fact that I accepted the astounding news of the bankruptcy as unquestioningly as Miss Lawton herself, unless they thought me an addlepated fool — but I didn't want to go ahead without direct instructions from you."

"I did not so direct you, Mr. Hamilton, for a distinct purpose. I wished the men we believe to be responsible for the present conditions to be slightly puzzled by your attitude, so that when the time came for you to begin your investigation, they would be more completely reassured. In order to make your questioning absolutely bona fide, I want you to go first this morning to the office of Anderson & Wallace, the late Mr. Lawton's attorneys, and question them as if having come with Miss Lawton's authority. Don't suggest any suspicion of there being any crookedness at work, but merely inquire as fully as possible into the details of Mr. Lawton's business affairs. They will, in their replies, undoubtedly bring in Mr. Mallowe, Mr. Rockamore and Mr. Carlis, which will give you a cue to go quite openly and frankly to one of the three — preferably Mallowe — for corroboration. Knowing that you come direct from the late Mr. Lawton's attorneys, he will be only too glad to give you whatever information he may possess or may have concocted — and so lay open to you his plan of defense."

"Defense? You think, then, Mr. Blaine, that they anticipate possible trouble — exposure, even? Surely such astute, far-seeing men as Mallowe and Rockamore are, at least, would not have attempted such a gigantic fraud if they'd anticipated the possibility of being discovered! Carlis has weathered so many storms, so many attacks upon his reputation and civic honor, that he may have felt cocksure of his position and gone into this thing without thought for the future, but the other two are men of different caliber, men with everything in the world to lose."

"And colossal, unearned wealth to gain — don't forget that, Mr. Hamilton. Men of different caliber, I grant you, but all three in the same whirlpool of crime, bound by thieves' law to sink or swim together. It is because they are astute and far-seeing that they must inevitably have considered the possibility of exposure and safeguarded themselves against it with bogus corroborative proof. If that proof is in tangible form, and we can lay our hands on it, we shall have them where we want them. Now go back to your office, Mr. Hamilton, and dictate this letter to your stenographer, having it left open on your desk for your signature. Don't wait for the letter to be typed, but proceed at once to the office of Anderson & Wallace. You, as a lawyer, will of course know the form of inquiry to use."

The detective handed Ramon Hamilton a typewritten sheet of paper from his desk; and the young man, after hastily perusing it, gazed with a blank stare of amazement into Blaine's eyes.

"I can't make this out," he objected. "Who on earth is Alexander Gibbs, and what has he to do with Miss Lawton's case? This letter seems to inform one Alexander Gibbs that I have retained you to recover for us the last will and testament of his aunt, Mrs. Dorothea Gibbs. I have no such client, and I know no one in — what's the address? — Ellenville, Sullivan County."

Blaine smiled.

"Of course you don't, Mr. Hamilton. Nevertheless, you will sign that letter and your secretary will mail it — that is, after it has lain open upon your desk for casual inspection for a considerable length of time. One of my operatives will receive it in Ellenville."

"But what has it to do with the matter in hand?" Ramon asked.

"Everything. I understand that you employ quite an office force, for an attorney who has so recently been admitted to the bar, and who has necessarily had little time yet to build up an extensive practice. There may be a spy in your office — remember that as Miss Lawton's fiancé and her only protector in this crisis, you are the one whom they would safeguard themselves against primarily. When I called you up this morning, to ask you to come here, you very indiscreetly mentioned my name over the telephone. Your entire office force will know that you have been to consult me — this letter will throw them off the track should there be a spy among them, and will also give you a legitimate excuse to call upon me frequently in the immediate future. You realize that we also must safeguard ourselves, Mr. Hamilton."

The young man reddened.

"Of course. I did not think — I called you by name inadvertently," he stammered. "I'll be more discreet in the future, Mr. Blaine."

"Memorize the gist of the letter on your way to your office — particularly the name and address — and place it securely in your vest pocket. When you have left your office to go to Anderson & Wallace, destroy it carefully. You had best, perhaps, stop in the lavatory of some restaurant or public bar and burn it, or tear it into infinitesimal pieces. Remember that everything depends upon you now — upon your discretion and diplomacy."

Hamilton followed Blaine's instructions to the letter, and an hour after he had left the detective he was closeted with the senior member of the firm of Anderson & Wallace.

"My dear Mr. Hamilton, we have had so little time," Mr. Anderson expostulated. "Remember that Mr. Lawton's death occurred little more than a fortnight ago, and even the most cursory examination has shown us that his affairs were in a most chaotic condition. It will take us weeks, months, to settle up so involved an estate.

"At present we can give you little information. It is by no means certain that Mr. Lawton was an absolute bankrupt — we have not yet assured ourselves that nothing can be saved from the wreckage. You cannot imagine how aghast, thunderstruck, we were, when this present state of affairs was made known to us. We have been Mr. Lawton's attorneys for more than twenty years, and we thought that we knew every detail of his multifarious transactions, but for some reason which we cannot fathom he saw fit, within the last two years, to change his investments without taking us into his confidence — and with disastrous results."

"Mr. Lawton was always conservative. He took no one fully into his confidence," Ramon Hamilton replied guardedly.

"You knew, of course, that he had ideas about the disposal of his vast wealth which many other financiers would consider peculiar. He would never invest in real estate, to our knowledge. His millions were placed entirely in stocks and bonds, and for years he had stated that his object was, in the event of his death, to save his daughter and the trustees from unnecessary trouble over real-estate matters. This makes his later conduct all the more inexplicable. Mr. Mallowe has told me that Mr. Lawton made several suggestions to him and to his associates, Mr. Rockamore and Mr. Carlis, to go with him into the unfortunate speculations which ultimately caused his ruin. They were far-seeing enough to refuse."

"Just what were these speculations, Mr. Anderson?"

"I can't tell you at this moment. You'll understand that we don't wish to make any statement until we can do so definitely, and we are still, as I said, quite at sea. We'll try to straighten everything out as soon as possible, and give you and Miss Lawton a full report. In the meantime, why not consult Mr. Mallowe? He can give you more explicit information concerning the late Mr. Lawton's speculation and final insolvency than we shall be able to do for some time; or possibly, Mr. Rockamore, or even Mr. Carlis might enlighten you. All three seem to have been more conversant with Mr. Lawton's affairs than we, his attorneys."

The dignified old gentleman's voice held a note of pained resentment, with which Ramon Hamilton could not help but sympathize.

"I will adopt your suggestion, Mr. Anderson, and call upon Mr. Mallowe at once. I can no more understand than you can how it happens that Mr. Lawton should have confided to such an extent in his business associates, to the exclusion of you and Mr. Wallace — to say nothing of his own daughter; but doubtless there were financial reasons which we'll learn. I will take up no more of your valuable time, but will try to see Mr. Mallowe immediately. If I learn any facts you're not now in possession of, I'll let you know at once."

Mr. Mallowe, when approached over the telephone, welcomed most cordially the proposed interview with Miss Lawton's fiancé. When the latter arrived, he was greeted with a warm, limp hand-clasp, and seated confidentially close to the president of the Street Railways.

"Mr. Anderson did well to suggest your coming to me, Mr. Hamilton," the magnate remarked unctuously. "I believe I am in a position to give you a more comprehensive idea of the circumstances which brought about my esteemed friend's unfortunate financial collapse at the time of his death than my colleagues, because I was closer to him in many ways, and I am confident that he regarded me as his best friend. However, I don't feel that I can, in honor, violate the confidence of the dead by giving any details just now — even to you and Miss Lawton — of matters which have not yet been fully substantiated by the attorneys. I know only from Mr. Lawton's own private statements that he was interested, to the point one might almost say of mania, in a gigantic scheme from which we, his friends, tried in vain to dissuade him. He urged me especially to go in on it with him, but because of the very position I hold, it would have been impossible for me to consider it, even if my better judgment hadn't warned me against it."

"Can't you give me some idea of the nature of this scheme?" Ramon asked. "I can't believe, any more easily than Miss Lawton can, that there could have been anything that was not thoroughly open and above-board about her father's dealings. Surely, there can be no reason for this extraordinary secrecy, particularly as the newspapers had given to the world at large the unauthorized statement, from a source unknown to Miss Lawton or myself, that Pennington Lawton died a bankrupt!"

The young man drew himself up sharply, as if fearful of having said too much, and for a moment there was silence. Then Mr. Mallowe leaned back easily in his chair and, removing his tortoise-shell rimmed eyeglasses, tapped the desk thoughtfully with them as he replied:

"That was regrettable, of course, Mr. Hamilton. It must have been distressing in the extreme to Miss Lawton, coming just at this time, but it would have had to be revealed sooner or later, you know — such a stupendous fact could not be hidden. There is no extraordinary secrecy about the matter. When the attorneys have completed their settlement of the estate, everything will be clear to you and Miss Lawton. I must naturally decline to give you any explanation which would be, just now, merely an uncorroborated opinion. I appreciate your feelings in this sudden, almost overwhelming trouble which has come to Miss Lawton, and I sympathize with both of you most heartily; but one must have patience. You will pardon me, but you are both very young, and that is the hardest lesson of all for you to learn."

His watery eyes beamed in fatherly benevolence upon

Ramon, and Anita's fiancé felt his gorge rising. The older man reminded him irresistibly of a cat licking its chops before a canary's cage, and it was with difficulty he restrained himself to remark coldly:

"You told me at the beginning of this interview, Mr. Mallowe, that I did well in coming to you, since you could give me a more comprehensive idea of the circumstances than anyone else, yet you have disclosed nothing beyond a few vague suggestions — to any other man I should have said, insinuations — and generalities which we were already familiar with. Can't you give me any real information?"

"My dear boy, I intend to tell you all that I know and can verify." The silky smoothness of the magnate's tones had deepened in spite of himself, with a steely undernote.

"I don't know when the project which spelled his ruin was first conceived by Mr. Lawton, but I believe that he started to put it into active operation over three years ago. He went into it with his usual cold nerve, and then, when the pendulum did not swing his way he kept heaping more and more of his securities on the pyre of his ambition and pride in himself, until he was forced to obtain large loans. That he did seek and obtain such loans I can prove to you at the present moment, in one instance at least, for it was through me the affair was negotiated. I think he fully realized his enormous error, but refused to admit it even to himself, and strove by sheer force of will-power to carry a hopeless scheme to success."

"Sought loans! He — Pennington Lawton required loans and obtained them through you?" Ramon almost started from his chair. "Mr. Mallowe, you will forgive me, but I can scarcely credit it. I know, of course, that financiers, even those who conduct their operations on a far lesser scale than Mr. Lawton, frequently seek loans, but your manner and your speech just now led me to believe that you had some other motive in doing what you did for Mr. Lawton. From what you have told me I gather that it was owing more to your friendship for him, than to your financial relations, that he called upon you at that time."

"And it was to my friendship at that time that he appealed, Mr. Hamilton."

"Appealed? I cannot imagine Pennington Lawton appealing to any man. Why should he appeal to you?"

"Because, my dear boy, he was in a mighty bad fix when he had need to call upon me. Oh, by the way, I have the letter here in my safe — I found it only the other day."

"The letter? What letter?"

"The letter Mr. Lawton wrote me from Long Bay asking me to get Mr. Moore's help in the matter — here it is."

Mallowe went to his safe, and opening it, withdrew from an inner drawer a paper which he presented to the young lawyer. After a cursory examination Ramon placed it upon the desk before him, and turning to Mr. Mallowe said:

"I am awfully sorry to have annoyed you with this matter, but you understand exactly how Miss Lawton and I feel about it — "

"Of course, Mr. Hamilton, I realize the situation fully. I am glad to have had this opportunity to explain to you how the matter stood as far as I personally was concerned. You know I will do anything that I can for Miss Lawton and I trust that you will call upon me."

He rose with ponderous significance as if to state tacitly that the interview was at an end, but the younger man did not stir from his chair.

"This letter came to you — when did you say, Mr. Mallowe?"

"When Pennington Lawton and his daughter were at The Breakers at Long Bay, about two years ago last August, as nearly as I can remember."

"If you still had the envelope, we could obtain the exact date from the postmark," Ramon suggested significantly. "The letter I see is only headed 'Saturday.'"

"Yes, it is unfortunate that I did not keep it," the magnate retorted a little drily. "It was by the merest, most fortunate chance that the letter itself came to light. However, I cannot see at this late date what difference it could possibly make when the letter was mailed, since it establishes beyond any possibility of doubt the fact that it *was* mailed. As to the matter of the negotiation of the loan, I would prefer that you apply to Mr. Moore himself for the particulars concerning it. I am sure that he will be quite as glad as I have been to give you such definite information as he possesses."

This time the dismissal could not be ignored, and Ramon Hamilton took his departure, but not before he had marked well the particular drawer within the safe from which the letter had been taken.

As he went down the corridor, a saucy, red-cheeked young woman with business briskness in her manner came from an inner office and smiled boldly at him. She was Loretta Murfree, the new filing clerk who had been installed only that morning in Mr. Mallowe's office.

Had Ramon known her to be the protégée of Anita Lawton and the spy of Henry Blaine, he might have glanced at her a second time.

The young man proceeded straight to the offices of Charlton Moore, the banker, and found that an interview was readily granted him. Mr. Moore remembered the incident of the loan, and his private accounts showed that it had been made on the sixteenth of August two years previously.

"Mr. Mallowe arranged the matter with you for Mr. Lawton, did he not?" Ramon asked.

"Yes, it was a purely confidential affair. Mr. Carlis came with him to interview me. They did not at first tell me that Mr. Lawton positively desired the loan, but they made tentative arrangements asking if I would be in a position to give it to him should he desire it, and they said they came to me at this early date desiring to make no definite statement. Mr. Lawton had told them that once before I had accommodated him by carrying a note confidentially at his request. Of course I did not care to commit myself, as you can readily understand, Mr. Hamilton, until I was assured the proposition was bona fide.

"Mr. Mallowe and Mr. Carlis suggested that I call Mr. Lawton up on the private wire in his office, but the matter was so delicate that as long as he had not come to me in person I did not care to telephone him. Mr. Mallowe showed me a letter which he had recently received from Pennington Lawton corroborating his statement. But in the matter of the amount desired we could not definitely distinguish the figures. Mr. Mallowe was sure that it was three hundred and fifty thousand dollars. Mr. Carlis was equally certain that it was three hundred and eighty-five thousand. To make certain of the matter they called Mr. Lawton up from my office here in my presence, and he stated that the sum desired was three hundred and fifty thousand dollars. There was only one odd thing about the entire transaction, and that was a remark Mr. Mallowe made as he was leaving. After the negotiations had been completed he turned and said, 'You understand, Mr. Moore, that Mr. Lawton is so careful, so secretive, that he does not wish this matter ever mentioned to him personally, even if you think yourself absolutely alone with him.'"

"Mr. Lawton was a very peculiar man in many ways," Ramon said meditatively. "His methods of conducting his affairs were not always easily understood. The negotiations were then completed shortly thereafter?"

"Yes, within a few days. I turned the amount required over to Mr. Mallowe and Mr. Carlis, and accepted Mr. Lawton's note. I will show it to you if you care to see it."

"That will not be necessary, Mr. Moore, but I am going to make a request that may seem very strange to you. Should it be necessary, would you be willing to show that note to some one whom I may bring here to you — some one who may prefer not to see you personally, but merely to be permitted to examine the note in the presence of some responsible people of your own choosing?"

"Certainly, Mr. Hamilton. I think I can safely promise that. But what does it mean — is there anything wrong with Pennington Lawton's note?"

"Not that I am aware of, Mr. Moore," Ramon answered, laughing rather shortly. "I am unable to explain just now, but I think the name of Pennington Lawton carries with it a sufficient guarantee that the note will be honored when it is presented."

An hour later, at the close of the busiest day he had experienced since his graduation from the law school, young Hamilton presented himself at Henry Blaine's office. The detective listened in silence to his story, and at its conclusion remarked quietly: "You did well, Mr. Hamilton. I am going to call one of my operatives and ask you to repeat to him in detail the location of that safe in Mallowe's office and the drawer which contains Mr. Lawton's letter from Long Bay."

"Anyone would think you meant to steal it, Mr. Blaine."

Young Hamilton's laugh was now unrestrained. "There couldn't possibly be anything wrong with the note or the entire transaction. Mr. Moore proved that when he told me how Mr. Mallowe and Carlis called up Mr. Lawton in his presence on his private wire and discussed the negotiations."

"Are you sure that they did, Mr. Hamilton?" The detective suddenly leaned forward across his desk, his body tense, his eyes alight with fervid animation. "Are you sure Pennington Lawton ever received that message?"

"He must have. According to Mr. Moore, the two men used Mr. Lawton's private wire, the number of which was known only to a few of his closest intimates and which of course was not listed."

"But some one who knew that the telephone message was coming might readily have been in Lawton's office seated at his desk, alone, and replied to it in the financier's name. Do you understand, Mr. Hamilton? The note may be a forgery, the letter may be a forgery; that we shall soon know. If it is, and the money so obtained from Moore has been converted to the use of the

77

three confederates whom we suspect to have formed a conspiracy to ruin Miss Lawton, then her father's entire fortune might have been seized upon in virtually the same way."

Henry Blaine rose and paced back and forth as if almost oblivious of the other's presence. "The mortgage of his was forged — we have proved that," he continued. "Why, then, should not every other available security have been stolen in practically the same way?" he continued.

"But how would anyone dare? The whole thing is too barefaced," Ramon expostulated. "A man like Mr. Moore could not have been imposed upon by a mere forgery."

"But if that note proves to be a forgery, Mr. Hamilton, and the letter as well — we shall have picked up a tangible clue at last. I think I am beginning to see daylight."

Late that night in the huge suite of offices of President Mallowe of the Street Railways, a very curious scene took place. The stolid watchman who had been on uneventful duty there for twenty years had made his rounds for the last time. With superb nonchalance, he settled himself for his accustomed nap in his employer's chair. From the stillness and gloom of the semi-deserted office-building two stealthy figures descended swiftly upon him, their feet sinking noiselessly into the rich pile of the rugs. A short, silent struggle, a cloth saturated with chloroform pressed heavily over his face, and the guardian of the premises lay inert. The shorter, more stocky of the two nocturnal visitors, without more ado switched on a pocket electric light and made a hasty but thorough survey of the room. The taller one shrank back inadvertently from the drug-stilled body in the chair, then resolutely turned and knelt beside his companion before the safe. He dreaded to think of what discovery might mean. If he, Ramon Hamilton, were to be caught in the act of burglarizing, his career as a rising young lawyer would be at an end. The risk indeed was great, but he had promised Henry Blaine every aid in his power to help the girl he loved.

After a minute examination, the operative proceeded to work upon the massive safe door. With the cunning of a *Jimmy*

Valentine he manipulated the tumblers. Ramon Hamilton, his discomfiture forgotten, watched with breathless interest while the keen, sensitive fingers performed their task. Soon the great doors swung noiselessly back and the manifold compartments within were revealed.

The young lawyer pointed out the drawer from which he had seen President Mallowe remove the letter that morning, and it, too, yielded quickly to the master-touch of the expert. There, on the very top of a pile of papers, lay the written page they sought.

"He'll be all right. We haven't done for him, have we?" Ramon Hamilton whispered anxiously, pointing to the watchman's unconscious form, as, their mission accomplished, they stole from the room.

"Surest thing you know. He'll come to in half an hour, none the worse," the operative responded. "We made a good clean job of it."

Henry Blaine could hardly suppress his elation when they laid the letter before him on their return to his office.

"It's a forgery, just as I suspected," he exclaimed, with supreme satisfaction. "Look, Hamilton; I'll show you how it was done."

"It is incredible. I can scarcely believe it. I know Pennington Lawton's handwriting as well as I know my own, and I could swear that his fingers guided the pen. His writing was as distinctive as his character."

"It's that very fact," the detective returned, "which would have made it easier to copy; but, as it happens, you are partially right. This was not a forgery in the ordinary sense. Those are Pennington Lawton's own words before you, in his own handwriting."

"Then how — " the young lawyer inquired, in a bewildered tone.

Henry Blaine smiled.

"You do not intend to specialize in criminal law, do you, Mr. Hamilton?" he remarked whimsically. "If you do, you will have to be up in the latest tricks of the trade. The man who forged this letter — the same man, by the way, forged the signature on that mortgage — accomplished it like this: He took a bundle of Mr. Lawton's old letters, cut out the actual words he desired, and pasted 'em in their proper order on the letter paper. Then he photographed this composite, and electrotyped it — that is, transferred it to a copperplate, and etched it. Then he re-photographed it, and in this way got an actual photograph of a supposedly authentic communication. There is only one man in this country who is capable of such perfect work. I know who that man is and where to find him."

"Then if you can locate him before he skips, and make him talk, you will have won the victory," Ramon exclaimed, jubilantly.

But the detective shook his head.

"The time is not yet ripe for that. The man is, in my estimation, a mere tool in the hands of the men higher up. He may not be able to give us any actual proof against them, and our exposure of him will only tip them off — put 'em on their guard. We needn't show our hand just yet."

"What's the next move to be, then?" the young lawyer asked. "I don't mean, of course, that I wish to inquire into your methods of handling the case — but have you any further commissions for me?"

"Only to accompany me to-morrow morning to the office of Charlton Moore and let me examine that note which Mr. Lawton presumably gave two years ago. Afterward, I have four little amateur detectives of mine to interview — then I think we'll be able to proceed straight to our goal."

The note also, as Henry Blaine had predicted, proved to be a forgery and to have been executed by the same hand as the letter.

With the cunning of a Jimmy Valentine he manipulated the tumblers. Ramon Hamilton, his discomfiture forgotten, watched with breathless interest.

The detective betrayed to the unsuspecting banker no sign of his elation at the discovery, but following their interview he returned to his office and sent for the four young girls whom he had taken from the Anita Lawton Club and installed in the offices of the men he suspected.

The first to respond was Margaret Hefferman, who had been sent as stenographer to Rockamore, the promoter.

"You followed my instructions, Miss Hefferman," asked Blaine. "You kept a list for me of Mr. Rockamore's visitors?"

"Yes, sir. I have it here in my bag. I also brought carbon copies of two letters which Mr. Rockamore dictated and which I thought might have some bearing on the matter in which you are interested — although I could not quite understand them myself."

"Let me see them, please."

Blaine took the documents and list of names, scanning them quickly and sharply with a practised eye. The names were those of the biggest men in the city — bankers, brokers, financiers and promoters. Among them, that of President Mallowe and Timothy Carlis appeared frequently. At only one did Henry Blaine pause — at that of Mark Paddington. He had known the man as an employee of a somewhat shady private detective agency several years before and had heard that he had later been connected in some capacity with the city police, but had never come into actual contact with him.

What business could a detective of his caliber have to do with Bertrand Rockamore?

The letters were short and cryptic in their meaning, and significant only when connected with those to whom they were addressed. The first was to Timothy Carlis; it read:

Your communication received. We must proceed with the utmost care in this matter. Keep me advised of any further contingencies which may arise. P. should know or be able to find out. The affair is to his interests as much as ours.

B. R.

The second was addressed to Paddington:

Have learned from C. that your assistants are under espionage. What does it mean? Learn all particulars at once and advise.

R.

"You have done well, Miss Hefferman," said Blaine as he looked up from the last of the letters. "I will keep these carbon copies and the list. Let me know how often Mr. Mallowe and Timothy Carlis call, and try particularly to overhear as much as possible of the man Paddington's conversation when he appears."

When the young stenographer had departed, Fifine Déchaussée appeared. She was the governess who had been sent to the home of Doctor Franklin, ostensibly to care for his children, but in reality to find, if possible, what connection existed between Carlis, Mallowe, Rockamore and himself. The young Frenchwoman's report was disappointingly lacking in any definite result — save one fact. The man Paddington had called twice upon the minister, remaining the second time closeted with him in his study for more than an hour. Later, he had intercepted her when she was out with the children in the park; but she had eluded his attentions.

"I wish you hadn't done so. If he makes any further attempt to talk with you, Mademoiselle Déchaussée, encourage him, draw him out. If he tries to question you about yourself and where you came from, don't mention the Anita Lawton Club, but remember his questions carefully and come and tell me."

"Certainly, m'sieur, I shall remember."

Agnes Olson and Laurette Murfree, the switchboard operator to Carlis and filing clerk to Mallowe, respectively, added practically the same information as had the two preceding girls. Mark Paddington, the detective, had been in frequent communication with each of their employers. When the young women had concluded their reports and gone, Blaine telephoned at once to Guy Morrow, his right-hand operative, and instructed him to watch for Paddington's appearance in the neighborhood of the little house in the Bronx, where they had located Brunell, the one-time forger.

CHAPTER VIII
GUY MORROW FACES A PROBLEM

Morrow, meanwhile, had slowly become aware that he had a problem of his own to face, the biggest of his life. Should he go on with his work? In the event that James Brunell proved, indeed, to be guilty of the forgeries of which he was suspected by the Master Mind, it would mean that he, Morrow, would have betrayed the father of the girl he felt himself beginning to care for. Dared he face such a tremendous issue?

His acquaintance with Emily Brunell had progressed rapidly in the few days since his subterfuge had permitted him to speak to her. He had met her father and found himself liking the tall, silent man who went about the simple affairs of his life with such compelling dignity and courteous aloofness. Brunell had even invited him to his little shop and shown him with unsuspecting enthusiasm his process for making the maps which were sold to the public schools.

Morrow had seen no evidence of anything wrong, either in the little shop or the home life of the father and daughter; nor had he observed Paddington — who was well known to him — in the neighborhood.

Even in these few mornings it had become a habit with him to watch for Emily and walk with her to her subway station, and as frequently as he dared, he would await her arrival in the evening. After his last telephone conversation with Blaine, he called upon the two in the little house across the way, determined to find out, if possible, if the man Paddington had come into their lives. He felt instinctively that James Brunell would prove a difficult subject to cross-examine. The man seemed to be complete master of himself, and were he guilty, could never be led into an admission, unless some influence more powerful than force could be brought to bear upon him.

But the girl, with her clear eyes and unsuspecting, inexperienced mind, could easily be led to disclose whatever knowledge she possessed, particularly if her interest or affections were aroused. It seemed cowardly, in view of his newly awakened feelings toward her, but he had committed far more unscrupulous acts without a qualm, in the course of his professional work.

Brunell was out when he called, but Emily led him into the little sitting-room, and for a time they talked in a desultory fashion. Morrow, who had brought so many malefactors to justice by the winning snare of his personality, felt for once at a loss as to how to commence his questioning.

But the girl herself, guilelessly, gave him a lead by beginning, quite of her own accord, to talk of her early life.

"It seems so strange," she remarked, confidingly, "to have been so completely alone all of my life — except for Daddy, of course."

"You have no brothers or sisters, Miss Brunell?" asked the detective.

"None — and I never knew my mother. She died when I was born."

Morrow sighed, and involuntarily his hand reached forward in an expression of complete sympathy.

"Daddy has been mother and father to me," the girl went on impulsively. "We have always lived in this neighborhood, ever since I can remember, and of course we know everyone around here. But with my downtown position and Father's work in the shop, we've had no time to make real friends and we haven't even cared to — before."

"Before when?" he asked with a kindly intonation not at all in keeping with the purpose which had actuated him in seeking her friendship.

"Before you brought my kitten back to me." She paused, suddenly confused and shy, then added hurriedly, "We have so few guests, you know. Daddy, somehow, doesn't care for people — as a rule, that is. I'm awfully glad that he has made an exception with you."

"But surely you have other friends — for instance, that young fellow I've noticed now and again when he called upon you."

Morrow's thoughts had suddenly turned to that unknown visitor toward whom he had taken such an unaccountable dislike.

"Young fellow — what young fellow?" Emily Brunell's voice had changed, slightly, and a reserved little note intruded itself which reminded Morrow all at once of her father.

"I don't know who he is — I'm such a newcomer in the neighborhood, you know; but I happened to see him from my window across the way — a short, dapper-looking young chap with a small, dark mustache."

"Oh! *that* man." Her lip curled disdainfully. "That's Charley Pennold. He's no friend of mine. He just comes to see Father now and again on business. I don't bother to talk to him. I don't think Daddy likes him very much, either."

She caught her breath in sharply as she spoke, and looked away from Morrow in sudden reserve. He felt a quick start of suspicion, and searched her averted face with a keen, penetrating glance.

If this Charley Pennold, whoever he might be, wished to see James Brunell on legitimate business, why did he not go to his shop openly and above-board in the day-time? Could he be an emissary from some one whom the old forger had reason to evade? If he were, did Emily know for what purpose he came, and was she annoyed at her own error in involuntarily disclosing his name?

"He is a map-maker, too?" leaped from Morrow's lips.

"He is interested in maps — he gives Daddy large orders for them, I believe."

Emily spoke too hurriedly, and her tones lacked the ring of sincerity which was habitual with them.

The trained ear of the detective instantly sensed the difference, and his heart sank.

So she had lied to him deliberately, and her womanly instinct told her that he knew it.

She began to talk confusedly of trivialities; and Morrow, seeing that it would be hopeless to attempt to draw her back to her unguarded mood, left her soon after — heartsick and dejected.

Should he continue with his investigations, or go to Henry Blaine and confess that he had failed him? Was this girl, charming and innocent as she appeared, worth the price of his career — this girl with the blood of criminals in her veins, who would stoop to lies and deceit to protect them? Yet had not he been seeking deliberately to betray her and those she loved, under the guise of friendship? Was he any better than she or her father?

Then, too, another thought came to him. Might she not be the tool, consciously or unconsciously, of a nefarious plot?

He felt that he could not rest until he had brought his investigations to a conclusion which would be satisfactory to himself, even if he decided in the end, for her sake, never to divulge to Henry Blaine the discoveries he might make.

A few days later, however, Morrow received instructions from Blaine himself, which forced his hand. The time had come for him to use the skeleton-key which he had had made. He must proceed that night to investigate the little shop of the map-maker and look there for the evidence which would incriminate him — the photographic and electrotyping apparatus.

Early in the evening he heard Emily's soft voice as she called across the street in pleasant greeting to Miss Quinlan, but he could not bring himself to go out upon the little porch and speak to her, although he did not doubt his welcome.

He waited until all was dark and still before he started upon his distasteful errand. It was very cold, and the streets were deserted. A fine dry snow was falling, which obliterated his footprints almost as soon as he made them, and he reached the now familiar door of the little shop without meeting a soul abroad save a lonely policeman dozing in a doorway. He let himself into the shop with his key and flashed his pocket lamp about. All appeared the same as in the day-time. The maps were rolled in neat cases or fastened upon the wall. The table, the press, the binder were each in their proper place.

Morrow went carefully over every inch of the room and the curtained recess back of it, but could find no evidence such as he sought. At length, however, just before the little desk in the corner where James Brunell kept his modest accounts, the detective's foot touched a metal ring in the floor. Stepping back from it, he seized the ring and pulled it. A small square section of the flooring yielded, and the raising of the narrow trap-door disclosed a worn, sanded stone stairway leading down into the cellar beneath.

Blaine's operative listened carefully but no sound came from the depths below him; so after a time, with his light carefully shielded, he essayed a gingerly descent. On the bottom step he paused. There was small need for him to go further. He had found what he sought. Emily Brunell's father was a forger indeed!

CHAPTER IX
GONE!

Guy Morrow, after a sleepless night, presented himself at Henry Blaine's office the next morning. The great detective, observing his young subordinate with shrewd, kindly eyes, noted in one swift glance his changed demeanor: his pallor, and the new lines graven about the firm mouth, which added strength and maturity to his face. If he guessed the reason for the metamorphosis, Blaine gave no sign, but listened without comment until Morrow had completed his report.

"You obeyed my instructions?" he asked at length. "When you discovered the forgery outfit in the cellar of Brunell's shop, you left everything just as it had been — left no possible trace of your presence?"

"Yes, sir. There's not a sign left to show any one had disturbed the place. I am sure of that."

"Not a foot-print in the earth of the cellar steps?"

"No, sir."

"And the outfit — was there any evidence it had been used lately?"

"No — everything was dust-covered, and even rusty, as if it had not even been touched in months, perhaps years. The whole thing might be merely a relic of Jimmy Brunell's past performances, in the life he gave up long ago."

Morrow spoke almost eagerly, as if momentarily off his guard, but Blaine shook his head.

"Rather too dangerous a relic to keep in one's possession, Guy, simply as a souvenir — a reminder of things the man is trying to forget, to live down. You can depend on it: the outfit was there for some more practical purpose. You say Paddington has not appeared in the neighborhood, but another man has — a man Brunell's daughter seems to dislike and fear?"

"Yes, sir. There's one significant fact about him, too — his name. He's Charley Pennold. It didn't occur to me for some time after Miss Brunell let that slip, that the name is the same as that of the precious pair of old crooks over in Brooklyn, the ones Suraci and I traced Brunell by."

"Charley Pennold!" Blaine repeated thoughtfully. "I hadn't thought of him. He's old Walter Pennold's nephew. The boy was running straight the last I heard of him, but you never can tell. Guy, I'm going to take you off the Brunell trail for a while, and put you on this man Paddington. I'll have Suraci look up Charley Pennold and get a line on him. In the meantime, leave your key to the map-making shop with me. I may want to have a look at that forgery outfit myself."

"You're going to take me off the Brunell trail!" Morrow's astonishment and obvious distaste for the change of program confronting him was all-revealing. "But I'll have to go back and make some sort of explanation for leaving so abruptly, won't I? Will it pay to arouse their suspicions — that is, sir, unless you've got some special reason for doing so?"

Blaine's slow smile was very kindly and sympathetic as he eyed the anxious young man before him.

"No. You will go back, of course, and explain that you have obtained a clerkship which necessitates your moving downtown. Make your peace with Miss Brunell if you like, but remember, Guy, don't mix sentiment and business. It won't do. I may have to put you back on the job there in a few days, and I know I can depend on you not to lose your head. She's a young girl and a pretty one; but don't forget she's the daughter of Jimmy Brunell, the man we're trying to get! Pennington Lawton had a daughter, too; remember that — and she's been defrauded of everything in the world but her lover and her faith in her father's memory." His voice had gradually grown deeper and more stern, and he added in brisk, businesslike tones, far removed from the personal element. "Now get back to the Bronx. Come to me to-morrow morning, and I'll have the data in the Paddington matter ready for you."

The young detective had scarcely taken his departure, when

Ramon Hamilton appeared. He was in some excitement, and glanced nervously behind him as he entered, as if almost in fear of possible pursuit.

"Mr. Blaine," he began, "I'm confident that we're suspected. Here's a note that came to me from President Mallowe this morning. He asks if I inadvertently carried away with me that letter of Pennington Lawton's written from Long Bay two years ago, in which I had shown such an interest during our interview the other day. He has been unable to find it since my departure. That's a rather broad hint, it seems to me."

"I should not consider it as such," the detective responded. "Guilty conscience, Mr. Hamilton!"

"That's not all!" the young lawyer went on. "He says that a curious burglary was committed at his offices the night after my interview with him — his watchman was chloroformed, and the safe in his private office opened and rifled, yet nothing was taken, with the possible exception of that letter. Mallowe asks me, openly, if I knew of an ulterior motive which any one might have possessed in acquiring it, and even remarks that he is thinking of putting you, Mr. Blaine, on the mysterious attempt at robbery. That would be a joke, wouldn't it, if it wasn't really, in my estimation at least, a covert threat. Why should he, Mallowe, take me into his confidence about an affair which took place in his private office? He did not make the excuse of pretending to retain me as his attorney. I think he was merely warning me that he was suspicious of me."

"Probably a mere coincidence," Blaine observed easily.

"I wonder if you'll think so when I tell you that twice since yesterday my life has been attempted." Ramon spoke quietly enough, but there was a slight trembling in his tones.

"What!" Blaine started forward in his chair, then sank back with an incredulous smile, which none but he could have known was forced. "Surely you imagine it, Mr. Hamilton. Since your automobile accident, when you were run down and so nearly killed on the evening you sent for me to undertake Miss Lawton's case, you may well be nervous."

As he spoke he glanced at the other's broken arm, which was still swathed in bandages.

"But these were no accidents, Mr. Blaine, and I have always doubted that the first one was, as you know. Yesterday afternoon, a new client's case called me down to the sixth ward, at four o'clock. In order to reach my client's address it was necessary to pass through the street in which that shooting affray occurred which filled the papers last evening. Two men darted out of a house, shot presumably at each other, then turned and ran in opposite directions without waiting to see if either of the shots took effect. You know that isn't usual with the members of rival gangs down there. Remember, too, Mr. Blaine, that it was prearranged for me to walk alone through that street at just that psychological moment. It seemed to me that neither man shot at the other, but both fired point-blank at me. I dismissed the idea from my mind as absurd, the next minute, and would have thought no more about it, beyond congratulating myself on my fortunate escape, had not the second attempt been made."

"The sixth ward — " Blaine remarked, meditatively. "That's Timothy Carlis' stamping ground, of course. But go on, Mr. Hamilton. What was the second incident?"

"Late last night, I had a telephone message from my club that my best friend, Gordon Brooke, had been taken suddenly ill with a serious attack of heart-trouble, and wanted me. Brooke has heart-disease and he might go off with it at any time, so I posted over immediately. The club is only a few blocks away from my home, so I didn't wait to call my machine or a taxi, but started over. Just a little way from the club, three men sprang upon me and attempted to hold me up. I fought them off, and when they came at me again, three to one, the idea flashed upon me that this was a fresh attempt to assassinate me.

"I shouted for help, and then ran. When I reached the club I found Brooke there, sitting in a poker game and quite as well as usual. No telephone message had been sent to me from him. I tried this morning, before I came to you, to have the number traced, but without success. Do you blame me now, Mr. Blaine, for believing, after these three manifestations, that my life is in actual danger?"

"I do not." The detective touched an electric button on his desk. "I think it will be advisable for you to have a guard, for the next few days, at least."

"A guard!" Ramon repeated, indignantly. "I'm not a coward. Any man would be disturbed, to put it mildly, over the conviction that his life was threatened every hour, but it was of her I was thinking — of Anita! I could not bear to think of leaving her alone to face the world, penniless and hedged in on all sides by enemies. But I want no guard! I can take care of myself as well as the next man. Look at the perils and dangers you have faced in your unceasing warfare against malefactors of every grade. It is common knowledge that you have invariably refused to be guarded."

"The years during which I have been constantly face to face with sudden death have made me disregard the possibility of it. But I shall not insist in your case, Mr. Hamilton, if you do not wish it; and allow me to tell you that I admire your spirit. However, I should like to have you leave town for a few days, if your clients can spare you."

"Leave town? Run away?" Ramon started indignantly from his chair, but Blaine waved him back with a fatherly hand.

"Not at all. On a commission for me, in Miss Lawton's interests. Mr. Hamilton, you have known the Lawtons for several years, have you not?"

"Ever since I can remember," the young lawyer said with renewed eagerness.

"Two years ago, in August, Pennington Lawton and his daughter were at 'The Breakers,' at Long Bay, were they not?"

"Yes. Anita and I were engaged then, and I ran out myself for the week-end."

"I want you to run out there for me now. The hotel will be

closed at this time of year, of course, but a letter which I will give you to the proprietor, who lives close at hand, will enable you to look over the register for an hour or two in private. Turn to the arrivals for August of that year, and trace the names and home addresses on each page; then bring it back to me."

"Is it something in connection with that forged letter to Mallowe?" asked Ramon quickly.

"Perhaps," the detective admitted. He shrugged, then added leniently, "I think, before proceeding any further with that branch of the investigation, it would be well to know who obtained the notepaper with the hotel letterhead, and if the paper itself was genuine. Bring me back some of the hotel stationery, also, that I may compare it with that used for the letter."

A discreet knock upon the door heralded the coming of an operative, in response to Blaine's touch upon the bell.

"There has been a slight disturbance in the outer office, sir," he announced. "A man, who appears to be demented, insists upon seeing you. He isn't one of the ordinary cranks, or we would have dealt with him ourselves. He says that if you will read this, you will be glad to assent to an interview with him."

He presented a card, which Blaine read with every manifestation of surprised interest.

"Tell him I will see him in five minutes," he said. When the operative had withdrawn, the detective turned to Ramon.

"Who do you think is waiting outside? The man who threatened Pennington Lawton's life ten years ago, the man whose name was mentioned by the unknown visitor to the library on the night Lawton met his death: Herbert Armstrong!"

"Good heavens!" Ramon exclaimed. "What brings him here now? I thought he had disappeared utterly. Do you think it could have been he in the library that night, come to take revenge for that fancied wrong, at last?"

"That is what I'm going to find out," the detective responded, with a touch of grimness in his tones.

"But you don't mean — it isn't possible that Mr. Lawton was murdered! That he didn't die of heart-disease, after all!"

"I traced Armstrong to the town where he was living in obscurity, and followed his movements." Blaine's reply seemed to be purposely irrelevant. "I could not, however, find where he had been on the night of Mr. Lawton's death. Now that he has come to me voluntarily, we shall discover if the voice Miss Lawton overheard in that moment when she listened on the stairs, was his or not.... Come back this afternoon, Mr. Hamilton, and I will give you full information and instructions about that Long Bay errand. In the meantime, guard yourself well from a possible attack, although I do not think another attempt upon your life will be made so soon. Take this, and if you have need of it, do not hesitate to use it. We can afford no half-measures now. Shoot, and shoot to kill!"

He opened a lower drawer in his massive desk and, drawing from it a business-like looking revolver of large caliber, presented it to the lawyer. With a warm hand-clasp he dismissed him, and, going to the telephone, called up Anita Lawton's home.

"I want you to attend carefully, Miss Lawton. I am speaking from my office. A man will be here with me in a few minutes, and I shall seat him close to the transmitter of my 'phone, leaving the receiver off the hook. Please listen carefully to his voice. I only wish you to hear a phrase or two, when I will hang up the receiver, and call you up later. Try to concentrate with all your powers, and tell me afterward if you have ever heard that voice until now; if it is the voice of the man you did not see, who was in the library with your father just before he died."

He heard her give a quick gasp, and then her voice came to him, low and sweet and steady.

"I will listen carefully, Mr. Blaine, and do my best to tell you the truth."

The detective pulled a large leather chair close to the telephone, and Herbert Armstrong was ushered in.

The man was pitiful in appearance, but scarcely demented,

as the operative had described him. He was tall and shabbily clothed, gaunt almost to the point of emaciation, but with no sign of dissipation. His eyes, though sunken, were clear, and they gazed levelly with those of the detective.

"Come in, Mr. Armstrong." Blaine waved genially toward the arm-chair. "What can I do for you?"

The man did not offer to shake hands, but sank wearily into the chair assigned him.

"Do? You can stop hounding me, Henry Blaine! You and Pennington Lawton brought my tragedy upon me as surely as I brought it upon myself, and now you will not leave me alone with my grief and ruin, to drag my miserable life out to the end, but you or your men must dog my every foot-step, spy upon me, hunt me down like a pack of wolves! And why? Why?"

The man's voice had run its gamut, in the emotion which consumed him, and from a menacing growl of protest, it had risen to a shrill wail of weakness and despair.

Henry Blaine was satisfied.

"Excuse me, Mr. Armstrong," he said gently. "The receiver is off my telephone, here at your elbow. It would be unfortunate if we were overheard. If you will allow me — "

But he got no further. Quick as he was, the other man was quicker. He sprang up furiously, and dashed the telephone off the desk.

"Is this another of your d — d tricks?" he shouted. "If it is, whoever was listening may hear the rest. You and Pennington Lawton between you, drove my wife to suicide, but you'll not drive *me* there! I'm ruined, and broken, and hopeless, but I'll live on, live till I'm even, do you hear? Live till I'm square with the game!"

His violence died out as swiftly as it had arisen, and he sank down in the chair, his face buried in his bony hands, his thin shoulders shaken with sobs.

Blaine quietly replaced the telephone and receiver, and seated himself.

"Come, man, pull yourself together!" he said, not unkindly. "I'm not hounding you; Lawton never harmed you, and now he is dead. He was my client and I was bound to protect his interests, but as man to man, the fault was yours and you know it. I tried to keep you from making a fool of yourself and wrecking three lives, but I only succeeded in saving one."

"But your men are hounding me, following me, shadowing me! I have come to find out why!"

"And I would like to find out where you were on a certain night last month — the ninth, to be exact," responded Blaine quietly.

"What affair is it of yours?" the other man asked wearily, adding: "How should I know, now? One night is like another, to me."

"If you hate Pennington Lawton's memory as you seem to, the ninth of November should stand out in your thoughts in letters of fire," the detective went on, in even, quiet tone. "That was the night on which Lawton died."

"Lawton?" Herbert Armstrong raised his haggard face. The meaning of Blaine's remark utterly failed to pierce his consciousness. "The date doesn't mean anything to me, but I remember the night, if that's what you want to know about, although I'm hanged if I can see what it's got to do with me! I'll never forget that night, because of the news which reached me in the morning, that my worst enemy on earth had passed away."

"Were you in Illington the evening before?" asked Blaine.

"I was not. I was in New Harbor, where I live, playing pinochle all night long with two other down-and-outs like myself, in a cheap hall bed-room — I, Herbert Armstrong, who used to play for thousands a game, in the best clubs in Illington! And I never knew that the man who had brought me to that pass was gasping his life away! Think of it! We played until dawn, when the extras, cried in the street below, gave us the news!"

"If you will give me the address of this boarding-house you mention, and the names of your two friends, I can promise that you will be under no further espionage, Mr. Armstrong."

"I don't care whether you know it or not, if that's all you want!" The gaunt man shrugged wearily. "I'm tired of being hounded, and I'm too weak and too tired to oppose you, even if it did matter."

He gave the required names and addresses, and slouched away, his animosity gone, and only a dull, miserable lethargy sagging upon his worn body.

When the outer door of the offices had closed upon him, Henry Blaine again called up Anita Lawton. This time her voice came to him sharpened by acute distress.

"I did not recognize the tones of the person's voice, Mr. Blaine, only I am quite, quite sure that he was not the man in the library with my father the night of his death. But oh, what did he mean by the terrible things he said? It could not be that my father brought ruin and tragedy upon any one, much less drove them to suicide. Won't you tell me, Mr. Blaine? Ramon won't, although I am convinced he knows all about it. I must know."

"You shall, Miss Lawton. I think the time has come when you should no longer be left in the dark. I will tell Mr. Hamilton when he comes to me this afternoon for the interview we have arranged that you must know the whole story."

But Ramon Hamilton failed to appear for the promised interview. Henry Blaine called up his office and his home, but was unable to locate him. Then Miss Lawton began making anxious inquiries, and finally the mother of the young lawyer appealed to the detective, but in vain. Late that night the truth was established beyond peradventure of a doubt. Ramon Hamilton had disappeared as if the earth had opened and engulfed him.

CHAPTER X
MARGARET HEFFERMAN'S FAILURE

The disappearance of Ramon Hamilton, coming so soon after the sudden death of his prospective father-in-law, caused a profound sensation. In the small hours of the night, before the press had been apprised of the event and when every probable or possible place where the young lawyer might be had been communicated with in vain, Henry Blaine set the perfect machinery of his forces at work to trace him.

It was dawn before he could spare a precious moment to go to Anita Lawton. On his arrival he found her pacing the floor, wringing her slim hands in anguish.

"He is dead." She spoke with the dull hopelessness of utter conviction. "I shall never see him again. I feel it! I know it!"

"My dear child!" Blaine put his hands upon her shoulders in fatherly compassion. "You must put all such morbid fancies from your mind. He is not dead and we shall find him. It may be all a mistake — perhaps some important matter concerning a client made it necessary for him to leave the city over night."

She shook her head despairingly.

"No, Mr. Blaine. You know as well as I that Ramon is just starting in his profession. He has no clients of any prominence, and my father's influence was really all that his rising reputation was being built upon. Besides, nothing but a serious accident or — or death would keep him from me!"

"If he had met with any accident his identity would have been discovered and we would be notified, unless, as in the case when he was run down by that motor-car, he did not wish them to let you know for fear of worrying you."

Blaine watched the young girl narrowly as he spoke. Was she aware of the two additional attempts only the day before on the life of the man she loved?

"He merely followed a dear, unselfish impulse because he

knew that in a few hours at most he would be with me; but now it is morning! The dawn of a new day, and no word from him! Those terrible people who tried to kill him that other time to keep him from coming to me in my trouble have made away with him. I am sure of it now."

The detective breathed more freely. Evidently Ramon Hamilton had had the good sense to keep from her his recent danger.

"You can be sure of nothing, Miss Lawton, save the fact that Mr. Hamilton is *not* dead," Henry Blaine said earnestly. "You do not realize, perhaps, the one salient fact that criminal experts who deal with cases of disappearance have long since recognized — the most difficult of all things to conceal or do away with in a large city is a dead body."

Anita shivered and clasped her hands convulsively, but she did not speak, and after a scarcely perceptible pause, the detective went on:

"You must not let your mind dwell on the possibilities; it will only entail useless, needless suffering on your part. My experiences have been many and varied in just such cases as this, and in not one in fifty does serious harm come to the subject of the investigation. In fact, in this instance, I think it quite probable that Mr. Hamilton has left the city of his own accord, and in your interests."

"In my interests?" Anita repeated, roused from her lethargy of sorrow by his words, as he had intended that she should be. "Left the city? But why?"

"When he called upon me yesterday morning I told him of a commission which I wished him to execute for me in connection with your investigation. I gave him some preliminary instructions and he was to return to me in the afternoon for a letter of introduction and to learn some minor details of the matter involved. He did not appear at the hour of our appointment and I concluded that he had taken the affair into his own hands and had gone immediately upon leaving my office to fulfill his mission."

"Oh, perhaps he did!" The young girl started from her chair, her dull, tearless eyes suddenly bright with hope. "That would be like Ramon; he is so impulsive, so anxious to help me in every way! Where did you send him, Mr. Blaine? Can't we telephone, or wire and find out if he really has gone to this place? Please, please do! I cannot endure this agony of uncertainty, of suspense, much longer!"

"Unfortunately, we cannot do that!" Blaine responded, gravely. "To attempt to communicate with him where I have sent him would be to show our hand irretrievably to the men we are fighting and undo much of the work which has been accomplished. He may communicate with you or possibly with me, if he finds that he can contrive to accomplish it safely."

"Safely? Then if he has gone to this place, wherever it is, he is in danger?" Anita faltered, tremblingly.

"By no means. The only danger is that his identity and purpose may be disclosed and our plans jeopardized," the detective reassured her smoothly. "I know it is hard to wait for news, but one must school oneself to patience under circumstances such as this. It may be several days before you hear from Mr. Hamilton and you must try not to distress yourself with idle fears in the meantime."

"But it is not certain — we have no assurance that he really did go upon that mission." The light of hope died in her eyes as she spoke, and a little sob rose in her throat. "Oh, Mr. Blaine, promise me that you will leave no stone unturned to find him!"

"My dear child, you must trust in me and have faith in my long years of experience. I have already, as a precautionary measure, started a thorough investigation into Mr. Hamilton's movements yesterday, and in the event that he has not gone on the errand I spoke of, it can only be a question of hours before he will be located. You did not see him yesterday?"

"No. He promised to lunch with me, but he never came nor did he telephone or send me any word. Surely, if he had meant to leave town he would have let me know!"

"Not necessarily, Miss Lawton." Blaine's voice deepened

persuasively. "He was very much excited when he left my office, interested heart and soul in the mission I had entrusted to him. Remember, too, that it was all for you, for your sake alone."

"And I may not know where he has gone?" Anita asked, wistfully.

"I think, perhaps, that is why Mr. Hamilton did not communicate with you before leaving town," the detective replied, significantly. "He agreed with me that it would be best for you not to know, in your own interests, where he was going. You must try to believe that I am doing all in my power to help you, and that my judgment is in such matters better than yours."

"I do, Mr. Blaine. Indeed I do trust you absolutely; you must believe that." She reached out an impulsive hand toward him, and his own closed over it paternally for a moment. Then he gently released it.

Anita sighed and sank back resignedly in her chair. There was a moment's pause before she added:

"It is hard to be quiescent when one is so hedged in on all sides by falsehood and deceit and the very air breathes conspiracy and intrigue. I have no tangible reason to fear for my own life, of course, but sometimes I cannot help wondering why it has not been imperiled. Surely it would be easier for my father's enemies to do away with me altogether than to have conceived and carried out such an elaborate scheme to rob me and defame my father's memory. But I will try not to entertain such thoughts. I am nervous and overwrought, but I will regain my self-control. In the meantime, I shall do my best to be patient and wait for Ramon's return."

Henry Blaine felt a glow of pardonable elation, but his usually expressive face did not betray by a single flicker of an eyelash that he had gained his point. He knew that Ramon Hamilton had never started on that mission to Long Bay, but if the young girl's health and reason were to be spared, her anxiety must be allayed. Courageous and self-controlled as she had been through all the grief and added trouble which besieged her on every hand, the keen insight of the detective warned him that she was nearing the breaking-point. If she fully realized the blow which threatened her in the sudden disappearance of her lover, together with the sinister events which had immediately preceded it, she would be crushed to the earth.

"You must try to rest." Blaine rose and motioned toward the window through which the cold rays of the wintry sun were stealing and putting the orange glow of the electric lights to shame. "See. It is morning and you have had no sleep."

"But you must not go just yet, Mr. Blaine! I cannot rest until I know who that man was whose voice I heard over your telephone this morning. What did he mean? He said that his wife committed suicide; that he himself had been ruined! And all through my father and you! It cannot be true, of course; but I must know to what he referred!"

"I will tell you. It is best that you should know the truth. Your father was absolutely innocent in the matter, but his enemies and yours might find it expedient to spread fake reports which would only add to your sorrow. You know, you must remember since your earliest childhood, how every one came to your father with their perplexities and troubles and how benevolently they were received, how wisely advised, how generously aided. Not only bankers and financiers in the throes of a panic, but men and women in all walks of life came to him for counsel and relief."

"I know. I know!" Anita whispered with bowed head, the quick tears of tender memory starting in her eyes.

"Such a one who came to him for advice in her distress was the wife of Herbert Armstrong. She was a good woman, but through sheer ignorance of evil she had committed a slight indiscretion, nothing more than the best of women might be led into at any time. We need not go into details. It is enough to tell you that certain unscrupulous persons had her in their power and were blackmailing her. She fell their victim through the terror of being misunderstood, and when she could no longer accede to their demands she came to your father, her husband's friend, for advice. Herbert Armstrong was insanely jealous of his wife, and in your father's efforts to help her he unfortunately incurred the unjust suspicions of the man. Armstrong brought suit for divorce, intending to name Mr. Lawton as corespondent."

"Oh, how could he!" Anita cried, indignantly. "The man must have been mad! My father was the soul of honor. Every one — the whole world — knows that! Besides, his heart was buried, all that he did not give to me, deep, deep in the sea where Mother and my little brother and sister are lying! He never even looked at another woman, save perhaps in kindness, to help and comfort those who were in trouble. But when did you come into the case, Mr. Blaine? That man whose voice I heard to-day must have been Herbert Armstrong himself, of course. Why did he say that you, as well as my father, were responsible for his tragedy?"

"Because when Mr. Lawton became aware of Armstrong's ungovernable jealousy and the terrible length to which he meant to go in his effort to revenge himself, he — your father — came to me to establish Mrs. Armstrong's innocence, and his, in the eyes of the world. Armstrong's case, although totally wrong from every standpoint, was a very strong one, but fortunately I was able to verify the truth and was fully prepared to prove it. Just on the eve of the date set for the trial, however, a tragedy occurred which brought the affair to an abrupt and pathetic end."

"A tragedy? Mrs. Armstrong's suicide, you mean?" asked Anita, in hushed tones. "How awful!"

"She was deeply in love with her husband. His unjust accusations and the public shame he was so undeservedly bringing upon her broke her heart. I assured her that she would be vindicated, that Armstrong would be on his knees to her at the trial's end. Your father tried to infuse her with courage, to gird her for the coming struggle to defend her own good name, but it was all of no use. She was too broken in spirit. Life held nothing more for her. On the night before the case was to have been called, she shot herself."

"Poor thing!" Anita murmured, with a sob running through her soft voice. "Poor, persecuted woman. Why did she not wait!

Knowing her own innocence and loving her husband as she did, she could have forgiven him for his cruel suspicion when it was all over! But surely Herbert Armstrong knows the truth now. How can he blame you and my father for the wreck which he made of his own life?"

"Because his mind has become unhinged. He was always excitable and erratic, and his weeks of jealous wrath, culminating in the shock of the sudden tragedy, and the realization that he had brought it all on himself, were too much for him. He was a broker and one of the most prominent financiers in the city, but with the divorce fiasco and the death of Mrs. Armstrong, he began to brood. He shunned the friends who were left to him, neglected his business and ultimately failed. Sinking lower and lower in the scale of things, he finally disappeared from Illington. You can understand now why I thought it best when you told me of the conversation you had overheard in the library here a few hours before your father's death, and of the mention of Herbert Armstrong's name, to trace him and find out if it was he who had come in the heart of the night and attempted to blackmail Mr. Lawton."

"I understand. That was why you wanted me to hear his voice yesterday and see if I recognized it. But it was not at all like that of the man in the library on the night of my father's death. And do you know, Mr. Blaine" — she leaned forward and spoke in still lower tones — "when I recall that voice, it seems to me, sometimes, that I have heard it before. There was a certain timbre in it which was oddly familiar. It is as if some one I knew had spoken, but in tones disguised by rage and passion. I shall recognize that voice when I hear it again, if it holds that same note; and when I do — "

Blaine darted a swift glance at her from under narrowed brows. "But why attribute so much importance to it?" he asked. "To be sure, it may have some bearing upon our investigation, although at present I can see no connecting link. You feel, perhaps, that the violent emotions superinduced by that secret interview, added to your father's heart-trouble, indirectly caused his death?"

Anita again sank back in her chair.

"I don't know, Mr. Blaine. I cannot explain it, even to myself, but I feel instinctively that that interview was of greater significance than any one has considered, as yet."

"That we must leave to the future." The detective took her hand, and this time Anita rose and walked slowly with him toward the door. "There are matters of greater moment to be investigated now. Remember my advice. Try to be patient. Yours is the hardest task of all, to sit idly by and wait for events to shape themselves, or for me to shape them, but it must be. If you can calm your nerves and obtain a few hours' sleep you will feel your own brave self again when I report to you, as I shall do, later to-day."

Despite his night of ceaseless work, Henry Blaine, clear-eyed and alert of brain, was seated at his desk at the stroke of nine when Suraci was ushered in — the young detective who had trailed Walter Pennold from Brooklyn to the quiet backwater where Jimmy Brunell had sought in vain for disassociation from his past shadowy environment.

"It has become necessary, through an incident which occurred yesterday, for me to change my plans," Blaine announced. "I had intended to put you on the trail of a young crook, a relative of Pennold, but I find I must send you instead to Long Bay to look up a hotel register for me and obtain some writing paper with the engraved letter-head from that hotel. You can get a train in an hour, if you look sharp. Try to get back to-night or to-morrow morning at the latest. Find out anything you can regarding the visit there two years ago last August of Pennington Lawton and his daughter and of other guests who arrived during their stay. Here are your instructions."

Twenty minutes' low-voiced conversation ensued, and Suraci took his departure. He was followed almost immediately by Guy Morrow.

"What is the dope, sir?" the latter asked eagerly, as he entered. "There's an extra out about the Hamilton disappearance.

Do you think Paddington's had a hand in that?"

"I want you to tail him," Blaine replied, non-committally. "Find out anything you can of his movements for the past few weeks, but don't lose sight of him for a minute until to-morrow morning. He's supposed to be working up the evidence now for the Snedecker divorce, so it won't be difficult for you to locate him. You know what he looks like."

"Yes, sir. I know the man himself — if you call such a little rat a man. We had a run-in once, and it isn't likely I'd forget him."

"Then be careful to keep out of his sight. He may be a rat, but he's as keen-eyed as a ferret. I'd rather put some one on him whom he didn't know, but we'll have to chance it. I wouldn't trust this to anyone but you, Guy."

The young operative flushed with pride at this tribute from his chief, and after a few more instructions he went upon his way with alacrity.

Once more alone, Henry Blaine sat for a long time lost in thought. An idea had come to him, engendered by a few vague words uttered by Anita Lawton in the early hours of that morning: an idea so startling, so tremendous in its import, that even he scarcely dared give it credence. To put it to the test, to prove or disprove it, would be irretrievably to show his hand in the game, and that would be suicidal to his investigation should his swift suspicion chance to be groundless.

The sharp ring of the telephone put an end to his cogitations. He put the receiver to his ear with a preoccupied frown, but at the first words which came to him over the wire his expression changed to one of keenest concentration.

"Am I speaking to the gentleman who talked with me at the working girls' club?" a clear, fresh young voice asked. "This is Margaret Heffernan, Mr. Rockamore's stenographer — that is, I was until ten minutes ago, but I have been discharged."

"Discharged!" Blaine's voice was eager and crisp as he reiterated her last word. "On what pretext?"

"It was not exactly a pretext," the girl replied. "The office boy accused me of taking shorthand notes of a private conversation between my employer and a visitor, and I could not convince Mr. Rockamore of my innocence. I — I must have been clumsy, I'm afraid."

"You have the notes with you?"

"Yes."

"The visitor's name was Paddington?"

"Yes, sir."

Blaine considered for a moment; then, his decision made, he spoke rapidly in a clear undertone.

"You know the department store of Mead & Rathbun? Meet me there in the ladies' writing-room in half an hour. Where are you now?"

"In a booth in the drug-store just around the corner from the building where Mr. Rockamore's offices are located."

"Very good. Take as round-about a route as you can to reach Mead & Rathbun's, and see if you are followed. If you are and you find it impossible to shake off your shadow, do not try to meet me, but go directly to the club and I will communicate with you there later."

"Oh, I don't think I've been followed, but I'll be very careful. If everything is all right, I will meet you at the place you named in half an hour. Good-by."

Henry Blaine paced the floor for a time in undisguised perturbation. His move in placing inexperienced girls from Anita Lawton's club in responsible positions, instead of using his own trained operatives, had been based not upon impulse but on mature reflection. The girls were unknown, whereas his operatives would assuredly have been recognized, sooner or later, especially in the offices of Carlis and Rockamore. Moreover, the ruse adopted to obtain positions for Miss Lawton's protégées had appeared on the surface to be a flawlessly legitimate one. He had counted upon their loyalty and zeal to outweigh their possible incompetence and lack of discretion, but the stolid German girl had apparently been so clumsy at her task as to bring failure upon his plan.

"So much for amateurs!" he murmured to himself, disgustedly. "The other three will be discharged as soon as excuses for their dismissal can be manufactured now. My only hope from any of them is that French governess. If she will only land Paddington I don't care what suspicions the other three arouse."

Margaret Hefferman's placid face was a little pale when she greeted him in the ladies' room of the department store a short time later.

"I'm so sorry, Mr. Blaine!" she exclaimed, but in carefully lowered tones. "I could have cut my right hand off before I would hurt Miss Lawton after all she has done for me, and already the first thing she asks, I must fail to do!"

"You are sure you were not followed?" asked the detective, disregarding her lamentations with purposeful brusqueness, for the tears stood in her soft, bovine eyes, and he feared an emotional outburst which would draw down upon them the attention of the whole room.

"Oh, no! I made sure of that. I rode uptown and half-way down again to be certain, and then changed to the east-side line."

"Very well." He drew her to a secluded window-seat where, themselves almost unseen, they could obtain an unobstructed view of the entrance door and of their immediate neighbors.

"Now tell me all about it, Miss Hefferman."

"It was that office boy, Billy," she began. "Such sharp eyes and soft walk, like a cat! Always he is yawning and sleepy — who would think he was a spy?"

Her tone was filled with such contempt that involuntarily the detective's mobile lips twitched. The girl had evidently quite lost sight of the fact that she herself had occupied the very position in the pseudo employ of Bertrand Rockamore which she derided in his office boy.

He did not attempt to guide her in her narrative of the morning's events, observing that she was too much agitated to give him a coherent account. Instead, he waited patiently for her to vent her indignation and tell him in her own way the substance of what had occurred.

"I had no thought of being watched, else I should have been more careful," she went on, resentfully. "This morning, only, he was late — that Billy — and I did not report him. I was busy, too, for there was more correspondence than usual to attend to, and Mr. Rockamore was irritable and short-tempered. In the midst of his dictation Mr. Paddington came, and I was bundled out of the room with the letters and my shorthand book. They talked together behind the closed door for several minutes and I had no opportunity to hear a word, but presently Mr. Rockamore called Billy and sent him out on an errand. Billy left the door of the inner office open just a little and that was my chance. I seated myself at a desk close beside it and took down in shorthand every word which reached my ears. I was so much occupied with the notes that I did not hear Billy's footsteps until he stopped just behind me and whistled right in my ear. I jumped and he laughed at me and went in to Mr. Rockamore. When he came out he shut the door tight behind him and grinned as if he knew just what I had been up to. I did not dare open the door again, and so I heard no more of the conversation, but I have enough, Mr. Blaine, to interest you, I think."

She fumbled with her bag, but the detective laid a detaining hand on her arm.

"Never mind the notes now. Go on with your story. What happened after the interview was over?"

"That boy Billy went to Mr. Rockamore and told him. Already I have said he was irritable this morning. He had seemed nervous and excited, as if he were angry or worried about something, but when he sent for me to discharge me he was white-hot with rage. Never have I been so insulted or abused, but that would be nothing if only I had not failed Miss Lawton. For her sake I tried to lie, to deny, but it was of no use. My people were good Lutherans, but that does not help one in a business career; it is much more a nuisance. He could read in my face that I was guilty, and he demanded my shorthand note-book. I had to give it to him; there was nothing else to be done."

"But I understood that you had the notes with you," Blaine commented, then paused as a faint smile broke over her face and a demure dimple appeared in either cheek.

"I gave to him a note-book," she explained naïvely. "He was quite pleased, I think, to get possession of it. No one can read my shorthand but me, anyway, so one book did him as much good as another. He tried to make me tell him why I had done that — why I had taken down the words of a private conference of his with a visitor. I could not think what I should say, so I kept silent. For an hour he bullied and questioned me, but he could find out nothing and so at last he let me go. If now I could get my hands on that Billy — "

"Never mind him," Blaine interrupted. "Rockamore didn't threaten you, did he?"

"He said he would fix it so that I obtained no more positions in Illington," the girl responded, sullenly. "He will tell Miss Lawton that I am deceitful and treacherous and I should no longer be welcome at the club! He said — but I will not take up your so valuable time by repeating his stupid threats. Miss Lawton will understand. Shall not I read the notes to you? I have had no opportunity to transcribe them and indeed they are safer as they are."

"Yes. Read them by all means, Miss Hefferman, if you have nothing more to tell me. I do not think we are being overheard by anyone, but remember to keep your voice lowered."

"I will, Mr. Blaine."

The girl produced the note-book from her bag and swept a practised eye down its cryptic pages.

"Here it is. These are the first words I heard through the opened door. They were spoken by Mr. Rockamore, and the other, Paddington, replied. This is what I heard:

"'I don't know what the devil you're driving at, I tell you.'

"'Oh, don't you, Rockamore? Want me to explain? I'll go into details if you like.'

"'I'm hanged if I'm interested. My share in our little business deal with you was concluded some time ago. There's an end of that. You're a clever enough man to know the people you're doing business with, Paddington. You can't put anything over on us.'

"'I'm not trying to. The deal you spoke of is over and done with and I guess nobody'll squeal. We're all tarred with the same brush. But this is something quite different. We were pretty good pals, Rockamore, so naturally, when I heard something about you which might take a lot of explaining to smooth over, if it got about, I kept my mouth shut. I think a good turn deserves another, at least among friends, and when I got in a hole I remembered what I did for you, and I thought you'd be glad of a chance to give me a leg up.'

"'In other words you come here with a vague threat and try to blackmail me. That's it, isn't it?'

"'*Blackmail* is not a very pleasant term, Rockamore, and yet it is something which even you might attempt. Get me? Of course the others would be glad to help me out, but I thought I'd come to you first, since I — well, I know you better.'

"'How much do you want?'

"'Only ten thousand. I've got a tip on the market and if I can raise the coin before the stock soars and buy on margin, I'll make a fine little *coup*. Want to come in on it, Rockamore?'

"'Go to the devil! Here's your check — you can get it certified at the bank. Now get out and don't bother me again or you'll find out I'm not the weak-minded fool you take me for. Stick to the small fry, Paddington. They're your game, but don't fish for salmon with a trout-fly.'

"'Thanks, old man. I always knew I could call on you in an emergency. I only hope my tip is a straight one and I don't go short on the market. If I do — '

"'Don't come to me! I tell you, Paddington, you can't play me for a sucker. That's the last cent you'll ever get out of me. It suits me now to pay for your silence because, as you very well know, I don't care to inform my colleagues or have them informed that I acted independently of them; but I've paid all that your knowledge is worth, and more.'

"'It might have been worth even more to others than to you or your colleagues. For instance — '

"Then Billy came up behind me and whistled," concluded Miss Hefferman, as she closed her note-book. "Shall I transcribe this for you, Mr. Blaine? We have a typewriter at the club."

"No, I will take the note-book with me as it is and lock it in my safe at the office. Please hold yourself in readiness to come down and transcribe it whenever it may be necessary for me to send for you. You have done splendidly, Miss Hefferman. You must not feel badly over having been discovered and dismissed. You have rendered Miss Lawton a valuable service for which she will be the first to thank you. Telephone me if anyone attempts to approach you about this affair, or if anything unusual should occur."

Scarcely an hour later, when Henry Blaine placed the receiver at his ear in response to the insistent summons of the 'phone, her voice came to him again over the wire.

"Mr. Blaine, I am at the club, but I thought you should know that after all, I was — what is that you say — shadowed this morning. Just a little way from Mead & Rathbun's my hand-bag was cut from my arm. It was lucky, *hein*, that you took the note-book with you? As for me, I go out no more for any positions. I go back soon as ever I can, by Germany."

CHAPTER XI
THE CONFIDENCE OF EMILY

All during that day and the night which followed it, the search for Ramon Hamilton continued, but without result. With the announcement of his disappearance, in the press, the police had started a spectacular investigation, but had been as unsuccessful as Henry Blaine's own operatives, who had been working unostentatiously but tirelessly since the news of the young lawyer's evanescence had come.

No one could be found who had seen him. When he left the offices of the great detective on the previous morning he seemed to have vanished into thin air. It was to Blaine the most baffling incident of all that had occurred since this most complex case had come into his hands.

He kept his word and called to see Anita in the late afternoon. He found that she had slept for some hours and was calmer and more hopeful, which was fortunate, for he had scant comfort to offer her beyond his vague but forceful reassurances that all would be well.

Early on the following morning Suraci returned from Long Bay and presented himself at the office of his chief to report.

"Here are the tracings from the register of 'The Breakers' which you desired, sir," he began, spreading some large thin sheets of paper upon the desk. "The Lawtons spent three weeks there at the time you designated, and Mr. Hamilton went out each week-end, from Friday to Monday, as you can see here, and here. They had no other visitors and kept much to themselves."

Blaine scanned the papers rapidly, pausing here and there to scrutinize more closely a signature which appeared to interest him. At length he pushed them aside with a dissatisfied frown, as if he had been looking for something which he had failed to find.

"Anything suspicious about the guests who arrived during the Lawtons' stay?" he asked. "Was there any incident in connection with them worthy of note which the proprietor could recall?"

"No, sir, but I found some of the employees and talked to them. The hotel is closed now for the winter, of course, but two or three of the waiters and bell-boys live in the neighborhood. A summer resort is a hot-bed of gossip, as you know, sir, and since Mr. Lawton's sudden death the servants have been comparing notes of his visit there two years ago. I found the waiter who served them, and two bell-boys, and they each had a curious incident to tell me in connection with the Lawtons. The stories would have held no significance if it weren't for the fact that they all happened to concern one person — a man who arrived on the eighth of August. This man here."

Suraci ran his finger down the register page until he came to one name, where he stopped abruptly.

"Albert Addison, Baltimore, Maryland," read Blaine. Then, with a sudden exclamation he bent closer over the paper. A prolonged scrutiny ensued while Suraci watched him curiously. Reaching into a drawer, the Master Detective drew out a powerful magnifying glass and examined each stroke of the pen with minute care. At length he swung about in his chair and pressed the electric button on the corner of the desk. When his secretary appeared in response to the summons, Blaine said:

"Ask the filing clerk to look in the drawer marked 'P. 1904,' and bring me the check drawn on the First National Bank signed *Paddington*."

While the secretary was fulfilling his task the two waited in silence, but with the check before him Henry Blaine gave it one keen, comparing glance, then turned to the operative.

"Well, Suraci, what did you learn from the hotel employees?"

"One of the bell-boys told me that this man, Addison, arrived with only a bag, announcing that his luggage would be along later and that he anticipated remaining a week or more. This boy noticed him particularly because he scanned the hotel register before writing his own name, and insisted upon having one of two special suites; number seventy-two or seventy-six.

115

Seventy-four the suite between, was occupied by Mr. Lawton. They were both engaged, so he was forced to be content with number seventy-three, just across the hall. The boy noticed that although the new arrival did not approach Mr. Lawton or his daughter, he hung about in their immediate vicinity all day and appeared to be watching them furtively.

"Late in the afternoon, Mr. Lawton went into the writing-room to attend to some correspondence. The boy, passing through the room on an errand, saw him stop in the middle of a page, frown, and tearing the paper across, throw it in the waste-basket. Glancing about inadvertently, the bell-boy saw Addison seated near by, staring at Mr. Lawton from behind a newspaper which he held in front of his face as if pretending to read. The boy's curiosity was aroused by the eager, hungry, expectant look on the stranger's face, and he made up his mind to hang around, too, and see what was doing.

"He attended to his errand and returned just in time to see Mr. Lawton seal the flap of his last envelope, rise, and stroll from the room. Instantly Addison slipped into the seat just vacated, wrote a page, crumpled it, and threw it in the same waste-basket the other man had used. Then he started another page, hesitated and finally stopped and began rummaging in the basket, as if searching for the paper he himself had just dropped there. The boy made up his mind — he's a sharp one, sir, he'd be good for this business — that the stranger wasn't after his own letter, at all, but the one Mr. Lawton had torn across, and in a spirit of mischief, he walked up to the man and offered to help.

"'This is your letter, sir. I saw you crumple it up just now. That torn sheet of paper belongs to one of the other guests.'

"According to his story, he forced Addison's own letter on him, and walked off with the waste-basket to empty it, and if looks could kill, he'd have been a dead boy after one glance from the stranger. That was all he had to tell, and he wouldn't have remembered such a trifling incident for a matter of two years and more, if it hadn't been for something which happened late that night. He didn't see it, being off duty, but another boy did, and the next day they compared notes. They were undecided as to whether they should go to the manager of the hotel and make a report, or not, but being only kids, they were afraid of getting into trouble themselves, so they waited. Addison departed suddenly that morning, however, and as Mr. Lawton never gave any sign of being aware of what had taken place, they kept silent. I located the second boy, and got his story at first hand. His name is Johnnie Bradley and he's as stupid as the other one is sharp.

"Johnnie was on all night, and about one o'clock he was sent out to the casino on the pier just in front of the hotel, with a message. When he was returning, he noticed a tiny, bright light darting quickly about in Mr. Lawton's rooms, as if some one were carrying a candle through the suite and moving rapidly. He remembered that Mr. Lawton and his daughter had motored off somewhere just after dinner to be gone overnight, so he went upstairs to investigate, without mentioning the matter to the clerk who was dozing behind the desk in the office. There was a chambermaid on night duty at the end of the hall, but she was asleep, and as he reached the head of the stairs, Johnnie observed that some one had, contrary to the rules, extinguished the lights near Mr. Lawton's rooms. He went softly down the hall, until he came to the door of number seventy-four. A man was stooping before it, fumbling with a key, but whether he was locking or unlocking the door, it did not occur to Johnnie to question in his own mind until later. As he approached, the man turned, saw him, and reeled against the door as if he had been drinking.

"'Sa-ay, boy!' he drawled. 'Wha's matter with lock? Can't open m' door.'

"He put the key in his pocket as he spoke, but that, too, Johnnie did not think of until afterward.

"'That isn't your door, sir. Those are Mr. Pennington Lawton's rooms,' Johnnie told him. 'What is the number on your key?'

"The man produced a key from his pocket and gave it to Johnnie in a stupid, dazed sort of way. The key was numbered seventy-three.

"'That's your suite, just across the hall, sir,' Johnnie said. He unlocked the door for the newcomer, who muttered thickly about the hall being d - - - - d confusing to a stranger, and gave him a dollar. Johnnie waited until the man had lurched into his rooms, then asked if he wanted ice-water. Receiving no reply but a mumbled curse, he withdrew, but not before he had seen the light switched on, and the man cross to the door and shut it. The stranger no longer lurched about, but walked erectly and his face had lost the sagged, vapid, drunken look and was surprisingly sober and keen and alert.

"The two boys decided the next day that Addison had come to 'The Breakers' with the idea of robbing Mr. Lawton, but, as I said, nothing came of the incident, so they kept it to themselves and in all probability it had quite passed from their minds until the news of Mr. Lawton's death recalled it to them."

Suraci paused, and after a moment Blaine suggested tentatively:

"You spoke of a waiter, also, Suraci. Had he anything to add to what the bell-boys had told you, of this man Addison's peculiar behavior?"

"Yes, sir. It isn't very important, but it sort of confirms what the first boy said, about the stranger trying to watch the Lawtons, without being noticed himself, by them. The waiter, Tim Donohue, says that on the day of his arrival, Addison was seated by the head waiter at the next table to that occupied by Mr. Lawton, and directly facing him. Addison entered the dining-room first, ordered a big luncheon, and was half-way through it when the Lawtons entered. No sooner were they seated, than he got up precipitately and left the room. That night, at dinner, he refused the table he had occupied at the first meal, and insisted upon being seated at one somewhere back of Mr. Lawton.

"This Donohue is a genial, kind-hearted soul, and he was a favorite with the bell-hops because he used to save sweets and tid-bits for them from his trays. Johnnie and the other boy told him of their dilemma concerning number seventy-three, as they designated Addison, and he in turn related the incident of the dining-room. The boys told me about him and where he could be found. He's not a waiter any longer, but married to one of the hotel chamber-maids, and lives in Long Bay, running a bus service to the depot for a string of the cheaper boarding houses. He corroborated the bell-hops' story in every detail, and even gave me a hazy sort of description of Addison. He was small and thin and dark; clean shaven, with a face like an actor, narrow shoulders and a sort of caved-in chest. He walked with a slight limp, and was a little over-dressed for the exclusive, conservative, high-society crowd that flock to 'The Breakers.'"

"That's our man, Suraci — that's Paddington, to the life!" Blaine exclaimed. "I knew it as soon as I compared his signature on this check with the one in the register, although he has tried to disguise his hand, as you can see. I'm glad to have it verified, though, by witnesses on whom we can lay our hands at any time, should it become necessary. He left the day after his arrival, you say? The morning after this boy, Johnnie, caught him in front of Mr. Lawton's door?"

"Yes, sir. The bell-hops don't think he came back, either. They don't remember seeing him again."

"Very well. You've done splendidly, Suraci. I couldn't have conducted the investigation better myself. Do you need any rest, now?"

"Oh, no, sir! I'm quite ready for another job!" The young operative's eyes sparkled eagerly as he spoke, and his long, slim, nervous fingers clasped and unclasped the arms of his chair spasmodically. "What is it? Something new come up?"

"Only that disappearance, two days ago, of the young lawyer to whom Miss Lawton is engaged, Ramon Hamilton. I want you to go out on that at once, and see what you can do. I've got half a dozen of the best men on it already, but they haven't accomplished anything. I can't give you a single clue to go upon, except that when he walked out of this office at eleven o'clock in the morning, he wore a black suit, black shoes, black tie, a black derby and a gray overcoat with a mourning band on the sleeve — for Mr. Lawton, of course. Outside the door there, he vanished as if a trap had opened and dropped him through into space. No one has seen him; no one knows where he went. That's all the help I can offer you. He's not in jail or the morgue or any of the hospitals, as yet. That isn't much, but it's something. Here's a personal description of him which the police issued yesterday. It's as good as any I could give you, and here are two photographs of him which I got from his mother yesterday afternoon. Take a good look at him, Suraci, fix his face in your mind, and then if you should manage, or happen, to locate him, you can't go wrong. I know your memory for faces."

The "shadow" departed eagerly upon his quest, and Blaine settled down to an hour's deep reflection. He held the threads of the major conspiracy in his hands, but as yet he could not connect them, at least in any tangible way to present at a court of so-called justice, where everyone, from the judge to the policeman at the door could, and inevitably would, be bought over, in advance, to the side of the criminals. It was a one-man fight, backed only with the slender means provided by a young girl's insignificant financial ventures, against the press, the public, a corrupt political machine of great power, the desperate ingenuity of three clever, unscrupulous minds brought to bay, and the overwhelming influence of colossal wealth. Henry Blaine felt that the supreme struggle of his whole career was confronting him.

The unheard-of intrepidity of conception, the very daring of the conspiracy, combined with the prominence of the men involved, would brand any accusation, even from a man of Henry Blaine's celebrated international reputation, as totally preposterous, unless substantiated. And what actual proof had he of their criminal connection with the alleged bankruptcy of Pennington Lawton?

He had established, to his own satisfaction, at least, that the mortgage on the family home on Belleair Avenue had been forged, and by Jimmy Brunell. The signature on the note held by Moore, the banker, and the entire letter asking Mallowe to negotiate the loan had been also fraudulent, and manufactured by the same hand. Paddington, the private detective with perhaps the most unsavory record of any operating in the city, was in close and constant communication with the three men Blaine held under suspicion, and probably also with Jimmy Brunell. Lastly, Brunell himself was known to be still in possession of his paraphernalia for the pursuit of his old nefarious calling. Paddington, on Margaret Heffernan's testimony, had assuredly succeeded in mulcting the promoter, Rockamore, of a large sum in a clear case of blackmail, but on the face of it there was no proof that it was connected with the matter of Pennington Lawton's insolvency.

The mysterious nocturnal visitor, on the night the magnate met his death, was still to be accounted for, as was the disappearance of Ramon Hamilton; and in spite of his utmost efforts, Henry Blaine was forced to admit to himself that he was scarcely nearer a solution, or rather, a confirmation of his steadfast convictions, than when he started upon his investigation.

Unquestionably, the man Paddington held the key to the situation. But how could Paddington be approached? How could he be made to speak? Bribery had sealed his lips, and only greed would open them. He was shrewd enough to realize that the man who had purchased his services would pay him far more to remain silent than any client of Blaine's could, to betray them. Moreover, he was in the same boat, and must of necessity sink or swim with his confederates.

Fear might induce him to squeal, where cupidity would fail, but the one sure means of loosening his tongue was through passion.

"If only that French girl, Fifine Déchaussée, would lead him on, if she had less of the saint and more of the coquette in her make-up, we might land him," the detective murmured to himself. "It's dirty work, but we've got to use the weapons in our hands. I must have another talk with her, before she considers herself affronted by his attentions, and throws him down hard — that is, if he's making any attempt to follow up his flirtation with her."

Blaine's soliloquy was interrupted by the entrance of Guy Morrow, whose face bore the disgusted look of one sent to fish with a bent pin for a salmon.

"I found Paddington, all right, sir," he announced. "I tailed him until a half-hour ago, but I might as well have been asleep for all I learned, except one fact."

"Which is — " the detective asked quickly.

"That he went to Rockamore's office yesterday morning, remained an hour and came away with a check for ten thousand dollars. He proceeded to the bank, had it certified, and deposited it at once to his own account in the Merchants' and Traders'. He evidently split it up, then, for he went to three other banks and opened accounts under three different names. Here's the list. I tailed him all the way."

He handed the Master Detective a slip of paper, which the latter put carefully aside after a casual glance.

"Then what did he do?"

"Wasted his own time and mine," the operative responded in immeasurable contempt. "Ate and drank and gambled and loafed and philandered."

"Philandered?" Blaine repeated, sharply.

"In the park," returned the other. "Spooning with a girl! Rotten cold it was, too, and me tailing on like a blamed chaperon! After he made his last deposit at the third bank, he went to lunch at Duyon's. Ate his head off, and paid from a thick wad of yellowbacks. Then he dropped in at Wiley's, and played roulette for a couple of hours — played in luck, too. He drank quite a little, but it only seemed to heighten his good spirits, without fuddling him to any extent. When he left Wiley's, about five o'clock, he sauntered along Court Street, until he came to Fraser's, the jeweler's. He stopped, looked at the display window for a few minutes, and then, as if on a sudden impulse, turned and entered the shop. I tailed him inside, and went to the men's counter, where I bought a tie-clasp, keeping my eye on him all the time. What do you think he got? A gold locket and chain — a heart-shaped locket, with a chip diamond in the center!"

"The eternal feminine!" Blaine commented; and then he

added half under his breath: "Fifine Déchaussée's on the job!"

"What, sir?" asked the operative curiously.

"Nothing, Guy. Merely an idle observation. Go on with your story."

"Paddington went straight from the jeweler's to the Democratic Club for an hour, then dined alone at Rossi's. I was on the look-out for the woman, but none appeared, and he didn't act as if he expected anybody. After dinner he strolled down Belleair Avenue, past the Lawton residence, and out to Fairlawn Park. Once inside the gates, he stopped for a minute near a lamp-post and looked at his watch, then hurried straight on to Hydrangea Path, as if he had an appointment to keep. I dropped back in the shadow, but tailed along. She must have been late, that girl, for he cooled his heels on a bench for twenty minutes, growing more impatient all the time. Finally she came — a slender wisp of a girl, but some queen! Plainly dressed, dark hair and eyes, small hands and feet and a face like a stained-glass window!

"They walked slowly up and down, talking very confidentially, and once he started to put his arm about her, but she moved away. I walked up quickly, and passed them, close enough to hear what she was saying: 'Of course it is lonely for a girl in a strange country, where she has no friends.' That was all I got, but I noticed that she spoke with a decidedly foreign accent, French or Spanish, I should say.

"Around a bend in the path I hid behind a clump of bushes and waited until they had passed, then tailed them again. I saw him produce the locket and chain at last, and offer them to her. She protested and took a lot of persuading; but he prevailed upon her and she let him clasp it about her neck and kiss her. After that — Good Lord! They spooned for about two hours and never even noticed the snow which had begun to fall, while I shivered along behind. About half-past ten they made a break-away and he left her at the park gates and went on down to his rooms. I put up for the night at the Hotel Gaythorne, just across the way, and kept a look-out, but there were no further developments until early this morning. At a little after seven he left his apartment house and started up State Street as if he meant business. Of course I was after him on the jump.

"He evidently didn't think he was watched, for he never looked around once, but made straight for a little shop near the corner of Tarleton Place. It was a stationery and tobacco store, and I was right at his heels when he entered. He leaned over the counter, and asked in a low, meaning tone for a box of Cairo cigarettes. The man gave him a long, searching glance, then turned, and reaching back of a pile of boxes on the first shelf, drew out a flat one — the size which holds twenty cigarettes. He passed it quickly over to Paddington, but not before I observed that it had been opened and rather clumsily resealed.

"Paddington handed over a quarter and left the shop without another word. He went directly to a cheap restaurant across the street, and, ordering a cup of coffee, he tore open the cigarette box. It contained only a sheet of paper, folded twice. I was at the next table, too far away to read what was written upon it, but whatever it was, it seemed to give him immense satisfaction. He finished his coffee, returned to his rooms, changed his clothes, and went directly to the office of Snedecker, the man whose divorce case he is trying to trump up. Evidently he's good for a day's work on that, so I thought I could safely leave him at it, and report to you."

"Humph! I'd like to have a glimpse of that communication in the cigarette box, but it isn't of sufficient importance, on the face of it, to show our hand by having him waylaid, or searching his rooms," Blaine cogitated aloud. "I'll put another man on tomorrow morning. Leave the address of the tobacconist with my secretary on your way out, and if there is another message tomorrow, he'll get it first. You needn't do anything more on this Paddington matter; I think the other end needs your services more; and since you've already broken ground up there, you'll be able to do better than anyone else. I want you to return to the Bronx, get back your old room, if you can, and stick close to the Brunells."

Back in his old rooms at Mrs. Quinlan's, Guy sat in the window-seat at dusk, impatiently awaiting the appearance of a slender, well-known figure. The rain, which had set in early in the afternoon, had turned to sleet, and as the darkness deepened, the rays from a solitary street lamp gleamed sharply upon the pavement as upon an unbroken sheet of ice.

Presently the spare, long-limbed form of James Brunell emerged from the gloom and disappeared within the door of this little house opposite. Morrow observed that the man's step lacked its accustomed jauntiness and spring, and he plodded along wearily, as if utterly preoccupied with some depressing meditation. A light sprang up in the front room on the ground floor, but after a few moments it was suddenly extinguished, and Brunell appeared again on the porch. He closed the door softly behind him, and strode quickly down the street. There was a marked change in his bearing, a furtiveness and eager haste which ill accorded with his manner of a short time before.

Scarcely had Brunell vanished into the encroaching gloom, when his daughter appeared. She, too, approached wearily, and on reaching the little sagging gate she paused in surprised dismay at the air of detached emptiness the house seemed to exude. Then a little furry object scurried around the porch corner and precipitated itself upon her. She stooped swiftly, gathered up the kitten in her arms and went slowly into the house.

Morrow ate his supper in absent-minded haste, and as soon as he decently could, he made his way across the street.

Emily opened the door in response to his ring and greeted him with such undisguised pleasure and surprise that his honest heart quickened a beat or two, and it was with difficulty that he voiced the plausible falsehood concerning his loss of position, and return to his former abode.

Under the light in the little drawing-room, he noticed that she looked pale and careworn, and her limpid, childlike eyes were veiled pathetically with deep, blue shadows. As he looked at her, however, a warm tint dyed her cheeks and her head drooped, while the little smile still lingered about her lips.

"You are tired?" he found himself asking solicitously, after she had expressed her sympathy for his supposed ill fortune. "You found your work difficult to-day at the club?"

"Oh, no," — she shook her head slowly. "My position is a mere sinecure, thanks to Miss Lawton's wonderful consideration. I have been a little depressed — a little worried, that is all."

"Worried?" Morrow paused, then added in a lower tone, the words coming swiftly, "Can't you tell me, Emily? Isn't there some way in which I can help you? What is it that is troubling you?"

"I — I don't know." A deeper, painful flush spread for a moment over her face, then ebbed, leaving her paler even than before. "You are very kind, Mr. Morrow, but I do not think that I should speak of it to anyone. And indeed, my fears are so intangible, so vague, that when I try to formulate my thoughts into words, even to myself, they are unconvincing, almost meaningless. Yet I feel instinctively that something is wrong."

"Won't you trust me?" Morrow's hand closed gently but firmly over the girl's slender one, in a clasp of compelling sympathy, and unconsciously she responded to it. "I know that I am comparatively a new friend. You and your father have been kind enough to extend your hospitality to me, to accept me as a friend. You know very little about me, yet I want you to believe that I am worthy of trust — that I want to help you. I do, Emily, more than you realize, more than I can express to you now!"

Morrow had forgotten the reason for his presence there, forgotten his profession, his avowed purpose, everything but the girl beside him. But her next words brought him swiftly back to a realization of the present — so swiftly that for a moment he felt as if stunned by an unexpected blow.

"Oh, I do believe that you are a friend! I do trust you!" Emily's voice thrilled with deep sincerity, and in an impetuous outburst of confidence she added: "It is about my father that I am troubled. Something has happened which I do not understand; there is something he is keeping from me, which has changed him. He seems like a different man, a stranger!"

"You are sure of it?" Morrow asked, slowly. "You are sure that it isn't just a nervous fancy? Your father really has changed toward you lately?"

"Not only toward me, but to all the world beside!" she responded. "Now that I look back, I can see that his present state of mind has been coming on gradually for several months, but it was only a short time ago that something occurred which seemed to bring the matter, whatever it is, to a turning-point. I remember that it was just a few days before you came — I mean, before I happened to see you over at Mrs. Quinlan's."

She stopped abruptly, as if an arresting finger had been laid across her lips, and after waiting a moment for her to continue, Morrow asked quietly:

"What was it that occurred?"

"Father received a letter. It came one afternoon when I had returned from the club earlier than usual. I took it from the postman myself, and as father had not come home yet from the shop, I placed it beside his plate at the supper table. I noticed the postmark — 'Brooklyn' — but it didn't make any particular impression upon me; it was only later, when I saw how it affected my father, that I remembered, and wondered. He had scarcely opened the envelope, when he rose, trembling so that he could hardly stand, and coming into this room, he shut the door after him. I waited as long as I could, but he did not return, and the supper was getting cold, so I came to the door here. It was locked! For the first time in his life, my father had locked himself in, from me! He would not answer me at first, as I called to him, and I was nearly frightened to death before he spoke. When he did, his voice sounded so harsh and strained that I scarcely recognized it. He told me that he didn't want anything to eat; he had some private business to attend to, and I was not to wait up for him, but to go to bed when I wished.

"I crept away, and went to my room at last, but I could not sleep. It was nearly morning when Father went to bed, and his step was heavy and dragging as he passed my door. His room is next to mine, and I heard him tossing restlessly about — and once or twice I fancied that he groaned as if in pain. He was up in the morning at his usual time, but he looked ill and worn, as if he had aged years in that one night. Neither of us mentioned the letter, then or at any subsequent time, but he has never been the same man since."

"And the letter — you never saw it?" Morrow asked eagerly, his detective instinct now thoroughly aroused. "You don't know what that envelope postmarked 'Brooklyn' contained?"

"Oh, but I do!" Emily exclaimed. "Father had thrust it in the stove, but the fire had gone out, without his noticing it. I found it the next morning, when I raked down the ashes."

"You — read it?" Morrow carefully steadied his voice.

"No," she shook her head, with a faint smile. "That's the queer part of it all. No one could have read it — no one who did not hold the key to it, I mean. It was written in some secret code or cipher, with oddly shaped figures instead of letters; dots and cubes and triangles. I never saw anything like it before. I couldn't understand why anyone should send such a funny message to my father, instead of writing it out properly."

"What did you do with the letter — did you destroy it?" This time the detective made no effort to control the eagerness in his tones, but the girl was so absorbed in her problem that she was oblivious to all else.

"I suppose I should have, but I didn't. I knew that it was what my father had intended, yet somehow I felt that it might prove useful in the future — that I might even be helping Father by keeping it, against his own judgment. The envelope was partially scorched by the hot ashes, but the inside sheet remained untouched. I hid the letter behind the mirror on my dresser, and sometimes, when I have been quite alone, I took it out and tried to solve it, but I couldn't. I never was good at puzzles when I was little, and I suppose I lack that deductive quality now. I was ashamed, too: it seemed so like prying into things which didn't concern me, which my father didn't wish me to know; still, I was only doing it to try to help him."

Morrow winced, and drew a long breath. Then resolutely he plunged into the task before him.

"Emily, don't think that I want to pry, either, but if I am to help you I must see that letter. If you trust me and believe in my friendship, let me see it. Perhaps I may be able to discover the key in the first word or two, and then you can decipher it for yourself. You understand, I don't wish you to show it to me unless you really have confidence in me, unless you are sure that there is nothing in it which one who has your welfare and peace of mind at heart should not see."

He waited for her reply with a suffocating feeling as if a hand were clutching at his throat. A hot wave of shame, of fierce repugnance and self-contempt at the rôle he was forced to play, surged up within him, but he could not go back now. The die was cast.

She looked at him — a long, searching look, her childlike eyes dark with troubled indecision. At length they cleared slowly and she smiled, a faint, pathetic smile, which wrung his heart. Then she rose without a word, and left the room.

It seemed to him that an interminable period of time passed before he heard her light, returning footsteps descending the stairs. A wild desire to flee assailed him — to efface himself before her innocent confidence was betrayed.

Emily Brunell came straight to him, and placed the letter in his hands.

"There can be nothing in this letter which could harm my father, if all the world read it," she said simply. "He is good and true; he has not an enemy on earth. It can be only a private business communication, at the most. My father's life is an open book; no discredit could come to him. Yet if there was anything in the cryptic message written here which others, not knowing him as I do, might misjudge, I am not afraid that you will. You see, I do believe in your friendship, Mr. Morrow; I am proving my faith in you."

CHAPTER XII
THE CIPHER

It was a haggard, heavy-eyed young man who presented himself at Henry Blaine's office, early the next morning, with his report. The detective made no comment upon his subordinate's changed appearance and manner, but eyed him keenly as with dogged determination Guy Morrow told his story through to the end.

"The letter — the cipher letter!" Blaine demanded, curtly, when the operative paused at length. "You have it with you?"

Morrow drew a deep breath and unconsciously he squared his shoulders.

"No, sir," he responded, his voice significantly steady and controlled.

"Where is it?"

"I gave it back to her — to Miss Brunell."

"What! Then you solved it?" the detective leaned forward suddenly, the level gaze from beneath his close-drawn brows seeming to pierce the younger man's impassivity.

"No, sir. It was a cryptogram, of course — an arrangement of cabalistic signs instead of letters, but I could make nothing of it. The message, whatever it is, would take hours of careful study to decipher; and even then, without the key, one might fail. I have seen nothing quite like it, in all my experience."

"And you gave it back to her!" Blaine exclaimed, with well-simulated incredulity. "You actually had the letter in your hands, and relinquished it? In heaven's name, why?"

"Miss Brunell had shown it to me in confidence. It was her property, and she trusted me. Since I was unable to aid her in solving it, I returned it to her. The chances are that it is, as she said, a matter of private business between her father and another man, and it is probably entirely dissociated from this investigation."

"You're not paid, Morrow, to form opinions of your own, or decide the ethics, social or moral, of a case you're put on; you're paid to obey instructions, collect data and obtain whatever evidence there may be. Remember that. Confidence or no confidence, girl or no girl, you go back and get that letter! I don't care what means you use, short of actual murder; that cipher's got to be in my hands before midnight. Understand?"

"Yes, sir, I understand." Morrow rose slowly, and faced his chief. "I'm sorry, but I cannot do it."

"You can't? That's the first time I ever heard that word from your lips, Guy." Henry Blaine shook his head sadly, affecting not to notice his operative's rising emotion.

"I mean that I won't, sir. I'm sorry to appear insubordinate, but I've got to refuse — I simply must. I've never shirked a duty before, as I think you will admit, Mr. Blaine. I have always carried out the missions you entrusted to me to the best of my ability, no matter what the odds against me, and in this case I have gone ahead conscientiously up to the present moment, but I won't proceed with it any further."

"What are you afraid of — Jimmy Brunell?" asked the detective, significantly.

The insult brought a deep flush to Morrow's cheek, but he controlled himself.

"No, sir," he responded, quietly. "I'm not going to betray the trust that girl has reposed in me."

"How about the trust another girl has placed in me — and through me, in you?" Henry Blaine rose also, and gazed levelly into his operative's eyes. "What of Anita Lawton? Have you considered her? I ought to dismiss you, Guy, at this moment, and I would if it were anyone else, but I can't allow you to fly off at a tangent, and ruin your whole career. Why should you put this girl, Emily Brunell, before everything in the world — your duty to Miss Lawton, to me, to yourself?"

"She trusted me," returned Morrow, with grim persistence.

"So did Henrietta Goodwin, in the case of Mrs. Derwenter's diamonds; so did the little manicure, in the Verdun blackmail affair; so did Anne Richardson, in the Balazzi kidnaping mystery. You made love to all of them, and got their confessions, and if your scruples and remorse kept you awake nights afterward, you certainly didn't show any effect of it. What difference does it make in this case?"

"Just this difference, Mr. Blaine" — Morrow's words came with a rush, as if he was glad, now that the issue had been raised, to meet it squarely — "I love Emily Brunell. Whatever her father is, or has done, she is guiltless of any complicity, and I can't stand by and see her suffer, much less be the one to precipitate her grief by bringing her father to justice. I told you the truth when I said that the cipher letter was an enigma to me. I could not solve the cryptogram, nor will I be the means of bringing it to the hands of those who might solve it. I don't want any further connection with the case; in fact, sir, I want to get out of the sleuth game altogether. It's a dirty business, at best, and it leaves a bad taste in one's mouth, and many a black spot in one's memory. I realize how petty and sordid and treacherous and generally despicable the whole game is, and I'm through!"

"Through?" Henry Blaine smiled his quiet, slow, illuminating smile, and walking around the table, laid his hand on Morrow's shoulder. "Why, boy, you haven't even commenced. Detective work is 'petty,' you said? 'Petty' because we take every case, no matter how insignificant, if it can right a wrong? You call our profession 'sordid,' because we accept pay for the work of our brains and bodies! Why should we not? Are we treacherous, because we meet malefactors, and fight them with their own weapons? And what is there that is 'generally despicable' about a calling which betters mankind, which protects the innocent, and brings the guilty to justice?"

Morrow shook his head slowly, as if incapable of speech, but it was evident that he was listening, and Blaine, after a moment's pause, followed up his advantage.

"You say that you love Miss Brunell, Guy, and because of

that, you will have nothing further to do with an investigation which points primarily to her father as an accomplice in the crime. Do you realize that if you throw over the case now, I shall be compelled to put another operative on the trail, with all the information at his disposal which you have detailed to me? You may be sure the man I have in mind will have no sentimental scruples against pushing the matter to the end, without regard for the cost to either Jimmy Brunell or his daughter. Naturally, being in love with the girl, her interests are paramount with you. I, too, desire heartily to do nothing to cause her anxiety or grief. Remember that I have daughters of my own. As I have told you, I firmly believe that the old forger is merely a helpless tool in this affair, but my duty demands that I obtain the whole truth. If you repudiate the case now, give up your career, and go to work single-handed to attempt to protect her and her father by thwarting my investigation, you will be doing her the greatest injury in your power. The only way to help them both is to do all that you can to discover the real facts in the case. When we have succeeded in that, we shall undoubtedly find a way to shield old Jimmy from the brunt of the blame.

"Don't forget the big interests, political and municipal, at work in this conspiracy. They would not hesitate to try to make the old offender a scape-goat, and you know what sort of treatment he would receive in the hands of the police. Play the game, Guy; stick to the job. I'm not asking this of you for my own investigation. I have a dozen, a score of operatives who could each handle the branch you are working up just as well as you. I ask it for the sake of your career, for the girl herself, and her father. I tell you that instead of incriminating old Jimmy, you may be the means of ultimately saving him. — Go back to Emily Brunell now, get that letter from her by hook or crook, and bring it to me."

The detective paused at length and waited for his answer. It was long in coming. Guy Morrow stood leaning against his desk, his brows drawn down in a troubled frown. Blaine watched the outward signs of his mental struggle warily, but made no further plea. At last the young operative raised his head, his eyes clear and resolute, and held out his hand.

"I will, sir! Thank you for giving me another chance. I do love the girl, and I want to help her more than anything else in the world, but I'll play the game fairly. You are right, of course. I can be of more assistance to her on the inside than working in the dark, and it would be better for everyone concerned if the truth could be brought to light. I'll get the letter, and bring it to you to-night."

Morrow was waiting at the foot of the subway stairs that evening when Emily appeared. The crisp, cold air had brought a brilliant flush to her usually pale cheeks, and her sparkling eyes softened with tender surprise and happiness when they rested on him. He thought that she had never appeared more lovely, and as they started homeward his hand tightened upon her arm with an air of unconscious possession and pride which she did not resent.

"May I come over after supper?" he asked, softly, as they paused at her gate. "I have something to tell you — to ask you."

"Won't you come in and have supper with me?" she suggested shyly. "Caliban and I will be all alone. My father will not be home until late to-night. He telephoned to me at the club and told me that he had closed the shop for the day and gone downtown on business."

A shadow crossed her face as she spoke, the faint shadow of hidden trouble which he had noticed before. It was an auspicious moment, and Morrow seized upon it.

"I will, gladly, if you will let me wash the dishes," he replied, with alacrity.

"We will do them together." The brightness which but an instant before had been blotted from her face returned in a warm glow, and side by side they entered the door.

With Caliban, the black kitten, upon his knees, Morrow watched as she moved deftly about the cheerful, spotless kitchen preparing the simple meal. He made no mention of the subject which lay nearest his heart and mind, and they chattered as gaily and irresponsibly as children. But when supper was over, and they settled themselves in the little sitting-room, a curious constraint fell upon them both. She sat stroking the kitten, which had curled up beside her, while he gazed absently at the rosy gleam of the glowing coals behind the isinglass door of the little stove, and for a long time there was silence between them.

At length he turned to her and spoke. "Emily," he began, "I told you out there by your gate to-night that I had something to ask of you, something to tell you. I want to tell you now, but I don't know how to begin. It's something I've never told any girl before."

Her hands paused, resting with sudden tenseness upon Caliban's soft fur, and slowly she averted her face from him. He swallowed hard, and then the words came in a swift, tender rush.

"Dear, I love you! I've loved you from the moment I first saw you coming down the street! You — you know nothing of me, save the little I have told you, and I came here a stranger. Some day I will tell you everything, and you will understand. You and your father admitted me to your friendship, made me welcome in your home, and I shall never forget it. It may be that some time I shall be able to be of service to you, but remember that whatever happens, no matter how you reply to me now, I shall never forget your goodness to me, and I shall try to repay it. I love you with all my heart and soul; I want you to be my wife, dear! I never knew before that such love could exist in the world! You have your father, I know, but, oh, I want to protect you and care for you, and keep all harm from you forever."

"Guy!" Her voice was a mere breathless whisper, and her eyes blurred with sudden tears, but he slipped his arm about her, and drew her close.

"Emily, won't you look at me, dear? Won't you tell me that you care, too? That at least there is a chance for me? If I have spoken too soon, I will await patiently and serve you as Jacob served for Rebecca of old. Only tell me that you will try to care, and there is nothing on this earth I cannot do for you, nothing I will not do! Oh, my darling, say that you care just a little!"

There was a pause and then very softly a warm arm stole about his neck, and a strand of rippling brown hair brushed his cheek lightly as her gentle head drooped against his shoulder.

"I — I do care — now," she whispered. "I knew that I cared when you — went away!"

The minutes lengthened into an hour or more while Morrow in the thrall of his exalted mood forgot for the second time in the girl's sweet presence his battle between love and duty: forgot the reason for his coming, the mission he was bound to fulfill — the letter he had promised his employer to obtain.

For many minutes Guy Morrow and Emily forgot all else but the new-found happiness of the love they had just confessed for each other. Morrow had even forgotten that most-important letter which, after many misgivings, he had solemnly promised his employer to obtain from Emily. It was a phrase which fell from her own lips that recalled him to the stern reality of the situation.

"My father!" she exclaimed, starting from Morrow's arms in sudden confusion. "What do you suppose Father will say?"

"We will tell him when he returns." Morrow spoke with reassuring confidence, but a swift feeling of apprehension came over him. What indeed would Jimmy Brunell say? The thought of lying to Emily's father was repugnant beyond expression, and yet what account could he give of himself, of his profession and earlier career? What credentials, what proof of his integrity and clean, honest life could he present to the man whose daughter he sought to marry? At the first hint of "detective" the old forger would inevitably suspect his motive and turn him from the house, forbidding Emily to speak to or even look upon him again. There was an alternative, and although he shrank from it as unworthy of her faith and trust in him, Morrow was forced to accept it as the only practicable solution to the problem confronting him.

"Oh, no, don't let us tell him — yet!" Unconsciously Emily smoothed the way for him. "I don't mean to deceive him, of course, or keep anything from him which it is really necessary that he know at once, but it seems too wonderful to discuss, even with Father, just now. It is like a fairy promise, like moonshine, which would be dispelled if we breathed a word of it to anyone."

"Of course, dearest, if it is your wish, we will say nothing now," he returned slowly. In his heart a fierce wave of self-contempt at his own hypocrisy surged up once more, but he forced it doggedly down. He had promised his chief to play the game, and after all it was for the sake of the girl beside him, that he might be able, when the inevitable moment of disclosure came, to be of real service to her and her unfortunate father, and to shield her from the brunt of the blow. "I should not like your father to think that we deceived him, but perhaps it would be as well if we kept our secret for a little time. Later, when I have succeeded in landing a good, permanent position with a prospect of advancement, I can go to him with greater assurance, and ask him for you."

"Poor Father!" sighed Emily, with a wistful, tremulous little smile. "We have been inseparable ever since I can remember. He has lived only for me, and I cannot bear to think of leaving him — especially now, when he seems weighed down with some secret anxiety, which he will share with no one, not even me. I feel that he needs me, more than ever before. It wrings my heart, Guy, to see him age before my very eyes, and to know that he will not confide in me, I may not help him! He seems to lean upon me, upon my presence near him, as if somehow I gave him strength. Although he maintains a steadfast silence, his eyes never leave me, and such a sad, hungry expression comes into them sometimes, almost as if he were going away from me forever, as if he were trying to say farewell to me, that I have to turn away to hide my tears from him."

"Poor little girl! It must make you terribly unhappy." Morrow paused, and then added, as if in afterthought: "Perhaps when we tell your father that we care for each other, that when I have proved myself you are going to be my wife, he may confide in me — that is, if he is willing to give you to me. You know, dear, it is easier sometimes for a man to talk to another of his private worries, than to a woman, even the one nearest and dearest to him in all the world. I may possibly be of assistance to him.

You told me last night that the change in him had been coming on gradually for several months. When did it first occur to you that he was in trouble?"

"I don't know. I can't remember. You see, I didn't realize it until that letter came, and then I began to think back, and the significance of little things which I had not noticed particularly when they occurred, was borne in upon me. Although I have no reason for connecting the two happenings beyond the fact that they coincided, I cannot help feeling that Mr. Pennold — the young man whom you have observed when he called to see my father — has something to do with the state of things, for it was with his very first appearance, more than two years ago, that my father became a changed man."

"Tell me about it," Morrow urged, gently. "Can you remember, dear, when he first came?"

"Oh, yes. We have so few visitors — Father doesn't, as a rule, encourage new acquaintances, you know, Guy, although he did seem to like you from the very beginning — that the reception of a perfect stranger into our home as a constant caller puzzled me. It occurred on a Sunday afternoon in summer. I was sitting out on the porch reading, when a strange young man came up the path from the gate, and asked to see my father. I called to him — he was weeding the flowerbed around the corner of the house — and when he came, I went up to my room, leaving them alone together. I didn't go, though, until I had seen their meeting, and one thing about it seemed strange to me, even then. The stranger, Mr. Pennold, evidently did not know my father, had never even seen him before, from the way he greeted him, but when Father first caught sight of his face, his own went deathly white and he gripped the porch railing for a moment, as if for support.

"'You wished to see me?' he said, and his voice sounded queer and hollow and dazed, like a person awaking from sleep. 'What can I do for you?'

"'This is Mr. James Brunell?' the young man asked. 'You are a map-maker, I understand. I have come to ask for your estimate on a large contract for wall-maps for suburban schools. If you can spare a half-hour, we can talk it over now, sir, in private. I have a letter of introduction to you from an old acquaintance. My name is Pennold.'

"'I know.' My father smiled as he spoke, an odd, slow smile which somehow held no mirth or welcome. 'I noted the family resemblance at once. A relative of yours was at one time associated with me in business.'

"The young man laughed shortly.

"You mean my uncle, I guess. He's retired now. Well, Mr. Brunell, shall we get to business?'

"I left them then, and when I came downstairs from my room, the young man had gone. Father was standing in the window over there, with a letter crushed in his hand. He turned when I spoke to him, and, oh, Guy, if you had seen his face at that moment! I almost cried out in fear! It was like one of the terrible, despairing faces in Dante's description of the Inferno. He looked at me blankly as if he scarcely recognized me; then gradually that awful expression was blotted out, and his old sweet, sunny smile took its place.

"'Well, little girl!' he said. 'Our Sunday together was spoiled, wasn't it, by that young fellow's intrusion?'

"'Not spoiled,' I replied, 'if he brought you work.'

"The smile faded from Father's face, and he responded very gravely, with a curious, halting pause between the words:

"'Yes. He has brought me — work.'

"I forgot all about that episode, in the weeks and months which followed. Charley Pennold called irregularly. Sometimes he would come three or four times a week, then again we would not see him for two or three months. Father was busier than ever in the shop, and, Charley Pennold's orders must have been very profitable, for we've had more money in the last two years than ever before, that I can remember. And yet Father has been melancholy and morose at times, as if he were brooding over something, and his disposition has changed steadily for the worse, although in the last few months the difference in his moods has become more marked. Then, when that letter came he seemed to give himself wholly up to whatever it is which has obsessed him."

"Emily, will you let me see the letter again?" Morrow asked suddenly. "If you really care for me, and will be my wife some day, your troubles and vexations are mine. I want you to let me take the letter home with me to-night. I feel that if I can study it for a few hours undisturbed, I shall be able to read the cipher. I'll promise, dear, to bring it back the very first thing in the morning."

"Of course, you may have it, Guy!" The young girl rose impulsively, and went to the little desk in the corner. "I hid it last night after you had gone, among some old receipts; here it is. You need not return it to-morrow. Keep it for several days, if you like, until you have studied it thoroughly. I don't see how you or any one could solve it without possessing the key, but I should feel as if a load were taken off my shoulders if you will try."

She gave him the letter, and after a long, tender farewell, he took his departure. Going straight to his room at Mrs. Quinlan's, he lighted the lamp, so that if Emily chanced to look over the way, she would fancy him at work upon the cryptogram. Morrow waited until the little house opposite was plunged in darkness; then very stealthily he crept down the stairs and let himself out, the precious letter carefully tucked into an inside pocket.

Morrow proceeded at once to Blaine's office and found his chief awaiting him.

"Here's the letter, sir," he announced, as he placed the single sheet of paper on the desk before the detective. "I can't make anything out of it, but you probably will. It's curious, isn't it! Why, for instance, are those little dots placed near some of the crazy figures, and not others?"

Blaine picked the letter up, and examined it with eager interest.

"It's comparatively simple," he remarked, as he spread it flat upon the desk, and taking up pen and paper, copied it rapidly. "Symbolic cryptograms are usually decipherable, with the expenditure of a little time and effort. There is a method which is universally followed, and has been for ages. For instance, the letter *e* is recognized as being the most frequently used, in ordinary English, of the whole alphabet; after that the vowels and consonants in an accepted rotation which I will not take up our valuable time in discussing with you now, since we will not even need to use it, in this case. — Here, take this copy, and see if you can follow me."

He passed the sheet of paper across to his operative and Morrow gazed again upon the curiously shaped characters which from close scrutiny had become familiar, yet still remained maddeningly baffling to him:

```
ⱯᴌɹF ᑎCᴜ ɹᑎᴧ
 ɹᗡᑐ ꓶᑎꓷᴌᴧ ᴜᑎꓶᗡꓶꓷ ꝛᑎ ᴧᑎᴠᴌFᑎꓶ
ᑎCᴜ ꝛᴜᑎFᴌ Cᴌᴌꝛ ᴠꓷᑎɹᗡᴜ
   ﹤ɹᴌꝛ ᗡꝛꓶᴧ ꝛɹɹFᴌ ᴌᑎF ᴜᑎCCᴌᴜꝛᗡꓶꓷ
ᴌᑎF ᴧᑎᴠ ꓶᑎ FᗡꝛC ﹤ᗡCC ᴜɹCC ᑎꓶ ᴧᑎᴠ
ꝛɹᴠFꝛᴜɹᴧ ɹꝛ ᴌᑎᴠF ᗡᴌꓶ
```

"Now," resumed Blaine, "presupposing that in an ostensibly friendly message beginning with a word of four letters, that word is *dear*, and we've two important vowels to start with. We know the letter was addressed to Brunell, from an old partner in crime. We will assume, therefore, that the two words of three letters each, following *dear* are either *old Jim, old man*, or *old boy*. Let us see how it works out."

The detective scribbled hastily on a pad for several minutes, then leaned back in his chair, with a sigh of satisfaction.

"It can only be *boy*," he announced. "That gives us a working start of eight letters. Add to that the fact that this character is printed twice consecutively in three different places" — he pointed to the figure as he spoke — "which confirms the supposition that it is *l,* and you have this result immediately."

Blaine handed the pad across to Morrow, who read eagerly:

Dear Old Boy.

B-- -o-ey -o---- -o yo- -ro- old --ore le-- ---a-d --a- ---y --are -or -olle----- -or yo--o r--- --ll -all o- yo- ---r-day a- -o-r -e-.

The operative started to speak, but checked himself, and listened while Henry Blaine went on slowly but steadily.

"Each letter gained helps us to others, you see, Guy. For instance *-o-ey* must be *money*; the character following *yo* three times in different places must be *u*; the word — *-r-day* can only be *Thursday*; *-all* is *call*; *a-* is *at*; and *-o-r* is *four*. That gives us eight more letters, and makes the message read like this." Blaine wrote it down and handed the result to Morrow, who read:

Dear Old Boy.

B-- money com-n- to you from old score left un-a-d -hat -s my share for collect-n- for you? No ris- --ll call on you Thursday at four. -en.

"It looks easy, now," admitted Morrow. "But I never should have thought of going about it that way. I suppose the sixth word is *coming.* That gives us *i* and *g.*"

"Right you are," Blaine chuckled. "Knowing, too, that the message came from Walter Pennold, we can safely assume that *-en* is *Pen.* Use your common sense alone, now, and you will find that the message reads: 'Dear old boy. Big money coming to you from old score left unpaid. What is my share for collecting for you? No risk. Will call on you Thursday at four. Pen.'

"The word *risk* was misspelled *risl.* Evidently Pennold was a little bit rusty in the use of the old code. Our bait landed the fish all right, Guy. The money we planted in the bank of Brooklyn and Queens certainly brought results. No wonder poor old Jimmy Brunell was all broken up when he received such a message. More crafty than Pennold, he realized that it was a trap, and we were on his trail at last. We've got him cinched now, but he's only a tool, possibly a helpless one, in the hands of the master workmen. We'll go after them, tooth and nail, for the happiness and stainless name of two innocent young girls, who trust in us, and we'll get them, Guy, we'll get them if there is any justice and honor and truth left in the world!"

CHAPTER XIII
THE EMPTY HOUSE

"Don't spare them now. Get the truth at all costs."

With the last instructions of his chief ringing in his ears, the following morning Guy Morrow set out for Brooklyn, to interview his erstwhile friends, the Pennolds, in his true colors.

Mame Pennold, who was cleaning the dingy front room, heard the click of the gate, and peered with habitual caution from behind the frayed curtains of the window. The unexpected reappearance of their young banking acquaintance sent her scurrying as fast as her palsied legs could carry her back to the kitchen, where her husband sat luxuriously smoking and toasting his feet at the roaring little stove.

"Wally, who d'you think's comin' up the walk? That young feller, Alfred Hicks, who skipped from the Brooklyn and Queens Bank!"

"Good Lord!" Walter Pennold took his pipe from his lips and stared at her. "What d'you s'pose brought him back? Think he's broke, an' wants a touch?"

"No-o," his wife responded, somewhat doubtfully. "He looked prosperous, all right, by the flash I got at him, an' he's walkin' real brisk and businesslike. Maybe he's back on the job."

"'Tain't likely, not after the way he left his boarding place, if that Lindsay woman didn't lie." Pennold laid aside his pipe and frowned thoughtfully, as steps echoed from the rickety porch and a knock sounded upon the door. "He's a lightweight, every way you take him — he'd never stick anywhere."

"Maybe he's come to try an' get you into somethin'," Mame suggested. "Don't you go takin' up with a bad penny at your time o' life, Wally. He might know somethin' an' try blackmail, if he's real up against it."

"Well, go ahead an' open the door!" ordered Walter impatiently. "We're straight with the bank. If he's workin' there again we ain't got nothin' to worry about, an' if he ain't, we got nothin' against him. Let him in."

With obvious reluctance, Mame shuffled through the hall and obeyed.

"Hello, Mrs. Pennold!" Guy greeted her heartily, but without offering his hand. He brushed past her half-defensive figure with scant ceremony, and entered the kitchen. "Hello, Pennold. Thought I might find you home this cold morning. How goes it?"

"Same as usual." Pennold rose slowly and looked at his visitor with swiftly narrowed eyes. There was a new note in the young man's voice which the other vaguely recognized; it was as if a lantern had suddenly flashed into his face from the darkness, or an authoritative hand been laid upon his shoulder. He motioned mechanically toward a chair on the other side of the stove, and added slowly: "S'prised to see you, Al. Didn't expect you'd be around here again after your get-away. Workin' once more?"

"Oh, I'm right on the job!" responded Guy briskly. He drew the chair close to the square deal table, so close that he could have reached out, had he pleased, and touched his host's sleeve. Pennold seated himself again in his old position, significantly half-turned, so that when he glanced slyly at his visitor it was over his shoulder, in the furtive fashion of one on guard.

"Ain't back with the Brooklyn and Queens, are you?" he asked.

"No. It got too slow for me there. I found something bigger to do."

Mame Pennold, who had been hovering in the background, came forward now and faced him across the table, her shrewd eyes fastened upon him.

"Must have easy hours, when you can get off in the morning like this?" she observed. "Didn't forget your old friends, did you?"

"No, of course not. I hadn't anything more important to do this morning, so I thought I'd drop in and see you both."

His hand traveled to his breast pocket, and at the gesture, Mame's gaunt body stiffened suddenly.

"Didn't come to inquire about our health, did you?" she shot at him, acrimoniously.

"I came to see you about another matter — "

"Not on the trail of old Jimmy Brunell still, on that business of the bonds found at the bank?" Walter's voice was suddenly shrill with simulated mirth. "Nothin' in that for you, Al; not a nickel, if that's what you're here for."

"I'm not on Brunell's trail. I've found him," Morrow returned quietly; and in the tense pause which ensued he added dryly: "You led me to him."

"So that's what it was, a plant!" Walter started from his chair, but Mame laid a trembling, sinewy hand upon his shoulder and forced him back.

"What d'you mean, young man?" she demanded. "What do we know about old Brunell?"

"You wrote him a letter — you knew where to find him."

"I only wish we did!" she ejaculated. "We didn't write him! You must be crazy!"

"'Big money coming to you from old score left unpaid. What is my share for collecting for you?'" quoted Morrow, adding: "I have a friend who is very much interested in ciphers, and he wanted me to ask you about the one you use, Pennold. His name is Blaine. Ever hear of him?"

"Blaine!" Mame's voice shrank to a mere whisper, and her sallow face whitened.

"Blaine! Henry Blaine? The guy they call the Master Mind?" Pennold's shaking voice rose to a breaking cry, but again his wife silenced him.

"Suppose we did write such a letter — an' we ain't admittin' we did, for a minute — what's Blaine got on us?" demanded

Mame, coolly. "It's no crime, as I ever heard, to write a letter any way you want to. Who are you, young man? You're no bank clerk!"

"He's a 'tec, of course! Shut up your fool mouth, Mame. An' as for you, d — n you, get out of this house, an' get out quick, or I'll call the police myself! We've been leadin' straight, clean, respectable lives for years, Mame an' me, an' nobody's got nothin' on us! I ain't goin' to have no private 'tecs snoopin' in an' tryin' to put me through the third degree. Beat it, now!"

He rose blusteringly and advanced toward Morrow with upraised fist, but the other, with the table between them, drew from his pocket a folded paper.

"Not so fast, Pennold. I have a warrant here for your arrest!"

"Don't you believe him, Wally!" shrilled Mame. "It's a fake! Don't you talk to him! Put him out."

"The warrant was issued this morning, and I am empowered to arrest you. You can look at it for yourselves; you've both seen them before." He opened the paper and spread it out for them to read. "Walter Pennold, alias William Perry, alias Wally the Scribbler, number 09203 in the Rogues' Gallery. First term at Joliet, for forgery; second at Sing Sing for shoving the queer. This warrant only holds you as a suspicious character, Pennold, but we can dig up plenty of other things, if it's necessary; there's a forger named Griswold in the Tombs now awaiting trial, who will snitch about that Rochester check, for one thing."

"Don't let him bluff you, Wally." Mame faced Morrow from her husband's side. "They can't rake up a thing that ain't outlawed by time. You've lived clean more'n seven years, an' you're free from the bulls. They can't hold you."

"I haven't any warrant yet for you, Mrs. Pennold," observed Morrow, imperturbably. "I admit that it's more than seven years since every department-store detective was on the look-out for Left-handed Mame. I believe you specialized in furs and laces, didn't you?"

"What's it to you? You can't lay a finger on me now!" the woman stormed, defiantly.

"Not for shop-lifting or forgery — but how about receiving stolen goods?"

The shot found an instant target. Walter Pennold slumped and crumpled down into his chair, his arms outspread upon the table. He laid his head upon them, and a single dry, shuddering sob tore its way from his throat. The woman backed slowly away, and for the first time a shadow as of approaching terror crossed her hard, challenging face.

"Stolen goods!" she repeated. "What are you tryin' to put over? Do you think we're so green at the game that you can plant the goods here an' get us put away on the strength of a past record? You're a — "

"Nothing like it!" Morrow leaned forward impressively. "We don't have to do any planting, Mame. It's a good deal less than seven years since the Mortimer Chase's silver plate lay in your cellar."

"Silver plate — in our cellar!" echoed Mame in genuine amazement.

She stepped forward again, her shrewish chin out-thrust, but Walter Pennold raised his face, and at sight of it she stopped as if turned to stone.

"It's no use!" he cried, brokenly. "They've got me, Mame!"

"Got you? They'll never get you!" her startled scream rang out. "Wally, d'you know what the next term means? It's a lifer, on any count! I don't know what he means about any silver plate, but it's a bluff! Don't let him get your nerve!"

"Is it a bluff, Pennold?" asked Morrow, with dominant insistence.

The broken figure huddled in the chair shuddered uncontrollably.

"No, it ain't," he muttered. "I — I held out on you, Mame! I knew you wouldn't risk it, so I didn't say nothin' to you about it, but the money was too easy to let get by. The old gang offered me five hundred bucks just to keep it ten days, and pass it on to Jennings. He came here with a rag-picker's cart, you remember? You wondered what I was givin' him, an' I told you it was some rolls of old carpet I got from that place I was night watchman at, in Vandewater Street. I hid the stuff under the coal — "

"Shut up!" cried Mame, fiercely. "You don't know what you're sayin'. Wally, hold your tongue for God's sake! Where's your spirit? Are you goin' to break down now like a reformatory brat, you that had 'em all guessin' for twenty years!"

The gaunt woman had recovered from the sudden shock of her husband's unexpected revelation and now towered protectingly over his collapsed form, her palsied hands for once steady and firm upon his shoulders, while her keen eyes glittered shrewdly at the young operative confronting them.

"Look here!" she said, shortly. "If you wanted us for receiving stolen goods, you wouldn't come around here with a warrant for Wally's arrest as a suspicious character, an' you wouldn't have worked that Brunell plant. What's your lay?"

"Information," responded Morrow, frankly. "The police don't know where the plate was, for those ten days, and there's no immediate need that they should. Blaine cleaned up that case eventually, you know — recovered the plate and caught the butler in Southampton, under the noses of the Scotland Yard men. I want to know what you can tell me about Brunell — and about your nephew, Charley Pennold."

Walter opened his lips, but closed them without speech, and his wife replied for him.

"We're no snitchers," she said coldly. "There's nothin' we can tell. Jimmy Brunell's run straight for near twenty years, so far as we know."

"And Charley?" persisted Morrow.

"It's no use, Mame," Walter Pennold repeated, dully. "If I go up again, it means the end for me. Charley's got to take his chance, same as the rest of us. God knows I tried to do the right thing by the boy, same as Jimmy did by his daughter, but Charley's got the blood in him. It's hell to peach on your own, but it's worse to hear that iron door clank behind you, and to know it's for the last time! After all, there ain't nothin' in what we can tell about Charley that a lot of other people wouldn't spill, an' nothin' that could land him behind the bars. I ain't the man I was, or I'd take my medicine without squealin', but I can't face it again, Mame, I can't! I'm an old man now, old before my time, perhaps, but it's been so long since I smelled the prison taint, so long since I had a number instead of a name, that I'd die now, quick, before I'd rot in a cell!"

The terrible, droning monotone ceased, and for a moment there was silence in the squalid little room. The woman's face was as impassive as Morrow's, as she waited. Only the tightening of her hands upon her husband's shoulders, until her bony knuckles showed white through the drawn skin, betrayed the storm of emotion which swept over her, at the memories evoked by the broken words.

"I'm not asking you to snitch, Pennold," Morrow said, not unkindly. "We know all we want to about Brunell's life at present — his home in the Bronx, and his little map-making shop — and we're not trying to rake up anything from the past to hold over him now; it is only some general information I want. As to your nephew, you've got to tell me all you know about him, or it's all up with you. Blaine won't give you away, if you'll answer my questions frankly and make a clean breast of it, and this is your only chance."

Pennold licked his dry lips.

"What do you want to know?" he asked, at last.

"When did Jimmy Brunell turn his last trick?"

"Years ago; I've forgotten how many. It's no harm speakin' of it now, for he did his seven years up the river for it — his first and only conviction. That was the time old Cowperthwaite's name was forged to five checks amounting to thirty thousand, all told, and Jimmy was caught on the last."

"Where was his plant?"

"In a basement on Dye Street. The bulls never found it. He was running a little printer's shop in front, as a blind — oh, he was clever, old Jimmy, the sharpest in his line!"

"What became of his outfit, when he was sent up?"

"Dunno. It just disappeared. Some of his old pals cribbed it, I guess, or Jimmy may have fixed it with them to remove it. He was always close-mouthed, and he never would tell me. I knew where his plant was, of course, and I went there myself, after he was sent up and the coast was clear, to get the outfit, to — to take care of it for him until he came out. Oh, I ain't afraid to tell now; it's so long ago! I could take you to the place to-day, but the outfit's gone."

"And when he had served his term, what happened?"

"He came out to find that his wife was dead, and Emily, the little girl that was born just after he went up, was none too well treated by the people her mother'd had to leave her with. He'd learned in the pen' to make maps, an' he opened a little shop an' made up his mind to live straight, an' — an' so far as I know, he has." Pennold faltered, as if from weakness, and for a moment his voice ceased. Then he went on: "I ain't seen him for a long time, but we kept track of each other, an' when you come with that cock-an'-bull story about the bonds, and the bank backed you up in it, why I — I went to see him."

"You wrote him first. Why did you send a cipher letter?"

"Because I suspicioned the whole thing was a plant, just like it turned out to be, an' I didn't want to get an old pal into no trouble. The cipher's an old one we used years ago, in the gang, an' I know he wouldn't forget it. I never thought he'd squeal on me to Blaine!"

"He didn't. The letter — er — came into Blaine's possession, and he read it for himself."

"He did?" Pennold looked up quickly, with a flash of interest on his sullen face. "He's a wonder, that Blaine! If he'd only got started the other way, the way we did, what a crook he would have made! As it is, I guess we ain't afraid of all the organized police on earth combined, as much as we are of him. It's a queer thing he ain't been shot up or blown into eternity long ago, an' yet they say he's never guarded. He must be a cool one! Anyhow, I'm glad Jimmy didn't squeal on me; I'd hate to think it of him. When I went to see him about the bonds, he wouldn't have nothin' to do with them. Swore they was a plant, he did, an' warned me off. He seemed real excited, considerin' he had nothin' to worry about, but I took his word for it, an' beat it. That's the last I seen of him."

"Did you send your nephew to him?"

"Me?" Pennold's tones quickened in surprise. "I ain't seen him in a long while, an' I don't believe he even remembers old Jimmy; he was only a kid when Jimmy went up the river. What would I send Charley for, when I'd gone myself an' it hadn't worked?"

It was evident to Morrow that the man he was interrogating was ignorant of Brunell's connection with the Lawton case, and he changed his tactics.

"Tell me about Charley. You say you tried to do right by him."

"Of course I did! Wasn't he my brother's boy?" Pennold hunched over the table, and continued eagerly: "Mame kept him clean an' fed, an' we sent him to public school, just like any other kid. But it wasn't no use. He had it in him to go wrong, without the wit to get away with it. He was caught pinchin' lead piping when he was sixteen, an' sent to Elmira for three years. Them three years was his finish. When he came out he'd had what you'd call a graduate course in every form of crookedness under the sun, from fellers harder an' cleverer than he'd ever thought of bein', an' he was bitter besides, an' desperate. There wasn't no chance for him then, an' he just drifted on down the line. I never heard of him turnin' a real trick himself, an' he never got caught at nothin' again, but he chummed in with the gang, an' he always seemed to have coin enough. I ain't seen him in more'n a year. The last I heard of him, he was workin' as a stool-pigeon an' snitcher for the worst scoundrel of the lot."

"Who was that?" asked Morrow.

Pennold hesitated and then replied with dogged reluctance.

"I dunno what that's got to do with it, but the feller's name is Paddington, an' he's the worst kind of a crook — a 'tec gone wrong. At least, that's what they say about him, but I ain't got nothin' on him; I don't believe I ever seen the man, that I know of. He's worked on a lot of shady cases; I know that much, an' he's clever. More'n a dozen crooks are floatin' around town that would be up the river if he told what he knew about 'em; so naturally, he owns 'em, body an' soul. Not that Charley's one that'd go up — he's only in it for the coin — but I'd rather see him get pinched an' do time for pullin' off somethin' on his own account, than runnin' around doin' dirty work for a man who ain't in his father's class, or mine. He's a disgrace; that's what Charley is — a plain disgrace."

Pennold's voice rang out in highly virtuous indignation. Morrow forbore to smile at the oblique moral viewpoint of the old crook.

"What does he look like?" he asked. "Short and slim, isn't he, with a small dark mustache?"

"That's him!" ejaculated Pennold disgustedly. "Dresses like a dude, an' chases after a bunch of skirts! Spreads himself like a ward politician when he gets a chance! He's my nephew, all right, but as long as he won't run straight, same as I'm doin' now, I'd rather he'd crack a crib than play errand boy for a man I wouldn't trust on look-out!"

"Where does Charley live?" asked Morrow.

"How should I know? He hangs out at Lafferty's saloon, down on Sand Street, when he ain't off on some steer or other — leastways he used to."

Morrow folded the warrant slowly, in the pause which ensued, and returned it to his pocket while the couple watched him tensely.

"All right, Pennold," he said, at last. "I guess I won't have to use this now. If you've been square, an' told me all you know, you won't be bothered about that matter of the Mortimer Chase silver plate. If you've kept anything back, Blaine will find it out, and then it's good-night to you."

"I ain't!" returned Pennold, with tremendous eagerness. "I've told you everything you asked, an' I don't savvy what you're gettin' at, anyway. If you're tryin' to mix Jimmy Brunell up in any new case you're dead wrong; he's out of the game for good. As for Charley, he wouldn't know enough to pick up a pocket-book if he saw one lyin' on the sidewalk, unless he was told to!"

"Well, I may as well warn both of you that you're watched, and if you try to make a get-away, you'll be taken up — and it won't be on suspicion, either. Play fair with Blaine, and he'll be square with you, but don't try to put anything over on him, or it'll be the worse for you. It can't be done."

Morrow closed the door behind him, leaving the couple as they had been almost throughout the interview — the woman erect and stony of face, the man miserable and shaken, crouched dejectedly over the table. But scarcely had he descended the steps of the ramshackle little porch when the voice of Mame Pennold reached him, pitched in a shrill key of emotional exultation.

"Oh, Wally, Wally! Thank God you ain't a snitcher! Thank God you didn't tell!"

The voice ceased suddenly, as if a hand had been laid across her lips, and after a moment's hesitation, Morrow swung off down the path, conscious of at least one pair of eyes watching him from behind the soiled curtains of the front room.

What had the woman meant? Pennold obviously had kept something back, but was it of sufficient importance to warrant his returning and forcing a confession? Whether it concerned Brunell or their nephew Charley mattered little, at the moment. He had achieved the object of his visit; he knew that Pennold himself had no connection with the Lawton forgeries, nor knowledge of them, and at the same time he had learned of Charley's affiliation with Paddington. The couple back there in the little house could tell him scarcely more which would aid him in his investigation, but the dapper, viciously weak young stool-pigeon, if he could be located at once, might be made to disclose enough to place Paddington definitely within the grasp of the law.

Guy Morrow boarded a Sand Street car, and behind the sporting page of a newspaper he kept a sharp look-out for Lafferty's saloon. He came to it at last — a dingy, down-at-heel resort, with much faded gilt-work over the door, and fly-specked posters of the latest social function of the district's political club showing dimly behind its unwashed windows.

He rode a block beyond — then, alighting, turned back and entered the bar. It was deserted at that hour of the morning, save for a disconsolate-looking individual who leaned upon one ragged elbow, gazing mournfully into his empty whisky glass at the end of the narrow, varnished counter. The bartender emerged from a door leading into the back room, with a tall, empty glass in his hand, and Morrow asked for a beer. As he stood sipping it, he watched the bartender replenish the empty unwashed glass he had carried with a generous drink of doubtful looking absinthe and a squirt from a syphon.

"Bum drink on a cold morning," he observed tentatively. "Have a whisky straight, on me?"

"I will that!" the bartender returned heartily. "This green-eyed fairy stuff ain't for me; it's for a dame in the back room — one of the regulars. She's been hittin' it up all the morning, but it don't seem to affect her — funny, too, for she ain't a boozer, as a general thing. Her guy's gone back on her, an' she's sore. I'll be with you in a minute."

He vanished into the back room with the glass, and before he returned, the disconsolate individual had slunk out, leaving Morrow in sole possession. If this place was indeed the rendezvous of the gang of minor criminals with which Charley Pennold had allied himself, he had obviously come at the wrong time to obtain any information concerning him, unless the voluble bartender could be made to talk, and that would be a difficult matter.

"Look here!" Morrow decided on a bold move, as the bartender reappeared and placed a bottle of whisky between them. He leaned forward, after a quick, furtive glance about him, and spoke rapidly, with a disarming air of confidential frankness. "I'm in an awful hole. I'm new at this game, and I've got to find a fellow I never saw, and find him quick. He hangs out here, and the big guy sent me for him."

"What big guy?" The cordiality faded from the bartender's ruddy countenance and he stepped back significantly.

"You know — Pad!" Morrow shot back on a desperate bluff. "The fellow's name's Charley Pennold, and Pad wants him right away. He didn't tell me to ask you about him, but he made it pretty plain to me that he'd got to get him."

"Say!" The bartender approached cautiously. He rested one hand upon the counter, keeping the other well below it, but Morrow did not flinch. "What's your lay?"

"Anything there's coin in," returned the operative, with a knowing leer. "Anything from planting divorce evidence to shoving the queer. I've been working for a pal of Pad's in St. Louis for three or four years — that's why I'm strange around here. Pad's up in the air about something, and wants this Charley-boy right away, and he tells me to look here for him and not come back without him, see? This is on the level. If you know where he is, be a good fellow and come across, will you?"

The bartender felt under the counter for the shelf, and then raised his hand, empty, toward the bottle.

"I guess you're all right," he remarked. "Anyway, I'll take a chance. What's your moniker?"

"Guy the Blinker," returned Morrow promptly. "Guess you've heard of me, all right. I pulled off — but I haven't got time to chin now. I got to find this boy if I want to keep in with Pad, and there's coin in it."

"Sure there is," the bartender affirmed. "But he's a queer one — the big guy, as you call him. What's his game? Why, only this morning, he tipped Charley off to beat it, and Charley did. Maybe he thinks the kid's double-crossed him."

Morrow's heart leaped in sudden excitement at this astounding news, but he controlled himself, and replied nonchalantly:

"Search me. He told me I'd find this Charley-boy here; that's all I know. He isn't talking for publication — not Pad."

"You bet not!" The bartender nodded. Then he jerked a grimy thumb in the direction of the back room. "Why, the dame in there, cryin' into her absinthe, is Charley's girl. She's a queen — straight as they make 'em, if she does work the shops now and then — and Charley was fixin' to hook up with her next month, preacher-fashion, and settle down. Now he gets the office and skips without a word to her, and she's all broke up over it!"

The door at the rear opened suddenly, and a girl stood upon the threshold. She was tall and slender, and her face showed traces of positive beauty, although it was bloated and distorted with weeping and dissipation, and her big black eyes glittered feverishly.

"What's that you're sayin' about Charley?" she demanded half-hysterically. "He's gone! He's left me! I don't believe Pad gave him the office, and if he did, Charley's a fool to beat it! They've got nothin' on him — it's Pad who's got to save his own skin!"

"Shut up, Annie!" advised the bartender, not unkindly. "Pad's sent this here feller for him, now!"

"Then it was a lie — a lie! Pad didn't tell him to beat it — he's gone on his own account, gone for good! But I'll find him; I'll — "

The girl suddenly burst into a storm of sobs, and, turning, reeled back into the inner room.

"You see!" the bartender observed, confidentially, as the door swung shut behind her. "She thinks he's gone off with another skirt; that's the way with women! I knew Pad had given him the office, though. I got it straight. You're right about Pad bein' up in the air. He must have bitten off more than he can chew, this time. I heard Reddy Thursby talkin' to Gil Hennessey about it, right where you're standin', not two hours ago. They're both Pad's men — met 'em yet?"

Morrow shook his head, not trusting himself to speak, and the loquacious bartender went on.

"It was Reddy brought the word for Charley to skip, and he dropped somethin' about a raid on some plant up in the Bronx. Know anything about it?"

For a moment the rows of bottles on their shelves seemed to reel before Morrow's eyes, and his heart stood still, but he forced himself to reply:

"Oh, that? I know all about it, of course. Wasn't I in on the ground floor? But that's only a fake steer; this Charley-boy hasn't got anything to do with it, that I know of. Maybe the big guy thought he hadn't got out of the way, and sent me to find out. No use my hanging round here any longer, anyhow. I'll amble back and tell Pad he's gone. Swell dame, that Annie — some queen, eh? Let's have one more drink and I'll blow!"

With assurances of an early return, Morrow contrived to beat a retreat without arousing the suspicions of the bartender, but he went out into the pale, wintry, sunlight with his brain awhirl. To his apprehensive mind a raid on a plant in the Bronx could mean only one place — the little map-making shop of Jimmy Brunell. Something had happened in his absence; some one had betrayed the old forger. And Emily — what of her?

Morrow sped as fast as elevated and subway could carry him to the Bronx. Anxious as he was about the girl he loved, he did not go directly to the house on Meadow Lane, but made a detour to the little shop a few blocks away.

Morrow's instinct had not misled him. Before he had approached within a hundred feet of the shop he knew that his fears had been justified.

The door swung idly open on its hinges, and the single window gave forth a vacant stare. Within everything was in the wildest disorder. The table which served as a counter, the racks of maps, the high stool, the printing apparatus, all were overturned. The trap door leading into the cellar was open, and Morrow flung himself wildly down the sanded steps. The forger's outfit had disappeared.

What had become of Jimmy Brunell? His purpose served, had Paddington betrayed him to the police, or had some warning reached him to flee before it was too late?

With mingled emotions of fear and dread, Morrow emerged from the little dismantled shop and made the best of his way to Meadow Lane. The Brunell cottage appeared much as usual as he neared it, and for an instant hope surged up within him. Emily would be at the club, of course. If her father had been arrested, or had succeeded in getting away safely alone, she would not know of it until she came back in the evening. He would wait for her, intercept her, and tell her the whole truth.

Instead of entering his own lodgings, he crossed the road, and paused at the Brunells' gate. Something forlorn and desolate in the atmosphere of the little home seemed to clutch at his heart, and on a swift impulse he strode up the path, ascended the steps of the porch and peered in the window of the living-room. Everything in the usually orderly room was topsy-turvy, and everywhere there was evidence of hurried flight. From where he stood the desk — her desk — was plainly visible, its ransacked drawers pulled open, the floor before it strewn with torn and scattered papers. Its top was bare, amid the surrounding litter, and even his photograph which he had recently given her, and which usually stood there in the little frame she had made for it with her own hands, was gone.

A chill settled about his heart. Had Brunell been captured, and police detectives searched the house, his picture could hold no interest for them. Had the old forger fled alone, he would not have taken so insignificant an object from among all his household goods and chattels. Emily alone would have paused to save the photograph of the man she loved from the wreckage of her home; Emily, too, had gone!

Scarcely knowing what he was doing, and caring less, Morrow rushed across the street, and descended upon Mrs. Quinlan, his landlady, at her post in the kitchen.

"What's happened to the Brunells?" he demanded breathlessly.

"Land's sakes, but you scared me, Mr. Morrow!" Mrs. Quinlan turned from the stove with a hurried start, and wiped her plump, steaming face on her apron. "I should like to know what's happened myself. All I do know is that they've gone bag and baggage — or as much of it as they could carry with them — and never; a word to a soul except what Emily ran across to say to me."

"What was it?" he fairly shouted at her. But there were few interests in Mrs. Quinlan's humdrum existence, and seldom did she have an exciting incident to relate and an eager audience to hang upon her words. She sat down ponderously and prepared to make the most of the present occasion.

"I thought it was funny to see a man goin' into their yard at five o'clock this mornin', but my tooth was so bad I forgot all about him and it never come into my mind again until I seen them goin' away. I sleep in the room just over yours, you know, Mr. Morrow, an' my tooth ached so bad I couldn't sleep. It was five by my clock when I got up to come down here an' get some hot vinegar, an' I don't know what made me look out my winder, but I did. I seen a man come running down the lane, keepin' well in the shaders, an' looking back as if he was afraid he was bein' chased, for all the world like a thief. While I looked, he turned in the Brunells' yard an' instead of knocking on the door, he began throwin' pebbles up at the old man's bedroom winder. Pretty soon it opened and Mr. Brunell looked out. Then he come down quick an' met the man at the front door. They talked a minute, an' the feller handed over somethin' that showed white in the light of the street lamp, like a piece of paper. Mr. Brunell shut the door an' the man ran off the way he had come. I come down an' got my hot vinegar an' when I got back to my room I seen there were lights in Mr. Brunell's room an' Emily's, an' one in the livin'-room, too, but my tooth was jumpin' so I went straight to bed. About half an hour after you'd left for business I was shakin' a rug out of the front sittin'-room winder, when Emily come runnin' across the street.

"'Oh, Mrs. Quinlan!' she calls to me, an' I see she'd been cryin'. 'Mrs. Quinlan, we're goin' away!'

"'For good?' I asked.

"'Forever!' she says. 'Will you give a message to Mr. Morrow for me, please? Tell him I'm sorry I was mistaken. I'm sorry to have found him out!'

"She burst out cryin' again an' ran back as her father called her from the porch. He was bringin' out a pile of suit-cases and roll-ups, and pretty soon a taxicab drove up with a man inside. I couldn't see his face — only his coat-sleeve. They got in an' went off kitin' an' that's every last thing I know. What d'you s'pose she meant about findin' you out, Mr. Morrow?"

He turned away without reply, and went to his room, where he sat for long sunk in a stupor of misery. She had found out the truth, before he could tell her. She knew him for what he was, knew his despicable errand in ingratiating himself into her friendship and that of her father. She believed that the real love he had professed for her had been all a mere part of the game he was playing, and now she had gone away forever! He would never see her again!

"By God, no!" he cried aloud to himself, in the bitterness of his sorrow. "I will find her again, if I search the ends of the earth. She shall know the truth!"

CHAPTER XIV
IN THE OPEN

Guy Morrow's resolve to find Emily Brunell at all costs, stirred him from the apathy of despair into which he had fallen, and roused him to instant action. Leaving the house, he went to the nearest telephone pay station, where he could converse in comparative privacy, and called up Henry Blaine's office, only to discover that the master detective had departed upon some mission of his own, was not expected to return until the following morning, and had left no instructions for him.

This unanticipated set-back left Morrow without definite resource. As a forlorn hope he telephoned to the Anita Lawton Club, only to learn that Miss Brunell had sent in her resignation as secretary early that morning, but told nothing of her future plans, except that she was leaving town for an indefinite period.

There was nothing more to be learned by another examination of the dismantled shop, and the young operative turned his steps reluctantly homeward. A sudden suspicion had formed itself in his mind that Blaine himself, and not the police, had been responsible for the raid on the forger's little establishment — that Blaine had done this without taking him into his confidence and was now purposely keeping out of his way.

When the early winter dusk came, Guy could endure it no longer, but left the house. Drawn irresistibly by his thoughts, he crossed the road again, and entering the Brunells' gate, he strolled around the deserted cottage, to the back. At the kitchen door a faint, piteous sound made him pause. It was an insistent, wailing cry from within, the disconsolate meowing of a frightened, lonely kitten.

Caliban had been left behind, forgotten! Emily's panic and haste must have been great indeed to cause her to forsake the pet she had so tenderly loved! Much as he detested the spiteful little creature, he could not leave it to starve, for her sake.

Morrow tried the kitchen door, but found it securely bolted from within. The catch on the pantry window was loose, however, and Morrow managed to pry it open with his jackknife. With a hasty glance about to see that he was not observed, he pushed up the window and clambered in, closing it cautiously after him. He stumbled through the semi-obscurity and gloom into the kitchen; instantly the piteous cry ceased and Caliban rose from the cold hearth and bounded gladly to him, purring and rubbing against his legs. Mechanically he stooped and stroked it; then, after carefully pulling down the shades, he lighted the lamp upon the littered table, and looked about him. Everything bore evidence, as had the living-room, of a hasty exodus. The fire was extinguished in the range, and it was filled to the brim with flakes of light ashes. Evidently Brunell or his daughter had paused long enough in their flight to burn armfuls of old papers — possibly incriminating ones.

On the table was the débris of a hasty meal. Morrow poured some milk from the pitcher into a saucer and placed it on the floor for the hungry kitten; then, taking the lamp, he started on a tour of inspection through the house. Everywhere the wildest confusion and disorder reigned.

Morrow turned aside from the door of Emily's room, but entered her father's. There, save for a few articles of old clothing strewn about, he found comparative order and neatness. The simple toilet articles were in their places, the narrow bed just as Jimmy Brunell had left it when he sprang up to admit his nocturnal visitor.

On the floor near the bureau on which the lamp stood, something white and crumpled met Morrow's eye; he stooped quickly and picked it up. It was a large single sheet of paper, and as the operative smoothed it out, he realized that it must be the message which had been hurriedly brought to Brunell in the early hour before the dawn. The paper had lain just where he had dropped it, crushed from his hand after reading the warning it contained.

Morrow turned up the wick of his own lamp and stared curiously at the missive. The sheet of paper was ruled at intervals, the lines and interstices filled with curious hieroglyphics, and at a first glance it appeared to the operative's puzzled eyes to be a mere portion of a page of music. Then he observed that old figures and letters, totally foreign to the notes of a printed score, were interspersed between the rest, and moreover only the treble clef had been used.

"Oh, Lord!" he groaned to himself. "It's another cryptogram, and I don't believe Blaine himself will be able to solve this one!"

He stared long and uncomprehendingly at it; then with a sigh of baffled interest he folded it carefully and placed it in his pocket. As he did so, there came a sudden sharp report from outside, the tinkle of a broken window pane, and a bullet, whistling past his ear, embedded itself in the wall behind him!

Instinctively Morrow flung himself flat upon the floor, but no second shot was fired. Instead, he heard the muffled receding of flying footsteps from the sidewalk, and an excited cry or two as neighboring windows were raised and curious heads were thrust out.

Hastily extinguishing the lamp, Morrow felt his way to the kitchen, where he pocketed Caliban with scant ceremony and departed swiftly the way he had come, through the pantry window. By scaling a back-yard wall or two he found an alley leading to the street; and making a detour of several blocks, he returned to his lodgings, to find Mrs. Quinlan waiting in great excitement to relate her version of the revolver shot.

Morrow listened with what patience he could muster, and then handed Caliban over to her mercy.

"It's Miss Brunell's cat," he explained. "You'll take care of it for a day or two, at least, won't you? I expect to hear from her soon, and I'd like to be able to restore it to her."

"Well, I ain't what you would call crazy about cats," the landlady returned, somewhat dubiously, "but I couldn't let it die in this cold. I'll keep it, of course, till you hear from Emily. Where did you find it?"

"Over in their yard," he responded, with prompt mendacity. "I was in the neighborhood and heard the shot fired, so I ran in to have a look around and see if anyone was hurt, and I came across this poor little chap yowling on the doorstep. I won't want any supper to-night, Mrs. Quinlan. I'm going out again."

Within the hour, Morrow presented himself at Henry Blaine's office. This time he did not wait to be told that the famous investigator was out, but writing something on a card, he sent it in to the confidential secretary.

In a moment he was admitted, to find Blaine seated imperturbably behind his desk, fingering the card his young operative had sent in to him.

"What is it, Guy?" he asked, not unkindly. "You say you have a communication of great importance."

"I think it is, sir," returned the other, stiffly. "At least I have the message which warned Brunell of your raid upon his shop. It's another cipher, a different one this time."

"Indeed? That's good work, Guy. But how did you know it was a warning to old Jimmy of the raid? Could you read it?"

Morrow shook his head.

"No, and I don't see how anyone else could! It must have been a warning of some sort, for it was what caused them both, old Jimmy and his daughter, to run away. Here it is."

He passed the cryptogram over to his chief, who studied it for a while with a meditative frown, then laid it aside and listened in a non-committal silence to his story. When the incidents of the day had been narrated, Blaine said:

"That was a close call, Guy, that shot from the darkness. It must have come from the opposite side of the street, of course, from before your own lodgings. The bullet glanced upward in its course, didn't it?"

"No, sir. That's the funny part of it! The spot where it is embedded in the wall is very little higher than the hole in the window pane."

"And Mrs. Quinlan's, where you board, is directly opposite?"

"Yes. It's the only house on the other side of the street for fifty feet or more on either side."

"Then you'd better look out for trouble, Guy. That shot came from your own house, probably from the window of your own room, if it is the second floor front, as you say. There's a traitor in camp. Any new lodgers to-day that you know of?"

"No, sir," Morrow replied, startled at the theory evolved by his chief. "But how do you account for the fact that I distinctly heard some one running away immediately after the shot was fired?"

"It was probably a look-out, or a decoy to draw investigation away from the house had a prompt pursuit ensued. Be careful when you go back, Guy, and don't take any unnecessary chances."

"I'm not going back, sir," the younger man returned, with quiet determination. "I'm sorry, but I'm through. I wanted to resign before, to protect the woman I love from just this trouble which has come upon her, but you overruled me, and I listened and played the game fairly. Now I've lost her, and nothing else matters under the sun except that I must find her again and tell her the truth, and I mean to find her! Nothing shall stand in my way!"

"And your duty?" asked Blaine quietly.

"My duty is to her first, last, and all the time! I know I have no right, sir, to ask that I should be taken into your confidence in regard to any plans you make in conducting an investigation, but I think in view of the exceptional conditions of this case that I might have been told in advance of the raid you intended, so that I might have spared Emily much of the trouble which has come upon her, or at least have told her the truth, and squared myself with her, and known where she was going. I've got to find her, sir! I cannot rest until I do!"

"And you shall find her, Guy. I promise you on my word

that if you are patient all will be well. It is not my custom to explain my motives to my subordinates, but as you say, this case is exceptional, and you have been faithful to your trust under peculiarly trying circumstances. I raided Jimmy's little shop last night and carried off his forgery outfit because I had received special information of a confidential nature that Paddington intended to make the same move and lay it to the work of the police, not only to scare poor old Jimmy out of town, but to obtain possession of the outfit himself and destroy the evidence, in case the old forger was caught and lost his spirit and confessed, implicating him. I did not know the raid would be discovered and the warning take effect so soon. I had arranged to have the Brunells watched and tailed later in the day, but they escaped my espionage.

"I shall at once set the wheels in motion to discover the number of the taxicab in which they went away, and I will leave no stone unturned to find their ultimate destination and see that no harm comes to either of them; you may depend upon that. I don't mind going a little further with this subject with you now than I have before, and I'll tell you confidentially that I believe whatever part Jimmy played in this conspiracy, in forging the letter, note, and signatures, was a compulsory one; and in the end we shall be able to clear him. You know that I am a man of my word, Guy. I want you to go on with this case under my instructions and leave the search for the Brunells absolutely in my hands. Will you do this, on my assurance that I will find them?"

"If I can have your word, sir, that at the earliest possible moment I may go to her, to Emily, and tell her the truth," Morrow replied, earnestly. "You don't know what it means to me, to have her feel that I have been such a dog as not to mean a word of all that I said to her, to have her believe that it was all part of a plan to trap her into betraying her father. It drives me almost mad when I think of it! This inaction, the suspense of it, is intolerable."

"Then go home and find out who fired at you from the window of your own house. Watch the Brunell cottage, too — there will be developments there, if I'm not mistaken. To-morrow I may want you to go out on another branch of this investigation — the search for Ramon Hamilton."

"Very good, sir, I'll try," Morrow promised with obvious reluctance. "I know how busy you are and how much every day counts in this matter just now; but for God's sake, do what you can to find the Brunells for me!"

Blaine repeated his assurances, and Morrow returned to the Bronx with considerably lightened spirits. The sight of the little cottage across the way, dark and deserted, brought a pang to his heart, but it also served to remind him of the duty which lay before him. He must find out whose hand had fired that shot at him from the house which had given him shelter.

Mrs. Quinlan had not yet retired. He found her reading a newspaper in the kitchen, with Caliban curled up in drowsy content beside the stove.

"Cold out, ain't it?" she observed. "I went round to the store, an' I like to've froze before I got back. They said they'd send the things, but they didn't."

"I'll go get them for you," offered Morrow. "Was it the grocery to which you went?"

"No, the drug store. I — I've got a new lodger upstairs at the back — an old gentleman who's kind of sickly and rheumatic, and he asked me to get some things for him. Thank you just the same, Mr. Morrow, but there ain't no hurry for them." Mrs. Quinlan's wide, ingenuous face flushed, and for a moment she seemed curiously embarrassed. Could she have guessed that the revolver shot which had created so much excitement that afternoon had been fired from beneath her roof?

"A new lodger!" repeated Morrow. "Came to-day, didn't he?"

"No, yesterday," she responded quickly — too quickly, the operative fancied. The ruddy flush had deepened on her cheek, and she added, as if unable to restrain the question rising irresistibly to her lips: "What made you think he came to-day?"

"I thought this afternoon that I heard furniture being moved about in the room directly over mine," he returned, with studied indifference.

"Oh, you did!" Mrs. Quinlan affirmed. "That's my room, you know. I was exchanging my bureau for the old gentleman's."

"Let me see; that makes four lodgers now, doesn't it?" Morrow remarked thoughtfully, as he toasted his back near the stove. "Peterson, the shoe clerk; Acker, the photographer; me — and now this old gentleman. What's his name, by the way?"

"Mr. — Brown." Again there was that obvious hesitation, followed by a hasty rush of words as if to cover it. "Yes, my house is full now, and I think I'm mighty lucky, considering the time of year. Just think, it's most Christmas! The winter's just flyin' along!"

The next morning, from his bed Morrow heard the clinking of china on a tray as Mrs. Quinlan laboriously carried breakfast upstairs to her new boarder. Guy rose quickly and dressed, and when he heard her descending again he flung open his door and met her face to face, quite as if by accident. She started violently at the sudden encounter and nearly dropped the tray.

"Land sakes, how you scared me, Mr. Morrow!" she exclaimed. "You're up earlier than usual. I'll have your breakfast ready in the dining-room in ten minutes."

She hurried on quickly, but not before the operative's keen eyes had noted in one lightning glance the contents of the tray. Upon it was a teapot, as well as one for coffee, and service for two. Peterson and Acker had both long since gone to their usual day's work. Mrs. Quinlan had lied, then, after all. She had two new lodgers instead of the single rheumatic old gentleman she had pictured; two, and one of them had entered his own room, and from the window fired that shot across the street at him, as he bent over the lamp in the Brunell cottage. He had one problematic advantage — it was possible that he had not been recognized as the intruder in the deserted house. He must contrive by hook or crook to obtain a glimpse of the mysterious newcomers, and learn the cause of their interest in the Brunells and their affairs. They were in all probability emissaries of Paddington's —

possibly one of them was Charley Pennold himself.

At that same moment Henry Blaine sat in his office, receiving the report of Ross, one of his minor operatives.

"I tried the tobacconist's shop yesterday morning, sir, but there wasn't any message there for Paddington, and although I waited around a couple of hours he didn't show up," Ross was saying. "This morning, however, I tried the same stunt, and it worked. I wasn't any too quick about it, either, for Paddington was just after me. I strolled in, asked for a package of Cairos and gave the man the office, as you told me. He handed it over like a lamb, and I walked out with it, straight to that little café across the way. I had four of the boys waiting there, and my entrance was a signal to them to beat it over and buy enough tobacco to keep the shopkeeper busy while I made a getaway from the dairy-lunch place. I only went three doors down, to a barber's, and while I was waiting my turn there I watched the street from behind a newspaper.

"In about ten minutes Paddington came along, walking as if he was in quite a hurry. He went into the tobacconist's, but he came out quicker than he had entered, and his face was a study — purple with rage one minute, and white with fear the next. I don't believe he knows yet who's tailing him, sir, but he looks as if he realized we had him coming and going. He went straight over to the little restaurant, with murder in his eye, but he only stayed a minute or two. I tailed him home to his rooms, and he stamped along at first as if he was so mad he didn't care whether he was followed or not. When he got near his own street, though, he got cautious again, and I had all I could do to keep him from catching me on his trail — he's a sharp one, when he wants to be, and he's on his mettle now."

"I know the breed. He'll turn and fight like any other rat if he's cornered, but meanwhile he'll try at any cost to get away from us," Blaine responded. "You have him well covered, Ross?"

"Thorpe is waiting in a high-powered car a few doors away, Vanner in a taxi, and Daly is on the job until I get back. He won't take a step to-day without being tailed," the operative answered, confidently. "Here's the cigarette box, sir. I opened it as soon as I got in the restaurant, to see if it was the real goods and not a plant, as you instructed. It's the straight tip, all right. There were no cigarettes inside, only this single sheet of paper covered with little marks — looks like music, only it isn't. I don't know much about sight-reading, but some of those figures couldn't be played on any instrument!"

Henry Blaine opened the little box and drew from it the bit of folded paper, which he spread out upon the desk before him. A glance was sufficient to show him that it was another cryptic message, similar to that which Guy Morrow had found in the Brunells' deserted cottage, and which he had vainly studied until far into the night.

"Very good, Ross. Get back on the job, now, and report any developments as soon as you have an opportunity."

When the operative had gone, Blaine drew forth the cryptogram received the previous evening and compared the two. They were identical in character, although from the formation of the letters and figures, the message each conveyed was a different one. The first had baffled him, and he scrutinized the second with freshly awakened interest:

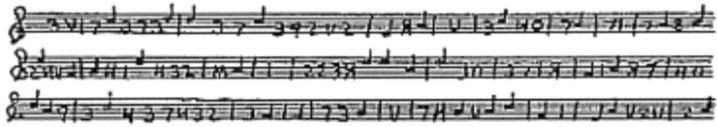

The three lines fascinated him by their tantalizing problem, and he could not take his eyes from them. The musical notes could be easily read in place of letters, of course, with the sign of the treble clef as a basic guide, but the other figures still puzzled him.

All at once, a word upon the lowest line which explained itself caught his eye; then another and another, until the method of deciphering the whole message burst upon his mind. One swift gesture, a few eagerly scrawled calculations, and the truth was plain to him.

Calling his secretary, he hastily dictated a letter.

"I want a copy of that sent at once, by special delivery, to every physician and surgeon in town, no matter how obscure. See to it that not one is overlooked. Even those on the staffs of the different hospitals must be notified, although they are the least likely to be called upon. Above all, don't forget the old retired one, those of shady professional reputation and the fledglings just out of medical colleges. It's a large order, Marsh, but it's bound to bring some result in the next forty-eight hours."

With the closing of the door behind his secretary, Henry Blaine rose and paced thoughtfully back and forth the length of his spacious office. The problem before him was the most salient in its importance of any which had confronted him during his investigation of the Lawton mystery — probably the weightiest of his entire career. Should he, dared he, throw caution to the winds and step out into the open, in his true colors at last?

It was as if he held within his hands the kernel of the mystery, yet surrounded still by an invulnerable shield of cunning and duplicity with which the master criminals had so carefully safe-guarded their conspiracy. He held it within his hands, and yet he could not break the shell of the mystery and expose the kernel of truth to justice. There seemed to be no interstice, no crevice into which he might insert the keen probe of his marvelous deductive power. And yet his experience told him that there must be some rift, some hiatus in the scheme. If only he could discover that rift, could prove beyond a shadow of a doubt the facts which he had circumstantially established, he would not hesitate to lay his hands upon the culprits, high in power and influence throughout the country as they were, and bring them before any court of so-called justice, however it might be undermined by bribery and corruption.

He had accomplished much, working as a mole works, in the dark. Could he not accomplish more by declaring himself; could he not by one bold stroke lay bare the heart of the mystery?

Seating himself again at his desk, he took the telephone receiver from its hook and called up Anita Lawton at her home — not upon the private wire he had had installed for her, but on the regular house wire.

"Oh, Mr. Blaine, what is it! Have you found him? Have you news for me of Ramon?" Her voice, faint and high-pitched with the hideous suspense of the days just past, came to him tremulous with eagerness and an abiding hope.

"No, Miss Lawton, I am sorry to say that I have not yet found Mr. Hamilton, but I have definite information that he still lives, at least," he returned. "I hope that in a few days, at most, I may bring him to you."

"Thank heaven for that!" she responded fervently. "I have tried so hard to believe, to have faith that he will be restored to me, and yet the hideous doubt will return again and again. These days and nights have been one long, ceaseless torture!"

"You have taken my advice in regard to receiving your visitors?"

"Oh, yes, Mr. Blaine. My three guardians have been unremitting in their attentions, particularly Mr. Rockamore, who calls daily. He has just left me."

"Miss Lawton, I have decided that the time has come for us to declare ourselves openly — not in regard to the mystery of your father's insolvency, but concerning the disappearance of Ramon Hamilton. I want you to call his mother up on the telephone as soon as I ring off, and tell her that you have resolved to retain me, on your account, to find him for you. Should she put forward any objections, over-rule her and refuse to listen. I will be with you in an hour. In the meantime, should anyone call, you may tell them that you have just retained me to investigate the disappearance of your fiancé. Tell that to anyone and everyone; the more publicity we give to that fact the better. The moment has arrived for us to carry war into the enemy's camp, and I know that we shall win! Keep up your courage, Miss Lawton! We're done with maneuvering now. You've borne up bravely, but I believe your period of suspense, in regard to many things, is past. Before this day is done, they will know that we are in this to fight to the finish — and to fight to win!"

CHAPTER XV
CHECKMATE!

Henry Blaine was allowed scant opportunity for reflection, in the hour which intervened between his telephone message to Anita and the time of his appointment with her. Scarcely had he hung up the receiver once more when his secretary announced the arrival of Fifine Déchaussée.

Had not Blaine been already aware of her success with Paddington, as the scene in the park an evening or two previously denoted, he would have been instantly apprised by her manner that something of vital import had occurred. There was an indefinable change, a subtle metamorphosis, which was conveyed even in her appearance. Her delicate, Madonna-like face had lost its wax-like pallor and was flushed with a faint, exquisite rose; the wooden, slightly vacant expression was gone; she walked with a lissome, conscious grace which he had not before observed, and the slow, enigmatic smile with which she greeted him held much that was significant behind it.

"You did not keep your appointment with me yesterday — why, mademoiselle?" asked Blaine, quietly.

"Because it was impossible, m'sieu," she returned. "I could not get away. Madame — the wife of M'sieu Franklin — would not allow me to leave the children. This is the first opportunity I have had to come."

"And what have you to report?" he asked, watching her narrowly.

She shrugged her shoulders.

"Very little, M'sieu Blaine. Yesterday the president of the Street Railways, M'sieu Mallowe, called on the minister, and remained for more than an hour. I could not hear their conversation — they were in the library; but just as M'sieu Mallowe was taking his departure I passed through the hall, and heard him say:

"'You must try to persuade her, Mr. Franklin; you have more influence over her than anyone else, even I. Miss Lawton must really go away for a time. It is the only thing that will save her health, her reason! She can do nothing here to aid in the search for young Hamilton, and the suspense is killing her. Try to get her to take our advice and go away, if only for a few days.'"

"What did Dr. Franklin reply?"

"I did not hear it all. I could not linger in the hall without arousing suspicion. Dr. Franklin agreed that Miss Lawton was ill and should go away, and he said he would try to induce her to go — that M'sieu Mallowe was undoubtedly right, and he was delighted that he took such an interest in Miss Lawton."

She paused, and after a moment Blaine asked:

"And that is all?"

"Yes, m'sieu." The French girl half turned as if to take her departure, but he stayed her by a gesture.

"You have nothing else to report? How about Paddington?" He shot the question at her tersely, his eyes never leaving her face, but she did not flinch.

"M'sieu Paddington?" she repeated demurely. "I have nothing to tell you of him."

"You didn't try, then, to lead him on, as I suggested — to get him to talk about Miss Lawton, or the people who were employing him? You have not seen him?"

"M'sieu Blaine, I could not do that!" she cried, ignoring his last question. "I would do much, anything that I could for Miss Lawton, but she would be the last to ask of me that I should lead a man on to — to make love to me, in order to betray him! I will do anything that is possible to find out for Miss Lawton and for you, m'sieu, all that I can by keeping my ears open in the house of the minister, but as to M'sieu Paddington — I will not play such a rôle with any man, even to please Miss Lawton."

"Yet you have been meeting him in the park." The detective leaned forward in his chair and spoke gently, as if merely reminding the girl of some insignificant fact which she had presumably forgotten, yet there was that in his tone which made her stiffen, and she replied impulsively, with a warning flash of her eyes:

"What do you mean, m'sieu? How do you know? I — I told you I had nothing to report concerning M'sieu Paddington, nothing which could be of service to Miss Lawton, and it is quite true. I — I did meet M'sieu Paddington in the park, but it was simply an accident."

"And was the locket and chain an accident, too? That locket which you are wearing at the present moment, mademoiselle?"

"The locket — " Her hand strayed to her neck and convulsively clasped the bauble of cheap, bright gold hanging there. "What do you know of my locket, M'sieu Blaine?"

"I know that Paddington purchased it for you two or three days ago — that he gave it to you that night in the park, and you allowed him to take you in his arms and kiss you!"

"Stop! How can you know that!" she stormed at him, stepping forward slightly, a deep flush dyeing her face. "He did not tell you! You have had me watched, followed, spied upon! It is intolerable! To think that I should be treated as if I were unworthy of trust. I have been faithful, loyal to Miss Lawton, but this is too much! I have not questioned M'sieu Paddington; I know nothing of his affairs, but I like him, I — I admire him very much, and if I desire to meet him, to receive his attentions, I shall do so. I am not harming Miss Lawton, who has been my *patronne*, my one friend in this strange, big country. M'sieu Paddington does not know that I am working at Dr. Franklin's under your instructions, and I shall never betray to him the confidence Miss Lawton has reposed in me. But I shall do no more; it is finished. That I should be suspected — "

"But you are not, my dear young woman!" interposed Blaine, mildly. "It was not you who was followed, spied upon, as you call it. For Miss Lawton's sake, because she is in trouble, we are interested just now in Paddington's movements, and naturally my operative was not aware that it was to meet you he went to the park."

"*N'importe!*" Fifine exclaimed. The color had receded from her face, and a deathly white pallor had superseded it. She retreated a step or two, and continued defiantly: "This afternoon I resign from the service of Dr. Franklin! I do not believe that M'sieu Paddington is an enemy of Miss Lawton; nothing shall make me believe that he, who is the soul of honor, of chivalry, would harm her, or cause her any trouble, and I do not like this work, this spying and treachery and deceit! That is your profession, m'sieu, not mine; I only consented because Miss Lawton had been kind to me, and I desired to aid her in her trouble, if I could. But that he — that I — should be suspected and watched, and treated like criminals, oh, it is insufferable. To-day, also, I leave the Anita Lawton Club. You shall find some one else to play detective for you — you and Miss Lawton!"

With an indignant swirl of her skirts, she turned and made for the door, in a tempest of rage; but on the threshold his voice stayed her.

"Wait! Miss Lawton has befriended you, and now, because of a man of whom you know nothing, you desert her cause. Is that loyalty, mademoiselle? We shall not ask you to remain at Dr. Franklin's any longer; Miss Lawton does not wish unwilling service from anyone. But for your own sake, go back to the club, and remain there until a position is open to you which is to your liking. You are a young girl in a strange country, as you say, and at least you know the club to be a safe place for you. Do not trust this man Paddington, or anyone else; it is not wise."

"I shall not listen to you!" she cried, her voice rising shrill and high-pitched in her excitement. "You shall not say such things of M'sieu Paddington! He is brave and good, while you — you are a spy, an eavesdropper, a delver into the private affairs of others. I do not know what this trouble may be, which Miss Lawton is in, and I am sorry for her, that she should suffer, but I shall have nothing more to do with the case, nor with you, m'sieu! *Au revoir!*"

"Whew!" breathed Blaine to himself, as the door closed after her with a slam. "What a firebrand! She may not have actually betrayed us to Paddington in so many words, but it isn't necessary to look far for the one who warned him that he was being watched, and put him on his guard, all unknowingly, that the whole scheme in which he is so deeply involved, was in jeopardy. Oh, these women! Let them once lose their heads over a man, and they upset all one's plans!"

Blaine arrived promptly within the hour at the house on Belleair Avenue. Anita Lawton received him as before in the library. He observed with deep concern that she was a mere shadow of her former self. The slenderness which had been one of her girlish charms had become almost emaciation; her eyes were glassily bright, and in the waxen pallor of her cheeks a feverish red spot burned.

She smiled wanly as he pressed her hand, and her pale lips trembled, but no words came.

"My poor child!" the great detective found himself saying from the depths of his fatherly heart. "You are positively ill! This will never do. You are not keeping your promise to me."

"I am trying hard to, Mr. Blaine." Anita motioned toward a chair and sank into another with a little gasp of sheer exhaustion. "You have never failed yet, and you have given me your word that you would bring Ramon back to me. I try to have faith, but with every hour that passes, hope dies within me, and I can feel that my strength, my will to believe, is dying, too. I know that you must be doing your utmost, exerting every effort, and yet I cannot resist the longing to urge you on, to try to express to you the torture of uncertainty and dread which consumes me unceasingly. That my father's fortune is gone means nothing to me now. Only give me back Ramon alive and well, and I shall ask no more!"

"I hope to be able to do that speedily," Blaine returned. "As I told you over the telephone, I have positive proof that he is alive, and a definite clue as to his whereabouts. You must ask me nothing further now — only try to find faith in your heart for just a few days, perhaps hours, longer. You 'phoned to Mrs. Hamilton, as I suggested?"

"Yes. She demurred at first, dreading the notoriety, and not — not appearing to believe in your ability as I do, but I simply refused to listen to her objections. Mr. Carlis called me up shortly afterward, and wanted to know if I would be able to receive him this afternoon, on a matter connected with my finances, but I told him I had retained you to search for Ramon, and was expecting you at any moment. He seemed greatly astonished, and warned me of the — he called it 'useless' — expense. He begged me not to be impatient, to wait until I had time to think the matter over and consult himself and Mr. Mallowe, saying that they were both doing all that could be done to locate Ramon, and Mr. Rockamore was, also, but I told him it was too late, that you were on your way here."

"That was right. I am glad you told him. The fact that you have retained me to search for Mr. Hamilton will appear as a scoop in every evening paper which he controls, now, and the more publicity given to it, the better. You told me over the 'phone that Mr. Rockamore calls upon you every day?"

"Yes. I try to be cordial to him, but for some reason which I can't explain I dislike him more than either of the others. I don't know why he comes so often, for he says very little, only sits and stares at that chair — the chair in which my father died — until I feel that I should like to scream. It seems to exert the same strange, uncanny influence over him as it does over me — that chair. More than once, when he has been announced, I have entered to find him standing close beside it, looking down at it as if my father were seated there once more and he was talking to him, I don't in the least know why, but the thought seems to prey on my mind — perhaps because the chair fascinates me, too, in a queer way that is half repulsion."

"You are morbid, Miss Lawton — you must not allow such fancies to grow, or they will soon take possession of you, in your weakened state, and become an obsession. Tell me, have you heard anything from the club girls we established in your guardian's offices?"

"Oh, yes! I had forgotten completely in my excitement and joy over your news of Ramon, vague though it is, that there was something important which I wanted to tell you. Since Margaret Hefferman's dismissal, all my girls have been sent away from the positions I obtained for them — all except Fifine Déchaussée."

"And she resigned not an hour ago," remarked the detective rather grimly, supplementing the fact, with as many details as he thought necessary.

Anita listened in silence until he had finished.

"Poor girl! Poor Fifine! What a pity that she should fancy herself in love with such a man as you describe this Paddington to be! She must be persuaded to remain in the club, of course; we cannot allow her to leave us now. I feel responsible for her, and especially so since it was indirectly because of me, or while she was in my service, at any rate, that she met this man. If she is all that you say, she could never be happy if she married him."

"There's small chance of that. He has a wife already. She left him years ago, and runs a boarding-house somewhere on Hill Street, I believe," Blaine replied. "I don't fancy he'll add bigamy to the rest of his nefarious acts. But tell me of the other girls. They did not report to me."

"Poor little Agnes Olson was dismissed yesterday. She is a spineless sort of creature, you know, without much self-assurance, or initiative, and I believe she had quite a scene with Mr. Carlis before she left. She was on the switchboard, if you remember, and as well as I was able to understand from her, he caught her listening in on his private connection. She reached the club in an hysterical condition, and I told them to put her to bed and care for her. I ought to be there myself now, at work, for I have lost my best helper, but I am too distraught over Ramon to think of anything else. My secretary — the girl you saw there at the club and asked me about, do you remember? — did not appear yesterday, but telephoned her resignation, saying she was leaving town. I cannot understand it, for I would have counted on her faithfulness before any of the rest, but so many things have happened lately which I can't comprehend, so many mysteries and disappointments and anxieties, that I can scarcely think or feel any more. It seems as if I were really dead, as if my emotions were all used up. I can't cry, even when I think of Ramon — I can only suffer."

"I know. I can imagine what you must be trying to endure just now, Miss Lawton, but please believe that it will not last much longer. And don't worry about your secretary; Emily Brunell will be with you again soon, I think."

"Emily Brunell!" repeated Anita, in surprise. "You know, then?"

"Yes. And, strange as it may seem, she is indirectly concerned in the conspiracy against you, but innocently so. You will understand everything some day. What about the Irish girl, Loretta Murfree?"

"President Mallowe's filing clerk? He dismissed her only this morning, on a trumped-up charge of incompetence. He has been systematically finding fault with her for several days, as if trying to discover a pretext for discharging her, so she wasn't unprepared. She's here now, having some lunch, up in my dressing-room. Would you like to talk with her?"

"I would, indeed," he assented, nodding as Anita pressed the bell. "She seemed the brightest and most wide-awake young woman of the lot. If anyone could have obtained information of value to us, I fancy she could. Did she have anything to say to you about Mr. Mallowe?"

"I would rather she told you herself," Anita replied, hesitatingly, with the ghost of a smile. "Whatever she said about him was strictly personal, and of a distinctly uncomplimentary nature. There is nothing spineless about Loretta!"

When the young Irish girl appeared in response to Anita's summons, her eyes and mouth opened wide in amazement at sight of the detective.

"Oh, sir, it's you!" she exclaimed. "I was going down to your office this afternoon, to tell you that I had been discharged. Mr.

Mallowe himself turned me off this morning. I'm not saying this to excuse myself, but it was honestly through no fault of mine. The old man — gentleman — has been trying for days to get rid of me. I knew it, so I've been especially careful in my work, and cheerful and smiling whenever he appeared on the scene — like this!"

She favored them with a grimace which was more like the impishly derisive grin of a street urchin than a respectful smile, and continued:

"This morning I caught him mixing up the letters in the files with his own hands, and when he blamed me for it later, I saw that it was no use. He was bound to get rid of me in some way or another, so I didn't tell him what I thought of him, but came away peaceably — which is a lot to ask of anybody with a drop of Irish blood in their veins, in a case like that! However, I learned enough while I was in that office, of his manipulations of the street railway stock, to make me glad I've got a profession and am not sitting around waiting for dividends to be paid. If the people ever wake up, and the District Attorney indicts him, I hope to goodness they put me on the stand, that's all."

"Why has he tried to get rid of you? Do you think he suspected the motive for your being in his employ?" asked Blaine, when she paused for breath.

"No, he couldn't, for I never gave him a chance," she responded. "He's a sly one, too, padding around the offices like a cat, in his soft slippers; and he looks for all the world like a cat, with the sleek white whiskers of him! Excuse me, Miss Lawton, I don't mean to be disrespectful, but he's trying, the old gentleman is! I think he got suspicious of me when Margaret Heffernan made such a botch of her job with Mr. Rockamore, and yesterday afternoon when Mr. Carlis caught Agnes Olson listening in — oh, I know all about that, too! — he got desperate. That's why he mixed up the files this morning, for an excuse to discharge me."

"How did you know about Agnes Olson?" asked Blaine quickly. "Did she tell you?"

"No, I heard it from Mr. Carlis himself!" returned Loretta, with a reminiscent grin. "He came right straight around to Mr. Mallowe and told him all about it, and a towering rage he was in, too! 'Do you think the little devil's sold us?' he asked. Meaning no disrespect to you, Miss Lawton, it was you he was talking about, for he added: 'She gets her girls into our offices on a whining plea of charity, and they all turn out crooked, spying and listening in, and taking notes. Remember Rockamore's experience with the one he took? Do you suppose that innocent, big-eyed, mealy-mouthed brat of Pennington Lawton's suspects us?'

"'Hold your tongue, for God's sake!' old Mr. Mallowe growled at him. 'I've got one of them in there, a filing clerk.'"

"'Then you'd better get rid of her before she tries any tricks,' Mr. Carlis said. 'I believe that girl is deeper than she looks, for all her trusting way. I always did think she took the news of her father's bankruptcy too d — n' calmly to be natural, even under the circumstances. Kick her protégée out, Mallowe, unless you're looking for more trouble. I'm not.'"

"What did Mr. Mallowe reply?" Blaine asked.

"I don't know. His private secretary came into the office where I was just then, and I had to pretend to be busy to head off any suspicion from him. Mr. Carlis left soon after, and I could feel his eyes boring into the back of my neck as he passed through the room. Mr. Mallowe sent for me almost immediately, to find an old letter for him, from one of the files of two years ago, and it was funny, the suspicious, worried way he kept watching me!"

"There is nothing else you can tell us?" the detective inquired. "Nothing out of the usual run happened while you were there?"

"Nothing, except that a couple of days ago, he had an awful row with a man who called on him. It was about money matters, I think, and the old gentleman got very much excited. 'Not a cent!' he kept repeating, louder and louder, until he fairly shouted. 'Not one more cent will you get from me. This systematic extortion of yours must come to an end here and now! I've done all I'm going to, and you'd better understand that clearly.' Then the other man, the visitor, got angry, too, and they went at it hammer and tongs. At last, Mr. Mallowe must have lost his head completely, for he accused the other man of robbing his safe. At that, the visitor got calm and cool as a cucumber, all of a sudden, and began to question Mr. Mallowe. It seems from what I heard — I can't recall the exact words — that not very long ago, the night watchman in the offices was chloroformed and the safe ransacked, but nothing was taken except a letter.

"'You're mad!' the strange man said. 'Why in h — l should anybody take a letter, and leave packets of gilt-edged bonds and other securities lying about untouched?'

"'Because the letter happens to be one you would very much like to have in your possession, Paddington,' the old gentleman said. Oh, I forgot to tell you that the visitor's name was Paddington, but that doesn't matter, does it? 'Do you know what it was?' Mr. Mallowe went on. 'It was a certain letter which Pennington Lawton wrote to me from Long Bay two years ago. Now do you understand?'"

"'You fool!' said Paddington. 'You fool, to keep it! You gave your word that you would destroy it! Why didn't you?'

"'Because, I thought it might come in useful some day, just as it has now,' the old gentleman fairly whined. 'It was good circumstantial evidence.'

"'Yes — fine!' Paddington said, with a bitter kind of a laugh. 'Fine evidence, for whoever's got it now!'

"'You know very well who's got it!' cried Mr. Mallowe. 'You don't pull the wool over my eyes! And I don't mean to buy it back from you, either, if that's your game. You can keep it, for all I care; it's served its purpose now, and you won't get another penny from me!'

"Well, I wish you could have heard them, then!" Loretta continued, with gusto. "They carried on terribly; the whole office could hear them. It was as good as a play — the strange man, Paddington denying right up to the last that he knew anything about the robbery, and Mr. Mallowe accusing him, and threatening and bluffing it out for all he was worth! But in the end, he paid the man some money, for I remember he insisted on having the check certified, and the secretary himself took it over to the bank. I don't know for what amount it was drawn."

"Why didn't you tell me that before, Loretta?" asked Anita, reproachfully. "I mean, about the — the names Mr. Carlis called me, and his suspicions. I wish I'd known it half an hour ago, when he telephoned to me!"

"That's just why I didn't tell you, Miss Lawton!" responded Loretta, with a flash of her white teeth.

"Mr. Blaine told me to report to him this afternoon, and I meant to, but he didn't tell me to talk to anyone else, even you. When you asked me to undertake this for you, you said I was to do just what Mr. Blaine directed, and I've tried to. It was on the tip of my tongue to tell you, but I thought I'd better not, at least until I had seen Mr. Blaine. I was sure that if I said anything to you about it, you would let Mr. Carlis see your resentment the next time he called, and then he and Old Mr. Mallowe would get their heads together, and find out that their suspicions of all of us girls were correct. You wouldn't want that."

"Miss Murfree is quite right," Blaine interposed. "You must be very careful, Miss Lawton, not to allow Mr. Carlis to discover that you know anything whatever of that conversation — at least just yet."

"I'll try, but it will be difficult, I am afraid," Anita murmured. "I am not accustomed to — to accepting insults. Ah! if Ramon were only here!"

Wilkes, the butler, appeared at the door just then, with a card, and Anita read it aloud.

"Mr. Mallowe."

"Oh, gracious, let me go, Miss Lawton!" exclaimed Loretta. "I've told you everything that I can think of, and if he sees me, it will spoil Mr. Blaine's plans, maybe?"

"Yes, he must not find you here!" the detective agreed hurriedly. "I'll communicate with you at the club if I need you again, Miss Murfree. You have been of great service to both Miss Lawton and myself."

When they were alone for the moment before the street-railway president appeared, Blaine turned to Anita.

"You will try to be very courageous, and follow whatever lead I give you?" he asked. "This interview may prove trying for you."

Anita had only time to nod before Mr. Mallowe stood before them. He paused for a moment, glanced inquiringly at Blaine and then advanced to Anita with outstretched hand. If he had ever seen the detective before, he gave no sign.

"My dear child!" he murmured, unctuously. "I trust you are feeling a little stronger this afternoon — a little brighter and more hopeful?"

"Very much more hopeful, thank you, Mr. Mallowe," returned the young girl, steadily. "I have enlisted in my cause the greatest of all investigators. Allow me to present Mr. Henry Blaine."

"Mr. Blaine," Mallowe repeated, bowing with supercilious urbanity. "Do I understand that this is the private detective of whom I have heard so much?"

Blaine returned his salutation coolly, but did not speak, and Anita replied for him.

"Yes, Mr. Mallowe, Mr. Blaine is going to find Ramon for me!"

Mallowe shook his head slowly, with a mournful smile.

"Ah! my dear!" he sighed. "I do not want to dampen your hopes, heaven knows, but I very much fear that that will be an impossible task, even for one of Mr. Blaine's unquestioned renown."

"Still, it is always possible to try," the detective returned, looking levelly into Mallowe's eyes. "Personally, I am very sanguine of success."

"Everything is being done that can be of any use now," the other man observed hurriedly. "Do I understand, Mr. Blaine, that Miss Lawton has definitely retained you on this case?"

Blaine nodded, and Mallowe turned to Anita.

"Really, my dear, you should have consulted me, or some other of your father's old friends, before taking such a step!" he expostulated. "It will only bring added notoriety and trouble to you. I do not mean to underestimate Mr. Blaine's marvelous ability, which is recognized everywhere, but even he can scarcely succeed in locating Mr. Hamilton where we, with all the resources at our command, have failed. Mark my words, my dear Anita; if Ramon Hamilton returns, it will be voluntarily, of his own free will. Until — unless he so decides, you will never see him. It is too bad to have summoned Mr. Blaine here on a useless errand, but I am sure he quite understands the situation now."

"I do," responded the detective quietly. "I have accepted the case."

"But surely you will withdraw?" The older man's voice rose cholerically. "Miss Lawton is a mere girl, a minor, in fact — "

"I am over eighteen, Mr. Mallowe," interposed Anita quietly.

"Until your proper guardian is appointed by the courts," Mallowe cried, "you are nominally under my care, mine and others of your father's closest associates. This is a delicate matter to discuss now, Mr. Blaine," he added, in calmer tones, turning to the detective, "but since this seems to be a business interview, we must touch upon the question of finances. I know that the fee you naturally require must be a large one, and I am in duty bound to tell you that Miss Lawton has absolutely no funds at her disposal to reimburse you for your time and trouble. Whatever fortune she may be possessed of, she cannot touch now."

"Miss Lawton has already fully reimbursed me — in advance," returned Henry Blaine calmly. "That question need cause you no further concern, Mr. Mallowe, nor need you have any doubt as to my position in this matter. I'm on this case, and I'm on it to stay! I'm going to find Ramon Hamilton!"

CHAPTER XVI
THE LIBRARY CHAIR

"Paddington's on the run!" Ross, the operative, announced to Henry Blaine the next morning, jubilantly. "He left his rooms about an hour after I got back on the job, and went to Carlis' office. He only stayed a short time, and came out looking as black as a thunder-cloud——I guess the interview, whatever it was, didn't go his way. He went straight from there to Rockamore, the promoter. I pretended an errand with Rockamore, too, and so got into the outer office. The heavy glass door was closed between, and I couldn't hear anything but a muffled growling from within, but they were both angry enough, all right. Once the stenographer went in and came out again almost immediately. When the door opened to admit her, I heard Paddington fairly shout:

"'It's your own skin you're saving, you fool, as well as mine! If I'm caught, you all go! Carlis thinks he can bluff it, and Mallowe's a superannuated, pig-headed old goat. He'll try to stand on his reputation, and cave in like a pricked balloon when the crash comes. I know his kind; I've hounded too many of 'em to the finish. But you're a man of sense, Rockamore, and you know you've got to help me out of this for your own sake. I tell you, some one's on to the whole game, and they're just sitting back and waiting for the right moment to nab us. They not only learn every move we make — they anticipate them! It's every man for himself, now, and I warn you that if I'm cornered in this — '

"'Hold your tongue!' Rockamore ordered. 'Can't you see — '

"Then the door closed, and I couldn't hear any more. The voices calmed down to a rumble, and in about twenty minutes I could hear them approaching the door. I decided I couldn't wait any longer, and got outside just in time to give Paddington a chance to pass me. He seemed in good humor, and I guess he got what he was after — money, probably, for he went to his bank and put through a check. Then he returned to his rooms, and didn't show up again until late afternoon, when he went away up Belleair Avenue, to the rectory of the Church of St. James. He didn't go in — just talked with the sexton in the vestibule, and when he came down the steps he looked dazed, as if he'd received a hard jolt of some sort. He couldn't have been trying to blackmail the minister, too, could he?"

"Hardly, Ross. Go on," Blaine responded. "What did he do next?"

"Nothing. Just went back to his rooms and stayed there. It seemed as if he was afraid to leave — not so much afraid to be found, but as if he might miss something, if he left. He even had his dinner sent in from a restaurant near there. Knowing him, I might have known what it was he was waiting for — he's always chasing after some girl or other."

"There was a woman in it, then?" asked the detective, quietly.

"You can bet there was — very much in it, sir!" the operative chuckled. "She came along while I watched — a tall, slim girl, plainly dressed in dark clothes, but with an air to her that would make you look at her twice, anywhere. She hesitated and looked uncertainly about her, as if she were unfamiliar with the place and a little scary of her errand, but at last she made up her mind, and plunged in the vestibule, as if she was afraid she would lose her courage if she stopped to think.

"For a few minutes her shadow showed on the window-shades, beside Paddington's. They stood close together, and from their gestures, he seemed to be arguing or pleading, while she was drawing back and refusing, or at least, holding out against him. At last they fell into a regular third-act clinch — it was as good as a movie! After a moment she drew herself out of his arms and they moved away from the window. In a minute or two they came out of the house together, and I tailed them. They walked slowly, with their heads very close, and I didn't dare get near enough to try to hear what they were discussing so earnestly. But where do you suppose he took her? To the Anita Lawton Club for Working Girls! He left her at the entrance and went back to his own rooms, and he seemed to be in a queer mood all the way — happy and up in the air one minute, and down in the dumps the next.

"He didn't stir out again last night, but early this morning he went down to the office of the Holland-American line, and purchased two tickets, first-class to Rotterdam, on the *Brunnhilde*, sailing next Saturday, so I think we have the straight dope on him now. He means to skip with the girl."

"Saturday — two days off!" mused Blaine. "I think it's safe to give him his head until then, but keep a close watch on him, Ross. The purchase of those tickets may have been just a subterfuge on his part to throw any possible shadow off the trail. Did you ascertain what name he took them under?"

"J. Padelford and wife."

"Clever of him, that!" Blaine commented. "If he really intends to fool this girl with a fake marriage and sail with her for the other side, he can explain the change of names on the steamer to her by telling her it was a mistake on the printed sailing-list. Once at sea, without a chance of escape from him, he can tell her the truth, or as much of it as he cares to, and she'll have to stick; that type of woman always does. She might even come in time to take up his line, and become a cleverer crook than he is, but we're not going to let that happen. We'll stop him, right enough, before he goes too far with her. What's he doing now?"

"Walking in the park with her. She met him at the gates, and Vanner took the job there of tailing them, while I came on down to report to you."

"Good work, Ross. But go back and take up the trail now yourself, if you're fit. And here, you'd better take this warrant with you; I swore it out against him several days ago, in case he attempted to bolt. If he tries to get the girl into a compromising situation, arrest him. Let me know if anything of importance occurs meanwhile."

As Ross went out, the secretary, Marsh, appeared.

"There's an elderly gentleman outside waiting to see you, sir," he announced. "He does not wish to give his name, but says that he is a physician, and is here in answer to a letter which he received from you."

"Good! They pulled it off, then! We were only just in time with those letters we sent out yesterday, Marsh. Show him in at once."

In a few moments a tall, spare figure appeared in the doorway, and paused an instant before entering. He had a keen, smooth-shaven, ascetic face, topped with a mass of snow-white hair.

"Come in, Doctor," invited the detective. "I am Henry Blaine. It was good of you to come in response to my letter. I take it that you have something interesting to tell me."

The doctor entered and seated himself in the chair indicated by Blaine. He carried with him a worn, old-fashioned black leather instrument case.

"I do not know whether what I have to tell you will prove to have any connection with the matter you referred to in your letter or not, Mr. Blaine. Indeed, I hesitated about divulging my experience of last night to you. The ethics of my profession — "

"My profession has ethics, too, Doctor, although you may not have conceived it," the detective reminded him, quietly. "Even more than doctor or priest, a professional investigator must preserve inviolate the secrets which are imparted to him, whether they take the form of a light under a bushel or a skeleton in a closet. In the cause of justice, only, may he open his lips. I hold safely locked away in my mind the keys to mysteries which, were they laid bare, would disrupt society, drag great statesmen from their pedestals, provoke international complications, even bring on wars. If you know anything pertaining to the matter of which I wrote you, justice and the ethics of your profession require you to speak."

"I agree with you, sir. As I said, I am not certain that my adventure — for it was quite an adventure for a retired man like myself, I assure you — has anything to do with the case you are investigating, but we can soon establish that. Do you recognize the subject of this photograph?"

The doctor drew from his pocket a small square bit of cardboard, and Blaine took it eagerly from him. One glance at it was sufficient, and it was with difficulty that the detective restrained the exclamation of triumph which rose to his lips. Upon the card was mounted a tiny, thumbnail photograph of a face — the face of Ramon Hamilton! It was more like a death-mask than a living countenance, with its rigid features and closed eyes, but the likeness was indisputable.

"I recognize it, indeed, Doctor. That is the man for whom I am searching. How did it come into your possession?"

"I took it myself, last night." The spare figure of the elderly physician straightened proudly in his chair. "When your communication arrived, I did not attach much importance to it because it did not occur to me for a moment that I should have been selected, from among all the physicians and surgeons of this city, for such a case. When the summons came, however, I remembered your warning — but I anticipate. Since my patient of last night is your subject, I may as well tell you my experiences from the beginning. My name is Alwyn — Doctor Horatius Alwyn — and I live at Number Twenty-six Maple Avenue. Until my retirement seven years ago I was a regular practising physician and surgeon, but since my break-down — I suffered a slight stroke — I have devoted myself to my books and my camera — always a hobby with me.

"Well — late last night, the front door-bell rang. It was a little after eleven, and my wife and the maid had retired, but I was developing some plates in the dark-room, and opened the door myself. Three men stood there, but I could see scarcely anything of their faces, for the collars of their shaggy motor coats were turned up, their caps pulled low over their eyes, and all three wore goggles.

"'Doctor Alwyn?' asked one of the men, the burliest of the three, advancing into the hall. 'I want you to come out into the country with me on a hurry call. It's a matter of life and death, and there's five thousand dollars in it for you, but the conditions attached to it are somewhat unusual. May we come into your office, and talk it over?'

"I led the way, and listened to their proposition. Briefly, it was this: a young man had fallen and injured his head, and was lying unconscious in a sanitarium in the suburbs. There were reasons which could not be explained to me, why the utmost secrecy must be maintained, not only concerning the young man's identity, but the location of the retreat where he was in seclusion. They feared that he had suffered a concussion of the brain, possibly a fractured skull, and my diagnosis was required. Also, should I deem an operation necessary, I must be prepared to perform it at once. They would take me to the patient in the car, but when we reached our destination, I was to be blindfolded, and led to the sickroom, where the bandage would be removed from my eyes. I was to return in the same manner. For this service, and of course my secrecy, they offered me five thousand dollars.

"Although that would not have been an exorbitant sum for me to obtain for such an operation in the days of my activities, it looked very large to me now, especially since some South American securities in which I invested had declined, but I did not feel that it would be compatible with my dignity and standing to accept the conditions which were imposed. I was, therefore, upon the point of indignantly declining, when I suddenly remembered your letter, and resolved to see the affair through.

"It occurred to me, while I was selecting the instruments to take with me, that it would not be a bad idea to take also my latest camera, and if possible obtain a photograph of the patient to show you. I managed to slip it into my vest pocket, unobserved by my visitors. Here it is."

Dr. Alwyn took the instrument case upon his knee and opening it, produced what looked like a large old-fashioned nickel-plated watch of the turnip variety. The doctor extended it almost apologetically.

"You see," he observed, "it is really more a toy than a real camera, although it served admirably last night. I have had a great deal of amusement with it, pretending to feel people's pulses, but in reality snapping their photographs. It takes very small, imperfect pictures, of course, as you can see from the print there on your desk, and only one to each loading, but it can be carried in the palm of one's hand, and it uses a peculiarly sensitive plate that will register a snap-shot even by electric light. It had fortunately just been reloaded before the advent of my mysterious visitors, and I resolved to make use of it if an opportunity offered.

"The curtains were tightly drawn in the car, and as the interior lights had been extinguished, we sat in total darkness. I could not, of course, tell in what direction we were going, although the car had been pointed south when we left my door. We appeared to be travelling at a terrific rate of speed and swung around a confusing number of curves.

"I tried at first to remember the turns, and their direction, but there were so many that I very soon lost count. I think they took me in a round-about way purposely, to confuse me. I have no idea how long we drove, but it must have been well over two hours. At last we struck a long up-grade, and one of my companions announced that we were almost there.

"They bound my eyes with a dark silk handkerchief, and a moment later the car swerved and turned abruptly in, evidently at a gateway, for we curved about up a graveled driveway — I could hear it crunching beneath the wheels — and came to a grinding stop before the door. They helped me out of the car, up some shallow stone steps and across the threshold.

"I was led down a thickly carpeted hall and up a single long flight of stairs, to a door just at its head. We entered; the door closed softly behind us; and the bandage was whipped from my eyes. There was only a low night-light burning in the room, but I made out the outlines of the furniture. There was a great bed over in the corner, with a motionless figure lying upon it.

"'There's your patient, Doc; go ahead,' my burly friend said, and accordingly I approached the bed, asking at the same time for more light. The young man was unconscious, and in answer to a question of mine the attendant who had sat at the head of the bed as we entered informed me that he had been in a complete state of coma since he had been brought there, several days before.

"I remembered the description in your letter of the subject for whom you were searching, and I fancied, in spite of the bandages which swathed his head, that I recognized him in the young man before me. The lights flashed on full in answer to my request, and on a sudden decision I drew the watch camera from my pocket, took the patient's wrist between my thumb and finger as if to ascertain his pulse, and snapped his picture. The result was a fortunate chance, for I did not dare focus deliberately, with the eyes of the attendant and the three men who had accompanied me, all directed at my movements.

"Then I gave the patient a thorough examination. I found a fracture at the base of the brain — not necessarily fatal, unless cerebral meningitis sets in, but quite serious enough. He was still bleeding a little from the nose and ears. I washed them out, and packed the ears with sterile gauze, leaving instructions that a specially prepared ice cap be placed at once upon his head and kept there. That was all which could be done at that time, but the patient should have constant, watchful attention. He must either have suffered a severe backward fall, or received a violent blow at the base of the skull, to have sustained such an injury.

"When I had finished, they blindfolded me again, led me from the room, and conveyed me home in the same manner in which I had come, with the possible exception that the car in returning seemed to take a different and more direct route; the journey appeared to be a much shorter one, with fewer twists and turns. The same three men came back to the house with me, and entered my office, where the burly one turned over to me ten five-hundred-dollar bills. They left almost immediately, and although it was close on to dawn, I went into my dark room, and developed the negative of the thumbnail photograph I had taken.

"The events of the night had been so extraordinary that when I did retire, it was long before I could sleep. In the morning, I made a couple of prints from the negative, then took the five thousand dollars down and deposited it to my account in the bank."

"When I decided to come here, I ran over in my mind every moment of the previous night's adventure, to catalogue my impressions. The habit of years has made me methodical in all things, and I jotted them down in the order in which they occurred to me, that I might not forget to relate them to you. Memory plays one sad tricks, sometimes, when one reaches my age. These notes may be of no assistance to you, sir, but they are entirely at your service."

"I am eager to hear them, Doctor. I only wish all witnesses were like you — my tasks would be lightened by half," Blaine said, heartily.

The elderly physician drew from his pocket a paper, at which he peered, painstakingly.

"I have numbered them. Let me see — oh, yes. First, the burly man walks with a slight limp in the right leg. Second, of the two men with him, all I could note was that one spoke with a decided French accent and had a hollow cough, tuberculous, I think; the other, who scarcely uttered a word, was short and stocky, and of enormous strength. He fairly lifted me into and out of the car when I was blindfolded at the entrance of the place they called a sanitarium. Third, the car had a peculiar horn; I have never heard one like it before. Its blast was sharp and wailing, not like a siren, but more like the howl of a wounded animal. I would know it again, anywhere. Fourth, there is a railroad bridge very near the house to which I was taken — I distinctly heard two trains thunder over the trestles while I was attending my patient. Fifth, I should judge the place to be more of a retreat for alcoholics or the insane, than for those suffering from accident, or any form of physical injury. A patient in some remote part of the house was undoubtedly a maniac or in the throes of an attack of delirium tremens. I heard his cries at intervals as I worked, until he quieted down finally.

"Sixth, the bedroom where my patient is lying is on the second floor, the windows facing south and east; there was a moon last night, and one of the curtains was partly raised. His door is just at the head of the stairs on your right as you go up, and the stairs are on a straight line with the front door — therefore the house faces south. Seventh, when we returned to my home, and were in my office, the burly man had to pull the glove off his right hand to get the wallet from his pocket in order to pay me my fee, and I saw that two fingers were missing — they had both been amputated at the middle joint. Also, when they were leaving, I heard the man who spoke with an accent address him as 'Mac.'"

"Mac! It's three-fingered Mac Alarney, by the Lord!" Blaine started from his chair. "Why did I not think of him before! Doctor, you have rendered to me and to my client an invaluable service, which shall not be forgotten. Mac Alarney is a retired prize-fighter, in close touch with all the political crooks and grafters in the city. He runs a sort of retreat for alcoholics up near Green Valley, and bears a generally shady reputation. Are you game to go back with me to-night for another call on your patient? You will be well guarded and in no possible danger, now or for the future. I give you my word for that. I may need you to verify some facts."

The doctor hesitated visibly.

"I am not afraid," he replied, at last, "but I scarcely feel that it is conformable with the ethics of my calling. I was called in, in my professional capacity — "

"My dear Doctor," the detective interrupted him with a trace of impatience in his tones, "your patient is one of the most widely known young men of this city. He was kidnaped, and the police have been searching for him for days. The press of the entire country has rung with the story of his mysterious disappearance. He is Ramon Hamilton."

"Good heavens! Can it be possible!" the physician exclaimed. "I assure you, sir, I had no idea of his identity. He was to have married Pennington Lawton's daughter, was he not? I have read of his disappearance, of course; the newspapers have been full of it. And he was kidnaped, you say? No wonder those ruffians maintained such secrecy in regard to their destination last night! Mr. Blaine, I will accompany you, sir, and give you any aid in my power, in rescuing Mr. Hamilton!"

"Good! I'll make all the necessary arrangements and call for you to-night at eight o'clock. Meanwhile, keep a strict guard upon your tongue, and say nothing to anyone of what has occurred. Have you told your wife of your adventure?"

"No, Mr. Blaine; I merely told her I was out on a sudden night call. I decided to wait until I had seen you before mentioning the extraordinary features of the case."

"You are a man of discretion, Doctor! Until eight o'clock, then. You may expect me, without fail."

Doctor Alwyn left, and Blaine spent a busy half-hour making his arrangements for the night's raid. Scarcely had he completed them when the telephone shrilled. The detective did not at first recognize the voice which came to him over the wire, so changed was it, so fraught with horror and a menace of tragedy.

"It is you, Miss Lawton?" he asked, half unbelievingly. "What is the matter? What has happened?"

"I must see you at once, *at once*, Mr. Blaine! I have made a discovery so unexpected, so terrible, that I am afraid to be alone; I am afraid of my own thoughts. Please, please come immediately!"

"I will be with you as soon as my car can reach your door," he replied.

What could the young girl have discovered, shut up there in that great lonely house? What new developments could have arisen, in the case which until this moment had seemed plain to him to the end?

He found her awaiting him in the hall, with ashen face and trembling limbs. She clutched his hand with her small icy one, and whispered:

"Come into the library, Mr. Blaine. I have something to tell you — to show you!"

He followed her into the huge, somber, silent room where only a few short weeks ago her father had met with his death. Coming from the brilliant sunshine without, it was a moment or two before his eyes could penetrate the gloom. When they did so, he saw the great leather chair by the hearth, which had played so important a part in the tragedy, had been overturned.

"Mr. Blaine," — the girl faced him, her voice steadied and deepened portentously, — "my father died of heart-disease, did he not?"

The detective felt a sudden thrill, almost of premonition, at her unexpected question, but he controlled himself, and replied quietly:

"That was the diagnosis of the physician, and the coroner's findings corroborated him."

"Did it ever occur to you that there might be another and more terrible explanation of his sudden death?"

"A detective must consider and analyze a case from every standpoint, you know, Miss Lawton," he answered. "It did occur to me that perhaps your father met with foul play, but I put the theory from me for lack of evidence."

"Mr. Blaine, my father was murdered!"

"Murdered! How do you know? What have you discovered?"

"He was given poison! I have found the bottle which contained it, hidden deep in the folds of his chair there. It was no morbid fancy of mine after all; my instinct was right! No wonder that chair has exerted such a horrible fascination for me ever since my poor father died in it. See!"

With indescribable loathing, she extended her left hand, which until now she had held clenched behind her. Upon the palm lay a tiny flat vial, with a pale, amber-colored substance dried in the bottom of it. Blaine took it and drew the cork. Before he had time to place it at his nostrils, a faint but unmistakable odor of bitter almonds floated out upon the air and pervaded the room.

"Prussic acid!" he exclaimed. "It has the same outward effect as an attack of heart-disease would produce, to a superficial examination. Miss Lawton, how did you discover this?"

"By the merest accident. I have a habit of creeping in here, when I am more deeply despondent than usual, and sitting for a while in my father's chair. It calms and comforts me, almost as if he were with me once more. I was sitting there just before I telephoned you, thinking over all that had occurred in these last weeks, when I broke down and cried. I felt for my handkerchief, but could not find it, and thinking that I might perhaps have dropped it in the chair, I ran my hand down deep in the leather fold between the seat and the side and back. My fingers encountered something flat and hard which had been jammed away down inside, and I dug it out. It was this bottle! Mr. Blaine, does it mean that my father was murdered by that man whose voice I heard — that man who came to him in the night and threatened him?"

"I'm afraid it does, Miss Lawton." Henry Blaine said slowly. "When you hear that voice again and recognize it, we shall be able to lay our hands upon the murderer of your father."

CHAPTER XVII
THE RESCUE

Precisely at the hour of eight that night, a huge six-cylinder limousine drew up at the gate of Number Twenty-six Maple Avenue. Half-way down the block, well in the shadow of the trees which gave to the avenue its name, two more cars and a motor ambulance had halted.

Doctor Alwyn, who had been excitedly awaiting the arrival of the detective, was out of his door and down the path almost before the car had pulled up at his gate. Within it were three men — Blaine himself and two others whom the Doctor did not know. Henry Blaine greeted him, introduced his operatives, Ross and Suraci, and they started swiftly upon their journey.

The doctor was plainly nervous, but something in the grim, silent, determined air of his companions imparted itself to him. The lights in the interior of the car had not been turned on, nor the shades lowered, and after a few tentative remarks which were not encouraged, Doctor Alwyn turned to the window and watched the brightly lighted cross streets dart by with ever-increasing speed. Once he glanced back, and started, casting a perturbed glance at the immovable face of the detective, as he remarked:

"Mr. Blaine, are you aware that we are being followed?"

"Oh, yes. Give yourself no uneasiness on that score, Doctor. They are two of my machines, filled with my men, and a Walton ambulance for Mr. Hamilton. We will reach Mac Alarney's retreat in an hour, now. There will be a show of trouble, of course, and we may have to use force, but I do not anticipate any very strenuous opposition to our removal of your patient, when Mac is convinced that the game is up. No harm will come to you, at any rate; you will be well guarded."

The Doctor drew himself up with simple dignity, quite free from bombast or arrogance.

"I am not afraid," he replied, quietly. "I am armed, and am

fully prepared to help protect my patient."

"Armed?" the detective asked, sharply.

For answer, Doctor Alwyn drew from his capacious coat pocket a huge, old-fashioned pistol, and held it out to Blaine. The latter took it from him without ceremony.

"A grave mistake, Doctor. I am glad you told me, in time. Fire-arms are unnecessary for your own protection, and would be a positive menace to our plans for getting your patient safely away. Gun-play is the last thing we must think of; my men will attend to all that, if it comes to a show-down."

The Doctor watched him in silence as he slipped the pistol under one of the side seats. If his confidence in the great man beside him faltered for the moment, he gave no sign, but turned his attention again to the window. They were now rapidly traversing the suburbs, where the houses were widely separated by stretches of vacant lots, and the streets deserted and but dimly lighted. Soon they rattled over a narrow railroad bridge, and Doctor Alwyn exclaimed:

"By George! This is the way we went last night! With all my careful thought, I forgot about that bridge until this moment!"

Minutes passed, long minutes which seemed like hours to the overstrained nerves of the Doctor, while they speeded through the open country.

All at once, from just behind them came a hideous, wailing cry, which swelled in volume to a screech and ended abruptly.

Doctor Alwyn grasped Blaine's arm.

"The motor-horn!" he gasped. "The car I was in last night!"

The detective nodded shortly, without speaking, and leaning forward, stared fixedly out of the window. A long, low-bodied limousine appeared, creeping slowly up, inch by inch, until it was fairly abreast of them. The curtain at the window was lowered, and the chauffeur sat immovable, with his face turned from them, as the two cars whirled side by side along the hard, glistening road. Blaine leaned forward, and pressed the electric bell rapidly twice, and there began a curious game. The other car put on extra speed and darted ahead — their own shot forward and kept abreast of it. It slowed suddenly, and made as if to swerve in behind; Blaine's driver slowed also, until both cars almost came to a grinding halt. Three times these maneuvers were repeated, and then there occurred what the detective had evidently anticipated.

The curtain in the other car shot up; the window descended with a bang and a huge, burly figure leaned half-way out. Henry Blaine noiselessly lowered their own window, and suddenly flashed an electric pocket light full in the heavy-jowled face, empurpled with inarticulate rage.

"Is that your man?" he asked, quickly.

"The one with the three fingers! Yes! That's the man!" whispered the Doctor, hoarsely.

"That's Mac Alarney." Blaine pressed the electric bell again, and their own car lunged forward in a spurt of speed which left the other hopelessly behind, although it was manifestly making desperate efforts to overtake and pass them.

"Do you suppose he suspected our errand?" the Doctor asked.

"Suspected? Lord bless you, man, he knows! He had already passed the two open cars full of my men, and the ambulance. He'd give ten years of his life to beat us out and reach his place ahead of us to-night, but he hasn't a chance in the world unless we blow out a tire, and if we do we'll all go back in the ambulance together, what's left of us!"

Even as he spoke, there came a swift change in the even drone of their engine, — a jarring, discordant note, slight but unmistakable, and a series of irregular thudding knocks.

"One of the cylinder's missing, sir." Ross turned to the detective, and spoke with eager anxiety.

"We'll make it on five." The quiet confidence in Blaine's voice, with its underlying note of grim, indomitable determination, seemed to communicate itself to the other men, and no further word was said, although they all heard the thunder of the approaching car behind.

The Doctor restrained with difficulty the impulse to look backward, and instead kept his eyes sternly fixed upon the trees and hedge-rows flying past, more sharply defined shadows in the lesser dark.

Then, all at once, the shriek of a locomotive burst upon his ears, and the roar and rattle of a train going over a trestle.

"The railroad bridge!" he cried, excitedly. "We're there, Mr. Blaine!"

The noise of the passing train had scarcely died away, when from just behind them the hideous shriek of Mac Alarney's motor-horn rose blastingly three times upon the night air, the last fainter than the others, as if the pursuing car had dropped back.

"He's beaten! He couldn't keep up the pace, much less better it," Blaine remarked. "Those three blasts sounded a warning to the guards of the retreat. It was probably a signal agreed upon in case of danger. We're in for it now!"

They swerved abruptly, between two high stone gateposts, and up a broad sweep of graveled driveway. Lights gleamed suddenly in the windows of the hitherto darkened house, which loomed up gaunt and squarely defined against the sullen sky.

"Your men, in the other cars — " Doctor Alwyn stammered, as they came to a crunching stop before the door. "Will they arrive in time to be of service? Mac Alarney will reach here first — "

"My men will be at his heels," returned Blaine, shortly. "They held back purposely, acting under my instructions. Come on now."

He sprang from the car and up the steps, and the Doctor found himself following, with Ross and Suraci on either side. The driver turned their car around and ran it upon the lawn, its searchlight trained on the circling drive, its engine throbbing like the throat of an impatient horse.

In response to the detective's vigorous ring, the door was opened by a short, stocky man, at sight of whom the Doctor gave a start of surprise, but did not falter. The man was clad in the white coat of a hospital attendant, beneath which the great, bunchy muscles of his shoulders and upper arms were plainly visible.

"Hello, Al!" exclaimed Blaine, briskly.

The veins on the thick bull neck seemed to swell, but there was no sign of recognition in the stolid jaw. Only the lower lip protruded as the man set his jaw, and the little, close-set, porcine eyes narrowed.

"You were a rubber at the Hoffmeister Baths the last time I saw you," went on the detective, smoothly, as he deftly inserted his foot between the door and jamb. "You remember me, of course. I'm Henry Blaine. My friends and I have come here tonight on a confidential errand, and I'd like a word in private with you."

The man he called "Al" muttered something which sounded like a disclaimer. Then he caught sight of the Doctor's face over Blaine's shoulder, and a spasm of black rage seized him.

"Oh, it's you, is it? You've snitched, d — n you! I'll do for you, for this!"

He lunged forward, but Blaine, with a strength of which the Doctor would not a moment before have thought him possessed, grasped the ex-rubber and flung him backward, advancing into the hall at the same time, while his two operatives and the Doctor crowded in behind him.

"Al" staggered, regained his balance, and came on in a blind rush, bull neck lowered, long, monkey-like arms taut and rigid for the first blow. Blaine set himself to meet it, but it was never delivered. At that instant the whirring roar of a high-powered car, unmuffled, sounded in all their ears, and a second machine drew up at the steps.

Its single passenger flung himself out and bounded up to the door.

"What in h - - l does this mean?" he bellowed. "Didn't you hear my horn?"

He stopped abruptly in sheer amazement, for Blaine had turned, with beaming face and outstretched hand.

"Mac Alarney!" he exclaimed. "Thank the Lord you've come! This thick-skulled boob wouldn't give me time for a word, and every minute is precious! Come where I can talk to you, quick!"

Then, as if catching sight of the car in which Mac Alarney had come, for the first time his eyes widened and he seemed struggling to suppress an outburst of mirth.

"Great guns! Is that *your* car, yours? Do you mean to tell me it was you I was playing with, back there on the road? When I flashed the light in your face I was sure you were Donnelley!"

As he uttered the name of the Chief of Police, Mac Alarney involuntarily stepped backward, and a wave of startled apprehension swept the amazement from his face, to be succeeded in turn by the primitive craftiness of the brute instinct on guard.

"And what may you be wanting here, Mr. Blaine?" he demanded, warily.

"To beat the police to it!" Blaine replied in a gruff whisper, adding as he jerked his thumb in the direction of the waiting Al. "Get rid of him! We haven't got a minute, I tell you!"

"The police!" repeated the other man, sharply. "Sure, I passed two cars full of plain-clothes bulls, with an ambulance trailing them! — You can go now, Al."

Without giving the burly proprietor of the retreat time to discover him for himself, Blaine pulled the astonished Doctor forward.

"Here's Doctor Alwyn, whom you brought here last night. The police trailed you, and got his number, but fortunately when they began to question him, he smelled a rat in the whole business and came to me. They told him a man named Paddington had double-crossed you, but of course I knew that was all rot, the minute I'd doped it out. You've got a fortune under your roof this minute, and you don't know it, Mac! That's the best joke of all! You're entertaining an angel unawares!"

"Say, what're you gettin' at, Mr. Blaine?" Mac Alarney's brows drew close together, and he stared levelly from beneath them at the detective's exultant face.

"That young man with the fractured skull in the corner room upstairs — the one you brought Doctor Alwyn to attend last night — when you know who he is you're going up in the air! I don't know who brought him here, or what flim-flam line of talk they gave you, but it's a wonder you haven't guessed from the start who he was, with the papers full of it for days! Of course they must have given you a lot of money to get him well, and hush it all up, when you were able to pay the Doctor, here, five thousand dollars, but whatever they paid, it's a drop in the bucket compared to the reward they expected to get. Mac, it's Ramon Hamilton you've got upstairs!"

Blaine stepped back himself, as if the better to observe the effect of what he manifestly seemed to believe would be astounding news, and clumsily and cautiously the other tried to play up to his lead.

"Ramon Hamilton!" he echoed. "You're crazy, Blaine! You don't know what you're talking about!"

"You'd better believe I do! See this photograph?" He held the tiny thumbnail picture before Mac Alarney's amazed eyes. "The Doctor took it last night, at the bedside of the young man upstairs, when you thought he was feeling his pulse. That watch of his was in reality a camera."

With a roar, the burly man turned upon the erect, unshrinking figure of the gray-haired doctor, but Blaine halted him.

"Not so fast, Mac. If it hadn't been for him, you'd be in the hands of the police now, remember, and they've only been waiting to get something on you, as you know. You can't blame Doctor Alwyn for being suspicious, after all the mysterious fuss you made bringing him here. I know Ramon Hamilton well, and I recognized his face the instant it was handed to me! I'm on the case, myself — Miss Lawton, the girl he's going to marry, engaged me. I might have come and tried to take him away from you, so as to cop all the reward myself, but as it is, we'll split fifty-fifty — unless the police get here while we're wasting time talking! Man, don't you see how you've been done?"

"You can bet your life I do — that is, if the young man I've got upstairs is the guy you think he is," he added, in an afterthought of cautious self-protection. The acid of the hint that Paddington had betrayed him to the police had burned deep, however, as Blaine had anticipated, and he walked blindly into the snare laid for him. "I'll tell you all about how he come to be here, later, and I'll fix them that tried to pull the wool over my eyes! Now, for the love of Heaven, Mr. Blaine, tell me what to do with him before the bulls come! Thank God, they can search the rest of the place, and welcome — I've got nothin' here but a half-dozen souses, and two light-weights, training."

"That's all right! You're safe if we can get him away without loss of time. That ambulance you saw don't belong to the police; it's mine. I saw them first, away back in the outskirts of the city, and I ordered it to drop behind and take the short cut up through Wheelbarrow Lane. It's waiting now under the clump of elms by the brook, up the road a little — you know the spot! Bring him down and we'll take him there in my car. You come too, of course, and Al, and help load him into the ambulance. Then Al can come back, if you don't want to trust him, and you go on with us, back to the city."

"Where you goin' to take him?" asked Mac Alarney, warily. "You can't hide him from them in town."

"Who's talking about hiding him!" Blaine demanded, with contemptuous impatience. "Your brain must be taking a rest cure, Mac! We'll go straight to Miss Lawton, deliver the goods and get the reward, before they beat us to it! It'll be easy to explain matters to her; she won't care much about the story as long as she's got him again alive, and at that you've only got to stick to the truth, and I'm right there to back you up in it. Any fool could realize that you'd have produced him and claimed the reward, if you had known who he actually was. Whoever brought him here gave you the wrong dope and you fell for it, that's all — For the Lord's sake, hurry!"

"You're right, Mr. Blaine. It's the only thing to do now. I fell for their dope, all right, but they'll fall harder before I'm through with them! Lend me your two men, here. There's no use having any of mine except Al get wise. You and the Doctor wait in the car, and we'll bring him out."

Henry Blaine motioned to his operatives, with a curt wave of his hand, to follow Mac Alarney, and turning, he went out of the door and down the steps to his car, with the Doctor at his heels.

"You don't suppose that he saw through your story, do you, Mr. Blaine?" the latter queried in an anxious whisper, as they settled themselves to wait with what patience they could muster. "Could that suggestion of his have been merely a ruse to separate your assistants from you?"

The detective smiled.

"Hardly, Doctor. It's part of my profession to have made a study of human nature, and Mac Alarney's type is an open book to me. Added to that, I've known the man himself for years, in an offhand way. I've got his confidence, and now that he realizes he is in a hole, he's a child in my hands, even if he thinks for the moment that as a detective I'm about the poorest specimen in captivity. Steady now, here they come!"

The large double doors had been thrown wide open and Mac Alarney, the burly Al, and the two operatives appeared, bearing between them a limp, unconscious, blanket-swathed form. As they eased it into the back seat of the limousine, Blaine flashed his electric pocket light upon the sleeping face.

"I knew I wasn't mistaken!" he whispered exultantly to Mac Alarney and the Doctor. "It's young Hamilton, all right. Now, let's be off!"

The others crowded in, and they whirled down the drive and out once more upon the wide State road, in the opposite direction to that in which they had come. A bare half-mile away, and they came abruptly upon the ambulance, screened by the clump of naked elms at the side of the road.

"You get in first, Doctor," ordered Blaine, significantly. "You've got to look after your patient now."

As the Doctor obeyed, Mac Alarney, with a shrewd gleam in his eyes, turned to the detective.

"I think I'd better ride with him, too, Mr. Blaine," he observed. "You don't know who you can trust these days. Your ambulance driver may give you the slip."

"All right, Mac!" Blaine assented, with bluff heartiness. "We'll both ride with him! Did you think I'd try to double-cross you, too? I can't blame you, after the rotten deal that's been handed to you, but we won't waste time arguing. Here's the stretcher. Come on, shove him in!"

The Doctor had been wondering when the dénouement of this adventure would be. Now it came without warning, with a startling suddenness which left him dazed and agape.

The inert body of his patient was laid carefully beside him, and he glanced out of the ambulance door in time to see Mac Alarney dismiss his burly assistant, and turn to enter the vehicle. His foot was already upon the lowest step, when the Doctor saw Blaine raise his hand to his lips. A short, sharp blast of a whistle pierced the air, and in an instant a dozen men had sprung out of the darkness and leaped upon the two surprised miscreants. Then ensued a struggle, brief but awful to the onlooker in its silent, grim ferocity, as the two separate knots of men battled each about their central orbit. The scuffle of many feet on the hard-packed road, the mutter of curses, the dull thud of blows, the hoarse, strangulated breathing of men fighting against odds to the last ounce of their strength, came to the Doctor's startled ears in a confused babel of half-suppressed sound, with the purring drone of the two engines as an undertone.

A minute, and it was all over. The thick-set Al went down like a felled ox, and Mac Alarney wavered under an avalanche of blows and crumpled to his knees. Handcuffed and securely bound, the two were bundled into Blaine's waiting car.

"Paddington never double-crossed me!" groaned Mac Alarney, before the door closed upon him. "But you did, Blaine! Just as I meant to get him, I'll get you! I fell for your d — d scheme, and since you've got the goods on me, I suppose I'll go up, but God help you when I come out! I can wait — it'll be the better when it comes!"

"But the others — " queried the Doctor, as he and Blaine, with the injured man between them, settled down in the ambulance for the slow, careful journey back to the city. "That third man who came for me last night — the one with the French accent and the cough — and the rest who are in this kidnaping plot? Will you get them, too?"

"Ross and Suraci are enough to guard Mac Alarney and Al on their way to the lock-up," the detective responded quietly. "The others will go on up to the sanitarium and clean the place out. They'll get French Louis, all right. And as for the rest who are concerned in this, Doctor Alwyn, be sure that I intend to see that they get their just deserts."

"And it is said that you have never lost a case!" the Doctor remarked.

"I shall not lose this one." Blaine spoke with quiet confidence, unmixed with any boastfulness. "I cannot lose; there is too much at stake."

Late that night, Anita Lawton was awakened from a tortured, feverish dream by the violent ringing of the telephone bell at her bedside. The voice of Henry Blaine, fraught with a latent tension of suppressed elation, came to her over the wire.

"Miss Lawton, I shall come to you in twenty minutes. Please be prepared to go out with me in my car. No, don't ask me any questions now. I will explain when I reach you."

His arrival found her dressed and restlessly pacing the floor of the reception-room, in a fever of mingled hope and anxiety.

"What is it, Mr. Blaine?" she cried, seizing his hand and pressing it convulsively in both of hers. "You have news for me! I can read it in your face! Ramon — "

"Is safe!" he responded. "Can you bear a sudden shock now, Miss Lawton? After all that has gone before, can you withstand one more blow?"

"Oh, tell me! Tell me quickly! I can endure everything, if only Ramon is safe!"

"I found him to-night, and brought him back to the city. I have come to take you to him."

"But why — why did he not come with you? Does he not realize what I have suffered — that every moment of suspense, of waiting for him, is an added torture?"

"He realizes nothing." Blaine hesitated, and then went on: "It is best for you to know the truth at once. Mr. Hamilton has suffered a severe injury. He is lying almost at the point of death, but the physicians say he has a chance, a good chance, for recovery, now that he is where he can receive expert care and attention. How he came by his shattered skull — he has a fracture at the base of the brain — we shall not know until he recovers sufficient consciousness to tell us. At present, he is in a state of coma, recognizing no one, nothing that goes on about him. He will not rouse to hear your voice; he will not know of your presence; but I thought that it would comfort you to see him, to feel that everything is being done for him that can be done."

"Ah, yes!" she sobbed. "Take me to him, Mr. Blaine! Thank God, thank God that you have found him! Just to look upon his dear face again, to touch him, to know that at least he still lives! He must not die, now; he cannot die! The God who has permitted you to restore him to me, would not allow that! Take me to him!"

So it was that a few short minutes later, Henry Blaine tasted the first real fruit of his victory, as he stood aside in the quiet hospital room, and with dimmed eyes beheld the scene before him. The wide, white bed, the silent, motionless, bandage-swathed figure upon it, the slender, dark-robed, kneeling girl — only that, and the echo of her low-breathed sob of love and gratitude. His own great, fatherly heart swelled with the joy of work well done, of the happiness he had brought to a spirit all but broken, and a sure, triumphant premonition that the struggle still before him would be crowned with victory.

CHAPTER XVIII
THE TRAP

"You are ready, Miss Lawton? Nerves steady enough for the ordeal?" asked Blaine the following morning.

"I am ready." Anita's voice was firm and controlled, and there was the glint of a challenge in her eyes. A wondrous change had come over her since the previous day. With the rescue of the man she loved, and the certainty that he would recover, all the latent, indomitable courage and fighting spirit which had come to her as an heritage from her father, and which had made of him the ruler of men and arbiter of events which he had been, arose again within her. The most crushing weight upon her heart had been lifted; hope and love had revivified her; and she was indeed ready to face the world again, to meet her enemies, the murderers and traducers of her father, and to give battle to them on their own ground.

"In a few moments, a man will enter this library — a man whom you know well. You will be stationed behind the curtains at this window here, and you must summon all your self-control to restrain yourself from giving any start or uttering a sound of surprise which would betray your presence. While I talk to him, I want you to try with all your might to put from your mind the fact that you know him. Do not let his personality influence you in any way, or his speech. Only listen to the tones of his voice — listen and try to recall that other voice which you heard here on the night of your father's death. If in his tones you recognize that voice, step from behind those curtains and face him. If not — and you must be absolutely sure that you do recognize the voice, that you could swear to it under oath in a court of justice, realizing that it will probably mean swearing away a man's life — if you are not sure, remain silent."

"I understand, Mr. Blaine. I will not fail you. I could not be mistaken; the voice which I heard here that night rings still in my ears; its echo seems yet to linger in the room." Her gaze wandered to the great leather chair, which had been replaced in its usual position. "Now that you have restored Ramon to me, I want only to avenge my father, and I shall be content. To be murdered, in his own home! Poisoned like a rat in a trap! I shall not rest until the coward who killed him has been brought to justice!"

"He will be, Miss Lawton! The trap has been baited again, and unless I am greatly mistaken, the murderer will walk straight into it. — There is the bell! I gave orders that you were to be at home to no one except the man I expect and that he was to be ushered in here immediately upon his arrival, without being announced — so take your place, now, please, behind the curtains. Do not try to watch the man — only listen with all your ears; and above all do not betray yourself until the proper moment comes for disclosing your presence."

Without a word Anita disappeared into the window-seat, and the curtains fell into place behind her. The detective had only time to step in the shadow of a dark corner beside one of the tall bookcases, when the door was thrown open. A man stood upon the threshold — a tall, fair man of middle age, with a small blond mustache, and a monocle dangling from a narrow black ribbon about his neck. From the very correct gardenia in his buttonhole to the very immaculate spats upon his feet, he was a careful prototype of the Piccadilly exquisite — a little faded, perhaps, slightly effete, but perfect in detail. He halted for a moment, as if he, too, were blinded by the swift change from sunshine to gloom. Then, advancing slowly, his pale, protruding eyes wandered to the great chair by the fireplace, and lingered as if fascinated. He approached it, magnetized by some spell of his own thoughts' weaving, until he could have stretched out his hand and touched it. A pause, and with a sudden swift revulsion of feeling, he turned from it in a sort of horror and went to the center-table. There he stood for a moment, glanced back at the chair, then quickly about the room, his eyes passing unseeingly over the shadowy figure by the bookcase. Then he darted back to the chair and thrust his hand deep into the fold between the back and seat. For a minute he felt about with frenzied haste, until his fingers touched the object he sought, and with a profound sigh of relief he drew it forth — a tiny flat vial.

He glanced at it casually, his hand already raised toward his breast-pocket; then he recoiled with a low, involuntary cry. The vial was filled with a sinister blood-red fluid.

At that moment Blaine stepped from behind the bookcase and confronted him.

"You have succeeded in regaining your bottle, haven't you, Mr. Rockamore?" he asked, significantly. "Are you surprised to find within it the blood of an innocent man?"

Rockamore turned to him slowly, his dazed, horror-stricken eyes protruding more than ever.

"Blood?" he repeated, thickly, as if scarcely understanding. Then a realization of the situation dawned upon him, and he demanded, hoarsely: "Who are you? What are you doing here?"

"My name is Blaine, and I am here to arrest the murderer of Pennington Lawton," the detective replied, his dominant tones ringing through the room.

"Blaine — Henry Blaine!" Rockamore stepped back a pace or two, and a sneer curled his thin lips, although his face had suddenly paled. "I've heard of you, of course — the international meddler! What sort of sensation are you trying to work up now, my man, by such a ridiculous assertion? Pennington Lawton — murdered! Why, all the world knows that he died of heart-disease!"

"All the world seldom knows the truth, but it shall, in this instance," returned Blaine, trenchantly. "Pennington Lawton was murdered — poisoned by a draught of prussic acid."

"You're mad!" Rockamore retorted, insolently. He tossed the incriminating little vial carelessly on the blotter of the writing-desk, and when he turned again to the detective his face, with its high, thin, hooked nose and close-drawn brows, was vulture-like in its malevolent intensity. "You don't deserve serious consideration! If you make public such a ridiculous statement, you'll only be laughed at for your pains."

"I shall prove it. The murderer's midnight visit, his secret conference with his victim, did not proceed unwitnessed. His motive is known, but his act was futile. It came too late."

"This is all very interesting, no doubt, or would be if it could be credited. However, I cannot understand why you have elected to take me into your confidence." Rockamore was livid, but he controlled himself sufficiently to speak with a simulation of contemptuous boredom. "I came here to see Miss Lawton, in response to an urgent call from her; I don't know by what authority you are here, but I do know that I do not propose to be further annoyed by you!"

"I am afraid that you will find yourself very seriously annoyed before this affair comes to an end, Mr. Rockamore," said Blaine. "Miss Lawton's butler summoned you this afternoon by my instructions, and with gratifying promptness you came and did just what I expected you would do — betrayed yourself irretrievably in your haste to recover the evidence which now will hang you!"

The other man laughed harshly, a discordant, jarring laugh which jangled on the tense air.

"Your accusation is too absurd to be resented. I knew that Miss Lawton herself could not have been a party to this melodramatic hoax!"

Blaine walked to the desk before replying, and taking up the crimson-tinged vial, weighed it in his hand.

"You did not find the poison bottle which you yourself thrust in that chair the night Pennington Lawton died, Mr. Rockamore, because his daughter discovered it and communicated with me," he said. "She anticipated you by less than twenty-four hours. We have known from the beginning of your nocturnal visit to this room; every word of your conversation was overheard. It's no use trying to bluff it; we've got a clear case against you."

"You and your 'clear case' be d - - - - d!" the other man cried, his tones shaking with anger. "You're trying to bluff me, my man, but it won't work! I don't know what the devil you mean about a midnight visit to Lawton; the last I saw of him was at a directors' meeting the afternoon before his death."

"Then why has that chair — the chair in which he died — exerted such a peculiar, sinister influence over you? Why is it that every time you have entered this room since, you have been unable to keep away from it? Why, this very hour, when you thought yourself unobserved, did you walk straight to this chair and place your hand deliberately upon the place where the poison bottle was concealed? Why did you recoil? Why did that cry rise from your lips when you saw what it contained?"

"I touched the chair inadvertently, while I waited for Miss Lawton's appearance, and my hand coming accidentally in contact with a hard substance, mere idle curiosity impelled me to draw it out. Naturally, I was startled for the moment, when I saw what it was." The man's voice deepened hoarsely, and he gave vent to another sneering, vicious laugh. As its echo died in the room, Blaine could have sworn that he heard a quick gasp from behind the curtains of the window-seat, but it did not reach the ears of Rockamore.

The latter continued, his voice breaking suddenly, with a rage at last uncontrolled:

"I could not, of course, know that that bottle of red ink was a cheap, theatrical trick of a mountebank, a creature who is the laughing-stock of the press and the public, in his idiotic attempts to draw sensational notoriety upon himself. But I do know that this effort has failed! You have dared to plant this outrageous, puerile trap to attempt to ensnare me! You have dared to strike blindly, in your mad thirst for publicity, at a man infinitely beyond your reach. Your insolence ceases to be amusing! If you try to push this ridiculous accusation, I shall ruin you, Henry Blaine!"

"No man is beyond my reach who has broken the law." The detective's voice was quietly controlled, yet each word pierced the silence like a sword-thrust. "I have been threatened with ruin, with death, many times by criminals of all classes, from defaulting financiers to petty thieves, but I still live, and my fortunes have not been materially impaired. I do not court publicity, but I cannot shirk my duty because it entails that. And in this case my duty is plain. You, Bertrand Rockamore, came here, secretly, by night, to try to persuade Mr. Lawton to go in with you on a crooked scheme — to force him to, by blackmail, if necessary, on an old score. Failing in that, you killed him, to prevent the nefarious operations of yourself and your companions from being brought to light!"

"You're mad, I tell you!" roared Rockamore. "Whoever stuffed you with such idiotic rot as that is making gammon of you! That conversation is a chimera of some disordered mind, if it isn't merely part of a deliberate conspiracy of yours against me! You'll suffer for this, my man! I'll break you if it is the last act of my life! Such a conference never took place, and you know it!"

"'Come, Lawton, be sensible; half a loaf is better than no bread,'" Blaine quoted slowly. "'There is no blackmail about this — it is an ordinary business proposition.'

"'It's a damnable crooked scheme, and I shall have nothing to do with it. This is final! My hands are clean, and I can look every man in the face and tell him to go where you can go now!'

"You remember that, don't you, Rockamore?" Blaine interrupted himself to ask sharply. "Do you also recall your reply? — 'How about poor Herbert Armstrong? His wife — '"

"It's a lie! A d - - - - d lie!" cried Rockamore. "I was not in this room that night! Such a conversation never occurred! Who told you of this? Who dares accuse me?"

"I do!" A clear, flute-like voice, resonant in its firmness, rang out from behind him as he spoke, and he wheeled abruptly, to find Anita standing with her slender form outlined against the dark, rich velvet of the curtains. Her head was thrown back, her eyes blazing; and as she faced him, she slowly raised her arm and pointed a steady finger at the recoiling figure. "I accuse you, Bertrand Rockamore, of the murder of my father! It was I who heard your conversation here in this room; it was I who found the vial which contained the poison you used when your arguments and threats failed! I am not mistaken — I knew that I could never be mistaken if I heard that voice again, shaken, as it was that night, with rage and defiance — and fear! I knew that I should hear it again some time, and all these weeks I have listened for it, until this moment. Mr. Blaine, this is the man!"

Her head was thrown back, her eyes blazing: and as she faced him, she slowly raised her arm and pointed a steady finger at the recoiling figure.

"Anita, you have lost your mind!" With the shock of the girl's appearance, a steely calm had come to the Englishman, and although a tremor ran through his tones, he held them well in leash. "My poor child, you do not know what you are saying.

"As for you," — he turned and looked levelly into Blaine's eyes, — "I am amazed that a man of your perception and experience should for a moment entertain the idea that he could make out a case of capital crime against a person of my standing, solely upon the hysterical pseudo-testimony of a girl whose brain is overwrought. This midnight conference, which you so glibly quote, is a figment of her distraught mind — or, if it actually occurred (a fact of which you have no proof), Miss Lawton admits, by the words she has just uttered, that she did not see the mysterious visitor, but is attempting to identify me as that person merely by the tones of my voice. She has made no accusation against me until this moment, yet since her father's death she has heard my voice almost daily for several weeks. Come, Blaine, listen to reason! Your case has tumbled about your ears! You can only avoid serious trouble for both Miss Lawton and yourself by dropping this absurd matter here and now."

"It is true that I did not recognize your voice before, but I have not until now heard it raised in anger as it was that night —" began Anita, but Blaine silenced her with a gesture.

"And the bottle of prussic acid which was found yesterday hidden in the chair where just now you searched for it?" he demanded, sternly. "The incontrovertible evidence, proved late last night by an autopsy upon the body of Pennington Lawton, which shows that he came to his death by means of that poison — how do you account for these facts, Rockamore?"

"I do not propose to account for them, whether they are facts or not," returned the other man, coolly. "Since I know nothing whatever about them, they are beyond my province. Unless you wish to bring ruin upon yourself, and unwelcome notoriety and possibly an official inquiry into her sanity upon Miss Lawton, you will not repeat this incredible accusation. Only my very real sympathy for her has enabled me to listen with what patience I have to the unparalleled insolence of this charge, but you are going too far. I see no necessity for further prolonging this interview, and with your permission I will withdraw — unless, of course," he added, sneeringly, "you have a warrant for my arrest?"

To Anita's astonishment, Henry Blaine stepped back with a slight shrug and Rockamore, still with that sarcastic leer upon his lips, bowed low to her and strode from the room.

"You — you let him go, Mr. Blaine?" she gasped, incredulously. "You let him escape!"

"He cannot escape." Blaine smiled a trifle grimly. "I'm giving him just a little more rope, that is all, to see if he will help us secure the others. His every move is under strict surveillance — for him there is no way out, save one."

"And that way?" asked Anita.

The detective made no reply. In a few minutes he took leave of her and proceeded to his office, where he spent a busy day, sending cables in cipher, detailing operatives to many new assignments and receiving reports.

Late in the afternoon replies began to come in to his cablegrams of the morning. Whatever their import, they quite evidently afforded him immense satisfaction, and as the early dusk settled down, his eyes began to glow with the light of battle, which those closest to him in his marvelous work had learned to recognize when victory was in sight.

Suraci noted it when he entered to make his report, and the glint of enthusiasm in his own eyes brightened like burnished steel.

"I relieved Ross at noon, as you instructed me, sir," he began, "in the vestibule of Mr. Rockamore's apartment house. It was a good thing that I had the six-cylinder car handy, for he surely led me a chase! Ten minutes after I went on duty, Rockamore came out, jumped into his automobile, and after circling the park, he turned south, zig-zagging through side streets as if to cut off pursuit. He reached South-end Ferry, but hovered about until the gates were on the point of closing. Then his chauffeur shot the car forward, but before I could reach him, Creghan stepped up with your warrant.

"'I'm sorry, sir,' I heard him say as I came up. 'I'm to use this only in case you insist on attempting to leave the city, sir. Mr. Blaine's orders.'

"Rockamore turned on him in a fury, but thought better of it, and after a minute he leaned forward with a shrug, and directed the chauffeur north again. This time he tried the Great Western Station, but Liebler was there, waiting for him; then the North

Illington branch depot — Schmidt was on hand. As a forlorn hope he tried the Tropic and Oriental steamship line, — one of their ships goes out to-night, — but Norris intercepted him; at last he speeded down the boulevard and out on the eastern post-road, but Kearney was on the job at the toll-gate.

"He gave it up then, and went back to his rooms, and Ross relieved me there, just now. The lights are flaring in the windows of his rooms, and you can see his shadow — he's pacing up and down like a caged animal!"

"All right, Suraci. Go back and tell Ross to have one of his men telephone to me at once if Rockamore leaves his rooms before nine. That will be all for you to-night. I've got to do the rest of the work myself."

At nine o'clock precisely, Henry Blaine presented himself at Rockamore's door. As he had anticipated he was admitted at once and ushered into the Englishman's presence as if his coming had been expected.

"I say, Blaine, what the devil do you mean by this game you're playing?" Rockamore demanded, as he stood erect and perfectly poised upon the hearth, and faced the detective. A faint, sarcastic smile curved his lips, and in his pale eyes there was no hint of trouble or fear — merely a look of tolerant, half-contemptuous amusement. Immaculate in his dinner-coat and fresh boutonnière, his bearing superb in his ease and condescension, he presented a picture of elegance. Blaine glanced about the rich, somber den before he replied.

"I'm not playing any game, Mr. Rockamore. Why did you try so desperately to leave the city?"

The Englishman shrugged.

"A sudden whim, I suppose. Would it be divulging a secret of your profession if you informed me why one of your men did not arrest me, since all had warrants on the ridiculous charge you brought against me this morning, of murdering my oldest and closest friend?"

"I merely wanted to assure myself that you would not leave the city until I had obtained sufficient data with which to approach you," the detective responded, imperturbably. "I have come to-night for a little talk with you, Mr. Rockamore. I trust I am not intruding?"

"Not at all. As a matter of fact, after to-day's incidents I was rather expecting you." Rockamore waved his unbidden guest to a chair, and produced a gold cigarette-case. "Smoke? You perhaps prefer cigars — no? A brandy and soda?"

"Thank you, no. With your permission, I will get right down to business. It will simplify matters for both of us if you are willing to answer some questions I wish to put to you; but, of course, there is no compulsion about it. On the other hand, it is my duty to warn you that anything you say may be used against you."

"Fire away, Mr. Blaine!" Rockamore seated himself and stretched out his legs luxuriously to the open wood-fire. "I don't fancy that anything I shall say will militate against me. I was an idiot to lose my temper this morning, but I hate being made game of. Now the whole situation merely amuses me, but it may become tiresome. Let's get it over."

"Mr. Rockamore, you were born in Staffordshire, England, were you not? Near a place called Handsworth?"

The unexpected question brought a meditative frown to the other man's brow, but he replied readily enough:

"Yes, at Handsworth Castle, to be exact. But I can't quite gather what bearing that insignificant fact has upon your amazing charge this morning."

"You are the only son of Gerald Cecil Rockamore, third son of the Earl of Stafford?" The detective did not appear to have heard the protest of the man he was interrogating.

"Precisely. But what — "

"There were, then, four lives between you and the title," Blaine interrupted, tersely. "But two remain, your father and grandfather. Your uncles died, both of sudden attacks of heart-disease, and curiously enough, both deaths occurred while they were visiting at Handsworth Castle."

"That is quite true." The cynical banter was gone from Rockamore's tones, and he spoke with a peculiar, hushed evenness, as if he waited, on guard, for the next thrust.

"Lord Ashfrith, your father's oldest brother, and next in line to the old Earl, was seated in the gun-room of the castle, sipping a brandy and soda, and carving a peach-stone. Twenty minutes before, you had brought the peaches in from the garden, and eaten them with him. He was showing you how, in his boyhood, he had carved a watch-charm from a peach-stone, and you were close at his side when he suddenly fell over dead. Two years later, your Uncle Alaric, heir to the earldom since his older brother was out of the way, dropped dead at a hunt breakfast. You were seated next him."

"Are you trying to insinuate that I had anything to do with these deaths?" Rockamore still spoke quietly, but there was a slight tremor in his tones, and his face looked suddenly gray and leaden in the glow of the leaping flames.

"I am recalling certain facts in your family history. When your Uncle Alaric died, he had just set down his cordial glass, which had contained peach brandy. An odd coincidence, wasn't it, that both of these men died with the odor of peaches about them, an odor which incidentally you had provided in both cases, for it was you who suggested the peach brandy as a cordial at the hunt breakfast, and induced your uncle to partake of it."

"It was a coincidence, as you say. I had not thought of it before." The Englishman moistened his lips nervously, as if they suddenly felt dry. "Uncle Alaric was a heavy, full-blooded man, and he had ridden hard that morning, contrary to the doctor's orders. I suggested the brandy as a bracer, I remember."

"An unfortunate suggestion, wasn't it?" Blaine asked, significantly. The other man made no reply.

"There was another coincidence." The detective pursued relentlessly. "The brandy-and-soda, which Lord Ashfrith was drinking at the moment of his death, was naturally a pale amber color. So was the brandy which your Uncle Alaric drank as he died. And prussic acid is amber-colored, too, Mr. Rockamore! Lord Ashfrith was carving a peach-stone when the end came, and the odor of peaches clung to his body. Your Uncle Alaric partook of peach brandy, and the same odor hovered about him in death. Prussic acid is redolent of the odor of peaches!"

Rockamore started from his chair.

"I understand what you are attempting to establish by the flimsiest of circumstantial evidence!" he sneered. "But you are away beyond your depth, my man! May I ask where you obtained this interesting but scarcely valuable information?"

"From Scotland Yard, by cable, to-day." Blaine rose also and faced the other man. "An investigation was started into the second death, upon the Earl's request, but it was dropped for lack of evidence. About that time, Mr. Rockamore, you decided rather suddenly, and for no apparent reason, to come to America, where you have remained ever since."

"Mr. Blaine, if I were in the mood to be facetious, I might employ your American vernacular and ask that you tell me something I don't know! Come to the point, man; you try my patience."

"In view of recent developments, I am under the impression that Scotland Yard would welcome your reappearance on British soil, but I fear that will be forever impossible," Blaine said slowly. "Just as you were beside your uncles when each met with his end, so you were beside Pennington Lawton when death came to him! That has been proved. Just as brandy and soda, and peach brandy, are amber-colored, so are Scotch high-balls, which you and Pennington Lawton were drinking. No odor of peaches lingered about the room, for Miss Lawton had lighted a handful of joss-sticks in a vase upon the mantel earlier in the evening, and their pungent perfume filled the air. But the odor of peaches permeated the room when the tiny bottle which you hid in the folds of the chair was uncorked — the odor of peaches rose above the stench of mortifying flesh, when the body of your victim was exhumed late last night for a belated autopsy! The heart would have revealed the truth, had there been no corroborative evidence, for it was filled with arterial blood — incontrovertible proof of death by prussic-acid poisoning."

There was a tense pause, and then Rockamore spoke sharply, his voice strained to the breaking point.

"If you are so certain of my guilt, Blaine, why have you come to me secretly here and now? What is your price?"

"I have no price," the great detective answered, simply.

"Then why did you not arrest me at once? Why this purposeless interview?"

"Because — " Blaine paused, and when he spoke again, a solemn hush, almost of pity, had crept into his tones. "You come of a fine old line, Mr. Rockamore, of a splendid race. Your grandfather, the aged Earl, is living only in the past, proud of the record of his forebears. Your father is a soldier and statesman, valuable to the nation; his younger brother, Cedric, has achieved deserved fame and glory in the Boer War. There remains only you. For the sake of the innocent who must suffer with you, I have come to you to-night, that you may have an opportunity to — prepare yourself. In the morning I must arrest you. My duty is plain."

As he uttered the words, the craven fear which had struggled through the malicious sneer on the other man's face faded as if an obliterating hand had passed across his brow, and a look of indomitable courage and resignation took its place. There was something akin to nobility in his expression as he turned to the detective with head proudly erect and shoulders squared.

"I thank you, Mr. Blaine," he said, simply. "I understand. I shall not fail them — the others! You have been far more generous to me than I deserve. And now — good-night. You will find me here when you come in the morning."

But in the morning Henry Blaine did not carry out his expressed intention. Instead, he sat at his desk, staring at the headlines in a paper spread out before him. The Honorable Bertrand Rockamore had been found dead on the floor of his den, with a bullet through his head. He would never allow his man to touch his guns, and had been engaged in cleaning one of them, as was his custom, in preparation for his annual shooting trip to Florida, when in some fashion it had been accidentally discharged.

"I wonder if I did the right thing!" mused Blaine. "He had the courage to do it, after all. Blood will tell, in the end."

CHAPTER XIX
THE UNSEEN LISTENER

"There's a man outside who wishes to speak to you, sir. Says his name is Hicks, but won't tell his business."

Blaine looked up from the paper.

"Never heard of him. What sort of a man, Marsh?"

"Old, white-haired, carries himself like an old family servant of some sort. Looks as if he'd been crying. He's trembling so he can scarcely stand, and seems deeply affected by something. Says he has a message for you, and must see you personally."

"Very well. Show him in."

"Thank you for receiving me, sir." A quavering old voice sounded from the doorway a moment later, and Blaine turned in his chair to face the aged, erect, black-clad figure which stood there.

"Come in, Hicks." The detective's voice was kindly. "Sit down here, and tell me what I can do for you."

"I bring you a message, sir." The man tottered to the chair and sank into it. "A message from the dead."

Blaine leaned forward suddenly.

"You were — "

"Mr. Rockamore's valet, sir, and his father's before him. I loved him as if he were my own son, if you will pardon the liberty I take in saying so, and when he came to this country I accompanied him. He was always good to me, sir, a kind young master and a real friend. It was I who found him this morning — "

His voice broke, and he bowed his head upon his wrinkled hands. No tears came — but the thin shoulders shook, and a dry sob tore its way from the gaunt throat.

Blaine waited until the paroxysm had ceased, and then

urged, gently:

"Go on, Hicks. You have something to tell me?"

"Yes, sir. The coroner and the press call it accidental death, but I — may God forgive me for saying it — I know better! He left word where none could find it but me, that you knew the truth, and he bade me give you — this!"

He produced a large, square envelope from an inner pocket, and extended it in his trembling hand to the detective. Without glancing at it, Blaine laid it on the desk before him.

"Where did you discover this?"

"There is a flat, oblong casket of old silver, shaped somewhat like a humidor — a family relic, sir — which stands upon the center-table in the den. Whenever Mr. Rockamore had any message to leave for me in writing, concerning his confidential business, which he did not wish the other servants to have access to, he always slipped it into the casket. After the coroner had come and gone this morning, and some of the excitement had died down, I went back to the den, to straighten it. I don't know why, but somehow I half suspected the truth. Perhaps it was the expression of his face — so peaceful and resigned, with all the hard, sneering lines the years had brought gone from it, so that he looked almost like a boy again, the bonny boy who used to ride helter-skelter on his pony through the lanes of Staffordshire, long ago."

The aged man spoke half to himself and seemed to have fallen into a reverie, which Blaine made no attempt to break in upon. At length he roused himself with a little start, and went on.

"At any rate, when I had the room in order, and was standing by the table taking a last look about, my hand rested on the casket, and quite without thinking, sir, I raised the lid. There within it lay a sealed envelope with my name on it! Inside was a certified check for two thousand pounds made out to me — he didn't forget me, even at the last — and that letter for you, together with a little note asking me to — to take him home. Is it true, sir, that you do know the whole truth?"

"I think I do," Blaine responded gravely. "I did the best I could for your late master, Hicks, all that I could do which was compatible with my duty, and now my lips are sealed. I cannot betray his confidence. You intend to accompany the body to England?"

"Of course, sir," the old man said simply. "It was his last request of me, who have never refused him anything in all his life. When I have seen him laid beside the others of the House of Stafford, I will go back to the castle, to his father, and end my days there. My course is nearly run, and this great new country has no place in it for the aged. I — I will go now, sir. I have much to attend to, and my master is lying alone."

When the old servant had taken his departure, Henry Blaine picked up the envelope. It was addressed in a firm, unshaken hand, and with a last touch of the sardonic humor characteristic of the dead man, it had been stamped with the seal of the renowned and honored House of Stafford.

The detective broke the seal, and lifting the flap, drew out the folded letter page and became immediately absorbed in its contents. He read:

In view of your magnanimity to-night, I feel that this explanation — call it a confession, if you will — is your due. If you consider it your duty to give it to the world at large, you must do so, but for God's sake be as merciful as you can to those at home, who will suffer enough, in all conscience, as the affair now stands.

Your accusation was justified. I killed Pennington Lawton in the manner and for the reason which you alleged. I made an appointment by telephone just after dinner, to call upon him late that night. I tried by every means in my power to induce him to go in on a scheme to which, unknown to him, I had already committed him. He steadfastly refused. His death was the only way for me to obviate exposure and ruin, and the disgrace of a prison sentence. I anticipated his attitude and had come prepared. During a heated period of our discussion, he walked to the desk and stood for a moment with his shoulder turned to me, searching for a paper in his private drawer. I saw my chance, and seized upon it. I was standing before his chair, I may explain, watching him over its high back. I took the vial of prussic acid from my pocket, uncorked it and poured a few drops into his high-ball glass. I had recorked the vial, and was on the point of returning it to its hiding-place, when he turned to me. Had I raised my hand to my pocket he would have noticed the gesture; as it was, the back of the chair screened me, and on a sudden desperate impulse I thrust the vial deep in the leather fold between the seat and back.

Lawton drank, and died. I left the house, as I thought, unnoticed and secure from detection. On subsequent visits to the house I endeavored to regain possession of the vial, but on each occasion I failed in my purpose, and at length it fell into the hands of Anita Lawton. I have no more to say. Of earlier events at home in England, which you and I discussed to-night, it is better that I remain silent. You, of all men, will appreciate my motive.

And now, Blaine, good-night. Please accept my heartfelt thanks for the manner in which you handled a most difficult situation to-night. You have beaten me fairly at my own game. It may be that we shall meet again, somewhere, some time. In all sincerity, yours,

Arthur Bertrand Rockamore.

The detective folded the letter slowly and returned it to its envelope. Then he sat for long buried in thought. Rockamore had taken the solitary loophole of escape from overwhelming disgrace left to him. He had, as far as in him lay, expiated his crimes. What need, then, to blazon them forth to a gaping world? Pennington Lawton had died of heart-disease, so said the coroner. The press had echoed him, and the public accepted that fact. Only two living persons beside the coroner knew the truth, and Blaine felt sure that the gentle spirit of Anita Lawton would be merciful — her thirst for vengeance upon her father's murderer sated by his self-inflicted death — to those of his blood, who, innocent, must be dragged in the mire by the disclosure of his infamy.

When Henry Blaine presented himself an hour later at her home, he found Anita inexpressibly shocked by the tragic event of the night.

"He was guilty!" she murmured. "He took his own life to escape falling into your hands! That gunshot was no accident, Mr.

Blaine. He murdered my father in cold blood, but he has paid. I abhor his memory, and yet I can find it in my heart to be sorry for him!"

In silence, the detective placed in her hands the letter of the dead man, and watched her face as she slowly read it. When she looked up, her eyes were wet, and a tiny red spot glowed in either cheek.

"Poor Father!" she moaned. "With all his leadership and knowledge of men, he was helpless and unsuspecting in the hands of that merciless fiend! And yet even he thought of his own people at the last, and wanted to spare them. Oh, how I wish we could! If we might only keep from them forever the knowledge of his wickedness, his crime!"

"We can, if you are willing."

Blaine met her look of startled inquiry, and replied to it with a brief résumé of his interview of the previous evening with Rockamore. When he added his suggestion that the matter of the way in which her father came to his death be buried in oblivion, and the public left to believe the first report, she was silent for a time.

"But the coroner who performed the autopsy night before last," she remarked, at length, hesitatingly. "He will make the truth public, will he not?"

"Not necessarily. That depends upon you. If you wish it, nothing will ever be known."

"I think you are right, Mr. Blaine. Father's death has been avenged; neither you nor I can do more. The man who killed him has gone to his last account. Further notoriety and scandal cannot help Father, or bring him back to me. It would only cause needless suffering to those who are no more at fault than we ourselves. If the coroner can be silenced, we will keep our secret, you and I."

"Unless," — Blaine's voice was very grave — "unless it becomes necessary to divulge it in order to get the rest of them within our grasp."

"The rest?" she looked up as if she had scarcely heard.

"Mallowe and Carlis and Paddington and the horde of lesser conspirators in their hire. We must recover your father's immense fortune, and find out how it was possible for them to divert it to their own channels. There is Mr. Hamilton to be thought of, too — his injury, his kidnaping! If we can succeed in unraveling this mysterious tangle of events without recourse to the fact of our knowledge of the murder, well and good. If not, we must make use of whatever has come to our hand. With the rest of the malefactors brought to justice, you can afford to be magnanimous even to the dead man who has done you the most grievous wrong of all."

"It shall be as you say — "

She broke off suddenly as her eyes, looking beyond Blaine's shoulder, fell upon a silent figure in the doorway.

"Mr. Mallowe!" she cried. "When did you come? How is it that Wilkes failed to announce you?"

"I arrived just at this moment." The smooth, unctuous tones floated out upon the strained tension of the air. "I told Wilkes I would come right up. He told me Mr. Blaine was with you, and I wish to congratulate him on his marvelous success. Surely you do not mind the liberty I took in announcing myself, my dear child?"

"Not at all," Anita responded, coldly. "To which success of Mr. Blaine's do you refer, Mr. Mallowe?"

"Why, to his discovery of Ramon, of course." Mr. Mallowe looked from one to the other of them as if nonplused by Anita's unexpected attitude. Then he continued hurriedly, with a show of enthusiasm. "It was wonderful, unprecedented! But how did Ramon come to be in Mac Alarney's retreat, and so shockingly injured?"

"The same people who ran him down the day Miss Lawton sent for him to come to her aid — the day she learned of her father's insolvency." Blaine spoke quickly, before the girl had an opportunity to reply. "The same people who on two other separate occasions attempted his life!"

"You cannot mean to tell me that there is some conspiracy on foot against Ramon Hamilton!" Mallowe's face was a picture of shocked amazement. "But why? He is the most exemplary of young men, quite a model in these days — "

"Because he is a man, and prepared to protect and defend to the last ounce of his strength the thing which he loved better than life itself — the thing which, but for him, stood helpless and alone, surrounded by enemies and hopelessly entangled in the meshes of a gigantic conspiracy!"

"You speak in riddles, Mr. Blaine." Mallowe's gray brows drew together.

"Riddles which will soon be answered, Mr. Mallowe. Miss Lawton's natural protector — her father — had been ruthlessly removed by — death. Only Mr. Hamilton stood between her and the machinations of those who thought they had her in their power. Therefore, Mr. Hamilton was also removed, temporarily. Do I make myself quite clear now?"

"It is impossible, incredible! What enemies could this dear child here have made, and who could wish to harm her? Besides, am I not here? Do not I and my friends stand in *loco parentis* to her?"

"As you doubtless are aware, one of Miss Lawton's pseudo-guardians, at least, has involuntarily resigned his wardenship," Blaine remarked.

"You refer to the sudden death last night of my associate, Mr. Rockamore?" Mallowe shook his head dolorously. "A terrible accident! The news was an inexpressible shock to me! It was to comfort Miss Lawton for the blow which the loss of this devoted friend must be to her that I came to-day."

"I fancy the loss itself will be consolation enough, Mr. Mallowe. The accident was tragic, of course. It takes courage to clean a gun, sometimes — more courage, perhaps, than to spill into a glass an ingredient not usually included in a Scotch highball, let us say."

"Mr. Blaine, if you are inclined to be facetious, sir, let me tell you this is neither the time nor place for an attempt at a jest! When Miss Lawton called you in, the other day, and engaged you to search for Mr. Hamilton — "

"Oh, she didn't call me in then, Mr. Mallowe! I've been on the case from the start, all this last month, in fact, and in close touch with Miss Lawton every day."

Mallowe started back, the light of comprehension dawning swiftly in his eyes, only instantly to be veiled with a film of craftiness.

"What case?" he asked. "Ramon Hamilton has not been missing for a month."

"The case of the death of Pennington Lawton! The case of his fraudulently alleged bankruptcy! The case of the whole damnable conspiracy to crush this girl to the earth, to impoverish her and tarnish the fair name and honored memory of her father. It's cards on the table now, Mr. Mallowe, and I'm going to win!"

"You must be mad!" exclaimed the older man. "This talk of a conspiracy is ridiculous, absurd!"

"Mr. Rockamore called me 'mad,' also, yesterday afternoon, standing just where you stand now, Mr. Mallowe." The detective met the lowering eyes squarely. "Yet he went home and — accidentally shot himself! A curiously opportune shot that! Miss Lawton's enemies depended too confidently upon her credulity in accepting without question the unsubstantiated assertion of her father's insolvency. They did not take into account the possibility that their henchman, Paddington, might fail, or turn traitor; that Mac Alarney might talk to save his own hide; that Jimmy Brunell's forgeries might be traced to their source; that the books in the office of the Recorder of Deeds might divulge interesting items to those sufficiently concerned to delve into the files of past years! You discharged your clerk on the flimsiest of excuses, Mr. Mallowe — but you did not discharge her quite soon enough.

Rockamore's stenographer, and the switchboard operator in Carlis' office, — who, like your filing clerk, came from Miss Lawton's club, — were also dismissed too late. As I have said, my cards are on the table now. Are you prepared to play yours?"

For answer, Mallowe turned slowly to Anita, his face a study of pained surprise and indignation.

"My dear girl, I do not understand one word of what this person is saying, but he is either mad, or intoxicated with his success in locating Ramon, to the extent that he is endeavoring to build up a fictitious case on a maze of lies. Any notoriety will bring him welcome publicity, and that is all he is looking for. I shall take immediate steps to have his incomprehensible and dangerous allegation suppressed. Such a man is a menace to the community! In the meantime, I must beg of you to dismiss him at once. Do not listen to him, do not allow him to influence you! You are only an impulsive, credulous girl, and he is using you as a mere tool for his own ends. I cannot imagine how you happened to fall into his clutches."

Anita faced him, straight and slim and tall, and her soft eyes seemed fairly to burn into his.

"I am not so credulous as you think, Mr. Mallowe. I never for a moment believed your assertion that my father died a pauper, and I took immediate steps to disprove it. Doctor Franklin was your tool, when he came to me with your message, but not I! And I shouldn't advise you to try, at this late date, to 'suppress' Mr. Blaine. Many other malefactors have attempted it, I understand, in the past, but I never heard of any of them meeting with conspicuous success. You and my other two self-appointed guardians must have been desperate indeed to have risked trying to hoodwink me with so ridiculous and vague a story as that of the loss of my father's fortune!"

"This is too much!" Mallowe stormed. "Young woman, you forget yourself! Because of the evil suggestions, the malevolent influence of this man's plausible lies, are you such an ingrate as to turn upon your only friends, your father's intimate, life-long associates, the people who have, from disinterested motives of the purest kindness and affection, provided for you, comforted you, and shielded you from the world? Anita, I cannot believe it of you! I will leave you, now. I am positively overcome with this added shock of your ingratitude and willful deceit, coming so soon after the blow of my poor friend's death. I trust you will be in a thoroughly repentant frame of mind when next I see you.

"As for you, sir!" He turned to the immovable figure of the detective. "I will soon show you what it means to meddle with matters which do not concern you — to pit yourself arrogantly against the biggest power in this country!"

"The biggest power in this or any other country is the power of justice." Blaine's voice rang out trenchantly. "When you and your associates planned this desperate *coup*, it was as a last resort. You had involved yourselves too deeply; you had gone too far to retrace your steps. You were forced to go on forward — and now your path is closed with bars of iron!"

"I will not remain here any longer to be insulted! Miss Lawton, I shall never cross the threshold of this house again — this house, which only by my charity you have been suffered to remain in — until you apologize for the disgraceful scene here this morning. I can only hope that you will soon come to your senses!"

As he strode indignantly from the room, Anita turned anxiously to Henry Blaine.

"Oh, what will he do?" she whispered. "He is really a power, a money-power, you know, Mr. Blaine! Where will he go now?"

"Straight to his *confrère* Carlis, and tell him that the game is up." The detective spoke with brisk confidence. "He'll be tailed by my men, anyway, so we shall soon have a report. Don't see anyone, on any pretext whatsoever, and don't leave the house, Miss Lawton. I will instruct Wilkes on my way out, that you are to be at home to no one. I must be getting back to my office now. If I am not mistaken, I shall receive a visit without unnecessary delay from my old friend Timothy Carlis, and I wouldn't miss it for the world!"

Blaine's prediction proved to have been well founded. Scarcely an hour passed, and he was deep in the study of some of his earlier notes on the case, when all at once a hubbub arose in his outer office. Usually quiet and well-ordered, its customary stillness was broken by a confused, expostulatory murmur of voices, above which rose a strident, angry bellow, like that of a maddened wild beast. Then a chair was violently overturned; the sudden sharp sound of a scuffle came to the detective's listening ears; and the door was dashed open with a jar which made the massive inkstand upon the desk quiver.

Timothy Carlis stood upon the threshold — Timothy Carlis, his face empurpled, the great veins upon his low-slanting forehead standing out like whipcords, his huge, spatulate hands clenched, his narrow, slit eyes gleaming murderously.

"So you're here, after all!" he roared. "Those d — d fools out there tried to give me the wrong steer, but I was wise to 'em. You buffaloed Rockamore, and that senile old idiot, Mallowe, but you can't bluff me! I came here to see you, and I usually get what I go after!"

"Having seen me, Carlis, will you kindly state your business and go? This promises to be one of my busiest days. What can I do for you?" Blaine leaned back in his chair, with a bland smile of pleased expectancy.

"It ain't what you *can* do; it's what you're *goin'* to do, and no mistake about it!" the other glowered. "You're goin' to keep your mouth shut as tight as a trap, and your hands off, from now on! Oh, you know what I mean, right enough. Don't try to work the surprised gag on me!"

He added the latter with a coarse sneer which further distorted his inflamed visage. Blaine, with an expression of sharp inquiry, had whirled around in his swivel chair to face his excited visitor, and as he did so, his hand, with seeming inadvertence, had for an instant come in contact with the under ledge of his desk-top.

"I'm afraid, much as I desire not to prolong this unexpected interview, that I must ask you to explain just what it is that I must keep my hands off of, as you say. We will go into the wherefore of it later."

Carlis glanced back of him into the empty hallway, then closed the door and came forward menacingly.

"What's the good of beating about the bush?" he demanded, in a fierce undertone. "You know d — n' well what I mean: you're butting in on the Lawton affair. You've bitten off more than you can chew, and you'd better wise yourself up to that, here and now!"

"Just what is the Lawton affair?"

"Oh, stow that bluff! You know too much already, and if I followed my hunch, I'd scrag you now, to play safe. Dead men don't blab, as a rule — though one may have, last night. I came here to be generous, to give you a last chance. I've fought tooth and nail, myself, for my place at the top, and I like a game scrapper, even if he is on the wrong side. You've tried to get me for years, but as I knew you couldn't, I didn't bother with you, any more than I would with a trained flea, and I bear no malice. D — d if I don't like you, Blaine!"

"Thank you!" The detective bowed in ironic acknowledgment of the compliment. "Your friendship would be considered a valuable asset by many, I have no doubt, but — "

"Look here!" The great political boss had shed his bulldozing manner, and a shade of unmistakable earnestness, not unmixed with anxiety, had crept into his tones. "I'm talking as man to man, and I know I can trust your word of honor, even if you pretend you won't take mine. Is anyone listening? Have you got any of your infernal operatives spying about?"

Blaine leaned forward and replied with deep seriousness.

"I give you my word, Carlis, that no human ear is overhearing our conversation." Then he smiled, and added, with a touch of mockery: "But what difference can that make? I thought you came here to issue instructions. At least, you so announced yourself on your arrival!"

"Because I'm going to make a proposition to you — on my own." Even Carlis' coarse face flushed darkly at the base self-revelation. "Pennington Lawton died of heart-disease."

He paused, and after waiting a full minute, Blaine remarked, quietly, but with marked significance:

"Of course. That is self-evident, isn't it?"

"Well, then — " Carlis stepped back with a satisfied grunt. "He didn't have a soul on earth dependent on him but his daughter. His great fortune is swept away, and that daughter left penniless. But ain't there lots of girls in this world worse off than she? Ain't she got good friends that's lookin' out for her, and seein' that she don't want for a thing? Ain't she goin' to marry a young fellow that loves the ground she walks on — a rich young fellow, that'll give her everything, all her life? What more could she want? *She's* all right. But the big money — the money Lawton made by grinding down the masses — wouldn't you like a slice of it yourself, Blaine? A nice, fat, juicy slice?"

"How?" An interested pucker appeared suddenly between the detective's expressive brows, and Carlis laughed.

"Oh, we're all in it — you may as well be! You're on the inside, as it is! The play got too high for Rockamore, and he cashed in; you've bluffed old Mallowe till he's looking up sailing dates for Algiers, but I knew you'd be sensible, when it came to the scratch, and divide the pot, rather than blow your whistle and have the game pulled!"

"But it was old Mallowe" — Blaine's tone was puzzled — "who succeeded in transferring all that worthless land he'd acquired to Lawton, when Lawton wouldn't come in and help him on that Street-Railways grab, which would have made him practically sole owner of all the suburban real estate around Illington, wasn't it?"

"Sure it was!" laughed Carlis, ponderously. "But who made it possible for Mallowe to palm off those miles of vacant lots — as improved city property, of course — on Lawton, without his knowledge, and even have them recorded in his name, but me? What am I boss for, if I don't own a little man like the Recorder of Deeds?"

"I see!" Blaine tapped his finger-tips together and smiled slowly, in meditative appreciation. "And it was your man, also, Paddington, who found means to provide the mortgage, letter of appeal for a loan, note for the loan itself, and so forth. As for Rockamore — "

"Oh, he fixed up the dividend end, watered the stock and kept the whole thing going by phony financing while there was a chance of our hoodwinking Lawton into going into it voluntarily. He was one grand little promoter, Rockamore was; pity he got cold feet, and promoted himself into another sphere!"

"All things considered, it may not be such a pity, after all!" Blaine rose suddenly, whirling his chair about until it stood before him, and he faced his amazed visitor from across it. "Now, Carlis, suppose you promote yourself from my office!"

"Wh-what!" It was a mere toneless wheeze, but breathing deep of brute strength.

"I told you when you first came in that this promised to be one of my busiest days. You're taking up my time. To be sure, you've cleared up a few minor points for me, and testified to them, but you haven't really told me anything I didn't know. The game is up! Now — get out!"

He braced himself, as he spoke, to meet the mountain of flesh which hurled itself upon him in a blind rush of Berserk rage — braced himself, met and countered it. Never had that spacious office — the scene of so many heartrending appeals, dramatic climaxes, impassioned confessions and violent altercations — witnessed so terrific a struggle, brief as it was.

"I'll kill you!" roared the maddened brute. "You'll never leave your office, alive, to repeat what I've told! I'll kill you, with my bare hands, first, d — n you!"

But even as he spoke, his voice ended in a surprised scream of agony, which told of strained sinews and ripped tendons, and he fell in a twisted, crumpled heap of quivering, inert flesh at the detective's feet, the victim of a scientific hold and throw which had not been included in his pugilistic education.

Instantly Blaine's hand found an electric bell in the wall, and almost simultaneously the door opened and three powerful figures sprang upon the huge, recumbent form and bound him fast.

"Take him away," ordered the detective. "I'll have the warrant ready for him."

"Warrant for what?" spluttered Carlis, through bruised and bleeding lips. "I didn't do anything to you! You attacked me because I wouldn't swear to a false charge. I got a legal right to try to defend myself!"

"You've convicted yourself, out of your own mouth," retorted Blaine.

The other looked into his eyes and quailed, but blustered to the end.

"Nobody heard, but you, and my word goes, in this town! What d'you mean — convicted myself?"

For answer Blaine again touched that little spring in the protruding under-ledge of his desk, and out upon the trenchant stillness, broken only by the rapid, stertorous breathing of the manacled man, burst the strident tones of that same man's voice, just as they had sounded a few minutes before:

"'But the big money — the money Lawton made by grinding down the masses — wouldn't you like a slice of it yourself, Blaine — a nice, fat, juicy slice.... Oh, we're all in it, you may as well be!... The play got too high for Rockamore, and he cashed in; you've bluffed old Mallowe till he's looking up sailing dates for Algiers, but I knew you'd be sensible, when it came to the scratch, and divide the pot, rather than blow your whistle and have the game pulled.... Who made it possible for Mallowe to palm off those miles of vacant lots — as improved city property, of course — on

Lawton without his knowledge, and even have them recorded in his name, but me? What am I boss for, if I don't own a little man like the Recorder of Deeds?'"

"What is it?" gasped the wretched Carlis, in a fearful whisper, when the voice had ceased. "What is that — infernal thing?"

"A detectaphone," returned Blaine laconically. "You've heard of them, haven't you, Carlis? When you asked me if we were alone, if any of my operatives were spying about, I told you that no human ear overheard our conversation. But this little concealed instrument — this unseen listener — recorded and bore witness to your confession; and this is a Recorder you do not own, and cannot buy!"

CHAPTER XX
THE CREVICE

"But I don't understand" — Guy Morrow's voice was plaintive, and he eyed his chief reproachfully, as he stood before Blaine's desk, twisting his hat nervously — "why you didn't nail him! You've got the goods on him, all right; and now, just because you only had him arrested on a charge of assault with intent to kill, he's gone and used his influence, and got himself released under heavy bail. Oh, why won't you go heeled or guarded? We can't afford to lose you, sir, any of us, and now he'll do for you, as sure as shooting!"

"Who — Carlis?" Blaine spoke almost absently, as if the portentous scene of two hours before had already almost slipped from his memory. "Oh, he won't get away, and I'm not afraid of him! I let him go for the same reason that I didn't have Mallowe arrested this morning — for the same reason why I haven't stopped Paddington's philandering with the French girl, Fifine: because a link is still missing in the chain; the shell, the exterior of the whole conspiracy is in the hollow of my hand, but I can't find the chink, the crevice into which to insert my lever and split it apart, lay the whole dastardly scheme irrefutably open to the light of day. I want to complete my case: in other words, Guy — I want to win!"

"And you will, sir; you've never failed yet! Only I — I don't have any luck!" The young man's haggard face grew wistful. "I want Emily Brunell; I need her — and I seem farther from finding her than ever!"

"I didn't know that was your job!" the detective objected, with a brusqueness which was not unkind. "I told you I'd take care of that, in my own way. I thought I assigned you to the task of finding out who fired at you, from the darkened window of your own room, when you were in Brunell's house across the street; also I wanted a line on those two mysterious boarders of Mrs. Quinlan's."

"Nothing doing on either count, sir," Morrow returned, ruefully. "I can't get a glimpse of them, or a line on either of them; and as for who tried to plug me — well, there isn't an iota of evidence, that I can discover, beyond the bare fact. I didn't come to report, for there's nothing to say, except that I'm sticking at it, and if I don't get a sight of those two before long I'm going to burn a red sulphur light some fine night, and yell 'fire!' I bet that'll bring the old codger out, for all his rheumatism!"

"Not a bad idea," Blaine commented, adding dryly: "What did you come for, then, Guy?"

"To find out if you had any news you were willing to tell me yet, sir — of Emily?"

"Yes." The detective's slow smile was quizzical. "The most significant news in the world."

"You've discovered their destination — hers and her father's?" the young operative cried eagerly. "You traced their taxi, of course!"

"No."

"Then what is it?"

"Just that, Guy — that I haven't been able to trace the taxicab in which they left their house. Think it over. Report to me when you've got anything definite to tell me."

With a curt nod Blaine dismissed him, but he glanced after the dejected, retreating figure with a very kindly, affectionate light in his fatherly eyes. It was dusk when he was aroused from a deep study of his carefully annotated résumé of the case by the excited jangle of the telephone bell, to hear Guy Morrow's no less excited but joyous voice at the other end of the wire.

"I've found her! I've found Emily! She loves me! She does! I made her listen, and she understands everything! She don't mind a bit about my hounding her father down, because she sees how it all had to be, and the old man's a regular brick about it!"

"Where — "

"It was the kitten did it — that blessed Caliban! And think of it, sir; I've always hated cats, ever since I was a kid! Emily says — "

"But how — "

"Maybe if the hall had been lighted — but Mrs. Quinlan's got that parsimony peculiar to all landladies — and I trod on its tail, and it was all up!"

"Morrow, are you a driveling idiot, or an operative? Are you reporting, or exploding? If you called me up to tell me that you trod on the tail of your landlady's parsimony, you don't need a job in a detective bureau; you need a lunacy commission!" Blaine's voice was vexed, but little smiling lines crinkled at the corners of his eyes.

"I beg your pardon, sir; I am almost crazy, I think — with happiness. I've found Mr. Jimmy Brunell and his daughter. They are the two mysterious boarders whom Mrs. Quinlan has been shielding all this time, and I never even suspected it! It was Jimmy Brunell who fired at me that night of the day they disappeared. He didn't recognize me, and thought I was one of his enemies — one of Paddington's men, like young Charley Pennold.

"You remember, I told you I found the kitten in the deserted house and brought it home for Mrs. Quinlan to take care of? Well, she never lights the gas until the very last minute, and late this afternoon, about half an hour ago, I was stumbling along the second-floor hallway to my room in the dark, when I stepped on the kitten. It yelled like mad, and Emily heard it from her room above. Forgetting caution and everything else, she opened the door and called it!

"Of course, when I heard her voice, I was upstairs two steps at a time, with the cat under my arm clawing like a vixen. She was perfectly freezing at first — not the cat; it's a he; I mean Emily. But after I explained that when I'd gotten to care for her I only tried to help her, she — oh, well, I'm going to let her tell you herself, if you're willing, sir! I'll bring them both down to you now, if you say so, she and her father. Jimmy Brunell's more than anxious to see you; he wants to make a clean breast of the whole affair — tell all he knows about the case; and I think what he's got to say will astonish you and finish the whole thing — crack that nut you were talking to me about this afternoon, provide the link in the chain, the crevice in the crime cube! May I bring them?"

Blaine acquiesced, and after issuing his orders to the subordinates about him, waited in a fever of impatience which he could scarcely control, and which, had he stopped to think of it, would have astonished him beyond measure. That he — who had daily, almost hourly, awaited unmoved the appearance of men famous and infamous, illustrious and obscure, should so agitatedly view the coming of this old offender, was incomprehensible.

Yet although he had really learned little that was conclusive from Guy's somewhat incoherent account, he felt, in common with his young operative, that the crux of the matter lay here, to his hand, that from the lips of this old ex-convict would fall the magic word which would open to him the inner door of this mystery of mysteries — which would prove, as the golden key of truth, absolute and unassailable.

After what seemed an incredibly long period of suspense, the door opened and Marsh ushered them in — Morrow, his face wreathed in triumph and smiles; a brown-haired, serene-eyed girl whom Blaine remembered from his memorable interview with her at the Anita Lawton Club; and a tall, grizzled, smooth-shaven man, who held himself proudly erect, as if the weight of years had fallen from his shoulders.

"Yes, sir, I'm Brunell," the latter announced, when the incidental salutations were over, " — Jimmy Brunell, the forger. I've lived straight, and tried to keep the truth from my little girl, for her own sake, but perhaps it is better as it is. She knows everything now, and has forgiven much, because she's a woman like her mother, God bless her! I've come of my own free will, to tell you all you want to know, and prove it, too!"

"Sit down, all of you. Brunell, you forged the signature to the mortgage on Pennington Lawton's home, at Paddington's instigation?"

"Yes, sir. And the signature on the note given for the loan from Moore, and the whole letter supposed to be from Mr. Lawton to Mallowe, asking him to procure that loan for him, and all the other crooked business which helped sweep Mr. Lawton's fortune away. But I didn't understand how big the job was, nor just what they were trying to put over, or I wouldn't have done it. I wish to heaven I hadn't, now, but it's too late for that; I can only do what's left me to help repair the damage. I wish I'd taken the consequences Paddington threatened me with, through Charley Pennold — curse them both!

"For it wasn't because of the money I did it, sir, although what they offered me was a small fortune, and would have been a mighty hard temptation in the old days. It was because if I refused they were going to strike at me through my little girl, the one thing on earth I've got left to love! They were going to have me sent up on an old score which no one else even had suspected I'd been mixed up in. I didn't know — until just now when this young friend here, Mr. Morrow, told me — that it had been outlawed long years ago, and I can see that they counted on my not knowing. How they found out about it, anyway, is a mystery to me, but that Paddington is the devil himself! However, if I didn't do the trick for them, they'd have me convicted, and once out of the way, my little girl would be helpless in their hands. They talked of sweatshops, and worse — "

The old man broke down, and shuddering, covered his face with his thin fingers. But in a moment, before the pitying, outstretched hand of his daughter could reach his shoulder, he had regained control of himself, and resumed:

"I did what they asked of me — all they asked. But I was suspicious, not only because they didn't take me fully into their confidence, but because I knew Paddington and his breed; and also, Miss Lawton had been kind to my little girl. If they meant any harm to Pennington Lawton's daughter, or if their scheme, whatever kind of a hold-up it was, failed to pan out as they expected, and they tried to make me the scape-goat — well, I meant to protect myself and Lawton. My word would have to be proof against theirs that they forced me into what I did, but I could fix it so that I could prove to anybody, without any doubt, that Lawton never wrote that note to Mallowe from Long Bay about that loan two years ago, and that would sort of substantiate my word that the signatures weren't his, either."

"How could you prove such a thing?" Blaine leaned forward tensely.

"Young Morrow, here, tells me that you've got that note — the note asking Mallowe to arrange the loan for Lawton. Will you get it, please, sir? I don't want to see it; I want you to read it to me, and then I'll tell you something about it. They thought they were clever, the rascals, but I fooled them at their own game! I cut out the words from a bundle of Lawton's old letters which they gave me, and I manufactured the note, all right. I did it, word for word, just like they wanted me to — but I put my *own private mark* on it, that they couldn't discover, so that I could prove anywhere, any time, that it was a forgery!"

In a concealed fever of excitement, the detective produced the fateful note from his private file.

"That looks like it!" chuckled old Jimmy. "It's dated August sixteenth, nineteen hundred and twelve, isn't it? Now, sir, will you read it out loud, please?"

Blaine unfolded the single sheet of hotel note-paper, and looked once more at the following message:

My Dear Mallowe:

Kindly regard this letter as strictly confidential. I desire to negotiate a private loan immediately, for a considerable amount, — three hundred and fifty thousand dollars, in fact, — but for obvious reasons, which you, as a man of discretion and financial astuteness second to none in this country, will readily understand, a public assumption of it by me would be disastrous to a degree, under the prevailing conditions. Ask Moore if he can arrange the matter for me, but feel him out tentatively first. If he does not see his way clear to it, let me know without delay, and I will come to Illington and confer with you.

I am prepared, of course, to give him my personal note for same, but do not desire any direct dealings with him. In fact, it would be ex-

ceedingly dangerous to my interests if he ever mentioned it to me personally, even when he fancied himself alone with me. Impress this upon him. I will pay far above the legal rate of interest, of course. You can arrange this with him. I will go into the whole matter of this contingency confidentially with you when I see you. In the meantime, I know that I can rely upon you.

Awaiting the earliest possible reply, and thanking you for the interest I know you will take in this affair,

Sincerely, your friend, Pennington Lawton.

After glancing at it a moment Blaine read the letter aloud in a calm, unemotional voice which gave no hint of the tumult within him. He had scarcely finished when Jimmy Brunell, greatly excited, interrupted triumphantly:

"That's it! That's the note! Don't see anything phony about it, do you, sir? Neither did they! Now, leave out the 'My dear Mallowe,' and beginning with the next as the first line, count down five lines. The last letter of the last word on that line is *f, isn't it*? Omit a line and take the last letter of the next, and so on for four letters — that is, the last words of the four alternate lines beginning with the fifth from the top are: *of, a, ask,* and *see,* and the last letters of those four spell a word. That word is *fake,* and so is the note, and the whole infernal business! *Fake,* from beginning to end! I put my mark on it, sir, so it could be known for what it is, in case of need. Now the need has come."

"By Jove, so it is!" Guy Morrow cried, unable to restrain himself longer. "You're a wonder, Mr. Brunell!"

"You have rendered us a greater service than you know," supplemented Blaine, the while his pulses throbbed in time to his leaping heart. The crevice! The rift in the criminal's almost perfected scheme, into which he had succeeded in inserting the little silver probe of his specialized knowledge, and disclosed to a gaping world the truth! He had found it at last, and his work was all but done.

"But what's to happen to me now?" The exultation had died out of his voice, and Jimmy Brunell looked suddenly pinched and gray and tired, and very, very old. "I don't care much what happens to me, but my daughter — Emily — "

"I'll take care of her, whatever happens!" Guy's heart was in his buoyant voice. "But you'll be all right. Don't you worry! Haven't you got Mr. Blaine on your side?"

"I'll try to see that you don't suffer for your enforced share in the Lawton conspiracy, Brunell. It seems to me that you've already gone through trouble enough on that score, great as was the damage you half-unwittingly wrought," Blaine remarked, reassuringly — adding: "But why didn't you come forward before, and give your testimony?"

"There wasn't any court action," the old man returned, hesitatingly. "And besides, I was afraid to come forward and tell what I knew, because of Emily. I would have done it, though, as soon as I learned they had robbed Miss Lawton of everything. I wasn't sure of that, you see."

"One thing more!" Blaine pressed the bell which would summon his secretary. "Why, if you had reformed, did you keep in your possession all these years your forging apparatus?"

"I had it taken care of for me while I served my term, meaning to use it again when I came out. I was bitter and revengeful, and I meant to do everybody up brown that I could. But when I was free and found my — my wife had gone and left me Emily, it seemed like a hostage from her gentle spirit given to the world, that I wouldn't do any more wrong. I kept the plant because I didn't know how to dispose of it so no one else could use it, and as the years went by, I got more and more scared at the thought of it.

"I was afraid both ways — afraid it would be discovered, but more afraid I'd be found out if I tried to get rid of it. So I buried it in the cellar of my little shop and did my level best to forget it. I'd almost succeeded when, God knows how, Paddington found me. You know the rest."

"You rang, sir?" Marsh, the secretary, had entered noiselessly.

"Yes. Have these two people — this young lady and her father — conducted in my own limousine to my house, and made comfortable there until I give you further directions as to what I wish done concerning them."

Blaine cut short the old forger's broken words of gratitude in his brusquely kind fashion, but his heart imaged always the light in the girl's soft eyes as she bent a parting glance upon him, like a benediction, before the door closed.

"What are you going to do with them, sir?" young Morrow asked anxiously when they were alone.

Henry Blaine paused a moment before replying.

"I might let him take his chance before the court, on the strength of his years, and his having turned State's evidence voluntarily, Guy, but he's an old offender, and Carlis' faction is strong. My racing car will make ninety miles an hour, easily, and it can do it unmolested, with my private sign on the hood. It can meet the Canadian express at Branchtown at dawn. I've a little farm in a nice community in Canada, not too isolated, and I'm going to make it over to you as part of your reward for your work on the Lawton case....

"No, don't thank me! I'm sworn on the side of law and order, but Justice is stern and sometimes blind because she will not see. Remember, the Greatest Jurist Himself recommended mercy!"

Soon afterward, as they sat discussing the wind-up of the case, the subject of the second set of cryptograms was broached, and Blaine smiled at Morrow's utter bewilderment concerning them.

"Still puzzling about those, Guy? They weren't as simple as the first one was, that of the system of odd-shaped characters and dots. The later ones were the more difficult because they were of no set system at all — I mean no one system, but a primitive conglomeration, probably evolved by Paddington himself, based on script music and also the old childish trick of writing letters shaped like figures, which can be read by reversing the paper, and holding it up to the light.

"Just a minute, and we'll look at the two notes, the one you found in Brunell's room in the deserted cottage, and the other which came to me in the cigarette box meant for Paddington, from Mac Alarney. Then we'll be able to see how they were worked out. And you'll see that though they look extremely meaningless and confusing, they are in reality extremely simple."

As he spoke, Blaine produced them from his desk drawer, and spread them out before him.

"Before you examine them," he went on, "let me explain the musical script idea on which they are fundamentally based, in case you are unfamiliar with it. The sign '&' before a bar of music means that music is written in the treble clef — that is, all the notes following it are above the central C on the piano keyboard. Thus" — here he drew rapidly on a scrap of paper and passed a scrawled scale over to the interested operative.

"The dot on the line below the five lines which are joined together by the sign of the treble clef is C. The dot on the space between that and the first of the five lines is D. The dot on the first line is E; on the next space is F, and so forth, in their alphabetical order on the alternating lines and spaces. Do you see how easily, they could be used as the letters of words in a cryptogram, by any one of an ingenious turn of mind? Of course, each bar — that is, each section enclosed by lines running straight up and down — represents a word. Now for the rest of it:

"Leaving the script music idea aside, and taking the characters not so represented in the cryptogram, we find that '3' when viewed from the under side of the paper will look very much like an English *E*; 7 like *T*; 9 like *P*; 2 like *S*, and so forth.

"Try it. Here is the first note, the one you found. Puzzle out the musical notes by their alphabetical nomenclature from the key I just gave you on the scrap of paper there; then hold the note up to the light, and read the other letters from the under side. Try it with both notes, and tell me what you find."

Guy took the papers, and wonderingly spelled out the letters represented by the musical notes, from the scale Blaine had given him. Then turning the pages over, he held them up to the light, an exclamation of absorbed interest escaping from him.

The great detective watched him in silence, until at last, with a glowing sense of achievement, Guy read:

"'Beat it at once. You are suspected. Detective on trail. Rite old address. I am sending funds as usual. If caught you get life sentence. Pad.'"

Blaine nodded.

"Now, the other."

"'Patient still unconscious. Consultation necessary at once to save life. Should he die advise Reddy what disposition to make of body. Mac.'"

The last cryptogram proved the more easily decipherable, and when the young operative had read it aloud, he looked up with a glowing face.

"By George, it's a world-beater! What put you on the right track?"

"The last one. I realized then that they were afraid the kidnaped man, Ramon Hamilton, who had been grievously wounded, would die on their hands, and that rather than face the results of such a contingency they would attempt to obtain some obscure but experienced medical aid, and in a way which would give the physician no inkling of his patient's identity or whereabouts. I therefore sent out that circular letter to every doctor in Illington, warning each one to come to me in the event of his having received a mysterious summons. It worked, as you know, and Doctor Alwyn responded."

"Well, if you hadn't been able to read the cryptogram, sir, the Lord knows what would have happened!"

"And if you hadn't trodden on the cat's tail — " Blaine suggested dryly.

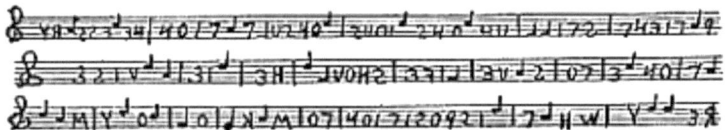

Guy glanced at him in sudden, swift comprehension.

"Why, look here, sir, I believe you knew that Emily and her father were the two mysterious boarders at Mrs. Quinlan's, all the time! You said it was significant that you hadn't been able to trace the number of the taxicab in which they had run away from the neighborhood! There never was a taxicab in all Illington which couldn't be traced by its number! You knew, of course, that that story of Mrs. Quinlan's was a fake, and then when I told you of the two concealed people there, you had it all doped out! Oh, why didn't you tell me?"

"Because I didn't want you to precipitate matters just then, Guy," the detective responded, kindly. "The house was watched — they couldn't get away."

"That's a good one!" Young Morrow looked his self-disgust. "Hire operatives on your staff, sir, and then have to set others to tail them, and see that they don't get into trouble! Heavens, what an idiot I am! I've found out one thing, though, from those cryptograms" — he pointed to the cipher notes on the desk. "Music's a cinch! I can read it already, and I'm going to start in and learn how to play on something or other, the first chance I get! There's a fellow next door to Mrs. Quinlan's with a clarinet — " He paused, and his face sobered as he added: "But I forgot! I sha'n't be there any more."

Before Blaine could speak, there was a knock upon the door, and Marsh entered with hurried circumspection. There was a look of latent, shocked importance upon his usually impassive face, and he carried in his hand a newspaper which was still damp from the press.

"I beg your pardon, sir, but I thought you would want to know at once. There's been a murder! Paddington, the private detective, was found in the Rhododendron Alley, just off the Mall in the park, stabbed to the heart!"

Henry Blaine took the paper and spread it out upon the desk before him, as Guy Morrow, with a soft, low whistle, turned away. The "extra" imparted little more than the secretary's announcement had done. There was no known motive for the crime, no clue to the murderer. When found, the man had been dead for some hours.

"Well, sir," observed Guy at last, when the secretary had withdrawn, "one by one they're getting away from us — and by the same route. First Rockamore, now Paddington!"

Blaine looked up with a grim smile.

"Putting a woman wise to anything is like lighting a faulty time-fuse: you never can tell when you're going to get your own fingers blown off! But tell me something, Guy. What was that tune you whistled a moment ago, when Marsh came in with the news? It had a vaguely familiar ring."

"Oh, that?" asked the operative, with a sheepishly guileless air. "It was just a bit from an English musical comedy of two or three years back, I think. It's got a silly-sounding name — something like 'There's a Boat Sails on Saturday — '"

Blaine's wry smile broadened to a grin of genuine appreciation, and rising, he clapped the young man heartily on the shoulder.

"Right you are, Guy! And it won't be our job to search the sailing lists. You may not always be able to see what lies under your nose, but your perspective is not bad. Hell has only one fury worse than a woman scorned, that I know of, and that is a woman fooled! We'll let it go at that!"

The evening had already grown late, but that eventful day was not to end without one more brief scene of vital import. Marsh presently reappeared, this time bearing a card.

"'Mr. Mallowe,'" read Blaine, with a half-smile. "Show him in, Marsh, and have your men ready. You know what to do. No, Guy, you needn't go. This interview will not be a private one."

"Mr. Blaine!" Mallowe entered pompously and then paused, glancing rather uncertainly from the detective to Morrow. It needed no keen observer to note the change in the man since the scene of that morning, at Miss Lawton's. He had become a mere shell of his former self. The smug unctuousness was gone; the jaunty side-whiskers drooped; his chalk-like skin fell in flabby folds, and his crafty eyes shifted like a hunted animal's.

"Mr. Blaine, I had hoped for a strictly confidential conference with you, but I presume this person to be one of your trusted assistants, and it is immaterial now — the matter upon which I have come is too pressing! Scandal, notoriety must be averted at all costs! I find that a frightful, a hideous mistake has been made, and I am actually upon the point of being involved in a conspiracy as terrible as that of which my poor friend Pennington Lawton was the victim! And I am as innocent as he! I swear it!"

"You may as well conserve your strength and your strategic ingenuity for the immediate future, Mr. Mallowe. You'll need both," Blaine returned, coolly. "If you've come here to make any appeal — "

"I've come to assert my innocence!" the broken man cried with a flash of his old proud dignity. "I only learned this evening of the truth, and that those scoundrels Carlis and Rockamore had implicated me! How a man of your discernment and experience could believe for a moment that I was a party to any fraudulent — "

Blaine pressed the bell.

"There is no use in prolonging this interview, Mr. Mallowe!" he said, curtly. "All the evidence is in my hands."

"But allow me to explain!" The flabby face grew more death-like, until the burning eyes seemed peering from the face of a corpse.

Two men entered, and at sight of them, the former pompous president of the Street Railways of Illington plumped to his fat, quaking knees.

"For God's sake, listen! You must listen, Blaine!" he shrieked. "I am one of the prominent men of this country! I have three married daughters, two of them with small children! The disgrace, the infamy of this, will kill them! I will make restitution; I will — "

"Pennington Lawton had one daughter, unmarried, unprovided for! Did you think of *her*?" asked Blaine, grimly. "I'm sorry for the innocent who must suffer with you, Mr. Mallowe, but in this instance the law must take its course. Lead him away."

When the wailing, quavering voice had subsided behind the closing door, Henry Blaine turned to young Morrow with a weary look of pain, age-old, in his eyes.

"Unpleasant, wasn't it?" he asked grimly. "I try to school myself against it, but with all my experience, a scene like this makes me sick at heart. I know the wretch deserves what is coming to him, just as Rockamore knew when he unfalteringly sped that bullet — just as Carlis knew when he heard his own voice repeated by the dictagraph. And yet I, who make my living, and shall continue to make it, by unearthing malefactors; I, who have built my career, made my reputation, proved myself to be what I am by the detection and punishment of wrong-doing — I wish with all my heart and soul, before God, that there was no such thing as crime in all this fair green world!"

CHAPTER XXI
CLEARED SKIES

Just as in autumn, the period of Indian summer brings a reminiscent warmth and sunshine, so sometimes in late winter a day will come now and then which is a harbinger of the not far-distant springtide, like a promise, during present storm and stress, of better things to come.

Such a day, balmy and gloriously bright, found four people seated together in the spacious, sunny morning-room of a great house on Belleair Avenue. A young man, pale and wan as from a long illness, but with a new steadiness and clarity born of suffering in his eyes; a girl, slender and black-robed, her delicate face flushing with an exquisite, spring-like color, her eyes soft and misty and spring-like, too, in their starry fulfillment of love that has been tried and found all-sufficing; another sable-clad figure, but clerically frocked and portly; and the last, a keen-faced, kindly-eyed man approaching middle-age — a man with sandy hair and a mustache just slightly tinged with gray. He might, from his appearance and bearing, have been a great teacher, a great philanthropist, a great statesman. But he was none of these — or rather, let us say, he was all, and more. He was the greatest factor for good which the age had produced, because he was the greatest instrument of justice, the crime-detector of the century.

The pale young man moved a little in his chair, and the girl laid her hand caressingly upon his blue-veined one. She was seated close to him — in fact, Anita was never willing, in these later days, to be so far from Ramon that she could not reach out and touch him, as if to assure herself that he was there, that he was safe from the enemies who had encompassed them both, and that her ministering care might shield him.

Doctor Franklin noted the movement, slight as it was, and cleared his throat, importantly.

"Of course, my dear children," he began, impressively, "if it is your earnest desire, I will perform the marriage ceremony for you here in this room at noon to-morrow. But I trust you have both given the matter careful thought — not, of course, as to the suitability of your union, but the — I may say, the manner of it! A ceremony without a social function, without the customary observances which, although worldly and filled with pomp and vanity, nevertheless are befitted by usage, in these mundane days, to those of your station in life, seems slightly unconventional, almost — er — unseemly."

"But we don't care for the pomp and vanity, and the social observances, and all the rest of it, do we, Ramon?" the girl asked.

Ramon Hamilton smiled, and his eyes met and held hers.

"We only want each other," he said quietly.

"But it seems so very precipitate!" the clergyman urged, turning as if for moral support to the impassive figure of Henry Blaine. "So soon after the shadow of tragedy has crossed this threshold! What will people say?"

A little vagrant breeze, like a lost, unseasonable butterfly, came in at the open window and stirred the filmy curtain, bearing on its soft breath the odor of narcissus from the bloom-laden window-box.

"Oh, Doctor Franklin!" cried the girl, impulsively. "Don't talk of tragedy just now! Spring is so near, and we love each other so! If he — my dear, dead father — can hear, he will understand, and wish it to be so!"

"As you will." The minister rose. "I gave you your name, Anita. I consecrated your father's soul to Heaven, and his body to the dust, and I will give his daughter in marriage to the man he chose for her protector, whenever it is your will. But, Mr. Blaine, what do you say? You seem to have more influence over Miss Lawton than I, although I can scarcely understand it. Don't you agree with me that the world will talk?"

"I do!" responded Henry Blaine fervently. "And I say — let it! It can say of these two children only what I do — bless you, both! Sorrow and suffering and tragedy have taken their quota of these young lives — now let a little happiness and joy and sunshine and love in upon the circumspect gloom you would still cast about them! You ministers are steeped in the spiritual misery of the world, the doctors in the physical; but we crime-specialists are forced to drink of it to its dregs, physical, mental, moral, spiritual! And there is so much in this tainted, sin-ridden world of ours that is beautiful and pure and happy and holy, if we will but give it a chance!"

Doctor Franklin coughed, in a severely condemnatory fashion.

"Now that I have learned your opinion, in a broad, general way, Mr. Blaine, I can understand your point of view in regard to that young criminal, Charles Pennold, when at the time of the trial you used your influence to have him paroled in your custody, instead of being sent to prison, where he belonged."

"Exactly." Blaine's tone was dry. "I firmly believe that there are many more young boys and men in our prisons, who should in reality be in hospitals, or in sheltering, uplifting, sympathetic hands, than there are criminals unpunished. And you, with your broadly, professionally charitable point of view, Doctor," he added with keen enjoyment, "will, I am convinced, be delighted to know that Charley Pennold is doing splendidly. He will develop in time into one of my most trusted, capable operatives, I have no doubt. He has the instinct, the real nose, for crime, but circumstances from his birth and even before that, forced him on the wrong side of the fence. He was, if you will pardon the vernacular, on the outside, looking in. Now he's on the inside, looking out!"

"I sincerely trust so!" the minister responded frigidly and turned to the others. "I will leave you now. If it is your irrevocable desire to have the ceremony at noon to-morrow, I will make all the necessary arrangements. In fact, I will telephone you later, when everything is settled."

"Oh, thank you, Dr. Franklin! I knew you wouldn't fail us!" Anita murmured. "Don't forget to tell Mrs. Franklin that she will hear from me. She must surely come, you know!"

When the door had closed on the minister's broad, retreating back, Ramon Hamilton turned with a suspicion of a flush in his wan cheeks, to the detective.

"If I'd gone to any Sunday school he presided over, when I was a kiddie, I'd have been a train-robber now!" he observed darkly. "I'm glad you lit into him about young Pennold, Mr. Blaine. He started it!"

"But think of the others!" Anita Lawton turned her face for a moment to the spring-like day outside. "Mr. Mallowe dead in his cell from apoplexy, Mr. Carlis imprisoned for life, Mac Alarney and all the rest facing long years behind gray walls and iron bars — oh, I know it is just; I remember what they did to my father and to me; and yet somehow in this glorious sunshine and with all the ages and ages just as bright, spreading before me, I can find charity and mercy in my heart for all the world!"

"Charity and mercy," repeated Ramon soberly. "Yes, dearest. But not liberty to continue their crimes — to do to others what they did to us!"

A spasm of pain crossed his face, and she bent over him solicitously.

"Oh, what is it, Ramon? Speak to me!"

"Nothing, dear, it's all right now. Just a twinge of the old pain."

"Those murdering fiends, who made you suffer so!" she cried, and added with feminine illogicality: "I'm *not* sorry, after all, that they're in prison! I'm glad they've got their just deserts. Oh, Ramon, I've been afraid to distress you by asking you, but did you tell the truth at the trial — all the truth, I mean? Was that really all you remember?"

"Yes, dear," he replied a trifle wearily. "When I left Mr. Blaine's office that day, I was hurrying along Dalrymple Street, when just outside the Colossus Building, a boy about fifteen — that one who is in the reformatory now — collided with me. Then he looked up into my face, and grasped my arm.

"'You're Mr. Hamilton, aren't you?' he gasped. 'Oh, come quick, sir! Mr. Ferrand's had a stroke or something, and I was just running to get help. You don't remember me, I guess. I'm Mr. Ferrand's new office-boy, Frankie Allen. You was in to see him about ten days ago, don't you remember?'

"Well, as I told you, 'Nita dearest, old Mr. Ferrand was one of my father's best friends. His offices were in the Colossus Building, and I *had* been in to see him about ten days before — so in spite of Mr. Blaine's warning, I was perfectly unsuspecting. Of course, I didn't remember his office-boy from Adam, but that fact never occurred to me, then. I went right along with the boy, and he talked so volubly that I didn't notice we had gotten into the wrong elevator — the express — until its first stop, seven floors above Mr. Ferrand's. They must have staged the whole thing pretty well — Carlis and Paddington and their crew — for when I stepped out of the express elevator, there was no one in sight that I remember but the boy who was with me. I pressed the button of the local, which was just beside the express — there was a buzz and whirring hum as if the elevator had ascended, and the door opened. As I stepped over its threshold, I felt a violent blow and terrific pain on the back of my head, and seemed to fall into limitless space. That was all I knew until I woke up in the hospital where Mr. Blaine had taken me after discovering and rescuing me, to see your dear face bending over mine!"

"One of Paddington's men was waiting, and hit you on the head with a window-pole, as you stepped into the open elevator shaft," Blaine supplemented. "It was all a plant, of course. You only fell to the roof of the elevator, which was on a level with the floor below. There they carried you into the office of a fake company, kept you until closing time, and got you out of the building as a drunkard, conveying you to Mac Alarney's retreat in his own machine. Nobody employed in the building was in their pay but the elevator man, and he's got his, along with the rest! Paddington's scheme wasn't bad; if he'd only been on the square, he might have made a very brilliant detective!"

"How terrible his death was!" Anita shuddered. "And how unexplainable! No one ever found out who stabbed him, there in the park, did they?"

Blaine did not reply. He knew that on the day following the discovery of the murdered man, one Franchette Durand, otherwise Fifine Déchaussée, had sailed for Havre on the ill-fated *La Tourette*, which had gone to the bottom in mid-ocean, with all on board. He knew also that an hour before the French girl's last tragic interview with Paddington, she had discovered the existence of his wife, for he himself had seen to it that the knowledge was imparted to her. Further than that, he preferred not to conjecture. The Madonna-faced girl had taken her secret with her to her swiftly retributive grave in the deep.

Blaine rose, somewhat reluctantly. Work called him, and yet he loved to be near them in the rose-tinted high noon of their happiness.

"I'll be on hand to-morrow, indeed I will!" he promised heartily, in response to their eager request.

"To-morrow! Just think!" Anita buried her glowing face in her lover's shoulder for an instant, and then looked up with misty eyes. "Just think, if it hadn't been for you, Mr. Blaine, there wouldn't be any to-morrow! I don't mean about your getting my father's money all back for me — I'm grateful, of course, but it doesn't count beside the greater thing you have given us! But for you, there would *never* have been any — to-morrow."

"That's true!" The young man's arm encircled the girl's slender waist as they stood together in the glowing sunlight, but his other hand gripped the detective's. "We owe life, our happiness, the future, everything to you!"

And so Henry Blaine left them.

At the door he turned and glanced back, and the sight his eyes beheld was a goodly one for him to carry away with him into the world — a sight as old as the ages, as new as the hour, as prescient as the hours and ages to come. Just a man and a maid, sunshine and happiness, youth and love! — that, and the light of undying gratitude in the eyes they bent upon him.